"It was just a run-of-the-mill, garden-variety trip to the supermarket. But everything changes when middle-aged, luck-starved Henry Puddester finds a baby in his shopping cart. Naturally, he panics and bolts, preferring the fire to the frying pan and an odyssey strewn with wild scenes and wacky characters. Award-winning writer and masterful storyteller Susan Flanagan has penned a memorable tale filled with humour and heart."

TERRY FALLIS, TWO-TIME WINNER OF
THE STEPHEN LEACOCK MEDAL FOR HUMOUR

"*Supermarket Baby* has excellent comic timing. I wonder if the author has worked in sketch comedy. Excellent grasp of narrative structure and how to keep a story moving along. . . . I often hooted with laughter while reading."

ADJUDICATION NOTES FOR
THE 2019 PERCY JANES AWARD

SUPERMARKET BABY

SUSAN FLANAGAN

a novel

FLANKER PRESS LIMITED
ST. JOHN'S

AN ENTRY FOR THE
Stephen Leacock Award
FOR HUMOUR FOR
2022

Library and Archives Canada Cataloguing in Publication

Title: Supermarket baby : a novel / Susan Flanagan.
Names: Flanagan, Susan, 1967- author.
Identifiers: Canadiana (print) 20200382675 | Canadiana (ebook) 20200382748 | ISBN 9781774570104 (softcover) | ISBN 9781774570111 (EPUB) | ISBN 9781774570128 (Kindle) | ISBN 9781774570135 (PDF)
Classification: LCC PS8611.L375 S87 2021 | DDC C813/.6—dc23

PRINTED IN CANADA

This paper has been certified to meet the environmental and social standards of the Forest Stewardship Council® (FSC®) and comes from responsibly managed forests, and verified recycled sources.

Cover design by Graham Blair   Edited by Charis Cotter, Robin McGrath

FLANKER PRESS LTD.
PO BOX 2522, STATION C
ST. JOHN'S, NL
CANADA

TELEPHONE: (709) 739-4477   FAX: (709) 739-4420   TOLL-FREE: 1-866-739-4420

WWW.FLANKERPRESS.COM

9 8 7 6 5 4 3 2 1

The publisher acknowledges the financial support of the Government of Canada through the Canada Book Fund (CBF) and the Government of Newfoundland and Labrador, Department of Tourism, Culture, Industry and Innovation for our publishing activities. We acknowledge the support of the Canada Council for the Arts, which last year invested $157 million to bring the arts to Canadians throughout the country. *Nous remercions le Conseil des arts du Canada de son soutien. L'an dernier, le Conseil a investi 157 millions de dollars pour mettre de l'art dans la vie des Canadiennes et des Canadiens de tout le pays.* We acknowledge the support of ArtsNL, which last year invested $3.9 million to foster and promote the creation and enjoyment of the arts for the benefit of all Newfoundlanders and Labradorians.

For Terry Kelly, who believed in me before I believed in myself

1

Henry Puddester Goes to City Hall for the Last Time

Henry Puddester turned heads. Had been doing so since the moment he slid out of his mother's womb. All present in the case room were goggle-eyed. "Have you ever seen such a perfect baby?" they asked one another. They all agreed they hadn't and warned the Puddesters that their son would grow up to be a "real looker."

By the time Henry began studying business marketing at Memorial University, students and profs alike could be seen appraising his looks. His perfect features, perfectly arrayed across his perfectly shaped face, sat on a well-seeded head atop a lean torso, forever trim. Women coveted his thick dark lashes and olive skin, and men felt inferior in his presence.

Henry himself, however, was oblivious to the power of his looks. He failed to notice the steady stream of girls who, between classes, slowed to a canter in the crushing throngs that scuttled their way through the tunnel system below the university buildings. It was in this underground maze that relationships were cemented, notes slipped into air vents, kisses stolen by locker doors, dates made in the ten minutes of freedom between classes.

"Isn't he to die for?" one girl asked.

"Yes, but I heard he's taken."

"Who's the lucky girl?"

The lucky girl, it turned out, was Millicent Pearlstein, a dark-haired firecracker of a woman who took one look into Henry's ocean eyes after he mistakenly trod on her foot outside the remains of the burning Thomson

Student Centre and fell under their spell. It was a crisp day in late September 1979. Maple leaves, not yet transformed into the gold and red hues of autumn, danced in the light breeze. Henry Puddester had been on campus for three weeks and was chuffed that he had successfully managed to find his way from class to his locker and then the Thomson Student Centre, where he located the microwave and placed his burrito on the thick glass plate, shut the door, and watched for a second as the flour tortilla rotated inside.

Spying a piano, Henry left the burrito for a moment and sat on a dented stool to pluck out Billy Joel's *Piano Man*. Just as he finished the last chords, water began spraying down on his head, as well as the heads of hundreds of his fellow students, who were now stampeding toward the exit. Henry paused to find the source of the acrid smoke that had begun stinging his eyes and noticed flames leaping out of the microwave and onto countertops and floors.

Henry joined the throng of students pushing through the doors into the quadrangle just as the first fire trucks arrived, and men in bunker gear ran into the burning building.

Outside, Henry stood transfixed with the crowd as the flames spread throughout the entire structure, licking the siding and nearby bushes. A fireman urged them back, roping off the perimeter as firefighters smashed windows and uncoiled thick grey hoses from the backs of trucks. A team mounted a ladder with an axe to cut a hole in the roof.

It was when a huge man in a haz-mat suit pushed by Henry that he took a step back, crushing the dainty feet of a female student standing directly behind him.

"Sorry, so sorry." Henry's heart raced like it did every time he came in contact with an attractive girl.

"It's okay," she answered. "I can always walk on my hands." Her eyes twinkled, and Henry saw that she was sexy in black tights and a short skirt, a cotton T-shirt with David Bowie's Aladdin Sane face stretched across her chest.

"What was that guy holding in his hand?" she asked.

"Geiger counter," said Henry, swallowing. "For measuring radiation."

"Radiation? You mean from the microwave?"

"I guess." Henry felt his stomach knot. *How did she know about the microwave?*

"Should we be moving farther away?" She blinked up at him, her dark hair falling over one eye.

"No, there's not enough radiation to harm us out here."

"Are you sure?"

Henry smiled. "I'm sure. You'd have to be mighty close to a microwave for it to cause damage."

The girl smiled and put a hand on Henry's arm, sending short electrical shocks to his heart and causing the hair to stand up, not only on his arm but all over his body.

"Can you believe some idiot put his burrito in for twenty minutes?" She removed her hand.

Henry shook his head, the electrical currents dimming and the hair flattening just as the last timbers collapsed and the building fell in on itself. A collective gasp rose from the crowd, and police began ushering the students away from the quadrangle.

"Come on, I'll walk you to your locker," she said, taking his hand and pulling him toward the tunnels.

Millicent—Millie Pearlstein—should not have been in the cafeteria at that time. She should have been in class discussing propositional probability and logic, but philosophy had been cancelled. Millie's analytical mind concluded that the odds of her meeting up with this impossibly attractive man were one in a billion, or maybe one in a trillion. Who knew? It surely had to be a sign that she and Henry were a perfect match. Perfectly compatible.

After the day the Thomson Student Centre burned to the ground, it seemed every time Henry went to his locker, there was Millie Pearlstein, fresh and lovely and sweet-smelling. His heart turned somersaults each time he laid eyes on her. She was so . . . clean. People would think this weird if Henry ever said it out loud, but he valued hygiene. There was a girl in his stats class who paid a lot of attention to him. She expressed intelligent views and had a wicked body and an amazing smile, but she dressed like a punk and her hair resembled a wasp nest. She once asked Henry to go to the Breezeway for a beer, but he declined. Millie Pearlstein, however, was unsoiled.

Their first official date was the Friday before Halloween, when she asked him to accompany her to a Doug and the Slugs concert, which had to be moved to downtown, seeing as the Thomson Student Centre no longer existed. For the rest of their years at Memorial University, the pair were inseparable.

Even years later, when Millie went off to law school in Nova Scotia and Henry stayed in St. John's to do his MBA and start a job at City Hall, he remained smitten. Despite the fact he knew she was dating other men while she was away, he stayed faithful to her.

And Millie, realizing that Henry was her true soulmate—he "completed" her, she said—always made her way back to him.

Henry couldn't quite figure out why she chose him. What Henry didn't realize was that for his entire life, he enjoyed the privilege of the intolerably attractive. What he hadn't grasped was that Millie overlooked his ineptitude and, despite her insight, could not see beyond his steely blue eyes, aquiline nose, and six-pack abs. What she saw was a perfect physical specimen and, she imagined, a perfect personality to match.

Now here they were, several decades later, she a criminal defence lawyer and Henry a househusband. Following thirty-five years of exemplary service, Henry Puddester had just given up his Director of Marketing position for the City of St. John's to be home after school for their ten-year-old son.

How this happened had blindsided Henry. Dash's after-school program announced in January that they'd be closing their doors the first week of April. There were no other facilities taking kids within a fifty-mile radius. Henry's mother had agreed to move in to be there for Dash after school, and Henry and Millie tacked an extra line of credit on their mortgage to rip out a section of their yard and build on a granny flat. Things went sideways after that. Just before she moved in, Granny was diagnosed with pancreatic cancer, and five weeks later she was dead.

Thinking there would be some equity in his mother's house, Henry gave up his job to let a young hire get his foot in the door and began performing his obligations of stay-at-home dad and executor of his mother's estate, only to find out, too late, that instead of being worth money, his mother's estate, and thus Henry, was on the hook for twenty years of back taxes, thrusting the couple into dire financial straits, their only real asset a brand new vacant mother-in-law suite that they would, no doubt, end up having to rent.

So, it was on a soulless spring day that Henry Puddester trudged up the steps to City Hall for what he knew would be the final time. The sun over Newfoundland had gone into hiding sometime in January and had not poked its face out since. Instead, a slate-grey sky had taken up permanent occupancy, tainting all enjoyment of life on the Avalon.

The northeasterly wind whipped off the water and cut through Henry's peacoat, and he struggled against its brute force to open the heavy glass door of City Hall. Henry didn't want to pick up his record of employment. He wished he could wind back the clock and still be employed.

He caught a glimpse of himself in the double panes. What he saw did not please him—a dishevelled version of what Millie kindly called his aging matinee-idol looks. She was forever telling him how handsome he was, but the face he saw this morning was weary, more chiselled old man than movie star. His nose was chilblained and his cheeks flushed. It was the grey hair that peeked out from under his Boston toque that never failed to shock him. Ever since the day Millie's new receptionist referred to him as the silver-haired gentleman, he had developed a complex. He ducked inside, pulled off his hat, wiped the rain off his horn-rimmed glasses, and did his best to sneak past the commissionaire, who was hammering away on his keyboard, index fingers pecking like two hens.

Don't look up. Don't look up, thought Henry.

"Henry Puddester, what're you doing here?" Wiener, who got his name after swallowing a dozen hot dogs at the staff barbecue, came out of the glass-encased booth and took in the windblown shape of his former colleague. "Man, you look like hell."

Henry blew out his breath, turned around, and smiled, showing all his teeth. "It's a bit blustery."

"I'll say. Wind's strong enough to blow Jesus Himself off the Cross." Wiener clapped Henry on the arm. "I can't believe you retired. One day you're there like always, slathering on that hand sanitizer, and next day I send old man Bates up to see you, and he comes back and says you're gone." Wiener paused to take a breath.

Henry eyed the concrete stairs and fingered the portable Purell in his pocket. He would wait until he was out of Wiener's sight to apply it, although thoughts of the germs on the front door made his skin crawl.

"How many years you have in? Gotta be over thirty."

"Two weeks off thirty-five."

"That's more years than I been on this earth. Good on ya, I say. You need to kick back, take life as it comes, know what I mean?" Wiener placed his crossed hands behind his head and stretched his arms as if he were sitting back in a chair, except he was standing up. "Mayor Jones always said you were too high-strung."

Henry gave a faint nod. Apparently, the mayor wasn't the only one who had this opinion. Millie was always telling him to relax, to be happy with what he had.

"Thought you'd be hitting the greens in Florida with the boys from Marketing." The phone rang in Wiener's glass booth. He raised his hand to Henry and made his way back inside.

No golf for Henry this spring, but he did hope to sneak away for a motorcycle trip . . . the Spring Tune-Up Ride from Montreal to St. John's to honour his deceased mother. He had yet to convince his wife of the merits of this idea. She argued that he could honour his mother in other ways that cost less money and were closer to home. As he made his way up the concrete stairs, her attorney voice entered his head. "Henry, we don't have two beans to rub together. Plus, you retired to take care of Dash, and you can't do that very well if you're on some highway between here and Quebec." She'd kissed him then and patted the top of his silver head.

Henry had long accepted the fact that he would never win an argument with his wife. So, while he adjusted to his new position of househusband, Millie continued to lead strategic planning sessions with her legal team and host power lunches for the jet-setters she worked with down at the Supreme Court of Newfoundland.

Henry waited until he was outside the opaque doors of Marketing and Communications before he pulled out the Purell. He inhaled as he rubbed in the alcohol-based sanitizer and then swallowed before going in. He liked his old co-workers—he just didn't want to see any of them. Luckily for him, what Wiener said was true, and the majority of them were now on the Boca Raton golf green while Henry was stuck in St. John's, enduring the most appalling spring on record. Make no wonder he had this vicious head cold.

Henry didn't really want to be golfing, though. All he wanted was to be out in his shed with his 1970 Triumph Bonneville, preparing for the Spring Tune-Up, rather than preparing after-school snacks for Dash.

Henry knew he shouldn't complain—he had hours to tinker with his bike while Dash was at school. And Dash was a good kid—a bit too addicted to video games, but all told, he was a fine example of what today's youth had to offer. Henry wouldn't trade him for anything.

It was just that Henry was too old to be a father to a ten-year-old. He didn't have the energy exhibited by the young parents. He didn't have the mental stamina to keep up with the new trends. In fact, Henry Puddester didn't have a clue about parenting.

2

Thursday: Two Weeks Later

Henry Puddester blinked at the baby carrier in the grocery cart and wondered how it got there.

He couldn't piece it together. Why would someone put an infant carrier in his shopping cart?

It *was* his cart. The lemon yogourt was there.

Henry's guts churned audibly. He liked children, but babies and baby-related things always gave Henry a sense of unease. He hadn't even trusted himself to pick up Dash until he was more than a year old.

Henry had felt woozy all morning, but not to the point of hallucinating a floral-patterned infant car seat. He gave the cloth a poke. It was real. But maybe it was empty. Maybe Sundries now sold baby carriers.

He studied his cart to see if anything else had changed.

What was this?

Instead of his hand-chosen pears, there was now a case of puréed baby food. Henry bent down to bring his bread up from the shelf underneath. "What the hey?" His Paradise Bakery loaves were MIA. Instead, there was a case of baby wipes and diapers. This was not good.

Henry came up quickly, and dizziness enveloped him. Good thing Millie said she'd get Dash off to school this morning. He held onto the handle of the shopping cart and took three deep breaths. In and out. In and out. In and out. He wanted to bolt. But at that moment, the carrier emitted a gurgle. He was afraid to look inside.

What on earth was going on?

Could a sleep-deprived mother have mistaken his cart for hers?

Or maybe someone had dumped the baby in his cart. Millie had been talking about an amber alert yesterday. What had she said? Henry wished he could remember. She was always telling him his mind was like a sieve, but this morning it had reached new proportions. Think, Henry, think. Something about an estranged father taking an infant while the mother slept. Police had advised the public to be on the lookout but not to approach the man. He was considered dangerous.

Henry gulped. In front of him, in line, an oversized man in a fedora loaded cases of soft drinks onto the conveyor.

Could it be him? He did not look menacing enough to have stolen an infant. Plus, if he were the one, what would he be doing looking casual at the checkout? Unless he was the type who liked to linger at crime scenes to see how things played out. Henry had seen a movie about that once.

Henry scanned his environs. A lean man with a flat cap, like the ones British cabbies wore, crouched in front of the magazines. Near him was a short, stout man who could lose a hundred pounds. A posse of come from aways was moving up front. But still no one who fit the bill of space cadet mother or dangerous offender.

Henry moved his tongue over his top teeth. It felt like sandpaper. Why was he so thirsty all of a sudden? He licked his lips and rewound his mind, back through the aisles of the supermarket. For some reason, it was like his brain synapses were not firing. Fleeting images flashed across his prefrontal cortex, like a commercial, the pictures too quick to properly focus on any one thing. A teenager with pink hair talking into her phone when he was in the back of the store searching for the eggs, but she, too, did not fit the picture of a human who had misplaced another human. Akela, the scout leader, in a long red coat with a logo on the chest, a coat that cost more than a month's worth of groceries. Frank's daughter had one like that.

Maybe this was an unsolvable mystery. He would just take his groceries and then ditch the cart and carrier at the door. But he couldn't do that. What about the baby? He had to save it in case the dangerous estranged father changed his mind and came back. Henry knew what to do. He would bring the baby to Millie. She was good with babies. She would make sure it was safe until it was reunited with its mother.

Henry bent again so he could peep under the cloth. An oval flap was Velcroed to the canopy, preventing a view of the contents. The flap was made of the same sunflower-patterned material as the rest of the tented area. He was familiar with this configuration from when Dash was born. Henry gently pulled back the Velcro to allow a sightline into the carrier. A whiff of baby powder escaped the cloth walls. The infant inside—a girl, judging from the pink hat and blanket that enveloped it—opened its oversized eyes and started to quiver. Next thing it was whimpering. Henry could tell from past experience that this was the buildup to a full-fledged cry. He had to act fast, survey the scene. Rubber pacifier was attached to the baby blanket by a tether. Henry grabbed hand sanitizer from his pocket, doused both hands, and quickly plugged the dummy into the baby's mouth. The baby looked worried but did what babies are programmed to do—it started sucking.

A fine sweat had broken out all over Henry's body. He felt like he was having one of Millie's hot flashes. Henry wiped his forehead with his sleeve and glanced at the man ahead. He was sliding his bank card out of the machine and packing his cases of drinks into his cart.

The cashier made eye contact, raising her left eyebrow at Henry. A silver ring pierced the middle part of her nose. She looked like a bull. "Sir, you can start loading your groceries on the belt."

Henry felt the presence of another cart pull up behind his. He was trapped. He had to get out of there.

3

Henry Goes Shopping, One Hour Earlier

Henry reluctantly left the half-polished Triumph in the shed and ran through the downpour to the driveway. He felt a bit woozy. He had taken a pill for his cold, something he rarely did because of the intense effect all medicine had on him. But still, he didn't usually react so strongly to cold and sinus meds. His heart was going two-forty, and his mind felt like it was battling its way out of deep fog. He wondered if he should even be driving.

Not only that, but his sinuses didn't seem any better. What was up with that? Usually the antihistamine medicine kicked in right away. Henry had to get out of this freezing wet weather. Under normal circumstances, he would have gone to Florida golfing with the boys. But these were not normal times. Don't think about it, he lectured himself. Instead, he thought about what he had done late last night. He had secretly booked a spot on the May 24 Spring Tune-Up road trip—the trip that his wife said that they couldn't afford. "Buttons or beach rocks?" were her exact words. Strange expression, but it was what Millie always said when they discussed large purchases.

Money was a minor detail to Henry, despite the fact he had none to pay the registration or the plane ticket to get to Montreal, where, come May 24 weekend, his shipped motorbike would be waiting for him. Ah, what a joy it would be to get clear of this foul weather and hit the pavement, feel the sun on his face, the wind in his hair.

He could certainly feel wind when he got out of the warm interior of the Ford Escape. In the supermarket parking lot, freezing rain catapulted sideways into his body, driven by savage earache-inducing gusts. These not-so-gentle breezes that April had been delivering with great glee were the reason Henry's nasal passages felt like they were going to explode. He shivered and pulled down his Boston Bruins toque, the black and gold stripes covering his ears.

A thin sheen of ice covered the parking lot as he scurried toward the cart corral, last fall's leaves whapping him in the face. Henry slowed his breathing and went over his game plan. He did this before entering any store so as not to waste time or come out with unnecessary purchases. His mind felt a bit like it was underwater, but he persisted. He was here at Sundries to pick up four dozen eggs for Dash's Cub Camp.

But, like every grocery shopping excursion since the dawn of supermarkets, getting in and out with just one foodstuff was virtually impossible. Henry's loving wife, Millie, had provided him with a list. "Just a coupla things," she said. Henry had rewritten Millie's haphazard version. The lined yellow paper in his pocket now neatly listed the products geographically, according to their location in the store. Therefore, Henry wouldn't have to backtrack.

So it was that Henry Puddester, wearing his leather driving gloves and favourite Boston toque, and feeling a bit lightheaded, jogged his way over to Sundries' automatic doors, with no inkling that this trip would change his life in unimaginable ways.

At least it was warm inside, recycled oxygen churning through the air exchange system. He placed his gloves in his yellow and black hat and dropped them in the little section of the cart where Dash used to sit when he was still a tiny human. Henry glanced at his silver wristwatch, a gift from the Marketing Department when he retired from City Hall. Seven thirty-five. Not bad. This time of day, there shouldn't be too many grocery shoppers. He would have plenty of time to make it to his 9:00 a.m. hair appointment at Fogtown Barber. He hoped Big Ernie—he was really big, with multiple tattoos on his tree-trunk arms—wouldn't notice his red, runny nose and send him packing.

Henry wrangled a Smart Car–sized cart from the indoor corral, pulled a wet wipe out of the dispenser, and wiped down the handle. You never knew who had touched the thing.

He went to move inside, but an old woman, four foot two with bluish hair, had come to a dead stop in the middle of the entranceway, causing the automatic doors to open and close, sending gusts of North Atlantic air in and out, negating the effects of the heating system. Henry opened his mouth to tell her to get a move on but then thought of his own mother and clamped his lips shut. She moved a few feet forward, took a piece of paper from her handbag, and stopped again.

Sweet Moses. The only way around her was to go through the flowers. Henry rolled between two banks of roses. He hated roses. They reminded him of his mother's funeral, and despite the fact that his nose was blocked, he could still smell them. Henry tried to squeeze the cart down the aisle but banged into a display of orchids. Two toppled to the floor, their delicate petals fanning out around fragile cracked stems.

"Jesus Murphy." Henry's words came out louder than he expected. Luckily for him, the old woman was hard of hearing and carried on her way, but other shoppers' heads turned among the perennials—a real estate agent Henry recognized from signs gave Henry a forced smile, her too-bright lipstick smearing her top teeth like a carnivore, and on her far side, Millie's yoga teacher, "Spring," and her daughter, "Tree," pretended not to recognize him. "The sixties are over, people." Shoot, did Henry just say that out loud? He really wasn't himself this morning.

Henry rolled his cart over the ruined orchids to produce, where he rifled through Cortland apples that had just been sprayed with great dollops of water. Henry was so thirsty, he felt like biting into one right there and then, but he could never eat any produce before washing it thoroughly first.

Pears were next. Henry selected six green Anjou, organized them next to the apples, and pushed his cart over to the wall of bread. He liked to look at the bread wall undisturbed, so he waited until a teenaged boy with three eyebrow piercings tossed four bags of hamburger buns into a basket. Once alone, Henry moved into position to perform the spring-back tests on several loaves from Paradise Bakery. He compressed the whole wheat slices and watched as they ever so slowly sprang back at him. He knew they delivered fresh to Sundries on Tuesdays and Thursdays, but you could never be too careful. The spring-back test was necessary before committing. Dash never tired of butter sandwiches for lunch, so Henry loaded the three loaves that had performed best onto the bottom shelf of the cart. Pleased with their arrangement, he headed west for lettuce.

Even though the E. coli outbreak was over, Henry hadn't bought lettuce in weeks. But yesterday Millie said she wanted salad and added romaine to the list. Henry expressed reservation. "Henry, I checked online. The scare is over." Henry had called the Canadian Food Inspection Agency to be certain. The nice woman assured him that Canadian supermarkets were only sourcing lettuce from unaffected countries, not those ones where farmers irrigated their crops with cow excrement.

So, today he decided to risk it and picked out three romaine hearts snuggled in one bag. They appeared crisp. Henry wondered what Sundries did with their lettuce when it wilted. His guess was that limp lettuce was spirited away under cover of darkness to the locked dumpster out back. Henry didn't like dumpsters. He had read a story in the paper recently about a dumpster diver in Vancouver who became stuck and got deposited into the back of a compactor garbage truck. Henry was happy he did not have to dumpster dive.

Yes, things might not be perfect, but they were looking up. This morning when he woke up and got Dash off to school, he had received a confirmation email saying he was booked for the Spring Tune-Up motorcycle trip. If he could only convince Millie that the registration was worth spending money on. That and shipping the bike, the plane ticket, and hotels and food while he was away. Oh, and babysitting. Millie worked long hours, so he had to come up with a babysitter for Dash. At ten, Dash was still too young to leave home alone after school while Henry rode from Montreal to St. John's on his Triumph.

Henry remembered the exact moment he decided he wanted a motorcycle. It was the day his mother rolled into the driveway on a 1972 Honda CB350. He was eleven, and it had been about six months since his father had skipped town. His mother slowed to a stop and passed him a full-face helmet that looked like something Marvin the Martian would wear. She patted the back seat. Henry's eyes were round. This was monumental. He climbed on back and held so tight around her waist that his arms were sore afterwards. Once, she gunned it from a stoplight. The momentum pulled him backwards, making his heart thud like a jackhammer until he realized he wasn't going to fly off onto the pavement. Funny, his heart was thudding here in the supermarket just like that day.

From then on, he dreamed about getting his own bike. His dream came true the day he turned sixteen. His mother upgraded to a Honda Gold Wing, and Henry inherited the '72 Honda four-stroke. After that, Henry and his mother went on rides together.

Millie thought it was sweet when she first met him, but it quickly began to wear thin when Henry would announce that instead of a Saturday picnic with Millie he was going on a ride with his mother. Then, once Dash came along, motorcycle rides took away from his parental duties. "Don't you think that it's somewhat ironic that your mother turned to motorcycles to forget about her husband abandoning her and her child, and now she encourages aforementioned son to accompany her on motorcycle trips resulting in his abandoning his wife and child?"

"I'm not abandoning you, Millie," Henry said. "I just like spending quality time with my mother. She won't be around forever, you know."

How true that was.

In response, Millie poured herself more and more into her work. Took on new clients. Cases that were deemed impossible to win. Yet somehow she always came out on top.

Now in the gluten-free aisle, Henry imagined a long stretch of winding highway. Quebec would be enjoying a real spring by the time he got there—unlike Newfoundland, which skipped spring altogether and just went from winter to summer in one day around mid-July. He pushed his cart toward the back of the store. Thud. He had run into someone in a long red coat. The cold and sinus pill was really throwing him for a loop. "Sorry. So sorry." Henry kept his eyes on the floor and put his cart in reverse.

"Mr. Puddester! Watch where you're going."

Dagnabit, it was Akela—Dash's smug old spinster of a Cub leader— looking at Henry like he was an insect she wanted to squash. How dare she? What was she doing just standing there? You couldn't just linger in the aisle like it was some sort of beach.

"Sorry," he repeated and scurried away. He had only nudged her, for God's sake. And here she was trying to make him feel bad. He refused. It was because of her that he was at the supermarket in the first place. It was because of her that he would be spending the weekend with a bunch of ten-year-olds, small humans who knew nothing about the important things in life, things like cleaning a carburetor.

He couldn't believe it when he found out he was responsible for pre-paring Ziploc omelets for twenty Cubs on Sunday morning. They had just had a Cub Camp in February. Now they were having another in April. Imagine the gall, springing an extra camp on them just because another group cancelled. Couldn't they just leave the place empty for one weekend?

That damn Akela. It was because of her he would not spend Saturday preparing the Triumph for the bike trip, and Saturday evening hove off drinking beer and watching the game with his neighbour, Frank. He took one last glance at her bundled in a huge red winter coat that ended mid-calf. She wasn't climbing Everest, for God's sake. And what was with those stupid scarves she always wore? They weren't outdoor scarves, but fifties-woman-in-a-convertible silk scarves. Yet Akela reminded Henry more of a man in a pickup rather than a woman in a convertible.

Calm down, he said to himself. No sense wasting any more time think-ing about her—he didn't even know her real name. Why did Cub leaders take names from *Jungle Book* characters, anyway?

Henry quickly wove the cart through a gauntlet of meat shoppers, his mood soured.

A woman with a wonky hairdo, like a wedding cake on top of her noggin, took his thoughts from Akela. Wedding Cake Woman and a group of about fifteen new Canadians were gathered around an end cooler over-flowing with discounted whole chickens. Henry had cooked one last week, but Dash wouldn't eat anything with bones in. He was strictly a nugget type of guy.

A thirty-something male worker with a buzz cut and a white butcher shirt led the group toward the upright coolers displaying cuts of meat. Al-though they looked African, they made Henry think of his wife. Last year,

Millie had pseudo-adopted a family of Syrians who loved the lamb carcasses at Costco. Millie had forked over a hundred dollars for membership just so she could take her new friends there. She was always blaming Henry for wasting money, but as far as he was concerned, she was the one dropping bucks all over town. Two weeks ago, she had a Union Jack sticker installed on the roof of her Mini, a hole cut out for the sunroof. And smaller Union Jacks on the backs of the mirrors. He knew they didn't come cheap. But he kept quiet since she was now the sole breadwinner in the family. Of course, he'd get his pension, but they were not living high on the hog ever since the mother-in-law suite fiasco.

Henry glanced at his watch. Seven fifty. Okay, back on track. Where was he?

He eased his cart past the margarine. He swore the last time he was here the eggs were right between the cheese and the sleeves of pre-made cookie dough. But where were they now?

Henry knew that the supermarket brass ordered the shelf stockers to place essentials in the farthest reaches of the store. Henry was in marketing—or at least he had been until very recently. The shocking series of events that had put an end to his thirty-five-year career with the City of St. John's flashed through his mind like a graphic novel. He might be addled from the cold medication, but these details were clear.

Panel 1: Dash's daycare suddenly going bust.

Panel 2: Futile search for another daycare.

Panel 3: Taking out a second mortgage for a mother-in-law suite so his mother could move in to babysit.

Panel 4: His mother's diagnosis and swift death.

Panels 5 and 6: The empty suite, the forced retirement.

Henry banished the thoughts from his mind. If he could just make it through Cub Camp, he could focus on getting his bike ready for shipping. Being on the road would dull the pain.

He blinked. What had taken him down that path? Ah yes, marketing.

He pondered asking another shopper where to find the eggs, maybe that young girl in the purple Chase the Ace T-shirt. How could she only be wearing a T-shirt on a day like this? No, he couldn't ask her. It would be like asking some pedestrian for driving directions to the next town. Total waste of time.

Maybe the eggs were still being off-loaded from a pallet in the back room. Henry watched as Price Gun Boy disappeared through the wettish-looking rubber flaps. His mood darkened even more—it always did when he found his efficiency challenged. The eggs had to be here somewhere.

Or did they?

His thoughts now turned ominous, foreboding.

But what could possibly happen in a grocery store?

4

Vanessa and the Whales

Ever since her father died, Vanessa Hannaford dreamed about whales. Whales the size of buses. Grey barnacle-covered ocean monoliths. Mostly humpback and fin, although she didn't remember identifying the genus in her dreams.

These dreams did not normally bother her. But then again, they usually occurred while she slept. Not while awake and cruising the meat section at Sundries on Torbay Road. This was not Vanessa's usual supermarket. She typically frequented Ledwells at the Lake, but when she heard Sundries had a sale on Ruby Rose whole chickens, she had driven up from downtown, bypassing her regular market, to stock up on the protein-rich meat. For some reason, Ruby Rose chickens were plumper than any other chickens on offer in and around St. John's.

The droning voice on the in-house speakers seemed to have hypnotized her. Vanessa had floated through produce and the bakery and gluten-free and was now down near the lobster tank. Yet she could have sworn she was at St. Vincent's Beach. She was with the whales—she was one of them—feeding fifty feet offshore. She was gliding expertly through the swells, scooping up huge mouthfuls of capelin, draining excess sea water through her baleen plates. When she reached the end of the bay, she turned with the others to make another slow pass in the opposite direction, the water rushing around her huge body as she turned into her own bubbles. She began to sing her full-belly song as she swished through the water with her pod. She was surprisingly agile despite her bulk. Hundreds of gannets were dive-bombing the water all around her.

"Dr. Hannaford, good morning." A male voice snapped Vanessa out of her reverie. She was not a massive filter feeder fattening up on capelin, but rather Dr. Vanessa Hannaford, research professor in Memorial University's Department of Biology, with an alter ego, Akela, the Cub leader.

Vanessa blinked. She had one hand on a shopping cart and the other squeezing a farmed salmon. It was Darryl, one of Vanessa's grad students from Bermuda.

Vanessa couldn't help but feel that Darryl might be able to see her dream, see her as a fin whale, gumming a gannet to death before spitting it out. She gave herself a shake. She did not like the whale dreams, whether asleep or awake. But she did like engaged students, especially those who fed off Vanessa's excitement when they were out in the field. And Darryl was one of the best, if not the brightest, a shining star in a sea of imbeciles. Students like Darryl made it a pleasure to come to work every morning. Vanessa loved working. In fact, she had planned to go directly to her office after the supermarket, even though it was reading week.

"I'm very grateful for the feedback you provided on the conference abstract." Darryl always spoke in a singsongy Bermudan accent that struck Vanessa as incongruous, as it was peppered with Canadian slang. Raised in Bermuda, he told her he had lived in Canada since he was fifteen.

"You deserved it. I hope you'll apply to be a teaching assistant for my field school the last two weeks in June, if you're not too busy with your thesis work, that is." Vanessa tightened the knot on her scarf.

"Where is that one?"

"Terra Nova. We'll be investigating the eastern extremity of black bear range on the island."

"Okay. I'll talk to the TA coordinator about that. I hope it's warmer by then." Darryl rubbed the ever-present Rastafarian hat on his head.

"Yes," Vanessa agreed, remembering the arctic chill that hit her when she had walked outside this morning. "Let's hope so. Regardless . . ." She almost said irregardless like her father used to. "It'll be interesting to see if the bear distribution has changed since the last major study nine years ago. Let me know in advance if you need camping gear."

"Thank you, Dr. Hannaford. See you in class."

And with that he was gone, leaving Vanessa standing in front of a cooler of farmed salmon. She quickly chose a five-pounder, embarrassed to think of how long she may have been fondling the fish when he came across her. She was hurrying through the meat section, past a group of African women with braided hair extensions and colourful dresses, when someone almost knocked her over with his shopping cart.

It was Dash's father. What a numbskull.

Dash Puddester was a sweet boy. She had no idea why his father bothered her so much. He was older than the other dads, but that wasn't it. There was something about him. She couldn't quite put her finger on it. He was shockingly handsome, like he was made of putty, but she always got the feeling he thought she was an idiot. Vanessa knew better, of course—she was the one with a Ph.D.

5

Introducing Millie Pearlstein Puddester

Millie Puddester, née Pearlstein, was fifty-six years old and, like her husband, desperate to feel a bit of heat on her skin. How many months had they been deprived of sun?

Millie couldn't remember the last time she had seen Cabot Tower on Signal Hill. It was always concealed in a wall of brume, the foghorn at Fort Amherst a constant companion no matter if she was at work or home in her bed.

She piloted her Mini Cooper Clubman east on Elizabeth Avenue toward Torbay Road and Sundries, where Henry was off getting groceries. Millie had to give him something to do. She couldn't have the man sitting around all day until Dash got off school.

The *CBC Morning Show* hosts were discussing a 1983 Ford LTD station wagon that was making its way across the province and was expected to arrive in the city within days. Not souped-up as in sporting a huge engine, but souped-up as in decorated on the inside and out with baubles and curios. Gewgaws, her mother used to call them. CBC reporter Gillian Gee's voice came through the dash. "If you have a favourite car, let us know. Sign into our Facebook page or send us a tweet."

There was only one other car Millie liked as much as her Mini Cooper Clubman—the '57 Ford she grew up with. But she'd be hard pressed to find time to tweet about it. She was off her head trying to keep on top of the backlog of court cases at the law firm where she worked as a criminal defence lawyer.

Traffic stalled just before Millie's right turn toward downtown. The Mini was steaming up, her defogger on the blink. She opened the windows a crack, and the smell of fried chicken flooded the car. A new billboard on Torbay Road said: CHASE THE ACE IN THE GOULDS. WILL THIS WEEK BE THE BIG ONE?

Millie wasn't a gambler. She was a low-risk person. Funny trait for a defence lawyer. But she removed any uncertainties from her work by preparing so well for cases that she blew most prosecutors out of the water. For this she had earned the nickname Missile Millie. Not many were brave enough to use it to her face, though.

Just as she reached the turn lane, Millie noticed a young mother in a hijab at the bus stop in front of Sundries. There was no shelter, and the incessant rain was hammering down on the woman. She had a kid on each side and, from the looks of her robes, another one on the way. The smaller child, a girl, slipped on the ice and grabbed at her mother before going down, the contents of the plastic grocery bag falling helter-skelter. The mother couldn't catch her daughter, not while holding two plastic grocery bags heavy enough to cut the skin.

Instead of making the right turn, Millie veered left at the last second. The owner of the Dodge Ram she had cut off leaned on the horn. Millie flipped him the finger, indicated right, and swung the car close to the sidewalk. The Dodge screeched around her, its driver screaming obscenities through a window. Millie didn't flinch. She heard much worse than that in court just about every day.

The woman gave a start when the Mini's right rear tire crunched over a can in one of the shopping bags. *Oops.* Millie flung open her door and smiled. She could see the mother was young—not yet twenty-five. Why wasn't she wearing a winter coat?

Millie's train ring tone sounded, but she sent it to voice mail. She ran around and opened the passenger door, cracking the sleet that had iced over the hinges. She motioned for the woman to get in, but the woman hesitated, looked to her children. A boy was about four, and the girl who slipped no more than three. They stared at Millie like she was a Martian. Millie opened the rear passenger door, removed a large accordion file, and brought it around to the double barn doors in the rear.

"I'll take you home." Millie tucked away the accordion file and mimicked lifting heavy bags. The woman didn't budge. Millie pointed at the children. The children started speaking quickly in Arabic. Millie only understood about ten words, but she knew they were begging their mother to take the offer of a ride home to get out of the horrid weather.

Again, Millie pointed to the bags. The children passed theirs over, and she loaded them in. The woman slowly pushed her groceries in beside the others, meeting Millie's gaze with her own. Millie smiled, and the woman's deep brown eyes softened. Millie took her hand and squeezed it.

"Do you live up this way?" Millie pointed north to where she knew many Syrians had apartments.

She knew this because she was defending a Syrian man who was up on charges of theft from the chicken plant where he worked—she had taken the case pro bono. Millie took on one free case per month. She figured it was her civic duty, her way of contributing to the cause.

The woman nodded, and Millie motioned for the children to climb into the back seat, where she fastened them in. The mother continued speaking to them, the Arabic clipped yet melodious. No booster seats, and they were tiny, but Millie had upgraded the front-wheel drive to four-wheel drive. They wouldn't hydroplane on her watch.

Back door closed, the woman scrambled in front, fumbling with her seat belt.

Millie walked around to the driver's door, remembering her own parents after the war. How many times had her mother recounted the small kindnesses that she and Millie's father had received when they arrived in Newfoundland from Poland? How they ended up in St. John's—Jews named Pearlstein in a town of 40,000 Murphys and Riches. They had lived on Victoria Street, so steep it was almost comical. Millie's eldest brother was born in 1952, ten years before Millie. The Pearlsteins had no car, and navigating the slippery streets with a babe in arms had proven challenging. One day Millie's mother was struggling up the hill with Joseph in her arms, when a shopkeeper on Bond Street came out rolling a pram and presented it to Millie's mother. She had never forgotten that selfless act.

Starting the engine, Millie touched her chest and said, "Millie." She turned to the children and smiled. "I'm Millie," she repeated. The little girl giggled, covering her mouth with a tiny hand. The boy still looked ill at ease. He took his sister's other hand in his.

Millie indicated left and moved into the traffic. She headed up the hill past the Irving gas bar and the McDonald's. With four people in the car, the windows began to steam up, and Millie had to open her window. "Do you know your address?" she asked.

"Twenty-four Fireweed Place." The woman looked proud of this foray into English.

Millie knew the cul-de-sac. Eight four-apartment brick row houses lined up across from a strip mall where a supermarket had once been. The building was now an empty shell, the reason the woman had to travel down the hill to get groceries.

Millie cut the engine in front of number twenty-four. She opened the back doors, and the children tumbled out onto the wet sidewalk. Millie took an umbrella out from under her seat and opened it. She passed it to the woman and dug a business card out of her purse. "Next time you go to the supermarket, call me." She put an imaginary phone to her ear and jabbed a painted nail at the card.

She then leaned into the Mini and opened the glovebox, producing four lollipops. She handed them to the mother. "I don't know your name?"

"Nariman," answered the woman, pointing to her chest and smiling. Then pointing to her son, she said, "Farid." Then her daughter. "Aleia." She went to pass back the umbrella, but Millie pushed her arm back. "You keep it," she said. "But it's not much good in this wind."

The family waited on the curb in the driving rain while Millie drove away. Her ring tone sounded again. She had missed several calls earlier, including two from Henry. He probably lost the shopping list. She sighed. The other call was from the lock-up. Her job was forever demanding.

A male voice she recognized as a sheriff's officer named Billy Breen filled the Mini. "Morning, Millie, I'm down at provincial court. Thought I'd let you know that they have your husband here. Not sure what's on the go, but you should probably get down here."

Oh, Henry, what have you done now?

6

Two Hours Earlier, Henry Searches for Eggs

Four dozen eggs. How hard could it be?

Henry looked again at his wristwatch and felt his forehead tighten. He had important things to do. First thing was his standing Tuesday appointment at Fogtown for his weekly side trim. Then, despite his head cold, he had planned to take his bike for a spin around the block. The silver thaw was not conducive to motorcycle riding, but he had to hear how she was running. He had discovered a problem with a gasket two weeks ago, and the courier company said they would have a replacement to him by today.

Dash would be home from school by two thirty. It only took him ten minutes to walk from Pius X. Who ever heard of letting children out of school before three o'clock?

Henry halted at the tubes of Easter Bunny cookie dough to refocus. He rubbed his temples. He would leave his cart to go on a reconnaissance mission. The eggs had to be here somewhere.

He grabbed a box of Triscuits. They weren't on the list, but originals were hard to come by. My God, was there anything in the box at all? Henry pushed his glasses above his eyes to read the number of grams in the box. The frames stuck to his forehead. The tiny words were swimming. Why couldn't he focus? He ditched the box on the nearest shelf and pulled down the glasses' frames. They had begun to permanently indent the soft skin above his eyebrows. Millie said he should consider graduated lenses, but they were for old people. He had arrived at the yogourt. Oh, how Henry loved lemon yogourt. He hip-checked a cardboard biscuit display. Marketing 101: keep the aisles clear. "This store is a freaking slalom course," he called to a grocery boy.

The worker, who wore a lime green T-shirt with SUNDRIES plastered across the chest, did not bother to look at Henry. Instead, he aimed his price gun at a bar code on a pack of liver. It beeped, and he moved one step to his left to zap the red light over a vacuum-packed leg of lamb. He reminded Henry of that video game Dash was always playing.

Cradling the yogourt, Henry returned to his cart. Odd, the right front wheel seemed to have developed a drag in his absence. Also, the front section was empty. Henry thought he had put his Boston hat and fruit up there. He remembered flipping up the plastic flaps so he wouldn't lose a glove. Not to worry. Millie liked to remind him that his mind was not the steel trap it once was. No, he knew it, too. This morning was a prime example. Or was his mind fog due to the sinus medication?

All he had left were the eggs, and he'd be done like dinner. Henry pushed around a figure clawing through a cart full of discount shampoo, female, judging by her size, but male according to the wardrobe, until he found what he was looking for. The eggs were well hidden in a cooler in the northwest corner. He opened four cartons to make sure there was no breakage. Henry turned several white ovals to make sure none were cracked. He would have preferred brown eggs. Why are some eggs white and others coloured? he wondered. He used to know. He dug around in the recesses of his mind for an answer. Maybe the white eggs come from hens who are cooped up, and brown eggs come from chickens who are out in the yard getting enough exercise and sunlight to turn their shells nice shades of brown and green. Hmm. He was so muddled this morning.

What difference does it make? he thought to himself. *Just get yourself up to the cash and out of Sundries.*

Henry gingerly cradled the eggs and placed them up front. He suddenly felt tired. Drugged. He'd be able to have a rest while the barber cut his hair. Then he could go home and go for a spin on his bike.

7

Delores Cowburn's Welcome to Newfoundland

"'I Am Woman,'" Delores announced. "Helen Reddy. *I Don't Know How to Love Him*, 1971." Delores sang along with the mix tape as she and Daisy hydroplaned their way east across Newfoundland. It had been raining for hours, a solid stream of sideways precipitation that alternated between light drizzle and scary slippery sleet, forcing hyper-vigilance on the part of Delores.

The worn tires on the Ford LTD dragged into yet another rut in the asphalt. Delores clutched the wheel and directed Daisy out of danger. It had been almost seven hours since she left the ferry in Port-O-Something. Delores prided herself on her positive attitude, but the long stretches of nothing and the constant concentration were affecting her mood. It's not like she didn't know how many kilometres it was across the island. The nice man on the ferry had warned her it would be a long haul.

"You're welcome to stay the night with us in Deer Lake," he'd said, smiling at his curly-haired wife. "You know, rest up a bit before you begin your final push."

Delores had received lots of offers like this in the past months and usually accepted them, but now she just wanted to get to the end of her journey.

"Thank you, sir. Ma'am." Delores nodded to the missus. "That's very kind, but Daisy and I will be on our way."

Delores and Daisy posed for a photo, and the man gingerly patted Daisy's hood.

"Okay. Just as long as you don't drive at night," he'd said.

"We'll be fine." She'd given Daisy a firm double tap for luck. "We've come this far."

"Well, read this just to be safe." He passed a brochure through her open window. She smiled and tossed it on the passenger seat.

"Safe travels," said his wife. "There'll be a hotel on the highway in Grand Falls."

"Grand Falls?" asked Delores. Hadn't she already stayed in a Grand Falls in New Brunswick?

"About halfway across." The lady raised her hand in a two-fingered salute.

That conversation seemed like a lifetime ago. It was hard to believe it was just that morning. Delores and Daisy were long past Grand Falls now. They didn't need a hotel. What they needed was a Walmart.

Delores checked her watch. It was 6:05 p.m., and for the first time, she caught glimpses of the sun behind the wooded hills to the west. She caught glimpses of water but didn't know if it was the Atlantic Ocean or lakes. She had to admit she was a bit tired of driving. Delores had been so looking forward to this trip across Canada, but now all she wanted was a break. She loved to drive, and she loved Daisy, was proud to show her off. She remembered how excited the crowd had been to meet her and Daisy in Halifax. Word had spread through the interwebs, and by the time she reached the Maritimes, people were lining the highway waiting for them to show up. And when they did, well, look out—they were the hottest ticket in town.

Delores couldn't quite figure out how so many people could know about their arrival. She expected the car aficionados, but ever since Toronto, wherever they stopped, they were met by hundreds and hundreds of well-wishers. Delores knew they had really come to see Daisy. She asked them how they heard about the trip. Facebook, Twitter, Instagram, Snapchat. Even TikTok, with teenagers dancing and lip-synching all around the car. No doubt about it, Daisy was a social media star. It was no surprise, given her fine lines.

But now on their final stretch, in the tenth province, all she and Daisy garnered was a curious look as other vehicles barrelled past them on this sorry excuse for a highway.

Delores had conquered the prairies with its big skies and endless flat plains. She had navigated her way through New York City with a police escort. She had connived her way out of a parking ticket in Montreal. But it was Newfoundland that threatened to defeat her soul. The island was ten times bigger than she had imagined.

"I am woman." Delores repeated her mantra.

Not only were the roads in rough shape, the island itself seemed to be deserted. Ever since she had started driving from the ferry terminal, Delores had not really seen any other communities. In fact, she had seen hardly anything at all besides a few dozen cars and endless stretches of trees.

Not majestic red cedars and Sitka spruce like she was accustomed to in BC, but much smaller white birch and larch. On this latest stretch, all she saw were bald maples and scraggly fir. They had withered grey trunks, thin as stop signs. Had they been hit by a blight?

Delores let out a tiny belch. The deep-fried fish 'n chips she'd wolfed down in Gander sat heavy in her stomach.

It was just as she entered Terra Nova National Park that she heard the pop. "Here we go, Daisy." She coasted to the shoulder and put the station wagon in park. Flat tires didn't stress Delores like they did some people. She pocketed her Minnie Mouse key ring and stepped out of the station wagon. The rain had calmed somewhat, and Delores was grateful for that. She pulled up her hood. The fresh air would ease her indigestion and wake her up. But jeepers, fresh wasn't the word. More like frigid. Could it really be April and this cold?

Something ran up a spindly spruce—it was the first wildlife they'd seen all day except for a pair of eagles near Grand Falls. It was smaller than a chipmunk but looked like a squirrel. A mutant chipmunk with no stripe? She took a brisk walk to get the circulation going before tackling the flat and almost walked in a mound of poop. Bear, definitely bear. Delores knew her scat.

She returned to the station wagon and got out the jack. Flat number thirty-six. Good thing her mother had taught her to change tires. They used to make a game of it. See how fast she could do it. Her best time was under eight minutes, providing she only had to install a spare. Now, her two spares looked more like patchwork rubber quilts than tires.

Delores sat back behind the wheel just as the rain started up again. The vinyl seat crunched under her weight. Merlin's beard, she was cold. Delores cleaned her hands on a rag before blowing on them. She consulted her handy-dandy map. "Man, oh man, Daisy. I thought we'd be closer to the city by now."

She guessed they had about three more hours before they'd reach St. John's. Delores resigned herself to the fact she would not get there today. Had they made a mistake coming this far? Maybe they should have ended their journey in Nova Scotia. They didn't start on Vancouver Island, so why the need to finish on an island in the east?

Daisy seemed none the worse for wear after their cross-country journey. Good, dependable Daisy. They had been together seven years now. She was her best friend. She'd never let Delores down.

"We can do it, Daisy." Delores looked at the map again. She had highlighted towns that had Walmarts. The next Walmart appeared to be in a place called Clarenville. Delores pulled her seat belt across her lap and turned the key in the ignition. Daisy purred to life. Janis Joplin was singing Kris Kristofferson's "Me & Bobby McGee."

"*Pearl Album*, released posthumously, January 1971." Janis reset Delores's default good mood.

Delores started singing along in her husky voice as she re-entered the highway, her windshield wipers "slapping time."

8

Henry at the Cash

Henry felt the presence of another cart pull up behind his. He glanced back and caught a glimpse of red polyester.

"Ahem," Akela said, raising her chin toward the girl behind the till, who was chewing a wad of gum like a cow in a field of clover. "I think it's your turn, Mr. Puddester." Of course, it had to be Akela, every word dripping with venom. Why couldn't she have chosen a different queue? Henry loaded the eggs onto the belt. The masticating clerk beeped them through and placed them into two plastic bags.

Henry stood stock still, pondering the car seat. What to do? Should he cut his losses and leave with the eggs? No, he couldn't abandon the helpless human in his shopping cart.

"Uh, sir . . . ?" The clerk nodded her head at the rest of the things in the cart. "You buying the rest or . . . ?"

Henry looked at Akela and placed the yogourt on the belt. The clerk whipped it through. He swallowed, feeling his Adam's apple bob dryly in his throat. The clerk widened her eyes.

Avoiding Akela's gaze, Henry slowly bent his knees and took the diapers and wipes from the bottom of the cart, placing them on the belt. There were little jars of baby food, too. And diaper cream. He felt Akela's eyes on him. He would not turn. The fact that a fifty-eight-year-old man was in unexpected possession of a baby was none of her business.

The cashier rang the last item through, and Henry slid his card in the machine. Savings or chequing? He couldn't remember. What was wrong with him? He had to get home and talk to Millie. She'd know what to do.

Heart pounding like the night he combined three Cokes with a painkiller, Henry packed the items in around the baby carrier as a disembodied female voice described to shoppers the benefits of kale. Henry caught a glimpse of

Akela's scarf as he started to move SWAT-team style past a display of buckets and mops. He was ten feet shy of the end of the automatic doors when he saw his childhood friend and neighbour, Dick Turner, enter the store. Frigging Dick Turner, what was he doing at Sundries on a Thursday morning?

Henry ducked behind a toilet paper display.

Dick Turner with his wonky eye. Henry knew the neighbourhood children, Dash included, called him Mad-Eye Turner after Brendan Gleeson's character in *Harry Potter*. Henry didn't really care for Dick, but it hadn't always been that way.

He had to act quickly. Dick would surely ask him what he was doing with a baby. He decided his best chance would be to exit another way.

Henry emerged from behind the toilet paper and began speed-walking toward the liquor store attached to the west side of Sundries. Back straight, head erect, upper arms perfectly parallel to his torso, bent at the elbows. He could do this. He was almost past customer service when he saw Dick Turner's right wonky eye do a double take. Henry did not wave hello but kept on going.

Just as Henry entered the liquor store, he heard an ear-piercing shriek, sounding as if it were emitted from a mature female.

For a few seconds, time stood still. Animation was suspended. He glanced back just in time to see a large glass container slip from Akela's manly hands. The jar smashed into a zillion pieces, bread and butter pickles oozing around her boots. Chunks of glass held together by the glue on the label bounced off her toe.

"Jumpin' Jesus in the garden." Henry pushed his shopping cart past a pyramid of Lamb's rum and bolted out into the freezing rain toward the Ford.

9

Frank Parrell and the Parking Meters

"Is everything all right, Mr. Parrell?" Frank's assistant leaned her head in the door, bearing witness to the decimation of that morning's newspaper.

"Fine, perfectly fine. Hunky dory, in fact." Frank Parrell was out of breath. He paused for a moment while Judy backed her head out of the room and shut the door. He then continued to beat the newspaper against his desk, something he had been doing for the better part of five minutes. He sat back for a moment, sweat dripping from his forehead onto his wrinkled shirt. He looked out his window at New Gower Street and the cars parked below. An ad for the *Telegram's* digital app filled a billboard near the gas station: THERE AND THEN, NEWS IN YOUR POCKET.

"Freakin' journalists. They're all wankers, the whole lot of them." Frank started to feed the newspaper into the shredder.

Frank Parrell had come to Newfoundland from Lancashire with his family when he was seventeen. The youngest of three children, his parents waited until Frank finished his A Levels in Wigan before embarking on what they referred to as their North American adventure. Frank's parents and siblings stayed in St. John's only a year or so before announcing their move to the warmer and more job-friendly pastures of Ontario, but by then Frank was firmly rooted in the capital city. He had been playing soccer with the Feildians only a month when his coach, recognizing talent when he saw it, made him striker and presented him with jersey number 9, and perhaps sensing that the Parrell family would eventually move on, the coach arranged for Frank to interview for a plum job with the City.

Before long, Frank Parrell met Patty Kelly, who liked not only his accent but also his magnificent physique, and Frank realized that his plans to move to Ontario with his family at the end of the following summer were not going to happen. That was how Lanky Franky, as he came to be called, ended up setting down roots in St. John's. But that was over thirty years ago. Frank was a lean machine back then with a full head of dark hair and only one chin. Now he was bald with a paunch and had taken to vaping to relieve life's stresses. The only thing that hadn't changed was his accent. That and the fact he clung to his British roots. He had no desire to return to Britain, but he found people acted more favourably when he spoke in his boyhood brogue.

In the three decades since he had started at City Hall, Frank had worked his way up from mailroom to traffic to operations. For the past ten years, he was in charge of parking meters. He liked parking meters. He appreciated their functionality. At least he used to. For many years, parking meters brought Frank great joy. Rather than be lumped in with engineering and planning, Frank was in his own little microcosm down at the bunker on New Gower Street. For a decade he had overseen the steady flow of quarters, loonies, and toonies that added up to millions in annual profit. He was a one-man show who single-handedly convinced Council of the merit of replacing the old coin and crank meters with digital ones.

Because the revenue that resulted from ticketing expired meters was a godsend for the City, it wasn't a hard sell. It was a known fact that, without the income from parking tickets, the City would be screwed. Frank had the higher-ups eating out of his hand. At least until 2014, when the digital state-of-the-art beauties became the bane of Frank's existence.

On June 1, Frank's men had all the new meters installed and working. On June 2, the complaints started to roll in. First, they came from people in wheelchairs who couldn't see the digital screens, which were far too high. So, Frank had to go and find a contractor to hack a foot off each and every one of the 2,547 metal meters in the Greater St. John's area and weld them back together. Two thousand five hundred and forty-seven. Bloody hell.

Then came the winter. The blasted snow and ice covered the solar panel screens so the sun couldn't power them up. The result: from December until May, people couldn't read the stupid things.

But the straw that broke the City's back, and started Frank vaping, came early last year when thieves began to nick the heads off the meters and spirit them away to access the change inside. It wasn't the loss of the coin—the estimate was only $22,000—but rather the repairs to the meters—$276,000—and the lost revenue while people parked for free.

Frank ordered new locking systems for every meter.

It took the bastards three weeks to figure out how to disassemble the new system. Three weeks? Did they have someone drawing up blueprints and holding seminars on how to crack off the heads? Frank spoke to one of his neighbours, a copper named Dick, to ask him how the thieves could be so cunning.

Dick shrugged his navy blue–sweatered shoulders. "They're good at what they do. What can I say?"

The pressure was catching up with Frank. He wasn't sleeping more than four hours at a stretch. He could feel kidney stones forming from his hopped-up homebrew. He needed to talk to his ex-wife, Patty. He convinced her to come have coffee with him.

"Yes, it's a bleedin' emergency," he said over the phone. "Can you meet me at Jumping Bean on Elizabeth in twenty minutes?"

Patty installed herself in the chair across the tiny table from Frank. She laid her bag and yoga mat under the table. She was wearing her blue plasticky-looking jacket over a long sweater and leggings. She had what he called her serious look on her face.

"You look good. You must be hitting the gym." Frank nudged the tea he had bought for Patty over to her side of the table.

"Frank," she said with little warmth to her voice. "I have things to do." She tapped her watch.

"I know, you're always busy." Frank took a sip of his coffee. He just needed to be in her presence to calm himself down. "You on your way to yoga?"

"Frank." The volume of Patty's voice had ratcheted up a couple of notches. Frank jumped.

Patty pushed away the untouched teacup with her left forearm like she thought she'd catch something if she made contact with her fingers. "Frank, what's wrong with Kaitlyn?"

"Kaitlyn?" An espresso machine gurgled behind the counter.

"Yes, Kaitlyn, you know, our daughter?"

"Oh. Nothing. No, Kaitlyn is best kind."

"So, what's the emergency?"

"It's me. I'm knackered." Frank looked pleadingly into Patty's green cat-like eyes. "The kidney stones are back, and I don't know what to do."

Frank's ex-wife looked at him, no doubt remembering why she'd left him. "You called me all the way across town to complain about your kidney stones?"

"Yes, Patty, you don't know how bad the pain is."

"Frank, I almost died giving birth to your child."

"Oh yeah, well, that was daft of me. I should've said you *do* know how bad the pain is, and that's why I need your advice. I have to do something before I throw myself off Signal Hill. I'm not over-egging the pudding, Patty. You have to tell me what to do."

"Okay," said Patty slowly, as if Frank were a child. "Remember the last time you had kidney stones?"

"Yes." Frank nodded.

Patty nodded, too. Frank was relieved she was showing some sympathy. "Do you remember what the doctor said?"

Frank's eyes travelled up and to the left. "She said to stop drinking so much homebrew. But that's bollocks. She didn't know what she was talking about. I mean, come on, the unfermented sugars in homebrew are no worse than in store-bought beer. You, of all people, know that's nothing but pork pies."

"Mmm hmm." Patty inhaled through her nose and stood up from the table. The smell of Screech coffee filled the place. "I'm going to go now, Frank. If you ever need to talk about Kaitlyn, don't hesitate to call."

Frank watched her pick up her things and push the door open with such force she almost creamed a man in a suit, who looked at her, disgusted.

Imagine agreeing with the doctor that he reduce his consumption of homemade beer. And he thought he knew Patty. Hmmph. She was obviously not the person to calm him down.

There was only one person who could do that. Henry Puddester, Frank's best friend and neighbour and, until recently, fellow municipal civil servant. Frank pulled out his phone. Henry would be up for a good hoppy beer, if not tonight, then the weekend.

10

Henry's Dilemma

Safe inside the Escape, Henry took some calming breaths. He looked at the floral car seat in the passenger seat and called his wife's cell. "Come on, Millie. Pick up, pick up."

No dice. His call went to voice mail.

"Millie, I'm in a bit of a pickle here. Need your advice. Call me soonest."

Henry looked at his cellphone. Had he just said "soonest"?

He pulled up the Velcro flap. The baby peered out at him and smiled around the pacifier.

Henry pulled the seat belt around the car seat. He knew it had to be backwards-facing. At least he remembered that. He blinked his eyes a few times to shake off the double vision, turned the key in the ignition, and pointed the Ford homeward.

Henry pulled in the driveway and ran up the front steps to unlock the door. He didn't know why he didn't want anyone to see the baby carrier. It's not like he had done anything wrong. He ran back and undid the seat belt. The baby was quiet. He removed the carrier from the seat and ran back in the sanctuary of his house, depositing the carrier on the floor next to the island. He made two more trips back out for the rest of the groceries and then closed the door and bolted it behind him. He tried Millie's cell again.

That's when the baby started to howl. Sheesh. Henry pulled open the Velcro and undid the harness. He picked up the tiny girl and rocked her in his arms. She stopped howling for a moment, until he went to put her back down. The howling started where it left off. Had Dash been that loud? "You hungry, little muffin?" he asked.

Holding the baby in his arms, he cracked open a jar of pears and found a teaspoon in the drawer. He sat on the wing chair at the end of the table and tickled the baby's lips with the mashed fruit. She opened her rosebud mouth and slurped it up. Half came back out, but Henry caught it with the spoon and fed it back in. God, he was thirsty. But he did not stop shovelling in the pears until the tiny human arched her back and screamed to high heaven. "Jesus Murphy," he said, flipping her onto his shoulder and patting gently. An enormous belch came from deep in the baby's innards, and she settled onto his shoulder.

Henry breathed a sigh of relief, went to the tap, and poured himself a tall glass of water. He was starting to feel a bit more like himself, although he still felt dizzy if he moved his head.

He had just settled the baby back into the carrier behind the island when the doorbell rang.

Shoot. He'd like to ignore it, but it would wake the baby. Henry closed the floral panel and padded to the door. Dick Turner stood on his front step. A second man sat in the passenger seat of a patrol car parked at the curb. "Wassup, Henry?" he asked. "How are things?" Dick spoke to him through the screen door.

"Fine. Fine. Everything is fine." Henry tended to repeat words when he was freaked out.

"Mind if I come in?"

"Well, actually . . ."

Dick opened the door and stepped inside. "Saw you at Sundries."

"Yes, yes, had to pick up some eggs." Henry still felt an unquenchable thirst. He went to the sink and filled his glass a second time and chugged down the cool liquid.

"Eggs . . . ?" Dick let the word linger, hoping, no doubt, that Henry would fill the empty space.

"Yes, well, uh . . . they only had white eggs. I wanted to get brown, uh, extra-large." Henry took a breath. "Farm fresh," he added. "Much better for you."

"Did you buy anything else?"

"Not much." Henry saw Dick's left eye take in the baby products on the table and moved closer.

"What do we have here?"

"Uh, nothing." Henry was happy he had placed the baby carrier on the floor out of Dick's line of sight. Sweat pooled on his forehead and began to drip down the front of his coat.

The other man was now out of the white police car and up the steps. "You need backup?"

"That's okay, Rupert. I'm just having a word with my man here."

Henry was not Dick's man. Had never been Dick Turner's man. A memory flashed through Henry's mind of ten-year-old Dick, ruddy-faced with pinball eyes, moving his wooden school desk away from Henry's and whispering, "Traitor." Henry could hear the word as if he had just uttered it now in his kitchen.

"A word about what?"

"Someone took a baby from Sundries. The mother is understandably upset." Dick's eyes shot off in different directions. "You happen to see anything strange while you were there?"

"No. Uh, is it related to that child abduction I heard about yesterday?"

"I don't think so. But I thought you might be able to help us." Dick pointed toward the patrol car at the curb.

"Me? How?"

"Well, the thing is, the cashier and another witness watched you leave Sundries with a baby in a car seat." Dick picked up the open jar of pears and slowly screwed the lid back on.

Words tumbled out of Henry's mouth before he even thought them. "That's ludicrous. What would I be doing with a baby?"

"That's what we came to find out."

Henry stood his ground.

"Henry, I have reason to believe you left Sundries with someone else's child."

"For God's sake, Dick. Why would you believe a cashier and a Cub leader over me?" Henry heard the rising volume of his voice.

"This." Dick held up a gold and black winter hat with gloves protruding from the inside. It was Henry's favourite Boston toque from the 2016 Outdoor Classic game in Foxborough, Massachusetts. The hat Henry never left home without. "Your toque was in an abandoned cart near where the mother last saw her child."

11

Tiny Taylor Navigates Chase the Ace

"Goddamn Chase the Ace." Tiny Taylor manoeuvred his Ford F150 down Old Petty Harbour Road, dodging pedestrians who popped out from between the vehicles parked on both sides of the two-laned street. "I've never seen so many people."

"They're out in droves," agreed Wally Burke, a fellow foreman at the chicken plant in the Goulds. Wally was short and compact with full lips and an enormous schnozz. He and Tiny normally worked different shifts, but tonight, their boss, Vik Morgan, or Vik the Prick, as most called him, needed them both there at the same time. For the past two months, a surplus of chickens had been causing the price to free-fall at grocery stores. People could only consume so much poultry. The market was saturated.

Chicken. Whenever he closed his eyes, Tiny saw plucked carcasses. When he was in his teens, he could eat chicken three times a day. His mother always said that's why he kept growing until he reached six foot seven. "It's all the steroids, sure. Them nuggets are just pumped full, Tiny. Make no wonder you're built like a skyscraper." Tiny imagined his mother's face in front of him, hovering just beyond the windshield.

Wally waved his hand in front of Tiny's eyes. "Helloooo. Pigs in space."

"What?" Tiny jolted a bit, causing the truck to drift slightly into the oncoming lane.

"I said, I wonder why there are so many more people out tonight?" Wally gestured toward the swarming crowds.

"Jackpot's at two point three million. Only nine cards left in the deck, apparently." Tiny swerved around a backhoe. "Who in their right mind would drive a tractor to a lottery?"

"We *are* in the Goulds." A headlight glinted off Wally's gold earrings, two hoops in one ear, none in the other.

"True enough. For the love of Jesus, someone better draw the stupid Ace of Spades tonight. I should have brought the bike."

"We'd have looked good, me tucked in behind the world's largest human."

"You would have found your own ride. Turn on the radio, will you?"

"What station?"

"CBC."

"You listen to CBC?"

"Why wouldn't I listen to CBC?"

"You've always struck me as the country type."

"And you strike me as a fucking Neanderthal."

"Neanderthal? That's the best you can come up with?"

"Let's just say that if you decide to get a nose job, the doctor is gonna need an excavator."

Wally laughed. "Not bad. All the same, I'm turning on VOCM."

"Listen, Gonzo. If you don't turn that radio to CBC, I'll throw you out of the truck and run over that nose of yours."

Wally switched on CBC.

"They've got to change the rules." A man's voice boomed simultaneously out of Tiny's front custom subwoofer and rear Polk speakers. "I understand St. Perpetua's needs a new roof, but they did not have to bring thousands of people into our community to play cards in order to get it."

"Okay, but Chase the Ace has already started. What do you propose the organizers do at this point to change things?" The reporter was the diminutive Gillian Gee, who Tiny liked to watch on the evening news. He fantasized about the children they would have, him with his six-foot-seven frame and her five-nothing.

"I can't stand her." Wally reached out to change the station.

Tiny smacked his hand away. "Stop it. I like her." He felt his cheeks flush.

"Saints alive, you're turning red. Tiny and Gilly up in a tree, K-I-S-S-I-N-G."

"I am not. Will you shut up and let me listen?"

"Right now, if a ticket number is called, the person has fifteen minutes to present themselves to the parish hall for verification and their chance to flip over a card. If they don't make it in that time period, then another ticket will be drawn."

Gillian Gee: "That's correct. Can you think of a better way of doing it?"

"They have to start letting winners call in their numbers rather than presenting in person at the church hall. The main street in the Goulds was not designed to accommodate five hundred cars."

Gillian Gee: "You make an excellent point. But aren't the businesses along that stretch benefiting from the money people are spending here?"

"That may be, but I can't get my car out of my effing driveway. 'Scuse my Latin."

"He's—" Wally began to speak.

Tiny held up his right index finger, silencing him.

Gillian Gee: "I thought the RNC posted no-parking signs all along the main road?"

"Yeah, a lot of good that did. I've got an effin' Winnebago parked on my lawn."

"Did anyone ask for permission?"

"No, they didn't ask for permission. It's like Armageddon here. Every ticket holder for himself."

Gillian Gee: "Besides the frustration, what's your major concern?"

"There's going to be an accident."

Gillian Gee: "It's my understanding there are emergency vehicles on site."

"Yes, but the roads are so blocked with people and cars and trucks and friggin' campers, they'd never make it out to get someone to the hospital.

Just last week, they had a close call. Mark my words. There'll be a death before someone draws the effing Ace of Spades." The man's voice faded out.

Gillian Gee: "This is Gillian Gee, reporting from St. Perpetua's Parish. We'll be back in fifteen minutes for more coverage of week twenty-eight of Chase the Ace in the Goulds. Now for the evening news."

A male voice came on. Reporter Hank Skanes. "Today's top story is another kidnapping in Clarenville. The incident has shaken up the entire community."

Tiny switched off the radio. "I am sick of kidnapping stories. That's all we've been hearing since last fall."

"You'd swear we were in LA," said Wally. "There are just as many people here."

They were passing St. Perpetua's Church and Parish Hall. It was every bit as bad as the man described, with tents and trailers squeezed higgledy-piggledy on every bit of unoccupied land.

"It's a refugee camp." Tiny retracted the truck mirrors so as not to scrape a particularly wide motorhome sticking into the road.

"My in-laws live in the Goulds, but the father-in-law works in town. The wife said he has to leave work at noon just to try and make it home before the madness begins."

"Fuck me sideways. How is Aggie, by the way?" asked Tiny.

"She got a new walker the other day and said she feels like a cheetah whenever she gets out of the wheelchair."

"That bad, is it?"

"They say it's MS. It's pretty serious. We don't know what to expect. I try not to think about it.. Anyway, the father-in-law told her they're expecting more than seventy thousand people tonight. Imagine. That's more than the Regatta."

"Forget the Regatta. That's more than the population of the Goulds."

"R. J. Mahone said he waited in line for over five hours to buy a ticket. And that was only for a chance to flip a card. He must be out of his mind."

"That's not news." Tiny laughed. "Anyone who works as a chicken catcher isn't dealing with a full deck."

"I heard he's working the forklift now." Wally scratched his head.

"Yep, wonders never cease. Did you hear someone dared him to eat three cooked chickens?"

"I can't stomach chicken anymore." Wally stuck out his tongue.

"I know what you're saying." Tiny pulled the truck around a group of kids playing soccer in the middle of the street. "Seeing a chicken in a supermarket cooler isn't the same as seeing them in the abattoir. All the blood and feathers."

"We should write a book. That's what Aggie says every time I complain about the simple minds I have to deal with at work."

"Yeah, we can call it *Last Cluck in Hell.*"

12

Pink-Clad Baby

"I was wondering where that went. I lost it when I got in the store. Someone must have picked it up." Henry reached for his Boston toque, but Dick Turner held it aloft with one hand and kept a firm grip on Henry's sleeve with the other.

"Let me go."

"Tell me what happened to the baby." Dick took a large Ziploc from his pocket and dropped in the hat.

"What are you doing? That's mine."

"Evidence."

"Evidence of what?" Henry's head was splitting.

"Evidence linking you to the kidnapping."

"Dick, how long have you known me? You know I'd never take a baby."

"I'm just trying to get the story straight."

"There is no story. I went to Sundries to pick up some eggs."

"You're telling me you didn't take someone else's shopping cart?"

"Dick, do I look like the type who'd take someone else's cart?" Henry thought back to just last week, when he had done that exact thing.

"Why do you have these baby things?" Dick touched the wet wipes.

Before Henry could answer, the guy in the car called out from the window. "They've issued an amber alert. They're setting up roadblocks within a ten-mile radius of Sundries."

Dick exhaled. "That's good. Any word on the mother?"

"Still freaking out."

"Okay, you hold tight. Me and Henry here are going to talk some more." He gripped Henry's arm tighter.

"Take it easy on the arm, Dick." Henry tried to wrench free of Dick's claws, but Dick did not loosen his grip. Henry was having trouble getting enough air in his lungs. Dick pushed Henry closer to the diapers and wet wipes. With his free hand, Dick picked up the tiny jar of puréed pears. Just as he did so, his toe came in contact with the carrier. Still holding Henry's sleeve, Dick reached down and pulled back the Velcro. The baby girl howled, her mouth forming a perfect O, obliterating her face.

"Now look what you did. You woke her up." Henry covered his mouth.

Dick released his grip on Henry's arm long enough to remove a walkie-talkie from his belt.

"I can explain," Henry said.

Dick held up his hand. "Rupert, I've got the baby. She appears fine. Can you go back to Sundries and bring the mother here?"

After that, things happened quickly.

In what seemed like seconds, a young mother appeared in Henry's kitchen. She wore a pair of denim overalls with a fisherman-knit sweater underneath. Over the top she wore a man's jacket. Like someone who worked in a garage would wear. Funny, Henry hadn't laid eyes on her before that moment. She must have been close to Henry at some point. When the woman's eyes lit on the baby, she started howling like a banshee. She picked up the pink-clad infant and held it in her arms so tight that Henry feared she would suffocate it. "Are you sure she can breathe?" asked Henry, stepping closer.

"Stay away from me." The mother screamed, backing up and pointing her left index finger at Henry. "Don't you come near her." She looked at Dick. "That's the bastard who kidnapped my baby."

"Oh, for God's sake. I didn't kidnap any baby." Henry shook his head and gave the girl an open-eyed glare.

"You're a monster, that's what you are."

"I told you, I would never . . ."

"I hope they lock you up and throw away the key," screamed the woman.

Dick had once again sunk his claws into Henry's forearm and pulled him away from the mother. "Rupert, can you please stay here with Miss Mooney and her baby until another patrol car arrives?"

"What are you going to do?"

"I am going to take the suspect down to the lock-up."

"You can't be serious, Dick." Henry tented his fingers over his eyes and rubbed his temples with his thumbs, Dick's left arm rising with Henry's right. "Let me just call Millie. She'll straighten this out."

Dick pulled Henry's arm back down and continued talking to Rupert, something about fingerprints on shopping carts. When he finished, he looked back to Henry.

"Henry, I'm going to cuff you. But I'll put the cuffs on the front. That way you can just walk out to the car like normal." He snapped the cuffs into position.

"You call this normal?" asked Henry, holding up his conjoined wrists. "I don't think Millie is going to be impressed."

But Dick wasn't listening. He was talking to his partner, the man named Rupert.

"While you're waiting, take Miss Mooney's statement. I'll catch up with you after I bring Mr. Puddester downtown."

He pushed Henry out in the hall and out the door. Henry took one last look at the pink bundle.

"Don't you look at her," the mother called out. "I hope you rot in hell." The frigid April air blasted Henry's ears. He didn't look back.

They did the perp walk out the door and across the lawn to the squad car. A woman was coming across the road toward them. Henry recognized the jacket. Was that Frank's ex, Patty? *Please God, let it not be Patty*. But it was. She was wearing a light blue jacket that looked like it was made out of plastic pop bottles.

"Hi, Patty." Dick raised his free arm to her. Henry tried to hide his face.

Patty twisted her neck as she walked by, trying to digest what she was seeing.

"It's not what you think," called Henry. "Just a little misunderstanding."

Dick was pushing Henry's head down into the back seat of the patrol car when a CBC van pulled into the cul-de-sac.

Geez Louise. Freaking reporters. How did they know where to come? There was no way they were going to get a picture of Henry for the evening news. He made sure of that.

13

Henry at the Lock-Up

Dick pulled the police cruiser up snug to the lower east side of the court-house. The rough stone building had to be more than a hundred years old. Henry had never before had reason to go inside.

"Sit tight." Dick's eyes ricocheted around a bit at Henry before he got out and rang the bell next to a steel door. A correctional officer appeared. Dick opened Henry's door.

Henry, his hands still cuffed, preceded Dick through the doorway in the thick granite walls. His head was splitting. He needed another decongestant. He needed water. He needed a new life.

Inside the musty-smelling lock-up, Dick unsheathed his Sig 9mm automatic and pushed it into a square black chamber.

"What are you doing?"

Dick's hands disappeared inside the chamber like he was performing a magic trick and would pull out a dove. "Removing the clip. Have to do it inside the unloading station. We don't want any stray bullets bouncing off the walls and hitting someone by mistake, now, do we?"

Dick grinned and pulled his hands back out. He placed the clip and gun in a small locker, shut the door, and turned the key, which he put in his pocket. He then led Henry to the counter, where one of the correctional officers came around to meet them.

"Are you okay if we take your cuffs off?" The female officer whose name tag read MARSHALL was the first to speak.

"Why wouldn't I be?"

The correctional officer looked to Dick, who nodded.

"He's all right." Dick kept his wonky eyes on TV monitors, which were angled so that Henry could not see them.

"What's going to happen now?" Henry felt his throat constrict.

Dick looked at him over the counter. "Let's see. You'll have to go before the judge within twenty-four hours, and he . . . who's on today? Hanrahan?"

CO Marshall shuffled a couple of pages in a black binder. "No, Hiscock. A sheriff's officer will bring you over to Atlantic Place this morning to see Judge Hiscock."

"You're lucky we made it here so soon. Otherwise you would have had to stay here until tomorrow." Dick smiled.

Henry refused to react. There was no question: Dick Turner was an asshole, through and through.

"What will the judge do?" Henry felt like he might throw up. He needed Millie.

"She'll set a date for you to answer to the charges." CO Marshall took Henry's hands and unlocked the cuffs.

"Which are?"

"Kidnapping, possibly child endangerment." Dick's wonky eye flipflopped a bit before settling on Henry.

"Come off it, Dick. Surely this little misunderstanding can be explained. You can't arrest me for taking a shopping cart with a baby in it."

"I thought you didn't take any baby . . . ?" Dick left Henry at the counter with CO Marshall.

"I didn't kidnap anybody, Dick. You know me."

But Dick was gone, leaving Henry to fend for himself.

"Keep your hands on the counter. I'm going to empty your pockets." CO Marshall motioned Henry closer to the desk.

Henry took a step closer, and she pulled out his wallet and flip phone from the left pocket. A pack of Juicy Fruit gum and his pocket knife followed. CO Marshall put them in a Ziploc.

"Other pocket."

She put her hand in Henry's right pocket and took out his little plastic bottle of hand sanitizer. He stiffened. "Do you have to take that?"

"Yep."

"Can I have a squirt first?"

CO Marshall opened the bottle, dripped a bit into Henry's waiting palm, and dropped the sanitizer into the bag. "Watch."

"Watch what?" Henry furiously rubbed in the sanitizing lotion.

"I'm going to take off your watch, Mr. Puddester." She undid Henry's silver retirement watch.

"Any other jewellery?"

He lifted his chin to reveal a thin silver chain with his mother's St. Christopher medal on it. CO Marshall dropped it in with the other things. "Shoelaces."

"They're slip-on." Henry showed her his feet.

"Belt." CO Marshall undid his Triumph buckle and slipped the belt off his khakis. She put it in a second bag, zipped it, and wrote up a receipt.

"What are you going to do with my things?"

"We'll keep them safe until you're released."

"When will that be?"

"No idea. Depends on what the judge says."

"Don't I . . . you know, get to make a call?"

"Sure. Calls cost twenty-five cents for twenty minutes."

"What happens after twenty minutes?"

"You get cut off. But you won't make it to twenty minutes."

"Why not?"

"Full house." CO Marshall swept her arm to indicate the packed wing. "Eleven cells, almost all triple-bunked. Plus the three female cells down there. That's thirty-three men and women who all like talking on the tel-ee-phone."

"Geesh, can I do it now?" Henry's temples throbbed. He had entered into a world of which he knew little, except by proxy from Millie. She would get him out of here.

CO Marshall called down to the penitentiary and got a code. Then she led Henry to an old-fashioned black wall phone. Two men were ahead of him. The one on the phone was at least 300 pounds with hands like catcher's mitts, one of which he flung through the air as he talked. The other guy was Henry's height and wore only a pair of sweatpants. He looked at Henry and smiled, showing a mouth in desperate need of orthodontic care.

Henry smiled back and felt compelled to say something. "Where's your shirt?"

"Buddy ripped it off me when he gave me this." The man turned, showing Henry an open wound in his side.

Henry felt the blood drain away from his brain.

"You okay, man? You're not lookin' too good." The man put the back of his hand to Henry's forehead. "Sit down, man. I won't be long. Just gotta talk to my boy, make sure I'm hooked up for when I go back in, know what I mean?"

Henry slid down on the concrete floor with his back to the wall and watched as Stab Man took the phone from Mr. Mitts. His sinuses dripped down the back of his throat. Why hadn't the stupid pill he had taken cleared up his nose?

"I don't care where he stuffs it, just make sure he gets himself arrested and shows up at the pen by the day after tomorrow. Else he's a dead man."

Stab Man hung up the phone and pulled Henry to his feet. He was so tired. And thirsty. Again. His tongue was sandpaper.

"Want me to stay here while you make your call? Make sure you're all right?"

"No, thank you," said Henry. "I appreciate your concern, but I think I can manage."

Henry dialled Millie's number. It went directly to voice mail again. She was probably in court upstairs in this very building. Dang. He hung up and dialled again, hoping for a different result.

"Millie Puddester. McLoughlan, McLoughlan and Mercer. Leave a message."

"Millie, call me as soon as you can." He sneezed, forgetting he no longer had his phone. Double dang, he needed different cold meds.

CO Marshall, who had returned from escorting Stab Man to his cell, led Henry away from the phone to the male wing of holding cells. They passed the drunk tank, a round room with three blanket-covered bodies sleeping on the concrete floor.

"They okay?" asked Henry. "They don't look very comfortable."

"Just sleeping it off."

CO Marshall walked on as if the scene were normal. My God, what century were they in?

Henry's cell was already occupied by a man sporting a swollen black eye and bandaged nose. He was rank, the top three buttons of his shirt were ripped off, and it looked like he may have pissed his pants, or worse.

The man held out his hand. Henry took it reluctantly. "I'm Henry."

"Charlie," Mr. Black Eye responded.

"Who's that?" Henry pointed to a second man, who was back-on in the corner. He looked no older than Frank's Kaitlyn.

"Get the spiders off me," he screamed.

"Aww, that's Hallucinating Harold. He'll be okay. He got a bit too much rat poison in his last hit."

Henry wasn't quite sure how to respond. "That's a shame." He tested the lower bunk. Firm. His stomach growled. How could his body be thinking of food when he was in this situation? He was still thirsty, too. Thirsty like he hadn't drunk in days. He turned to Black-Eyed Charlie. "Can we order something to eat and drink in here?"

"Yeah, they got a direct line to Big Bite. CO Marshall'll order in a donair for ya."

"Excellent. I am so hungry. I was afraid there'd be no food."

Black-Eyed Charlie shook his head. "I'm just pulling your leg. You are green, aren't ya? Green like the pasture. You missed breakfast, but if you're remanded, you'll probably make it back here for lunch." Black-eyed Charlie smiled, showing several brown teeth.

"Remanded." That was a term Henry heard on the news. "What . . . what exactly does that mean?"

"That means you can kiss your bed goodbye for a while. Until they figure out what to do with you. What are you in here for, anyway?"

Henry looked at his shoes and wished he had his Purell. "I was at the supermarket, and a baby appeared in my shopping cart. I didn't know what to do, so I . . ."

CO Marshall unlocked the door, cutting him off. "Fingerprint time, cowboy," she said.

"You'll have to excuse me." Henry waved to Black-Eyed Charlie and followed CO Marshall back out near the desk and into a small room, where a civilian member of the RNC stood Henry against a carpeted wall for his mug shot. The woman, H. BROWNE, her name tag read, picked up his right hand and pushed each finger individually into an ink pad. It was like an out-of-body experience, as if Henry were above, witnessing this happening to someone else. The fingerprints of his left hand pressed onto the paper. Then the right. A small blur on his right index fingerprint caused her to inspect Henry's hand. She wiped off the ink and held it up to the light.

"I burned it when I was nine," he said, remembering how his mother had run the water cold and made Henry keep his hand in the sink.

H. Browne did not speak but placed his hand back in his lap.

14

Henry, Time Is Ticking

On his way back to his cell, Henry saw the clock. Nine thirty. Shoot. He had forgotten his hair appointment. "I wonder if you'd be so kind as to call Fogtown to let them know I'll be a bit late?"

H. Browne laughed. "Hear that, Marshall?"

"No, what?"

"Mr. Puddester would like you to let the barber know he's been detained."

CO Marshall laughed so hard she hiccoughed.

Henry sighed. He was tired. He had never felt so tired in all his born days. He felt like putting his head down and having a rest. But it was so germy in this place.

"Put your hands in front," CO Marshall said when she stopped laughing. She cuffed Henry.

"How come you need to put them on again?"

"You're taking a little trip."

"Where?"

"To the courthouse."

Henry's two cellmates shuffled up. Their handcuffs were attached to a nylon restraint belt, which was in turn attached to leg irons. Black-Eyed Charlie was wearing a pair of clean grey sweatpants and didn't seem the least bit perturbed. Hallucinating Harold seemed sedated, his head lolling to one side.

"Oh." Henry was pleased he only had the cuffs.

CO Marshall moved Henry in line with the others, shackled his feet, and chained them to his wrist restraints.

"You thought you were free to waltz out in just handcuffs?" Black-Eyed Charlie laughed.

Under the direction of a sheriff's officer named Breen, Henry shuffled along with the seven others, daycare style. Once outside, Henry felt the frigid air. Before he had a chance to get cold, he was loaded into a high-ceilinged white Mercedes-Benz Sprinter van. The three men in Henry's compartment, his two roommates and one other short man with a goatee, pushed him along the bench.

Henry sat and sized up the seat belts. He struggled to pull the belt across his lap. It was bad enough to be in a paddy wagon. He didn't want to end up in an accident, too.

Black-Eyed Charlie laughed. "Check it out, b'ys." Then he directed a look at Henry. "You're not going to go anywhere. If you do, you're taking all of us with you."

Black-Eyed Charlie banged on the side of their compartment, dragging Henry's arm with him. "Imelda, you in there?"

"No, I'm down on the beach in Mexico." A gruff bottle-a-day female voice came from behind the metal wall.

"How're you doing? How is the eye?"

"You did a good job on it."

"Sorry about that." Black-Eyed Charlie shrugged. "You got me pretty good, too. Who's in there with you?"

"Geraldine."

"Hi, Geraldine. Long time, no see."

"Not long enough."

"I guess she's not over my last visit." Black-Eyed Charlie grinned at Henry.

"Bastard put a hole in my front door." Geraldine's tinny voice came through the wall. "They took it out of my cheque."

"You should answer your door next time someone knocks on it, then. It's polite."

Henry's stomach rumbled like an incoming storm.

"What was that?" Geraldine's voice.

"Fresh Fish here wants a pizza." Black-Eyed Charlie laughed and started to say more, but three bangs from the front wall of the van interrupted him.

"Get ready. You're in for a bumpy ride."

The men in the back listed left as the van began to move. They continued to lurch back and forth until the van came to a sudden halt just five minutes later. Henry could hear the front door open, and next thing, Sheriff's Officer Breen was opening the side door. The wind lifted Henry's hair upwards off his hatless head. He looked around. He felt like he hadn't seen the city in years. They were at Beck's Cove next to Atlantic Place, approximately 400 metres as the crow flies from where they started their van journey.

The sheriff's officer pulled the first man out of the van, and the rest followed. Once unloaded, they were marched, along with the two women, into a special elevator that Henry had no idea existed. Henry chanced a look at the damage Charlie had done to Imelda's eye. Jesus in the garden.

"What are you looking at, Fishy?" Imelda smiled a seductive smile.

"Charlie shouldn't have done that to a lady."

Charlie and Imelda and all the others laughed until the tears rolled, laughed until the elevator spat them out in what appeared to be a special holding cell.

"Where are we?" Henry tried to fathom what other secret rooms were hidden in the downtown that he had never heard of.

"Fourth floor Atlantic Place."

"You mean where you come to pay your parking tickets?"

"Close enough."

"What happens now?"

"You wait until they call you to see the judge." Sheriff's Officer Breen took Henry's hands, inserted the small key into his cuffs, and released his upper body from the coffle. After he undid all the hands, he moved down to the leg irons.

Henry did like the others and sat down to wait.

Sheriff's Officer Breen brought Geraldine in first. She was a bosomy woman with smoke-dried skin and a hacking cough. She had an open sore on her lip. A door in the side of the room opened, and Sheriff's Officer Breen led Geraldine inside. The door closed, swallowing them. Before it did, Henry heard, over the roar of his innards, the clerk announcing the judge.

"Judge Hiscock presiding. All rise."

15

Millie, the Lawyer

Henry could hear his wife, or more accurately he could hear her black ankle-high boots tapping down the tiles outside the holding cell in Atlantic Place, making her 120 pounds sound more like 200. He had bought her those boots for their twenty-fifth wedding anniversary. Italian leather. Funny, they didn't have a rubber sole. She had spied them down a tiny alleyway in Croatia. They had only cost a fraction of what they would have in Canada, but it still added up to more than a week's rent in the villa.

Henry didn't need to see Millie to know what she looked like, because Millie had only one look on workdays: don't-mess-with-me-or-I'll-chew-you-up-and-spit-you-out lawyer. Black power suit over a white blouse. Not one treated blonde hair out of place. Her blemish-free face set in an expression just daring someone to cross her.

The thought of Millie working with these lowlifes seemed incongruous, but Henry knew her work frequently involved visits here to meet with clients who ran into a bit of trouble by using a tire iron to beat the person they were ordered to stay away from, perhaps, or stealing a car to make it on time to a court appearance.

Millie always represented the downtrodden. Whatever gene was responsible for saving the world, Millie had it in triplicate. Equally strange, and Henry recognized this, he was born without it.

The noise of distant doors squeaking open and closed was interrupted by a sheriff's officer talking into his walkie-talkie. "Puddester, you're outta here."

Millie came within view in a whiff of breath-freshening mint. She looked laminated.

"Damn," said Black-Eyed Charlie when he caught sight of her. "I'd like to get me a piece o' that."

Henry glowered at him. Charlie responded with a thumbs-up and a wink.

"At least you didn't have far to come," said Henry, once the boots had stopped their clicking. Provincial court was less than a block from the lock-up on Water Street, where Dick had brought Henry that morning, and Millie's firm, McLoughlan, McLoughlan and Mercer, was only three doors down from the front of the courthouse on Duckworth Street, and it was either there, here, or in the courthouse that Millie spent virtually all of her working hours.

Millie did not respond to her husband. She was a trial lawyer, and Henry knew she was purposely mute so as not to encourage him to say anything that might cause him trouble later. "Thanks, Billy. See you tomorrow. They're bringing in Hutton."

"That should be interesting." Sheriff's Officer Breen smiled, revealing an upper row of shark-like overlapping incisors and cuspids. "Last time he was in, the whole building went into lockdown."

Henry fished around in his frontal lobes for something to add to this exchange but came up with nothing. Finally, he said, "Millie, I'm seeing double, and I've never been so desperate for a drink of water."

Sheriff's Officer Breen raised his eyebrows in a silent question.

"See ya, Fishy." Imelda and Geraldine waved as Henry left the holding cell.

Black-Eyed Charlie showed off his black grin. "Yeah, maybe on the outside. Or who knows, maybe down at the pen."

Henry felt a flush rising from his collar. He slipped a sideways glance at Millie. She was hard to read. Henry required a better view of her face, but she was already past the guards and the metal detector, out the door.

Once outside provincial court, Henry relaxed a little and automatically felt in his pocket for his hand sanitizer. "Millie, do you have any Purell in your purse?"

Millie didn't as much as grunt. She did not look at Henry. Nor did she open her bag. Henry followed her onto the escalator, rubbing his dry lips together. His stomach growled again, but he did not mention it. His sinuses were about to explode. He pinched the upper sides of his nose.

Henry had been confident Millie would realize that it was all just a misunderstanding. Looking at her tight little butt now, though, stalking ahead of him through the Atlantic Place parking garage, he was unable to shake the sneaking suspicion that his wife of twenty-seven years might think *he* had been the one to do something wrong.

He followed her outside and instinctively put his hands up to cover his ears. He wished he had his hat. The biting wind hadn't calmed any since he had come in. Salt water hung in the air, and vehicles, coated in coarse road salt, sent up waves of frosty slush as they drove along the waterfront.

Henry worried about what was going on inside Millie's head. The wheels were always turning, and from the look on her face, they weren't turning in a carefree manner. His stomach churned.

He wished he knew how much Millie had been told about what had happened at the grocery store. Henry didn't want to mention that it was Dick who brought him in. He didn't care for Dick, but he didn't wish him dead, and dead he would be if Millie got her hands on him.

Why wasn't she talking? She must have had a hard morning at work. But she talked to Sheriff's Officer Breen. They arrived at Millie's cobalt-blue Mini Clubman. Henry had just closed the passenger door when his wife turned on him like a rabid dog.

"Why didn't you tell me what was going on? I could have probably nipped this thing before it escalated."

"I did. I called and left messages on your phone."

"'Call me soonest,'" she said. "Henry, your message failed to mention you were *in custody*. I called home and got voice mail. Then I called your cell and got the same."

"They took my flip phone from me, Millie."

"So, let me get this straight. You were at the supermarket . . ." Millie inhaled, exhaled, and started the engine.

"Yes, getting the eggs for Cub Camp . . ."

Henry's voice was drowned out as Millie continued.

"You were at the supermarket getting eggs for Cub Camp and somehow ended up with a baby that you decided to bring home?" Her breath came out in little snorts through her nostrils. She peeled out of the parking spot, coming dangerously close to the truck parked in front. Henry held the door handle. Facing Judge Hiscock had been easier than this.

"I couldn't just leave it there."

Henry thought Millie would be on his side, but right now, his wife was more frightening than Dick or Sheriff's Officer Breen or any police officer or Supreme Court judge. In fact, his wife was more frightening than any human he had ever known. Henry didn't look up. Instead, he busied himself with the seat belt.

"Okay, where were you when you noticed the baby?"

"At the cash."

"Where did you think the baby came from?"

"I thought maybe it was the baby from the amber alert you told me about yesterday. I thought someone had abandoned it."

"Abandoned the baby in your shopping cart? Why would they do that?"

"So I would make sure it was safe."

Millie peered over at him, giving him the paralyzing appraisal she had given countless criminals over the years. "It didn't occur to you that maybe you had just switched carts with someone?"

Henry sank deeper into his seat.

"Henry, for God's sake, look at me. No one would put a baby in your shopping cart."

"I didn't know where it came from."

"Well, it didn't just appear out of the heavens."

"No," he whispered. He wanted to say that a baby would definitely not come from the heavens. It would more likely come from the devil down below. He decided to leave it alone.

Millie's eyes continued to bore into him like diamond drill bits working their way into solid rock. Henry wished she'd concentrate a little more on the waterfront traffic that she had just entered. He shrank farther down into the leather, willing it to close over him and save him from the inquisition.

"So . . . why didn't you just bring the baby to customer service and explain that a baby had appeared in your shopping cart? Surely they are accustomed to other absent-minded men frequenting the premises. What were you thinking?"

Right now, Henry was thinking he would rather get hit by a Mack Truck than deal with this. "I didn't think," he said.

"You didn't think?" Millie spat.

"No. I haven't been thinking clearly all morning."

"Henry, the only reason you're out of the lock-up is because Judge Hiscock did me a favour. She was going to remand you to the Waterford for an assessment, but I managed to talk her out of it."

"Come on, Millie. There's no way any judge would send someone for a psychiatric assessment for a switched shopping cart."

"Henry, she could have had you committed for a month."

"No way. It was just a silly mistake."

"Henry, switching a shopping cart might be a silly mistake, but removing a child from its mother is not. You may end up in jail, Henry. Judge Hiscock also could have sent you directly to the pen to await trial. The only reason she let you go is because I convinced her you were not a flight risk and not a risk to yourself or others. And I vouched that you would be in court on whatever date she sets."

"How come everyone is blaming me? How do you know it was me who took the wrong cart?"

"Because I've lived with you for twenty-seven years."

"Point taken."

16

Back to the Lock-Up

Millie pulled the Mini into the lock-up lot between a cop car and a white paddy wagon.

"What are we doing back here? I thought we were going home." Henry's heart began palpitating. He did not want to go back in a holding cell.

"You have to pick up your property."

Henry took note of the *pick up your property*, not *collect your things*. Millie did not move. Henry assumed it was up to him to venture into that snake den all by himself.

"Of course." He felt his breathing passages closing in. "I'll be out in a jiffy."

Henry had to hold himself together. He felt like throwing up. He was afraid that CO Marshall would put him back in a cell.

"How dee doo, Mr. Puddester. How did you enjoy your first foray into the court system?"

"Nice," was all Henry could manage. He didn't make eye contact. The drunk tank smelled like vomit, and he wanted to get out as quickly as possible.

"Sign here," she said.

When Henry got back to the car, he squirted Purell on both hands. He would clean off his wallet and pocket knife when he got home.

"How can they stand working in there all day?"

"That's their job, Henry."

Millie didn't say anything more on the drive home. It took less than ten minutes but felt long enough to have got them to Port aux Basques. She deposited Henry in the driveway of 10 Pine Place without so much as a goodbye kiss. He got out of the car and shut the door but knocked on the window before Millie backed out.

"I'm worried."

"I'm worried, too," she said. "I'll ask Gloria if she'll represent you."

"Gloria with the glasses?"

"Yes, Gloria with the glasses. What other Gloria is there?"

"I'd rather it was you."

"It can't be me."

"Why not?"

"Poor optics." Millie motioned for him to move away from the car. "We'll talk more when I get home."

Henry was afraid of Gloria, but he didn't have time to dwell on it, because just as Millie charged off in the Mini, Dash and Stella Turner emerged from the asphalt path that connected Pine Place Park to the cul-de-sac. Since his retirement two weeks ago, Henry's new responsibilities included being home to greet Dash when he came from school. Even though he resented the fact it was he, and not Millie, who had to give up work to be home at two thirty every day, Henry was happy Dash was not one of those latchkey kids he read about in the paper. You never knew what could happen.

Today, for the first time, Henry was happy to be here, safe from the dangers of the supermarket and the lock-up, safe from wayward infants and their theatrical mothers, safe from Dick Turner. Surely, though, Dick, who had moved onto the cul-de-sac a decade ago after his marriage broke up, understood that the whole thing was some silly mix-up and was just punishing Henry for childhood misunderstandings.

Dick and Henry went back a long way. In grade two they were as inseparable as Siamese twins. They sat next to each other in class and spent every minute while not in school playing in the woods behind their houses. Henry could hear Dick's mother calling out to Dick to come home for supper. She called him Richard. Mrs. Turner, God . . . Henry hadn't thought about her in years.

Henry called over to the Turners' one day to see if Dick wanted to go to the store. Mrs. Turner picked up the phone. "Hi, Mrs. Turner, this is Henry. Dick there?"

"No one here by that name." She clicked down the receiver with a perfunctory clunk.

Henry called back.

"Hi, Mrs. Turner, is Richard there?"

"Certainly, Henry. I'll get him for you."

Mrs. Turner never had trouble making her point. Henry never called Richard Dick again within earshot of his mother.

Now, Mrs. Turner's lovely son was getting his revenge for a grudge he'd held for almost four decades.

Don't think about Dick, Henry told himself. *Do not think about Dick Turner.*

Henry watched Stella Turner with her cat's-eye glasses, her jet-black hair in braids. He liked Stella. She was a good kid. She and Dash had been best friends since they could walk. He knew Dick didn't like the fact that his precious little girl thought the sun shone out of Dash's arse, but you can't choose your kid's friends.

Stella stopped on the sidewalk to perform some weird manoeuvre that involved swinging her hips and arms in a mechanical fashion. She looked like a spastic crab. Dash tried to replicate her movements. This made Stella throw back her head and laugh. They said things Henry couldn't hear and separated, Dash heading toward Henry, and Stella walking to her house across the street. She waved at Henry. "Hi, Mr. Puddester."

Henry waved back. Just before he turned, he caught a glimpse of Dick Turner's profile in the front window.

17

Dash

"Hey, buddy, did you have a good day?" Henry ruffled his ten-year-old's curly blond hair. He was never so happy to lay eyes on him. Even the pain in his head seemed to dissipate upon seeing Dash.

Dash pulled a Caramel Log bar from his pocket. Henry salivated, snatched the bar from his son's hand, and gobbled it in two bites.

"Daa-aad! I traded my Goldfish for that."

Henry's cheeks were too full of toasted coconut and biscuit to answer. God, he was famished.

"Was that Mom I saw driving off?"

Henry swallowed. "Yes, she forgot something for work." How easily the lie rolled off his tongue. "How was school?"

"Scrumpdiddlyicious."

Henry cocked his head. Did that even make sense?

Dash zipped past him, pulling off his hoodie as he went. Henry followed his son into the house. Dash threw his hoodie over the hook and disappeared into the basement with a backward salute. Henry was disappointed. He had hoped Dash might stay upstairs for a bit instead of descending into his lair.

Henry didn't want to be alone. He still felt the humiliation of Dick Turner pushing him into the back seat of the cruiser. He knew Millie and Gloria with her glasses would get things straightened out for him in jig time, but still, he needed a distraction from the monkeys in his mind. Henry could hear Dash stoking up the computer. The drone of the hard drive reverberated through the floor. Jesus Murphy, that boy spent too much time online.

"Want a snack?" called Henry from the top of the stairs.

"Nope, new update today."

"Update?"

"Yeah, on Fork-Knife."

Ah yes, Fork-Knife. Even in his drugged state, Henry knew this was the nickname Dash had given to Fortnite, the world's most popular video game until the next one came along. He had looked it up as a diligent parent should. Four players form a team to battle zombies that have risen up after a storm has wiped out ninety-eight per cent of the population of the world. The players don't have to be physically together in the same room. In fact, Dash often formed teams with players in other countries.

Henry chugged water directly from the tap. His mind was returning to normal, but he was afraid to take another pill. He made himself a peanut butter and banana sandwich, which he inhaled in eight bites. Then he laid out some carrot sticks and spread peanut butter on celery. He had googled healthy snacks for growing tweens. He was just adding raisins to the peanut butter when Dash appeared, a jagged hole in the right knee of his jeans.

"What happened to your pants?"

"*Happened* to them?"

"Yes, what happened?"

Dash looked down at his legs as if he were aware of them for the first time.

"There are holes," said Henry, pointing. "In both knees."

"Oh, Dad."

Henry could have sworn they were the new pants he had bought at Walmart only a week ago. He pointed to the table. Dash went right for the celery. Henry inwardly congratulated himself. Sometimes his parenting skills were exemplary. Peanut butter on celery was a great way to sneak protein into his meat-rejecting son, who Henry now noticed seemed to be wearing the same T-shirt he had slept in.

Dash spoke through a mouthful of peanut butter. "Stella's going to Chase the Ace this week."

"That's good."

It was not, really. Henry hated backyard fundraisers like Chase the Ace. Even if they did have a pot of over a million bucks. It was all anyone had talked about for the past ten months. First dates and evening strolls had been replaced with gambling trips to the Goulds. Grown adults standing around waiting for numbers to be called over loudspeakers.

"Can we go, too?"

"Dash, you know I hate crowds."

"Aww, Dad, it'd be fun."

"Why don't you see if you can go with Stella?" Henry smiled at his offspring and quickly changed the subject. He didn't want Dash anywhere near Dick Turner right now, but the thought of going to Chase the Ace was even more appalling. "So, what's happening in Fortnite?"

"I just played my first game in Save the World. We usually play Battle Royale."

"What's the difference?"

"In Save the World mode, you have to survive for two weeks."

"Ah, so that's why it's called Fortnite?"

"What?"

"Never mind." Henry wondered if that meant two real-time weeks or two game-time weeks. "Did your team do a good job of fighting off the zombies?" Henry was imitating the hip young fathers he had seen at the parent-teacher meeting. But if he were honest, it actually hurt to wrap his brain around the intricate details of video games. Why would anyone bother? There was enough conflict in real life without having to go looking for more online.

"Yup, and the new update is awesome. It's called Solid Gold. They launched a new chiller grenade that freezes people. You need mats to buy 'em from the vending machines. But . . ." Dash stopped to bite off another piece of celery. "The grenade freezes your teammates, too, and vehicles can slip around on the ice for seven seconds."

Mats? Dash was losing him, but Henry was happy to engage in any discussion that did not involve babies and shopping carts.

"Did you know that Stella won a contest for dancing the floss?"

"The floss?" Henry's puzzlement knew no bounds.

"Yeah, it's one of the official Fortnite dances." To illustrate, Dash stood up and started to swing his hips while whipping his arms back and forth in front of and behind his waist like a pendulum gone off the rails. It was the same manoeuvre Stella had performed on the sidewalk.

"There are dances on Fortnite?"

"About a hundred and fifty."

To Henry, the fact that children submitted dances to a shoot-'em-dead video game just did not compute.

"You should play, Dad."

Henry would sooner stick pins in his eyes. "No, I have stuff to do. You go ahead. I'll set the timer, and then I'll call you up to pack for Cub Camp tomorrow."

Dash was gone before Henry finished his sentence.

18

Henry Changes the Oil

As soon as Dash had gone downstairs to play Fortnite, a knock came at the door. It was a courier holding a heavily taped, flat envelope. The gasket Henry had ordered for his Triumph. He felt like kissing the guy. If anything could banish thoughts of supermarket babies from his mind, it was his motorcycle. Henry practically skipped out to the shed to install it.

Two weeks earlier, the first day of his retirement, Henry got Dash off to school, and then attempted a simple oil change on his motorcycle. It did not go as planned.

He drained the old oil when it was hot. He cleaned the sump screen at the bottom of the oil pan. He was always meticulous when it came to mechanics.

Visualize set-up, remove part, clean, inspect, replace if required. Repeat with every component.

It was a process. But something was wrong.

Not enough oil pressure. He checked and rechecked the oil in the tank. All good.

Viscosity? Thirty weight, the only type he had on the shelf. All good.

He took off the timing cover, disassembled the feed pump, and removed the oil pump gasket. *Ah, will you look at that*, Henry said to himself, *a small tear in the gasket*. Proud of this discovery, he ordered a new one.

Now in the shed, with the new gasket installed, Henry reassembled the pump, checked the petcock, tickled the carbs, and kicked her over with great optimism. The bike started on the second kick. She sounded beautiful. Like a 747. Or maybe a prop plane.

But the oil pressure gauge still read low pressure.

Usually calm, Henry slammed his hand down on the seat, hard. What was up with this day? He meticulously went through the whole process again. Even drained the oil into a clean jug.

Removed the feed pump. Inspected the gasket. Disassembled it and washed all parts in kerosene.

Reassembled.

Removed the sump screen. Washed it and the gasket in kerosene. Blew all dry with compressed air.

He inspected the oil pump. It was operational.

Ready for reassembly. All good.

Once again, the bike started on the second kick, the roar of the engine music to his ears. Gauge reading, still low.

He killed the engine and left the workshop.

Back in the house, he called over the stairs to Dash. "Time's almost up, Dash." In reality, he was way past overdue.

"One last game." This was the pat response to any request to get off the computer. Today, Henry didn't protest. Instead, he logged into a Triumph forum. He read posts describing everything he had just done, plus a couple of hillbilly fixes.

He viewed an enlarged schematic of the components. Pump, gasket, seal. He read "seal" in disbelief. Crankshaft feed seal? He'd completely missed it.

Henry enlarged the schematic even more and looked harder. There it was, a tiny seal that allowed oil to flow to the crankshaft. Prone to failure, it said. Henry recognized that little piece of rubber. He had a spare.

Eureka.

Things were back on track. He went back to the shed and fixed his bike, forgetting for another while the mess he had got himself into.

19

Henry, More Issues than *Vogue*

Henry flushed the ensuite toilet and came out yawning, making for the Triumph Bonneville owner's manual lying on the duvet. It was early, but it had been a long day. He and Millie agreed not to discuss the supermarket incident while Dash was up. But as soon as he was tucked in, they retired to the privacy of their bedroom to plan their next move.

"Uh oh," Millie said. She was sitting sideways high up on the bed, her left foot on the pillow and her right hand suspended mid-air, lavender nail polish dripping on the white towel spread below. Henry followed her gaze to their sixty-five-inch wall-mounted TV.

"This morning, a six-month-old baby girl was kidnapped from this east-end supermarket."

CBC's chirpy Gillian Gee, microphone in hand, was gesturing to the massive green letters above the brick facade: SUNDRIES FOR ALL YOUR HOUSEHOLD NEEDS. The words FOURTH CHILD ABDUCTION IN AS MANY MONTHS scrolled across the bottom of the screen in nine-inch letters.

"What started out as a terrifying ordeal ended quickly when a police officer in the right place at the right time apprehended the kidnapping suspect and safely returned the child to her frantic mother."

Gillian turned to the young mother, who wore a bomber jacket over denim overalls. The jacket had BOB embroidered on the left chest. No more horror-movie screaming. The baby cooed. The little pink beanie and blanket appeared far less menacing on the TV screen than they had in real life.

"What did you do when you realized someone had taken your baby?" Gillian asked the mother.

"I completely freaked out." She had that right, thought Henry. "I don't know how the police officers knew where to find Jade, but I am, like, so grateful. Thank you so much." She looked directly at the camera, touched the fingers on her right hand to her lips, and blew a kiss to the TV audience.

"Britney, this must have been a traumatic experience." Gillian brought the microphone close to Britney's mouth. The baby smiled and tried to grab the cord.

"Only a mother can know the horror." Britney shivered and put her cheek to the baby's forehead.

"How did you feel when you heard the police had apprehended the man responsible?"

"I was soooo, you know, like, relieved to know that he's off the streets so he can't do any more harm." Tears rolled down her teenaged cheeks.

"What would you say to him right now if you could talk to him?"

"I wouldn't say anything. I would cut off his balls."

"This is Gillian Gee, *CBC News*, St. John's."

"Jesus on the wharf, what was that?" Henry exhaled the breath that he hadn't realized he had been holding. He sank into the king-sized Sealy Posturepedic mattress.

"Shhh," Millie hissed and flicked from CBC to NTV.

Different reporter. Same story. Britney is wearing a different outfit. She's sitting in a living room, a bookshelf behind her filled with plastic-wrapped packs of diapers and rectangular containers of wet wipes. Her face looks strikingly different, globs of makeup trowelled on. The blue eye-liner and fake lashes make her look like a Barbie doll. Britney has pulled up her sleeves to reveal a tattoo of the Tasmanian Devil on her inner wrist. She rocks the baby, who sleeps peacefully in the floral-patterned car seat. One look at that car seat makes Henry feel nauseous.

"Ms. Mooney, can you tell us what happened this morning?"

"I was picking up some baby food for Jade—she likes the mashed pears at Sundries. Anyways, I saw this shampoo on sale. I was digging around in the cart to see if there was any conditioner, and when I turned back, someone had taken Jade." A plump tear drops from her fake lashes and plops onto the sofa.

"What happened then?"

"I screamed . . . like you would, right?"

"Was there anyone around?"

"Yes, a lady in a Canada Goose coat." She squinted her eyes. "And there were these two men. Like, a big one and a little one."

"Were either of these men the one who had taken Jade?"

"No, definitely not. The guy who took Jade had already gone. He left the store and took her home."

"Did you see the man who took Jade?"

"Only when the policeman took me to his house to get my baby." Britney wiped one fake lash with two fingers. The lashes were so long and thick, they actually cast a shadow on her face. "He was so scary-looking, like that creepy old man in *Silence of the Lambs*. I just know he's the one who took the others. I'm afraid to go out with Jade anymore."

"Do you have any advice for other parents of young children?"

"If that man gets out of prison, this town is not safe. Never, ever take your eyes off your children. I hope they keep him locked away for a long, long time."

"After the break, we'll hear from the police officer who made the arrest. With this man arrested, are our streets now safe? Also coming up on *The Nightly*, we'll tell you all about the Chase the Ace fundraiser in the Goulds. And an interesting station wagon that has been making its way across the island. Motor vehicle or piece of art? Yours to decide. Stay tuned."

Millie muted the sound.

Henry collapsed on the bed, sending a useless orange throw pillow and his manual to the floor. "You're looking at me like I'm some kind of vermin," he said.

Millie began jabbing the screen on her pink iPhone, her half-painted nails pinging off the protective cover. "Henry, this is the top story on all the news websites: VOCM, CBC, *Telegram*, NTV, allNewfoundland." She began mashing her thumbs even harder into the tiny screen. "There are 2,343 people reading this one story on Facebook right now."

Henry took a deep breath. He was not a fan of Facebook. He was not a fan of any social media. In fact, you could say he hated social media. "They'll have forgotten about it by tomorrow."

Millie kept poking, the soft bubble sounds coming faster as she typed.

"I don't think so. On the heels of yesterday's child abduction and that abduction and murder in Paradise last fall, it's all anyone is going to talk about."

"What are you talking about? What murder in Paradise?"

"Henry, do you live in a bubble? A little girl was taken in October. Plucked off the street while she was trick-or-treating. They found her body three days later. Raped and strangled."

"Jesus, Mary, and Joseph." Henry cupped his nose with his fingers and inhaled. "But I didn't abduct anyone."

"Henry, you removed a baby from a supermarket and took it home."

"But only to keep it safe."

Millie raised her eyebrows before sinking back into her own pillows. "Tell that to a jury. Any judge is going to feel obliged to give you a harsh sentence."

Henry looked at the paisley bed cover. "Gillian Gee called here this afternoon. I know CBC had a van outside the house, but I can't understand where she got my name and number."

"Well, who did you see at the supermarket that you know?"

"Uh . . ." Henry tried to think. "I don't know. I saw a bunch of people. I saw your yoga teacher and her kid."

"You saw Spring and Tree?"

"Mmm hmm." Henry nodded. "Not sure why Tree wasn't in school."

"She's home-schooled. Who else?"

"Uh, I saw Dash's Cub leader."

"Akela? The university professor?"

"Didn't know she was a prof. But yeah, she was there."

"Who else?"

"I don't know." Henry didn't want to tell Millie about Dick. It was too humiliating. "I'm having trouble conjuring up details. It doesn't even feel like the same day."

"You're going to have to, Henry."

"I just want to go to sleep."

"You can't. Judge Hiscock is going to feel immense pressure to come down hard on you in light of these other child abduction cases. We have to establish what happened in the supermarket while it's still fresh."

Henry tried to picture himself just before he found the eggs. Where had he left his cart? It all hurt his head. He stopped trying when he noticed Millie fanning a hand in front of his face.

"Henry!"

"What?" He had almost forgotten she was there.

"Just think. What do you remember most?"

"That my head was going to burst from sinus pressure, and I couldn't figure out why the cold and sinus medication hadn't kicked in. The pill I took made me woozy but didn't help with my cold."

"What pill? Show me. I don't think we have any cold medication."

Henry went to the medicine cabinet, brought out a pill bottle, and tossed it on the bed, narrowly missing Millie's freshly painted toes. Millie screwed the top on the nail polish and picked up the bottle.

"Henry, this isn't cold medication. It looks nothing like cold medication."

"Are you sure? It was in the spot on the bottom shelf where you usually keep cold medicine."

"I'm sure." Millie peered inside at tiny green pills each embossed with a capital D. "This is Dilaudid."

"What's Dilaudid?"

"It's an opioid. It's more powerful than morphine."

"What are we doing with opioids in our medicine cabinet?"

"They were your mother's. I didn't get around to disposing of them yet."

"Well, that explains why I was so dopey this morning. I'm going to pitch them."

"No."

"What do you mean, no? We can't have drugs like this around the house. Dash might find them."

"Give them to me. We're going to need them as evidence."

"Evidence?"

"Yes, Henry, for your case." Millie was tapping her phone screen again.

"What are you doing now?"

"Looking up the side effects of Dilaudid."

"What are they?"

"Dizziness, drowsiness, dry mouth, dehydration, excessive sweating, headache."

She patted the bed. Henry sat down.

"Did you feel any of these side effects?"

"Yes."

Millie took a pen and paper from her side table. "Which ones?"

"I have never been so thirsty in my life."

"What else?"

"I was dizzy, and a couple of times I saw two of whatever I was looking at."

"This is great, Henry. Gloria can use this for your defence."

"I'd be calmer if it was you asking me questions." Henry reddened, remembering the humiliation of going to court in the leg irons and handcuffs, attached to Charlie Black Eye and the guy who had ingested the bad mushrooms. He wondered how those guys were doing. "Court was horrible," he squeaked.

Millie shushed him and patted his leg as a truck commercial finished. Dick Turner's face replaced the Ford F150. Henry sank back on the bed.

"Constable Turner, can you tell us the status of the kidnapper?"

"You didn't tell me it was Dick," said Millie. "I will tie that bastard's bowels into reef knots."

"We apprehended the suspect and took him in for questioning."

"Is he still in custody?" Gillian Gee was in her element.

"No, we released him on his own recognizance with explicit orders that he not go anywhere until the investigation is complete."

"Friggin' Dick," said Henry, relieved Millie was on his side.

Millie reached for the remote, just in time to see Dick pushing her husband's head into the back of a patrol car. Just before the story ended, the camera showed Henry fumbling with something off camera. When he reappeared, his head was covered with a reusable orange bag that said: MORE ISSUES THAN *VOGUE*.

20

Friday: Delores and Daisy Reach St. John's

With Sir Elton serenading her from Daisy's speakers, Delores relaxed. "Levon" was the perfect song. What power and intensity.

"*Madman Across the Water*, November 1971."

She sometimes surprised herself with her musical trivia prowess. Delores's therapist had suggested she come up with a subtle way of calming herself when her mind began to spin out of control. Verbalizing song titles worked astonishingly well.

"Just don't say them too loud," her therapist said.

Delores smiled and moved into the passing lane. She missed their visits, but she'd have plenty of time for therapy after her adventure with Daisy.

The miles were speeding by, and Delores knew she was getting close to the city. It had been about an hour since she had crossed the narrow isthmus that connected the middle part of the island to what the map referred to as the Avalon Peninsula. Not that she could see much through the rain, but signs had begun to sprout up alongside the road advertising bars and restaurants. There was a Volkswagen Beetle perched precariously on a cliff, a huge silver windup key protruding out the back.

Trucks towing all-terrain vehicles and pleasure boats barrelled down the highway in the opposite direction. Delores had to pee, but she knew she was less than ten kilometres from downtown. She had already skirted around an industrial park where a sign said: WELCOME TO MOUNT PEARL. She didn't know what Mount Pearl was, but she did know they had a Walmart. St. John's had to be just a little farther along. *Come on, Daisy. We can do it.* Through the ever-present drizzle, she could see the outskirts of the city to her left and large hills to her right. Not quite mountains, but substantial all the same. In the distance she saw some sort of tower on a hill and a dozen or so high-rises. Nothing over ten storeys.

The divided highway, its two sides separated by yellow street lights and a concrete wall, came to an abrupt end, and she veered right, following the signs to downtown, passing above a dry dock shipyard. Some of the wooden houses on her left had widow's walks on the roof like in New England. The houses were painted bright shades of red and yellow, in vivid contrast to the doomsday sky. They were just like she had seen in the tourism ads.

She and Daisy cruised down a potholed off-ramp onto a sad-looking street that she thought couldn't possibly be her welcome to Canada's most easterly city. Elton was replaced by REM singing about losing their religion.

"*Out of Time*, February 1991," she said, wondering how she managed to record songs two decades apart on the same cassette tape. Delores opened her window a hand's width to gauge the temperature. She withdrew it quickly.

As if propelled by a giant fan, a thick fog scuttled across the road, limiting visibility to about fifty feet. The rain had slowed to a drizzle but still required the wipers on intermittent. The lines dividing the lanes were non-existent. Delores hugged the curb, which followed a graffitied wall and then skirted a fenced yard stocked with huge cranes moving blue shipping containers, all marked OCEANEX.

Just before the road veered right again, she noticed two men standing in the middle of her lane. What were two men doing in the middle of the road? She hit the brakes, straining to see through the blanket of fog. She screamed *Move out of the way*, but the men did not move. Daisy's rear end fishtailed, frayed rubber burning as it sought purchase with the asphalt. Holy moly, the two men weren't men at all, but rather two sets of long legs with a huge brown oil tank of a body parked on top. A frightened set of eyes gleamed yellow in the headlights, dewlap swinging gently in the breeze. Delores closed her eyes tight and instinctively ducked.

The thud that followed was what one would expect from an impact with a 2,000-pound animal. The moose's body hit the windshield and peeled back part of the roof. The windshield remained intact but separated into small blue cubes. Delores's rib cage hit the steering wheel. The seat belt cut into her abdomen, and several low-lying organs ascended into her chest.

Her breath coming in starts, Delores sat stunned in the middle of the lane and watched as the moose rolled off the roof, shook himself, and, despite several bloodied patches of fleshless skin, hobbled off into the mist. Delores had seen moose in BC, and she would bet her last $300 that they were nowhere near as big as this thing.

With shaking hands, she managed to pull into a parking spot on the waterfront. The smell of the animal had filled the vehicle. It was gamey and raw. She put the station wagon in park and fell back onto the cracked vinyl seat. Chunks of moose fur were stuck at the top of the windshield where the roof was open to the drizzle. She exhaled, her throat gritty.

Delores felt her head for signs of blood, but it appeared unscathed. Only her chest and abdomen hurt. She decided not to move until her breathing was under control. Delores closed her eyes and pressed rewind in her mind to replay the scene. She could still see the coarse brown fur, the long legs . . . she even saw the moose's breath on the windshield just before the impact. Her last glimpse of it was the massive coat rack balanced on top of its head, the tassel swaying under its chin.

Slowly, her heart returned to a normal rate. She expected someone to come see if she was okay, but there was no one around. How could that be? St. John's was the capital, wasn't it? She squinted into the roiling fog. It did not appear to be a booming metropolis.

Delores leaned into the seat, thinking she'd just sit there for a bit and let the cool damp air blow in through the open space between the roof and windshield. She picked up the yellow brochure from the passenger seat, where it lay on top of a half-eaten Charleston Chew. *Think moose at night. Think moose at night*, it chided.

21

Frank's Shed

Frank Parrell picked up the can of enamel spray paint and with even strokes began covering the red on the telephone booth with blue. Overwhelmed by the odour, he backed out of the booth, straight into the parking meter propping open his shed door. "Bollocks."

The vandalized meter toppled over, denting a portion of the 35,000 bottle caps that made up the floor. Frank collapsed next to it and removed his mask. "Double bollocks."

"What's going on over there, Frank?" It was his next-door neighbour, Henry Puddester.

"Henry, mate, you're just the person I need to see."

Henry's face appeared around the hedge and crossed the threshold into the oversized shed. His salt and pepper head looked like he had been electrocuted. "Uh, Frank, why do you have a telephone booth in your shed?"

Paper was taped over all the windows, and everything else in the shed was covered with white drop sheets. Frank stayed where he was on the floor and stoked up his vape pen. His shaking hands clutched the silver canister.

"I'm painting it blue."

"I see that. Why?"

"I'm trying to take my mind off the news." Frank's cheeks became concave as he inhaled deeply and let a cloud of smoke emerge from his lungs.

"By repainting a telephone booth?"

"Yeah, I thought I'd build a Tardis and go back in time to when I was in good shape and Patty still lived here."

"Good luck with that. I saw Patty yesterday. She was here on the cul-de-sac."

"Yeah, she wasn't coming to visit. She was just dropping some of Kaitlyn's uni bills in the mailbox."

"Maybe you should consider dating other people."

"I'm not like you, Henry. I don't have those movie-star looks. Anyway, I think Patty will eventually come to her senses."

Henry lifted his nose to the roof. "Besides spray paint, I smell . . ." Henry sniffed. "Cotton candy."

"I know." Frank put down the spray can, pulled the sheets into a heap on the floor, and inhaled more smoke. "Cotton candy is the new flavour at Smokin' Guns. It's the only flavour I buy now . . . reminds me of the Regatta."

"You know that stuff is going to kill you." Henry raised his eyebrows.

"I know, I know. If the beer doesn't kill me first." Frank patted his belly. "Fancy a cold one?"

Frank crawled to the tiny fridge that was now wedged under the workbench to make room for the telephone box. He had removed all the shelving so the fridge could house a twenty-litre stainless steel beer keg. After letting some gas escape from the keg chamber, he pulled out a chilled A&W mug, and filled it halfway, head filling the rest.

"That's the darkest stout I've seen since Dublin."

Henry took a long, hard pull on the beer and exhaled his appreciation. Now that Frank had put away his vape pen, the shed went back to smelling like spray paint mingled with a full-blown brewery on production day. He sat in his chair, and his eyes followed Henry's to the drying hops, slightly blue, hanging from the window winder, and then to a mangled copy of the *Telegram* sitting on top of Frank's biggest brew tank.

"I thought you didn't read the paper," said Henry.

"Blimey. I try not to. It aggravates my kidney stones, but my 'communications team'"—Frank put his fingers in the air to indicate the quotation marks—"insists. Have a butcher's at page three."

Henry looked underneath an ad for a Chase the Ace fundraiser in the Goulds. Ongoing vandalism of parking meters cost the City of St. John's more than $1.3 million in 2017.

"Jesus Murphy. That is bad," Henry said. "But not as bad as this." He flipped the paper back to page one, where a two-inch headline ran across the top: KIDNAPPED SUPERMARKET BABY LOCATED UNHARMED.

"Bloody hell. You're right," said Frank. "Blimey, Henry." Frank thought about the glee in Dick Turner's wonky eyes when he strolled out of his driveway on Pine Place and recounted the details of Henry's greengrocer saga.

"How'd you know it was me?"

Frank was afraid to admit that Dick had told him. Dick and Henry had some sort of long-lasting feud that did not need reinforcement. "I, uh . . . heard it on the radio."

"But they didn't use my name."

"Yes, you're lucky. My name is always front and centre in every miserable piece of news about parking meters, be it TV, radio, print, or the web."

"Have you ever pulled a cart switch?" asked Henry.

"What, at the greengrocers? Can't say I have. Though once I came across this trolley parked at the end of the aisle, you know, fifty per cent off this, seventy-five per cent off that. I thought it was the sale bin, started picking through it, there were some pretty good deals. Then this missus comes up and starts shouting, 'What the hell are ya doing taking my stuff?' Next thing, she calls over her man. He was about six foot ten and dressed in combat clothes."

"I take it it wasn't the sale bin?" Henry sipped his foam.

"Nope. So, what's gonna happen, you know, about the ... uh ... supermarket incident?" Frank blew imaginary dust off the workbench.

Henry coughed. "Don't want to discuss it."

"Okay." Frank held up his hands. Maybe Henry was embarrassed.

Henry took another pull on the beer and flipped the paper back to the meter story. "Is it really going to cost one point three million to replace the damaged meters?"

"Naw, it's all gobshite. You know how those gits love to inflate the figures." Frank rolled his eyes. "Wiener is the one who prepared the report for Council before his position became redundant."

"I saw him two days ago. Had to go pick up my ROE."

"Did you know he can regurgitate on request?" Frank mimicked swallowing a hot dog and vomiting it back up.

"Gross." Henry shook his head and looked down at the damaged Quidi Vidi Brewery section of bottle caps on the floor. "What happened?"

"The freaking meter tipped over and damaged the floor." Frank pointed at several dozen mutilated bottle caps.

Henry lifted his chin to the parking meter. "I told you to get rid of that thing. You're obsessed."

"You'd be obsessed, too, if some ijit was making you look like a fool." Frank put his heel to the meter and pushed it out the doors and shut them. "It's brass monkeys out there. How's the bike? Did you figure out what's wrong?"

"Yeah. It was a seal ... a ten-dollar part. She runs like a charm now." Henry leaned back, and Frank followed his eyes to the plastic-framed print of Foghorn Leghorn that peered down at them from over the spotless workbench. Foghorn Leghorn was quaffing an ale, while Henery, the little chicken hawk, sat on the beer keg. Henry had given him that poster as a shed-raising present. The caption read: GO, I SAY, GO AWAY, BOY, YOU BOTHER ME.

Frank liked the fact that they could sit there sometimes in amiable silence. For the moment, he even forgot about his kidney stones. But then Henry spoke.

"So, what's the bottom line?"

"What? With the parking meters?"

"Yeah. What are you in for?"

"After spending over six hundred thousand dollars to swap out all the meters in 2014, I now find myself in the most uncomfortable position of replacing them all again." Frank burped and patted his protruding belly. He leaned out of his chair to fling open the fridge door in order to reach the hose attached to the tank they were currently enjoying. He refilled his glass. The first one had only been filled enough to confirm that the ale was up to snuff.

"You should go back to the manufacturer for reimbursement." Henry placed his mug under the spout for a top-up.

"I tried." Frank pulled out his vape pen again, and clouds of cotton candy–flavoured smoke filled the air, once again overpowering the aroma of hops. "They said no other municipalities had a problem with thieves whopping the tops off meters with baseball bats or steel rods or whatever the heck the dimwits are using. They suggested more surveillance."

"So," said Henry. "Did you put up more cameras?"

Frank sucked the air over his bottom teeth. "You know we did, and we got the cops on board, too, doing extra patrols in the worst-hit areas, like the waterfront and Churchill Square."

"And?"

"Nada. It's like the thieves can detect surveillance cameras and coppers. I don't know how they know, but they do. They move to another area of town as soon as we set up. It's killing me."

"There has to be a way to catch them." Henry rubbed his day-old stubble.

"Well, whatever it is, it's eluding me. I should just pack it in and retire."

"Retirement is not what it's cracked up to be," said Henry, belching loudly.

"I know. I tried it last year, remember?" Frank had taken a leave of absence for six months when the parking meter stuff got too hard to handle. *The heart palpitations are due to stress*, his doctor said after Frank ended up in the back of an ambulance, thinking he was having a heart attack. *You have to learn to relax.* He sure as hell couldn't relax at work, so Frank had gone to his boss and announced he was taking stress leave. Six months. Tops. He'd de-stress and be back—fresh as one of the daisies growing up through the asphalt in front of the bunker.

The six-month leave had not been a stress reducer—in fact, it had ultimately resulted in the end of his marriage. Frank's wife, Patty, was a freelancer who worked out of their home office, a glass-doored room that gave onto the back deck and raised flower beds decorated with solar lights for evenings in the garden. She argued that if both of them were home all day, it would be a recipe for divorce. She was right. The sunroom not only housed Patty's workstation; it also housed the pantry. And while Patty tried to write, Frank beat a path to and from the pantry to obtain his favourite Purity Family Cookies.

"Frank, if you don't stay out of my office, I'm going to have to find somewhere else to work."

"You can move to the den upstairs."

"You know how I like the light in the sunroom."

Frank did know, but come on, their house was huge, especially for three people. Their bedroom alone was the size of a small bungalow. Patty refused to budge, and Frank refused to move the cookies to a cupboard in the kitchen.

"That would be like giving me the green light to eat them," he protested.

"But you're eating them all the time." Patty shook her head.

They were at an impasse. Patty stayed working next to the pantry, and Frank kept parading through.

He knew he had to give up the cookies. He kept telling himself he would. When he was younger, he used to be able to eat whatever he liked. That was while he was running a hundred kilometres a week. When his knee gave out, a strange thing happened: the less he ran, the more he ate, until he was a bald, 225-pound version of his old self.

Of course, things hadn't been perfect in their marriage for years, but Frank was naive. That fall, when Patty told Frank about the spiffy old loft apartment she'd found on Hayward Avenue, he thought, *Great, she'll enjoy working there.* He had no idea that she planned to live there, too. Their daughter, Kaitlyn, took it hard, but not as hard as Frank did when Kaitlyn chose to live with her mother. He was flabbergasted. What the heck had happened? Sure, he and Patty had their problems, but no more than any other couple.

Once Patty moved out and they figured out the finances, she cut all ties. She never spoke to Frank unless it concerned Kaitlyn. Frank didn't know how he ended up being the bad guy. The whole mess left him a ghost padding around their 3,000-square-foot house. Since the breakup, he spent most of his time in the shed. He went back to work early, despite the fact he still had a month of leave.

"Frank, you still with me?" Henry was waving his hand back and forth, sending a few pieces of dust floating.

Frank blinked and focused on Henry. "Yes, I just wandered there for a bit. What were we talking about?"

"How you took a leave of absence . . ."

"Right-o, definitely don't want to do that again, but maybe I could move to another role."

"Like what?"

"Well, I don't quite know. The trouble is, I don't want to be in the crosshairs of all the young whippersnappers trying to get a start down at the bunker."

"You could be a consultant. That's what a lot of guys are doing."

Millie's voice penetrated the sanctuary. "Henry, you out there?" Even though she was in the next yard and behind the hedge, it sounded like she was right there in the shed with them. "Henry, you have to get a move on. You'll be late for camp. I laid the eggs on the counter."

"No need to get Millie a microphone any time soon." Frank's belly started to quake as he tried to suppress a laugh.

"Bloody Cub Camp," muttered Henry.

"I feel for ya, man. See ya Sunday. We can watch the game."

Henry backed out the shed door, taking a last long pull before depositing his A&W root beer mug on the workbench. "See you Sunday—if I make it out alive."

22

Delores and a Damaged Daisy

"Journey. *Infinity* album, 1978." Even in times of great stress, Delores was getting better at saying the album names under her breath like her therapist taught her. "'When the Lights go Down.'"

The sun wasn't shining on the bay, however. In fact, the low-lying fog that had settled over the hills surrounding the harbour made for a most dreary scene. Delores got out of the station wagon on shaky legs. There was no sign of the moose. Had she imagined it?

She walked around to the front of the Ford and decided the moose was definitely not a figment of her overtired imagination. The bumper was bashed in and the grill crumpled. The windshield was smashed and the roof peeled back two inches. Orange plastic shards stuck up like stalactites from the right indicator. Or was it stalagmites? Drat it all, that was the original cover. But anything could be had on eBay for a price. Delores had $337 left in her bank account. She would have to cash in the last of the savings bonds her mother had given her as a child. They were worth about $50 each. That might just cover a new indicator casing and bumper, but no way would it pay for repairs to the windshield and roof.

Delores picked up pieces of the light casing and sighed. The worst part was the damage to her precious toy collection. Two plastic squirrels alongside a half-dozen mushrooms were flattened and covered with coarse hair. Plastic fruit, Curious George, Twiddle Bugs, all damaged beyond saving.

She laid everything that was loose on the passenger seat on top of the moose brochure and took in her immediate surroundings. She appeared to be near the main harbour, although with the fog so thick, she could have been anywhere. A chest-high stainless-steel guardrail with four bars separated her and Daisy from a dozen or so fishing boats lolling in the mist. The boats were tied to fluorescent orange bollards a dozen yards from where she had pulled in. Back over her shoulder, she could barely make out the blue rectangular shipping containers anymore. A large billboard read: WHO'LL BE THE NEXT MILLIONAIRE? CHASE THE ACE, THURSDAYS 8 PM, ST. PERPETUA'S, GOULDS.

Delores scanned up and down the sidewalk, but the moose was nowhere to be seen. She looked back at the harbour just in time to see the creature's tremendous bulk jump in and swim between two longliners.

"Well, I'll be crackerjacked." She shook her head to clear it and took a moment to thank the Good Lord for saving her from being flattened under a two-ton ruminant. She then took stock of herself. It hurt to inhale, but arms and legs seemed all right. She swivelled her neck around. All good. "Daisy . . ." she said. "We have cheated death."

She was digging in her purple bag for some change when she noticed a hooded man arrive out of nowhere and begin swinging a massive mallet through the air. The top of a parking meter, which a moment ago had been decidedly fixed to its metal pole, was now airborne. Delores ducked for the second time in fifteen minutes. The meter head missed her but lobbed off at least ten toys, including her See-No-Evil monkey that was stuck to the hood. The young man, who had red hedgehog hair peeking out from his black hoodie, followed the flight path with his head.

See-No-Evil, who had been a gift from her mother when Delores was twelve, flew through the air like a home run ball and landed either on the deck of a boat called the *Sikuvut* or in the water below. Maybe it hit the moose. It was hard to tell in the fog. Delores didn't hear any splash or thud.

The hooded human hedgehog did not appear perturbed that someone had witnessed this act of vandalism. In fact, he turned to look Delores straight on, a tiny blue teardrop tattoo under his right eye. "What the fuck was that?"

"See-No-Evil," she answered as if they were having a conversation about the weather.

He stood there for a full minute—looking Daisy over bumper to bumper, taking in her accoutrements, as Delores liked to think of them. "Sick ride," he said. "Sorry about the monkey."

He smirked as he picked up the top of the meter he had just bludgeoned before turning to sprint away with the meter head cradled in one arm and the mallet swinging from the other. He sped away from the water past a large grey building that looked like it had been dropped in the middle of the street, some sort of horse or iceberg painted on the side. Seconds later, the encroaching fog reached the building, and the red-headed man with the mallet and the metal meter box disappeared into it.

Delores quietly sang the lyrics to "I Am Woman" by Helen Reddy. Above the bumper where See-No-Evil had once sat, Delores saw long tufts of scraggly beige fur—or was it hair?—clumped around the remaining two monkeys.

"Daisy, I am too tired to find See-No-Evil. Please join me in wishing him farewell."

She closed her eyes and raised her hands in prayer pose before making her way around to open the back of the station wagon. There was no need to feed the meter. There was no place to put the coins. Rummaging in a suitcase, she found a pair of floral pants, much like the pair she was wearing. Then, swinging her purple vinyl bag over her shoulder, Delores Cowburn began ambling up the waterfront in search of a bathroom. She had wet her pants.

23

Millie Meets Mad-Eye Turner

"Constable Turner in?" Millie stood in front of the Formica counter near the front entrance of the police station. She was wearing her Friday special, a black suit that looked like all her other black suits except it was made of silk and cost twice as much. As a twist she had added a lamé scarf, the copper threads glinting in the light every time she moved.

"Is he expecting you?" The clerk scrutinized Millie's face. Millie knew she recognized her as a lawyer who came in on a regular basis to speak to clients.

"No, but it has to do with an arrest he made." Millie didn't offer any more than that. Nor did she give her name. She had decided it would be better to confront Dick at work rather than on the cul-de-sac.

The clerk left her chair and disappeared behind a wall. Two minutes later, Dick Turner appeared through the door to the right of the counter. Millie could tell that he regretted coming out.

"Millie, what a surprise."

"Dick, what in Christ's name are you playing at?" With her three-inch heels, Millie was taller than Dick.

"I'm not sure what you mean." Dick's right eye went left, and his left eye went right.

"You know what I mean, Dick. What did you go and arrest Henry for?"

"He broke the law."

"He would never harm a baby. He brought it home to ask me what to do. You know he's a space cadet. Anyone who's ever met him knows he's a space cadet. Plus, he had inadvertently taken Dilaudid that morning."

"Dilaudid is a controlled substance."

"It was a prescription."

"Be that as it may . . ."

Millie moved a step closer to Dick. "This has something to do with that old grudge, doesn't it?"

"I don't know what you're talking about." Dick moved back a step but banged into the counter.

"You do. Something to do with senior hockey back at Gonzaga."

Two police officers came through the door trying to manage a struggling man wearing nothing but pyjama bottoms. "You'll have to excuse me, Millie. I have to get back to work."

"And I have a case to prepare. See you in court."

24

Cub Camp, Henry and the Sasquatch

"Spadoodle." Dash hit the ceiling of the Escape with his right hand. Henry swerved but corrected the Ford's trajectory before crashing into a wooden garbage box. "Dash, you can't be hitting the roof. I could have an accident."

"Sorry, Dad." Dash was sitting behind him in the back seat of the Ford Escape as they made the hour-long drive to Tors Cove on the Southern Shore. They had quietly been listening to an audiobook about a sasquatch until Henry noticed that his son's face had gone pasty white, and he had his fingers in his ears. He was disappointed to turn it off, but he was relieved when the colour had slowly returned to his son's face.

"What does Spadoodle even mean?" Henry slowed behind a left-turning Honda.

"Only one headlight was working on that Jeep. Didn't you see?"

"Yes, I saw, but I wasn't expecting you to hit the roof and scream something in Swahili. I almost went off the road."

Dash laughed. "Dad, you're such a dingus. When you see a car with one headlight, the first one to hit the roof and say 'spadoodle' wins."

Henry filed away this information in the cramped corner of his mind reserved for parenting. "Best play that game when it's not snowing." Ever since they passed Bay Bulls, large flakes had begun falling out of the April sky.

"Cool," said Dash. "Maybe there'll be enough to go sledding."

Henry hoped not. Last year, the snow had continued falling until May. If it stayed on the ground that late this year, Henry was going to suggest to Millie that they pack up and spend the winters in Florida, like most sane Newfoundlanders. Or maybe Arizona. It was drier there.

"Did you know I played Fortnite with someone in Azerbaijan today?" Dash always hopped from one topic to the next.

"Do you even know where Azerbaijan is?"

"No."

"It's near Turkey."

"I don't know where Turkey is."

"I know what to get you for your eleventh birthday."

"A trip to Turkey?"

"No, a globe . . ." Henry glanced in the rear-view to give Dash a raised eyebrow, but he was looking out the window. "So, how does Fortnite work? How do you form a team with people you don't even know?" Henry navigated around a car flipped on its side in the ditch. The intense rain earlier in the week had eroded the shoulder.

"I do know lots of them. We jump out of a plane and land on an island, and then we work together to build forts and get weapons. Some guys are really good snipers. Stella is the best I know."

"Stella is a sniper? That's a good one." Henry shook his head.

"She's wicked with a P.A.S. You know, a pump-action shotgun. There are four types of shotguns: pump-action, tactical, heavy, and double-barrelled."

Henry wished he hadn't asked. The fact his son played a game where a hundred people fought to the death was too much for him.

Thankfully, they had just arrived at Camp D. Henry pulled the Ford alongside the other cars. Several mothers and children were slogging garbage bags and duffels through the snow and up the steps toward the bunkhouse. Oh no . . . was Henry the only father who had signed up?

Henry got out of the car. Did he imagine it, or had a hush come over the crowd, which ten seconds before had been nattering on about useless things?

One woman, dressed in a yellow rainsuit complete with sou'wester, stopped in mid-yank of a duffel. The woman next to her abandoned the task of carrying boxes of food to the cookhouse and drew her child closer to her. The leader, Akela, turned and saw Henry standing by the Escape. Had Millie really said she was a professor at the university? Akela frowned and looked down at her clipboard. The pages flapped in the caustic wind. She nodded at someone to take over ticking off the arriving children and approached the Ford. Dash tumbled out of the back seat like a bear cub and began tugging on her arm.

"Hi, Akela. Do you think we'll be able to go sledding like last time?" Dash's smile was like how you'd draw a cartoon smile. His curly hair was alive, dancing in the wind. He continued to pull on the Cub leader's sleeve. When she ignored him, he ran off to find his friends.

"Glad to have that drive over." Henry forced himself to smile at Akela and the other leader, Raksha or Mufasa or whatever the heck her name was. Why couldn't they just use their real names? Cubs *was* a cult. Neither answered, so Henry tried again.

"Did you see that car in the ditch just outside Mobile?"

Was he imagining it, or did Akela give Henry a funny look?

"Mr. Puddester." She paused for dramatic effect. "We weren't expecting you this evening."

"Why on earth not? I'm sure I answered the SurveyMonkey." Henry hated computer surveys. He preferred to just call someone up and say he was coming. But he had to admit that SurveyMonkey was useful.

"Well, you know . . ."

"No, I don't know. You'll have to tell me." Henry was breathing hard, in and out through his nose.

"Do I have to spell it out?" Akela adjusted her scarf.

"Yes." Henry could see all the other mothers leaning in to listen. Luckily for him, the children were goofing off, rolling in the wet snow, soaking the first of their many camp clothing outfits. But among the adults, you could hear a snail yawn.

Uh oh, thought Henry. *They know.*

Of course, anyone who saw last night's news would know about the supermarket—Henry couldn't even think the word "kidnapping." They were all young enough to be of the phone-addicted generation. They would all have seen the story on their bloody iPhones. What was it that Millie said? The story is *trending*.

But, except for Akela, they had no way of knowing Henry was in any way related to those events. The news report hadn't mentioned him by name, although Frank somehow knew it was him. You definitely couldn't tell who it was with the bag over his head in the patrol car.

She wouldn't mention it to the others. Or would she? He remembered Akela with her stupid neckerchief behind him in the lineup at the cash.

"In light of the—uh—incident . . ." Akela coughed. ". . . at the supermarket, I hope you don't mind, but until you get a new vulnerable sector check from the police, we'll have you sleep in the cookhouse."

"Excuse me?" Jesus in the garden. How dare she segregate him. How dare she say something like that within earshot of the other parents and children.

Dash had overheard. "Dad, I want you to sleep in the bunk under mine."

Akela raised her eyebrows at him.

Geez Louise. Henry and Millie hadn't even discussed what happened with Dash, who was now looking at him with a questioning expression.

"What's Akela talking about? What supermarket?"

"It's nothing, buddy," said Henry, tousling Dash's wild hair. "A silly misunderstanding. There aren't enough bunks in the bunkhouse for everyone, so I'll sleep in the other room."

"But there are lots of beds. There's always bunks left over."

Henry felt his blood pressure rising. He felt like wringing Akela's manly neck. *Breathe, Henry, breathe.* Dash dragged his duffel with his sleeping bag and pillow toward the clubhouse door. Henry flung his duffel over his shoulder and followed Dash inside. As Dash passed under the door frame, something fell through a hole in the ceiling and scurried under a bunk.

"Look, Dad, a mouse." Dash smiled, showing a gap where a tooth had recently been.

Great, thought Henry. *Just great.*

Once the Cubs were settled—well, Henry had seen war zones that were better organized—Akela gathered the Cubs. "Pack, Pack, Pack."

The Cubs, who one second earlier had looked like they were acting out the landing at Normandy, stopped moving. In whatever position they were in, they held it, like a frieze.

"Listen up. We can't do the campfire tonight because of the rain and snow." It was true. The incessant rain, now wet snow, had turned the ground into muck.

"Instead, we're going to have a Beyblade competition."

The children ramped up the frenzy level by several thousand percentage points. Henry felt himself hyperventilating. It was bad enough having to endure the little monsters in the school gym where they usually met for meetings. But this bunkhouse was another thing altogether. It was narrow and dimly lit and, despite the wood stove that stuck out from the wall in the centre of the room, smelled of dampness and mould.

The children screamed and ran to find their Beyblades. Henry was happy Millie hadn't pitched them. Henry had spin tops as a child, but Beyblades were spin tops on speed. Dash and the two other boys who had brought Beyblade Stadiums set up the plastic arenas, which were about two feet wide and would, at least half the time, contain the battles. Six boys and girls knelt on the grubby floor and faced off while the others crowded around them, their backs to the small wood stove. Dash chose his old favourite to start.

Dash and Stella Turner—thank God Dick wasn't here—pulled back on their rip cords, sending their Beyblades into the arena. Stella's fluorescent yellow and orange top knocked Dash's into a corner, where it came to a sad stop, while Stella's continued spinning with great force, bumping into the sides and careening off again. Stella got up and did her crazy Fortnite dance. What was it called? The floss, that was it. Within minutes, children were having battles outside the arenas.

Henry didn't cope well with chaos. Holy Mother—the air was close. Once Henry established that Dash didn't need him, he backed himself away from the crowd and over toward the door. He suddenly felt like he couldn't breathe. He felt like he needed a cigarette, even though he didn't smoke. His buddy Frank—it had only been two hours since he had seen Frank, but it felt like days—that's what he would have done. Frank would have gone outside in the rain, left the twenty little Cub Scouts to the much more qualified younger leaders, and lit up a smoke. Well, not a smoke, really, but that little silver canister of flavoured juice. Henry had come to associate the smell of Frank's vape pen with stress relief.

Henry slipped out of the bunkhouse and went to the sink for a drink. He was still thirsty. Was the tap water even safe to drink? Henry didn't care. He filled a huge plastic cup and wandered out on the deck. Huddled under the cabin eave, he pulled up his collar. He dug around in his red padded coat pocket for a piece of Juicy Fruit. What he found instead was a Tilley hat. How long had that been in there? He pulled it out and considered putting it on. He'd look like his father if he did, and that was not happening. Nope. No sirree, Bob. Henry did not want to look like Henry Puddester, Sr. About that, he was certain. His father shared the same birthday as Alex Tilley himself and had received his Tilley hat when he noticed an ad in Canadian Geographic offering anyone who was born on January 8, 1938, a free Tilley hat if they sent along a copy of their birth certificate.

One month later, Henry's father was the proud owner of a classic off-white model, complete with drawstring. It was while wearing that hat that Henry Puddester, Sr., announced he would be heading to Thailand and not coming back. Two weeks after that, Henry's mother had a visit from the RCMP explaining that her husband had been riding an elephant across a raging river when he was swept off the beast's back and never seen again. His hat, however, washed up downstream, where the same elephant had eaten it and later pooped it out with the 500 pounds of leaves and branches it had ingested that day. The tour leader scooped up the hat from the jungle floor, gave it a rinse in the Mai Ping River, and noticed a tiny compartment. Inside a tiny waterproof bag was Henry Puddester's name and address. With great ceremony, the RCMP officer, in his red serge, bestowed Henry Puddester, Sr.'s Tilley hat upon his only son, Henry Puddester the second. It was two days before Henry's twelfth birthday. The memory made Henry's skin crawl. Henry would never wear his father's hat.

What would Henry's parents have thought of his predicament?

Who cares? They were both gone now.

Breathing slowly, Henry thought if he could just make sense of the past two days, everything might be okay. He decided to review the facts.

1. He had mistakenly taken narcotics. He should always check the label before ingesting.
2. An infant had magically appeared in his shopping cart and derailed his life.
3. His wife and Glasses Gloria were preparing to defend him.
4. His son was addicted to video games and prone to punching the ceiling of vehicles and crying out "Spadoodle."
5. His neighbour, Frank, had begun construction of a Tardis in his shed.
6. Henry was tired.

Henry knew what he would have done differently. He should have left the supermarket baby where he found it. He should have never, ever, under any circumstances, have allowed himself to be cajoled into coming to Cub Camp. He should have had his vasectomy checked every day for the past decade and not just that one time six months after the operation, when the doctor, who looked no older than nineteen, confirmed he was shooting blanks.

Of course, Henry didn't really mean that. He loved Dash . . . he was just too darn old to be the father of an elementary-school-aged child. Also, he didn't have a patronly bone in his body. How could he, when his own father had discarded his wife and son? You need a role model for these things.

An extra loud whoop came out of the cabin behind Henry, jarring him back to the present. The Beyblade tournament was still in full swing. Henry had to admit that asking the children to bring Beyblades was a stroke of genius. Somebody had obviously taken note that the forecast this weekend called for sideways rain and light whipping snow.

Henry tried to think back on how he got roped into attending camp. He was sure it wasn't Dash who had asked. It was Millie. He should have said no. N-O. Millie should have been the one to come.

"I have a discovery to prepare for." As if that made things all right. But surely some other sucker could've come and had fun hiking through puddles and making bloody Ziploc omelets.

But no, the other parents were too busy with work. They had lives. Henry did not. Henry now spent his days learning the words to the Addams Family Grace. *Da da da da. Cluck, cluck. Da da da da. We thank You for our dinner. . . .* The words were on a constant loop in his head. He had to think about something else. He wished his mind had channels he could just turn on and off.

As Henry tried to sink deeper into his coat, he jammed the Tilley hat back into his pocket and thought about what Millie said as he headed out the door with the dratted eggs. "If you just paid a bit more attention to the world around you, you'd save yourself a lot of grief," she'd said. He knew she was referring to the judge having to give him a harsh sentence. But she made it about the omelets. "Make sure you listen to what each child wants in their baggy BEFORE you start cooking."

Henry sighed. That's when he heard the scream. Through the window, Henry could see that at least one child was on fire—a navy blue Cub hoodie shooting flames.

Henry ran around the corner of the building just as something large and rank-smelling skirted off into the woods. He had no time to investigate. He pulled open the door, just in time to see Akela dive on the flaming child, knock him to the floor, and roll him in a blanket. It would have made a fine fire-prevention video.

What would the parent of this child say when they heard the news that their kid had lit up like a firecracker at Camp D? It had lawsuit written all over it. Henry stayed back outside the outer ring and shuddered. That is until he noticed the curly blond hair sticking out of the blanket.

Henry got to Dash in seconds. He pushed through the circle of stunned children and knelt down. He caught a sideways look from Akela, who was kneeling on the other side. Her eyes were round, and she wasn't moving. In fact, no one was moving except Henry. Smoke was rising from Dash's hoodie. Henry pulled off the blanket and patted Dash down. Hair was singed. No burn marks on his face. He pulled off the hoodie. Arms okay. Legs appeared intact. Dash was shaking, and Henry could feel his heart beating through his T-shirt.

"What happened, Dasher?" Henry knew Dash didn't like him using his nickname outside the house, but it did the trick. Dash managed to hold back the dam of tears threatening to leak out the corners of his eyes while thirty sets of eyes bored into him like a dentist drill.

"I was just getting ready to launch my Beyblade when this big hairy face looked at me right there," said Dash, indicating the picture window just around the corner from where Henry had just been standing. "It looked like Bigfoot." This last bit came out softer than the first part. On the first bit of the drive up the Southern Shore, Henry had turned on a book on CD about a sasquatch. Henry knew it had Dash a bit freaked out because he hadn't talked at all after Henry turned it on. Normally, Dash talked over everything. When the story approached its climax, Henry looked in the rear-view and Dash was white, so Henry turned it off. That was just before Dash screamed "Spadoodle."

Akela broke the silence. "Someone left the door open on the wood stove, and an ember must have jumped out on his hoodie."

"I thought I saw something out there, too . . . a black bear, maybe." Henry wasn't just saying this. He had seen something.

"No bears on the Avalon Peninsula," piped up Akela, sticking out her chest. "There hasn't been a black bear sighting east of the isthmus since . . ."

Henry shot her a look.

She looked from him to Dash. "It could have been a coyote." She snapped the scorched blanket to give it a shake before folding it.

Henry lowered his voice. "Do you mind? This is a private conversation."

Dash looked up at his father. "Was it a bear, Dad?"

Henry looked at the militant Akela and was happy he wasn't a Cub.

"Akela says it wasn't a bear." He scowled at the Cub leader, put his arm around Dash, and gave him a squeeze before leading him out of the sleeping quarters. "Come on, buddy. Let's go to the cookhouse for a bit of breathing room."

"I want to call Mom." A huge shiver ran the length of Dash's body.

"Sorry, buddy, no service."

Henry took a flashlight off Dash's bunk and led Dash out to the cookhouse. He could hear Akela muttering, "Even if there were bears on the Avalon, they'd still be hibernating."

When they ventured outside, the night was dark. In fact, no moon or stars could be seen. The snow had stopped, but a thin layer remained on the sheltered passageway. Henry shone the light on the deck, and there before him and his son were what appeared to be prints of a large animal.

"Akela," Dash called. "Come look at this."

Thirty bodies crowded quickly onto the deck, wiping out any evidence of the footprints. Henry looked on the ground at the bottom of the steps, but the snow had soaked into the earth.

"There were big footprints." Dash's pupils were huge.

Akela shone her flashlight on the trampled snow. Only a small part of what could have been an animal print had survived the onslaught of Cub feet. "Could be a coyote," she said, patting Dash on the head.

"It was bigger than a coyote." Henry hugged Dash closer.

Akela shook her head at him. "Let's go back inside and get ready for bed," she said to the other Cubs. She held her mouth open, upper teeth jutting outwards like she was paralyzed. "We'll let Dash have time to unwind. He's had a bit of a scare."

With that, Akela gave Henry a look that said *I'll be keeping an eye on you*, turned on her booted heel, and dragged the unburned children inside.

25

Saturday: Frank Ponders Consulting

"Dad, did Mom tell you I've been accepted into medicine?" Kaitlyn gave him a peck on the cheek.

Frank blinked. "What do you mean, medicine? I haven't even finished paying for your engineering." Frank, who had hated school, could not understand how he had produced a serial student. He himself was never happier than the day he finished his studies.

"I realized engineering wasn't going to fulfill me." Frank's daughter sat in the swivel chair in front of the sunroom balcony doors and put her legs up on the desk.

"You said engineering was where your heart was."

"Yeah, well, things change. Tuition is due next week."

Frank sighed. "How much do you need?" He opened the drawer to take out his chequebook.

Kaitlyn flipped a finger over her phone screen. "Five thousand, one hundred and twenty-five dollars."

"Bloody hell," said Frank. "Are you actually planning to practise medicine after you finish?"

"Maybe."

"Kaitlyn, darling, I am not going to dish out over five thousand for a degree you may not use."

"Five thousand is just for the first term." She blinked up at her father.

Frank backed up out of the pantry to a stool at the island in the kitchen, sat down, and began inhaling like a Japanese yakuza, air over clenched teeth.

"It's not so bad, Dad. Mom said she'd cover books."

"That's nice of her." Frank tried not to be hostile toward Patty. He knew that since the divorce, Patty was having a hard time making ends meet. Although he had bought out her share of the house, he knew she had a mortgage with a nasty interest rate and that she was bringing in less salary than normal. Ever since the decline in oil, demand for Patty's corporate writing had dropped off considerably. Frank took out his vape pen.

"Dad, don't even think about smoking while I'm here." Kaitlyn Parrell did not raise her head from her phone. She thumb-typed as if the future of the world depended on her next text.

"It's not smoking, Kaitlyn darling. It's vaping. Much healthier."

Kaitlyn rolled her eyes as she continued to jab at her touch screen.

Frank did an about-face on his journey to the back deck, even though he desperately needed a smoke. He always felt the need to fortify himself for his twenty-year-old daughter's monthly post-divorce visit. But the last time he vaped in her presence, she had called 911 and asked for fire trucks to come to 8 Pine Place. She then promptly drove away and left Frank to explain to Payson, his firefighter neighbour, and the team from Station No. 2 what had transpired.

He was pretty sure Kaitlyn only visited to ensure that his bank account would continue to put her through school. But he tried to tell himself otherwise. He tried to tell himself she cared.

Frank pocketed his vape pen and swung open the pantry door next to Patty's old desk, the desk where Kaitlyn was now sitting, the desk that Patty hadn't bothered taking with her when she moved out. Patty's Sharpies and Post-it Notes still fanned out over the shelf above.

Maybe a cookie would do the trick. Frank's eyes scanned the pantry shelves. Same old, same old. He reached in and plucked a couple of oatmeal cookies from their Cellophane nest. He offered one to Kaitlyn.

"I'm not eating that crap. Have you looked at the ingredients? The fourth is lard. No wonder you've put on, like, twenty-five pounds in the past year."

Okaaaay. Frank decided to change the subject. "I was thinking about setting up a consulting business." He braced himself for his daughter's reaction.

"Consulting?" asked Kaitlyn. "What would you consult on?" Her questions weren't really questions. Just attacks in question form.

Frank cleared his throat. "Parking meters."

"Are you out of your mind? There are only four major municipalities in this province that even have parking meters. St. John's, Mount Pearl, Grand Falls, and Corner Brook. Count them. Four." She held up her fingers and counted them off, leaving out her thumb. "And every one of those jurisdictions is well aware of your history with meters."

Frank should have known better than to bring it up with her. "Maybe I could offer my services on the mainland."

"Not a chance." Kaitlyn swivelled on the office chair to face her father. "You could probably set up a business somewhere abroad, somewhere with no access to Google. China? North Korea? We can make a vacation of it."

"I'm being serious, Kaitlyn," he mumbled.

"I'm sorry. I shouldn't be so facetious. But think about it. Once any-one googles your name, they'll see stories about the fiasco here. No offence, Dad, but your reputation is a touch tarnished in the area of parking meters."

"Maybe I should reconsider."

"Uh, yeah." Kaitlyn went on texting.

Frank should just bite the bullet and retire like Henry. At fifty-eight, Henry was only three years older than Frank. Lucky bastard.

Wait a minute. Henry wasn't lucky. He had retired to take care of Dash, the surprise child, all because government cuts had shut down his daycare, and all the other daycares had waiting lists as long as the Trans-Canada. Naw, Henry wasn't lucky. He was cursed.

When Henry had told Frank that Millie was pregnant, Frank blanched and booked a recheck for his vasectomy. Imagine never wanting children, and then boom, you're into diapers and bottles in your late forties. Harsh, ever so harsh. The shock was bad enough for Frank. He could only imagine how hard it was for Henry and Millie.

Frank wished he could take a jaunt over to Henry's shed for a smoke, but Henry was still at Cub Camp. Frank wouldn't see him until Sunday evening.

Kaitlyn was waving her hand in the air in front of his face. He had forgotten she was there.

"Dad . . . don't forget the cheque."

"Of course. Tell me the exact amount again."

Kaitlyn laid her phone face up on the desk and vacated the chair so Frank could sit down. Very considerate of her. Frank filled in the amount and the date, signed his name, and passed the paper over to his daughter.

"Thanks, Dad. You know what you should do? You should open a mi-crobrewery. You're good at making beer."

A microbrewery. Now there was an idea, if he could manage to finance it and still pay for Kaitlyn's whimsical education.

The phone rang, and when Frank picked up, Kaitlyn took the oppor-tunity to disappear. "Bye, Dad. Love you." Not even a hug before her de-signer shoes slipped out the door.

It was Wiener from down at the bunker. His accounting job had be-come redundant, and he now worked as a commissionaire. Could Frank come down immediately?

"It's Saturday, for crying out loud."

"I know, but I got this tourist here who wants to talk to you."

"A tourist? Why does a tourist want to speak to me?"

"She says she can identify the meter thief."

"Butter my butt and call me a biscuit. I'll be right down," said Frank, not even bothering to change out of his maggoty shed jacket before he ran out the door.

26

Frank Meets Delores at City Hall

Frank may have had an extortionist daughter, but he would not let that ruin his day. Someone had seen a meter thief in action. There was a God after all. Frank was too excited to call a cab. He pulled on his trainers and sprinted out the door and down Pine Place. He ran all the way to City Hall. It had been years since he'd moved like that. It was exhilarating.

Wiener's eyebrows disappeared into his bangs when Frank presented himself in front of the glass window. Sweat rolled down his forehead and neck and disappeared under his collar. Frank could see Wiener's eyes travelling the length of his torso, taking in his grey sweatpants and shredded shed jacket; the outer layer had disintegrated from the ribs down, the honeycomb padding exposed for the world to see.

"Geez, you didn't have to go and dress up, you know. Between you and the meter missus, you could start a mummers' troupe."

"Wiener, I don't give a rat's ass how I look. Where is she?"

Wiener indicated up the stairs, where a floral-clad woman with periwinkle hair and a purple beach bag gazed up at a picture of Alcock and Brown on the concrete wall of the bunker.

"Blimey, I see what you mean. What's she doing?" Frank whispered.

"She's been looking at that picture for the past ten minutes."

"Is she for real?" Frank blinked, but the blue hair and flowery clothes were still there.

"She says she can identify your meter thief, if that's what you mean." The eyebrow over Wiener's left eye nudged upwards while the right stayed in place.

"What'd you say her John Henry is?"

Weiner raised an eyebrow. "I didn't get her autograph. She said her name is Cowburn. Delores Cowburn."

Frank straightened his shed coat and took the stairs two at a time.

"Frank Parrell," he said when he reached her, extending his hand.

She did not seem put off by his attire and, taking his hand in hers, shook with the speed of a blender. A big smile unveiled a leafy green lodged between her two front teeth. A neighbouring tooth was absent.

"I'm the bloke in charge of parking meters."

"I'm the woman who was almost beheaded by one."

"I am happy you were not beheaded. Miss Cowburn, my colleague . . ."

"Call me Delores. If you call me Miss Cowburn, I'll think you're talking to my mother, and if you're talking to her, well, let's just say you have the gift."

"Well, uh, Delores, my colleague . . ." Here Frank tilted his head to Wiener down in the glass booth. Wiener waved. "He said you may be able to provide me with some information about the person or persons who've been damaging meters throughout the city."

"Yes, sir."

When Delores didn't offer more, Frank spoke again. "Can you tell me what happened?"

"I had my station wagon vandalized."

"How so?"

"Well, first of all, I hit a moose."

"Oh, no, that's terrible." Frank didn't give two hoots about the moose. "Then what happened?"

"I pulled into a parking space on the waterfront and was sizing up the damage from the moose when this young guy comes along with a sledgehammer. He lobs off the meter and my See-No-Evil monkey, among other things."

"Blimey." Frank tried to sound sympathetic. He had no idea what this wacko was on about, but he knew what he needed. "You saw his face?"

"Yes, sir."

"And you would be able to identify him?"

"Yes, sir. He had freckles and short red hair."

"Excellent," said Frank, taking a small piece of wood out of his shed coat pocket and making notes with a carpenter's pencil. "Go on. Did he have any facial hair, earrings, that sort of thing?"

"No, sir, no beard or moustache, if that's what you're asking. And I didn't notice any earrings, but . . ."

"But what?" Frank was leaning in closer.

"He had a tattoo on his cheek."

"A tattoo?"

"Yup, shaped like a teardrop."

"A teardrop, you say. Doesn't that indicate he's killed someone?"

"He killed See-No-Evil."

Frank cleared his throat. "How old would you say he was?"

"Somewhere between twenty and thirty, but I'd wager closer to twenty."
"Height?"
"Average."
"Weight?"
"Lean, good runner."
"How did he remove the meter head?"
"Like I said, he had a huge mallet like the one my mamma used to use to pound in the fence posts back home."

Frank smiled. "Let's go have a gander at your car, size up the damage."

Wiener saluted as Frank led Delores Cowburn by the arm down the concrete steps to the car park.

27

Frank Meets Daisy

"Blimey. Wait till Henry gets a look at this." Frank stopped in his tracks when he saw the estate car. The Ford LTD was so covered in trinkets, you hardly noticed the smashed windscreen and damaged front end. Everything, from the roof to the hood, the sides, the tailgate, the bumpers, was completely blanketed with small toys, some retro, some modern. You could glimpse the original pink paint only around the door handles and wheel wells.

When they got closer, Frank could see that the interior was also adorned with similar kitsch. He whistled. "That's a lot of McDonald's toys."

"There are some toys from McDonald's, but many predate that era . . . from my childhood collection." The blue-haired Delores puffed out her floral chest.

Frank touched a Smurf's hat.
"You like her?"
"Sure, I mean, yes. Good gravy, what possessed you?"
"It just came to me one day in the Walmart back home in Williams Lake."
"Where's Williams Lake?"
"BC. That's where I bought the first bottle of Gorilla Glue."
"What's that? Like Super Glue?"

"Better. If you want something to stay where it is, Gorilla Glue is your adhesion product of choice."

"How many, uh, things are on here?" Frank walked slowly around the Ford.

"Since the accident, just under four thousand on the outside and eight hundred on the inside."

"Get out."

"Get out of where?"

"I mean there's no way there's that many toys on this thing."

"You're welcome to count them."

"I trust you." Frank looked closer at a snow globe on the hood. Miniature polar bears slid down a hill into an igloo. Next to it sat Mickey and Minnie Mouse and four Ninja Turtles.

"Can I get your phone number?"

"Are you being fresh with me?" Delores pulled her chin into her chest.

"No . . . no, it's so I can get you to give a description to the police."

"I'm pulling your leg. I don't have a phone." Delores opened the driver's door, allowing Frank a better view of hula girls surrounding a rubber Gumby and Pokey.

"So, how can I get in touch with you?"

"I'm at the Walmart on Stavanger." She pronounced Stavanger with a soft G. "See you around, Mr. Frank." With that, she got in the Country Squire and drove away.

"Cheers." Frank didn't even question why Delores would be at Walmart.

She rolled down the window as she drove out of the lot. Snippets of Billy Ray Cyrus singing about his achy breaky heart streamed out the window, and Frank smiled. As the Ford LTD disappeared, Frank could hear Delores Cowburn muttering something under her breath.

28

Millie Under Pressure

Millie sat at her desk, hands moving at lightning speed over the keyboard, while she spoke into the microphone attached to the earpiece tucked in her left ear. She had been working every waking moment since Henry and

Dash had gone off to camp. It took her until Saturday evening to get on top of all her files. She had just begun working on Henry's defence when she was interrupted by a senior partner.

"I told you, Bill. I can't take on any more cases right now."

"We can't afford to lose this one, Millie."

"Send Eleanor. She's up to speed."

"Eleanor is in Toronto working on the Freake case."

"Okay. I'll do it."

Millie sighed and ended the call. How was she going to find time to work on a defence for Henry if senior partners kept piling on more work? Millie was delighted Gloria had agreed to represent Henry, but Millie still had to prepare the case. Everyone at McLoughlan, McLoughlan and Mercer was working eighty-hour weeks trying to get through a backlog of cases.

Millie googled Dilaudid. Side effects included all Henry's symptoms: dizziness, drowsiness, dry mouth, and dehydration. As well as low blood pressure, nausea, temporary redness of face and neck, vomiting, confusion, rapid heartbeat, double vision, nervousness, trouble breathing, even hallucinations.

Hallucinations. Hmm. Millie might just be able to build a case yet.

29

Sunday: Akela Shuts Down Camp Sasquatch

When it was time to choose a camp name before closing, Dash suggested Camp Sasquatch. Stella drew what looked like a skinny ape on the woodcut, and Akela hung it on the wall next to all the other plaques from previous camps.

"I've never been so happy to see the end of a Cub Camp," Akela said to her right-hand woman, Baloo. The rain, mixed with snow, sleet, and hail, had persisted until—wouldn't you know it—Sunday morning, when the sun appeared on the horizon as if to say, *Ha, did you miss me?*

"How many have been picked up?" Baloo looked over Akela's shoulder to see where she was ticking off names on a clipboard.

"Four."

Yes, four Cubs had already dragged their maggoty, waterlogged clothes and bedding out to vehicles and were gone. Gloriously gone. Timmy F., who peed the bed every night without fail but luckily had a waterproof liner in his sleeping bag and plenty of spare clothes in his duffel; Sarah R., who it turned out was afraid of the dark and had to sleep in the bunk closest to Akela and the night light; Molly C., who had survived another Cub Camp despite a life-threatening allergy to peanuts; and Rourke D., who had been surprisingly quiet all weekend. Akela would have to see if there was something going on at home.

"Sixteen left to go," said Baloo.

Akela visualized more vehicles appearing and whisking away the children. She often used visualization as a tool when things weren't going exactly as planned.

"So, not counting the ten whose parents are here with them, who does that leave?" Baloo scanned the crowd. Most of the parents who had stayed at camp were in the final stages of getting on the road.

"Let's see. There's Leo A., Sam B., Ryder D. and Iggy K." Akela scrolled her finger down the list. "And Frankie M.'s father is taking home Stella T."

"Doesn't Stella live on the same street as Dash? I wonder why she's not getting a ride home with him, considering his father is here and all?"

Akela's hand paused over the clipboard. "I don't think Constable Turner likes Mr. Puddester very much."

"Why? He did a great job with the omelets." That was true. Henry Puddester had done an excellent job with breakfast. In fact, Akela couldn't remember a time when all the Cubs were happy with their omelets.

"Not sure."

Akela didn't know how much she should confide in Baloo. All the leaders knew that Henry Puddester was the man who had been led away in handcuffs after taking that baby from the supermarket. Akela couldn't believe she was right there standing behind him at the cash and hadn't done something. She thought it strange that Mr. Puddester had a baby with him but didn't question it. She remembered back to when he ran into her with his shopping cart. Had the baby been with him then? Akela shook her head. At least the baby was safely reunited with her mother, and Akela heard charges had been laid. But why wasn't Mr. Puddester behind bars instead of at her Cub Camp? She would find out the details, but for now she had been keeping an eagle eye on Mr. Puddester all weekend. She had taken note when he silently slipped out of the bunkhouse on Friday night. What was he doing out there, anyway? *God knows. Maybe it was him looking in the window freaking out his son and then making up the bear story after Dash went up in flames.*

She should have put her foot down and not allowed him to sleep over. Akela would tell him he wasn't welcome back without a new police check. There was no way he'd be allowed to volunteer with youth after a botched kidnapping.

Akela realized Baloo was still talking. "He was a bit over the top when he said he saw a black bear." Baloo shook her head.

"Yes, I can now say unequivocally that he is Looney Tunes." Akela/Vanessa knew whatever there was to know about black bears in Newfoundland. She was the expert. Vanessa knew the Newfoundland black bear better than she knew people. Except maybe her Cub Scouts. "Everyone knows black bears live all over the island of Newfoundland *except* the Avalon Peninsula. There would no more likely be a black bear here in Bauline East than a skunk or porcupine.

"Didn't someone just find a dead skunk in their backyard out in Dannyland recently?"

"Yes, but that was someone who carted it here from the mainland."

"Why would they do that?"

"Media attention. Remember the pranksters who dumped a bear cub carcass on the side of the road in PEI? Same thing. If Dash's father had found a bear belly-up dead, I would agree that yes, there is a bear on the Avalon, but I would argue that it did not come here on its own. Someone would have dragged its sorry carcass across the isthmus and deposited it here."

"Hmm." Baloo kicked at a small mound of snow.

Sam B.'s mother pulled in, and he tumbled into the van already occupied by several younger siblings. With each departing child, Akela breathed a sigh of relief that they had made it through camp without any more incidents. She was anxious to begin the trek north to St. John's. Akela waved and ticked off his name. She then turned back to Baloo and picked up where they left off.

"There are no bears on the Avalon Peninsula, with the exception of the odd polar bear who drifts in on an ice floe in the spring."

Akela stared up at the window through which the bear, or whatever it was, was supposed to have been looking. She knew it was impossible. But not in Henry Puddester's world. In Mr. Puddester's world, a bear was upright on his hind legs, peering in a window at Camp D in April. Maybe the man was psychotic. "I'm pretty sure Mr. Puddester made up the bear story so that Dash wouldn't be embarrassed after he set himself on fire."

"Maybe," said Baloo. "It's still not as bad as the year we baked cakes in tinfoil pans on the ground over hot coals. Remember that? When Kelvin M. bit into a meadow vole?"

"Oh, yes, I remember. He was so hysterical that two leaders had to leave at midnight for the hour ride back to St. John's. As soon as they reached the main road, their truck nosedived into a ditch." Akela had tried to shake that one out of her memory banks, but it refused to budge.

"I find Mr. Puddester all right," said Baloo. "He's better than the helicopter parents."

"He's definitely more the hands-off type. Look how relaxed he was when Dash got burned."

"True. Quick thinking with the stop, drop, and roll, by the way. I hadn't heard that since the seventies."

"That was the first time in fifteen years that a Cub has caught fire on my watch." Akela straightened up, raising her head on her neck.

"Thank goodness the burns were superficial. You performed due diligence questioning him before he went to bed and again this morning to make sure he was okay."

Akela knew all that psycho mumbo-jumbo was rubbish. It was no doubt some irrational fear of Bigfoot that had set Dash off, but she asked all the same. "Did you hear his answer when I asked if he had any dreams?"

"No."

"He said, 'Yes, I dreamed about marshmallows.'" They laughed.

"It is odd that Mr. Puddester wouldn't let Dash call his mother. He told him there was no cell reception. Reception was perfect. I had just called to ask Matilda to pick up some more garbage bags before she made her way down this morning."

"Maybe he was afraid once Dash heard his mother's voice he'd want to go home."

"Maybe."

Both leaders scanned the yard for Dash and his father. They were on the far end of the bunkhouse. Dash made a running start and ran up the trunk of a thirty-foot maple until he got hold of a branch. From there he climbed up close to the top. His father shaded his eyes with his hand and looked up.

"He's going to break his back if he falls."

"Guaranteed."

The leaders paused to listen to the conversation between father and son.

"You should come up, Dad."

"Dash, you promised your mother you wouldn't climb so high."

"You can see everything from up here. Even the ocean."

"Dash, I'm going to start the car now. You can come with me or stay in the tree."

Vanessa watched as Dash's father turned his back on his monkey son and trudged through the mud toward his red Escape. Dash zipped down and came over and gave Baloo a hug.

"Bye, Baloo, see you next week."

He then did the same to Akela. "Catch ya later, alligator."

She hugged the boy back. Akela had no children of her own. The Cubs were her surrogates. She was an only child herself and was such a tomboy that they let her go through Cubs with the boys before it was an official thing. She had vowed she'd be a Cub leader one day. Ever since she could remember, Cub meetings and camps were her happy place.

When Dash hugged her, that unconditional hug—he didn't care if she wasn't as feminine as some of the other leaders—he loved her just the way she was. Something sparked in her, like the Grinch whose heart has grown. Maybe she was too severe with Dash's father. Could it be possible that he had really seen a bear?

Akela shook her head. No, not possible. She banished the thought from her mind and pulled her coat around her. Although the sun was bright enough to split the rocks, the wind had picked up something terrible. She was looking forward to going home for a nice hot bath, where she could morph back into Dr. Hannaford, respected and oft-quoted university professor.

30

Sunday Evening in Henry's Shed

The Triumph Bonneville thundered up Pine Place and turned in the drive-way of number 10. The replaced seal worked perfectly. Henry eased the bike around the side of the house and along the paved walkway to the little grassy knoll up to the shed. He had gone for a ride to try and erase the con-versation he'd had with Millie after she saw Dash's singed hair.

"You should have come home right away." Millie had her hands plant-ed firmly on her hips. Lightning bolts zinged from her pupils.

"No need." Henry shrugged weakly and picked up a teacup out of the drainer and began to dry it slowly, methodically. "Dash was fine."

"Henry, your son was on fire."

"Yes, but he was lucky," said Henry, remembering the flames engulf-ing Dash.

"Lucky? How was he lucky, might I ask?"

"His hoodie must be fire-resistant. There was hardly a mark on him."

"What about his hair?"

Henry smiled his twitchy smile. "It'll grow back."

Millie looked at Henry, shaking her head. "Where were you . . . when it happened?"

"Outside." He slowly turned a teacup on the shelf so that the flower pattern faced out.

"Oh, I see, pondering the meaning of life, as usual, I suppose?"

Henry took the last plate from the drying rack and brought it to the cupboard. Millie's last question must have been rhetorical.

"You still should have called." Millie took the plate from his hands and put it in the stack with the others.

"If I called, you would have been worried." Henry sighed. "Listen, Millie. It's been quite few days. I can't turn back the clock. Dash is fine. He'd have been sad if he had to come home early and miss camp. Plus, he'll have a good story to tell."

"That's what you always say when there's a disaster. There'll be a good story to tell. Well, guess what, Henry? I don't want any more stories to tell."

Ever since they arrived home just after noon, Millie had been coddling Dash and treating Henry like a delinquent father. As soon as she left to take Dash to the Republic of Yogourt for a treat, Henry hightailed it to the shed and got the Triumph out for a ride. It wasn't his fault Millie hadn't taken the news well about her only child igniting. Henry had to stay in her good books, however, if he hoped to make it through the court case and on the plane to meet his bike in Montreal.

Henry rolled the bike up the ramp into the shed. The wind screamed through a hole in the vinyl siding, but it didn't matter. Henry's shed was his sanctuary, his nirvana. While he was in it, he was safe from the world. Even Millie knew not to pop her head in. Once, she came in trying to gather the recycling, but Henry shooed her out with a fan belt. Empty beer bottles were a requirement of any man cave.

The only thing he had left to do was drain the gas out of the tank and oil out of the engine, and then the bike was ready to go. Henry cast a glance at his mother's Ducati Monster peeking out from under the tarp. She was a beauty. Black and sleek. Only 3,500 klicks on her. They wouldn't need to ship that one after all.

He was re-polishing the forks when he caught a whiff of cotton candy. He looked out the window just in time to see Frank rounding the end of the fence and hopping over the holly bush. No doubt to vent some more of his parking meter frustrations. Henry didn't mind. Frank made Henry forget his own problems. He'd be frustrated, too, if he had to deal with the constant barrage of criticism that Frank had to put up with at work. Henry hadn't worked in the same office as Frank, but he had worked at City Hall for thirty-five years, and the culture was the same in every department down at the bunker. He missed his work, but there were times he appreciated the fact that he had gotten out when he had.

The cotton candy cloud entered the shed before Frank's red cheeks appeared around the door. He was smiling so hard his face looked like it was going to split. "I heard the Triumph before you turned into the cul-de-sac. She running well?"

"Yep. Just have to drain the fluids, and she'll be ready to pack up."

"Ah, jolly good day, isn't it?" Frank's British accent became even more pronounced when he was in a good mood.

"Haven't seen you so jovial in a long time." Henry always knew that, with Frank, it was either Armageddon or Christmas—no in-between. "What happened?"

"This estate car pulled into the car park at City Hall yesterday." Frank took a puff just like the caterpillar in Alice in Wonderland.

"Estate car? How many years have you been on this side of the drink, again?"

"Thirty-two. That's neither here nor there. A 1983 Ford LTD. Remember those boats with the wooden panels?"

"Yeah, I learned to drive in one. A Country Squire. Green. Hand me that wrench over there, will you?"

"What, this one?" Frank picked up a half-inch.

"No, that one." Henry indicated the nine-sixteenths.

Frank passed over the wrench and then wiped his oily hands on his shed coat. "Same car, but this one's pink. Except you can't see the paint job because there are about ten thousand knick-knacks stuck on it." Frank's thunderous laugh overshadowed the wind.

"What do you mean, knick-knacks?" Henry opened the gas tank and stuck in the dipstick. Fumes filled the shed.

"Just that. You know, like old ceramic figurines and plastic McDonald's toys."

"That's plain weird." Henry screwed the cover back on the tank. He wiped his hands in a handkerchief. There wouldn't be too much gas to drain.

"I know," Frank laughed.

Henry was astounded to see how much Frank's beer gut had grown in the last year or so. The hard-packed skin moved up and down, his shirt going with it. When he first met him, Frank had a six pack. He was one of the fittest boys at the bunker, sought after for any sports team.

"What was a Ford LTD with *knick-knacks* doing at City Hall?"

"I—"

"Wait," Henry interrupted. "This question is a two-header. More importantly, what were you doing at that fine establishment on a Saturday?"

"I got a call from Wiener to come meet the owner of the LTD. She drove the thing all the way across the continent."

"That's impressive. If I remember correctly, our Country Squire was prone to engine overheating."

"She didn't mention overheating, but get this . . . as soon as she arrives in St. John's, she hits a moose."

"Oooh, bad luck."

"Wait, it gets better." Frank was practically spitting. "She's freaked out, so she pulls in on Harbour Drive. And boom. Her station wagon gets hit again, but this time it's not a moose."

"What was it?"

"Some twit nicking the head off a parking meter."

"Noooo!"

"Yes, oh yes."

"Did she say how he did it?"

"Yeah."

Henry can tell how much Frank is enjoying this moment. "So . . . ?"

"Mr. Twit did it with a mallet on the waterfront."

"Now, that is interesting. Did the kind lady happen to get a look at the thief?"

"Why, yes, indeed she did. And get this, she's already been to the cop shop and provided a description."

"Get outta town." Henry whistled.

"I'm serious. I haven't been this happy since the brew store had a sale on Australian hops."

"Much damage to her car?"

"A good bit from the moose, but only minor damage from the mallet . . . a couple of monkeys knocked off the hood."

"Monkeys?" Henry's curiosity was piqued.

"Yeah, you know, See-No-Evil, yada, yada. I'm telling you, this wagon is completely covered in junk."

"Where's the car now?"

"Walmart on Stavanger."

"What the heck is it doing up there?"

"The missus who owns it, the one I met at the bunker. From what I deduced, she camps out at Walmart."

"What do you mean she camps at Walmart?"

"She stayed in Walmart car parks all across Canada. They welcome it, apparently. She can use the loo. Pick up her groceries. And from what I understand, her car always draws a crowd. And I guess the crowd shops at Walmart, too."

"That's insane." Henry opened a bag of rags and grabbed a new one to remove a speck of grease.

"Come on, Henry. Let's go up and see it."

"I'm not going anywhere. I'm busy."

"Bollocks. You're not busy. You're just hiding from your wife. I know what it's like. I had one, too, remember?"

"No, I really am. I gotta have her ready to go. Oceanex is coming to crate her Tuesday suppertime."

"You've thousands of time. You can finish tomorrow. I want you to see the estate car."

"No." Henry wiped a hand on his immaculately clean coveralls. "You just want me to drive you to Walmart so *you* can see the car."

"No, really, I want you to see it, too."

"Frank, don't you think it odd that someone who works for the municipal department of transportation does not possess a driver's licence?"

"Not at all. Henry, you'll be kicking yourself if you don't go."

"No way, monkeys on the hood or not. That place is hell on earth." Stavanger Drive had some of the highest winds on the island.

"Come on. Where's your sense of adventure?"

"Frank, the wind out there tonight . . ." He stopped for a minute to listen to the maple branches beating against the shed window. ". . . will blow us off the Outer Ring Road before we make it to Stavanger."

"Naw, we'll be fine. Just take Torbay Road. Plus, it's calmed a bit. Stick your head out and see."

Henry poked out his head for ten seconds before pulling it back in. He looked at the reflection of his salt and pepper hair in the bike mirror. "It's like a wind tunnel experiment out there. It almost took the shed door. Plus, what about the ten thousand crazed shoppers?"

"They won't be out on a Sunday night. Everyone will be heading home in an hour to watch the hockey game."

"That's what I'll be doing." Henry's eyes lit up. "Maybe I could hook up a TV in the shed, you know, run a cable. . . . After the game, I could watch an old Henry Fonda movie. Did you know my mother named me after Henry Fonda? She loved him in *12 Angry Men*."

"Henry, you're getting off topic. Why can't you just watch in the basement like you always do?"

Henry looked Frank straight in the eyes and blurted, "Dash accidentally set himself on fire at Cub Camp."

"Oh, I see. That's a cock-up, for sure." Frank rubbed his chin. "What happened?"

"A spark from the wood stove caught his sweatshirt. He's fine, but Millie's on the warpath."

"Blimey, I hope it wasn't too serious."

"He was pretty lit up." Henry's eyes widened as he remembered the scene.

"How did you put it out?"

"I didn't. That's half the problem. It was the psycho Cub leader who put out the fire."

"You mean the one with the man hands?"

"Yeah, did I tell you about her?"

"Yeah, said she was Lola."

"Lola?"

"You know . . . L-O-L-A, Lola. Anyway, where were you at the time?"

"I was outside when my offspring decided to engulf himself in flames."

"Bloody hell. I can just imagine Millie's reaction." Frank shuddered.

"Yeah, she said next time I decide to 'ponder the meaning of life' to do it where there's no open fire."

"Come with me to Stavanger, Henry. It'll take your mind off things. And we can watch the game in my basement when we get back. It'll be brilliant."

Henry slowly peeled himself out of the coveralls, hung them neatly on their hanger, and pulled his Escape keys out of his pocket.

If he only knew how much he was going to regret having gone.

31

Henry and the Walmart Wind

Henry pulled the Ford Escape into the Walmart lot just in time to see an errant shopping cart take out a middle-aged woman with a head of cropped blue hair. The cart was careening across the parking lot, heading east, when it took a turn to the south, and *bam*, down she went. Henry pulled into the nearest space.

"Bloody hell, did you see that?"

Frank jumped out of the SUV and ran to where the shape lay prone on the asphalt, the cart on its side next to her, the contents of her purple purse strewn around her like an art installation, anything lighter than a pound taking flight toward Robin Hood Bay. Henry jumped out and forced the door shut against the wind.

"Chris' Almighty, that's her," Frank screamed over the howling gusts. "That's Delores—the station wagon lady. I recognize the pants."

"But not the hair?" Henry's eyes travelled the length of the motion-less figure, moving down from the blue hair and red lipstick to the pink jacket and floral pants, which he had to admit were indeed memorable. No movement came from the lump, despite the wind gusts lifting the ends of the jacket and floral pant legs as well as some strands of aqua hair.

"She's out cold," said Frank, looking around as if hoping a doctor would materialize through the automatic doors in the distance. "Check her pulse, would you?"

"She's your friend. You check."

"She's not my friend, but she is the only person alive able to identify the meter thief."

"So, why don't you feel it?"

"I'm scared."

Henry rolled his eyes, squirted on some hand sanitizer, and took the woman's wrist in his. "Pulse is fine." His eyes roamed the parking lot for the LTD. There was a group of people standing around something in the far corner of the lot. Maybe that was the mysterious station wagon.

"I'm calling 911." Frank pulled out his phone.

Henry surveyed the contents of the purse that had not yet taken flight. A large plastic bottle of Gorilla Glue lay on the ground near a box of Flakies.

Frank started to key in the numbers.

"Frank, wait a minute. Looks like she's coming around."

The woman opened her eyes, but she did not seem to register Henry at her side. Frank crouched beside Henry and nudged him out of the way. "Delores, it's me, Frank from City Hall. Remember?"

The woman turned her head ever so slightly to bring Frank into focus. She blinked.

"See-No-Evil." She closed her eyes.

"Yes, we know all about the monkey."

"See-No-Evil," she repeated, eyes still shut.

"Don't worry, Delores, we're going to call an ambulance."

At the word "ambulance," it was like a lightning bolt passed through Delores's body. Her eyes flew open, and she shrieked. "No ambulance."

"Okaaay." Henry rubbed his thumb and forefinger up and down along the scruff on his chin. "What now?"

"We'll bring her to the hospital ourselves."

"I came here to see a souped-up station wagon, not play good Samaritan to some nutbar."

"She's not a nutbar. . . . Well, maybe she is, but we can't just leave her here."

"I got enough on my plate between Millie and Dash and bloody babies left in shopping carts. I'm going home to watch the game."

"Come on, Henry. It won't take any time. We'll still catch the game. And I have eight tins of scrummy Guinness."

Henry raised one eyebrow. It wasn't like Frank to buy Guinness. "I don't know what scrummy means, but if you have Guinness . . ."

"Yes, I do occasionally stock beer brewed by someone other than myself, although I'm sure it's far inferior to my latest batch."

"Is it cold?"

"Ice."

"Okay. I'll pick up her stuff."

Frank stood up to disperse the small crowd that had migrated from the station wagon to the accident scene. "Show's over, everyone." They grumbled but moved on.

He bent down to grab the Flakies and a hairbrush before they blew away while Henry wrestled the catch-all from the lady's arm and opened it wider to put in the Gorilla Glue. It looked like maple syrup. He motioned to Frank to drop the other things inside. The last thing Frank picked up was a Mickey Mouse key ring with at least twenty keys on it. He pitched them in the bag, and Henry swung it over his shoulder.

"Looks good on you." Frank laughed that thundering laugh of his. Henry did not laugh. He threw the bag in the Escape and drove as close as he could to the woman so they could load her inside.

"She's no lightweight." Frank wrestled the woman into a sitting position before taking her under the arms. Henry took her legs, and together they heave-hoed her into the back seat in much the same way Henry had loaded in a forty-pound bag of sushi rice a few days before.

Henry stretched to strap on her seat belt and placed her purse on the seat next to her lifeless form.

32

Henry at the Hospital with Delores

Henry did not get to see the game. He did not get to enjoy a cold Guinness. He did not even really get to see the Ford LTD. What he did was call his incredulous wife from the emergency department of the Health Sciences Centre to tell her he was waiting for a dowdy, blue-haired, floral-clad lady to be seen by a doctor after he and Frank witnessed her getting clobbered by a Walmart cart.

"We were supposed to go over your defence, and then Dash was waiting for you to watch the game." Millie's voice came through the phone like a chainsaw. Henry could tell she still wasn't over the fact that Dash had caught fire.

"I know, but we couldn't just leave her there."

"But who is she?" When Millie was irritated, there was no disguising it in her tone.

"I don't know . . . some lady Frank knows."

"Henry, what is the woman's name?"

"Uh . . ." Henry looked up to the left. "Delores, I think. A bit of a nutbar, really. She covered an old wood-panelled station wagon with plastic toys and drove it across the country."

"Oooh," said Millie, her tone suddenly changing. "*That* Delores. I saw her on *The National* a little while ago. She was in Quebec. I had no idea she had made it here already. How does Frank know her?"

"He met her yesterday. She went to City Hall to complain about damage to her car."

"You mean Daisy?"

"Is that the car's name?"

"Yes, we watched a story about her last Saturday night, remember?"

"No."

"What happened to Daisy?"

"Well, first she hit a moose."

"Oh, no." A gasp came out of Millie. "Is Delores all right?"

"Not since she was run over by a shopping cart." It was no surprise to Henry that his wife would be into the retro station wagon—she always loved funky cars—but he was surprised by her interest in the crackpot woman driving it.

"Okay, back up a bit. I don't understand what she was doing at City Hall."

Henry was experiencing information overload. "A thief was ripping the head off a parking meter and ended up damaging the station wagon, too."

"The plot thickens. So, she went down to the bunker, and they called Frank."

"Ipso facto. Then Frank insisted we had to bring her to the hospital. So here we are—at least I am. Not sure where Frank disappeared to." A stretcher pushed by a short male porter with a mohawk trundled by.

"Okay, keep me posted. I'd love to meet her sometime and see Daisy."

"Uh . . . gotta go, Millie. They're calling her name."

The woman had come to when Henry and Frank rolled her out of the Escape and onto the sidewalk outside emerg. They dragged her into triage, where she groggily spouted some gibberish that sounded like "Jumpin' Jack Flash" before passing out again, her aqua head listing to one side. Henry dug around in the tote until he produced a Hello Kitty wallet containing a licence and a British Columbia health card. DELORES COWBURN, it read. DOB 1975/02/24.

The triage nurse reappeared, indicating that Henry should bring Delores into a curtained room. Henry tried to drag the woman to her feet. He almost collapsed under the sudden burden of her full weight.

"I think we need a wheelchair here," he said. The nurse scurried off.

Where had Frank gone? Henry owled his head around and saw him talking to a man near the back of the packed room. The man held his left index finger aloft like a flaming torch. It was bundled in gauze, ruby blood seeping through.

"It's not right that people who park on damaged meters for more than two hours get tickets," the bloody-fingered man was saying.

Frank and his blasted meters. What was he doing talking shop while Henry risked whiplash? Delores still had hold of his side, so he couldn't fully turn his body. Jesus in the garden.

"I know. We'll all be lynched. They'll set the bunker ablaze." Frank imitated someone striking a match and dropping it to the floor.

"Uh, Frank, I hate to interrupt, but, uh, I need your help here." The nurse had reappeared with a wheelchair that looked like it was out of a World War II field hospital and was waiting for Henry to hoist in the station wagon lady. Frank took the hint and left Bleeding Finger Man.

The station wagon lady groaned as they each took her under an arm and yanked her into the chair. Henry straightened her shirt. The nurse then started in on a stream of questions that, beyond her name and date of birth, neither Frank nor Henry had any idea how to answer. They both looked to the station wagon lady, who began mumbling under her breath. "'I Want to Hold Your Hand.' *Meet the Beatles*, 1964."

"What's she saying?" asked Frank.

Henry put his ear close and struggled to make out the words.

"'Piano Man.' Album same name. Billy Joel, 1973."

"Sounds like song titles." Henry looked to the nurse for confirmation. She shrugged.

The station wagon lady continued. "'Respect.' Aretha Franklin. 'I Never Loved a Man the Way I Love You.' 1967. Written by Otis Redding, 1965."

The nurse leaned in and made a note on a tiny pad she produced from the pocket of her scrubs. Henry looked down to see the song titles written in tiny cursive.

"We'll leave her in your capable hands," said Henry, and he and Frank left the station wagon lady and headed back to the Escape.

It was nowhere in sight.

33

Monday: Frank Invites Henry to Breakfast at the Cabot Tower Diner

Bloodshot eyes stared back at Frank from the mirror. Bloody hell. He felt like he had been sucked into a vortex. It was past midnight by the time the cab dropped him and Henry home from the hospital last night. If only Henry's Escape hadn't been towed, they might have caught the end of the hockey game.

Frank pulled a pair of jeans off the shelf and attempted to force the button closed. It popped off and rolled under a dresser. Must have shrunk. He pulled them off and threw them down with the growing mound of laundry on the floor of the walk-in closet. In their place he picked up the blue stretch-top trousers he was wearing the day before and slid them on. He didn't understand why the workplace did not embrace comfortable clothing.

Staggering out of the bathroom, he made the voyage through his cavernous home, down the winding stairs and into the living room. He tried to avoid eye contact with the 11 x 14 wedding picture that taunted him from the landing, but it was impossible. Frank had threatened to do something about the picture and decided today was the day to take action. He removed the gilt frame. The photography sitting had cost a fortune. Frank began to undo the wire on one side of the frame. The sharp metal cut his finger, and he almost dropped it.

"Bollocks."

He balanced the frame on one thigh, pulled the loose wire across the front of the picture, and reattached it to the hook before re-hanging the image of marital bliss backwards on the wall. Frank descended the rest of the stairs, went to the shelves in the library, removed a utility knife from the reading desk drawer, and cut the cover off *Peter Pan*. He had always liked that book. Stopping by Patty's old office, he pulled some Cello off the roll and returned to the landing. Frank taped the *Peter Pan* cover to the back of the frame and then stood back to admire his redecorating efforts.

Straightening the frame, he noticed big red drops dripping onto the beige carpet. He shoved his finger in his mouth and sucked the metallic blood. He needed a plaster, but more urgently, he needed to feel tobacco in his lungs. However, he fought the urge. "The day I can't make it past breakfast without a fag is the day I go on the patch," he said as if addressing someone in the room. Frank had taken to talking to himself since Patty's departure.

When he reached the bottom step, he tried to steer himself into the kitchen for coffee, or the bathroom for a plaster if Patty hadn't taken them all, but his legs kept going until they went out the front door and halted at the mailbox. He did not want to look at the newspaper. But he couldn't help himself. An outside force was propelling his body.

RESIDENTIAL PERMITS DOUBLE, screamed the front page.

"Those bastards. I should've left the blasted newspaper in the blasted box." Frank began banging it against the rustic wooden post, making his finger bleed more. Dick's wife was just driving out of her garage, so Frank took his untreated anger into his own house.

Band-Aid in place, he sat at the kitchen table and pushed the toaster to one side. He didn't bother putting things away anymore. He spread the mutilated *Telegram* on the table and skimmed the paragraphs as he ate Honey Nut Oatie-Os right out of the box. Frank thought about brewing coffee, but it was too much work. He'd have to wait until he went out.

After Friday's stories on the meter thefts, he thought the hacks at the *Telegram* would leave him alone for a while, but no, now they were going to crucify him over changes to residential parking. Christ Almighty, didn't they know that the whole downtown core was built before cars were on the island, and people did not park their horses next to their homes? So, most houses downtown—3,600, to be exact—had no off-street parking, and their car-driving residents were forced to leave their vehicles on the street.

Frank flipped past pages two and three, which featured a retrospective piece about missing children, including famous international cases. On the bottom of page five, he found the second half of the parking permit story.

> The City collects $54,000 a year for parking permits. In order to recoup the $46,000 lost on the administration of the residential parking program, the City has decided to increase the cost of parking permits from $15 to $27.50 for those living downtown.

Frank let out an audible breath and read the words attributed to him by his communications staff.

> "Newfoundland has more registered vehicles than people," said Frank Parrell, Director of Transportation and Works. "Downtown residents will just have to pay the increased fees or give up their cars."

Frank choked. He looked at his hand, surprised to find it full of Oatie-Os on their way to his mouth. He grabbed his WORLD'S BEST DAD mug, but it contained only week-old coffee stains.

Oh my God. He was going to be lynched. Frank knew his staff were doing their best to shield him, but Lord Almighty, couldn't they come up with something better than that? Where were their communications skills? He would have to insist on signing off on quotes from now on. Bloody hell.

At least the writer had buried the hourly rate increase from twenty-five to seventy-five cents for meters in Churchill Square. Churchill Square was a nightmare for the City. What was supposed to be a noteworthy example of excellent urban planning went to hell in a handbasket once Ledwells pulled out of the square, leaving students and seniors with no supermarket. And then last year, the whole east side of the square flooded, shuttering businesses and forcing seniors out of the apartments they had waited years to obtain. Any increase in the price of parking might just make the Churchill Square residents revolt.

Frank tossed the paper in the bin, took a clean pair of socks from the breadbasket on the table, and bent down to pull them on. He kept the bread in the microwave. It wouldn't do to look as if he couldn't cope when Kaitlyn came by. He navigated his arms around his ever-expanding girth to pull the socks over his bunions. His back and legs protested every inch of the way.

There was no way he could face the office this morning. He must heed his doctor's warning. *Stress, Mr. Parrell, will send you to an early grave.* But Frank had to keep on top of things. If he wasn't careful, he was going to lose his job and, more importantly, his pension.

He called his secretary. "I've an off-site meeting. I'll see you after lunch."

Frank then poked at the BlackBerry to open Don't Tell Me the Score and brought it over to Henry's yard. He tapped on the shed window, through which he could see Henry gazing into space. Millie was at work. Dash was sequestered at school. What was Henry doing?

Frank moved sideways between the motorcycles. "You're looking a bit scruffy, Henry. You forget to shave again?"

"I've given up shaving. No need."

"Okay, Wolfman. Maybe I'll do the same when I retire. We can be like a pair of alley cats."

"Sounds good."

"Have you finished draining the oil?"

"Nope, I'll do it this afternoon."

"Excellent. Fancy a breakfast? My treat . . . to make amends for last night."

"Have you forgotten that my Escape has been impounded?"

"I'll call us a people mover."

Henry sighed. "Frank, you know that I still don't understand half of what you say. But I'm not one to turn down a second breakfast."

Frank pressed the cab company number into his phone and inwardly applauded his success at convincing Henry to come out. That was one of the best things about Henry. He was incapable of holding a grudge. Even that time last summer when Frank had trimmed his prized Japanese maple, Henry had forgiven him. Between that and the fact that he was able to eat in the face of extreme stress, he made a perfect best mate.

Ten minutes later they were sitting in a deep corner of the Cabot Tower Diner. Tucked away in a dark booth sheltered by plants, the smell of deep-fried everything permeating their pores, Frank stretched his legs and watched the steam spiral up from Henry's coffee.

Frank stoked up the game highlights on his phone, and they watched in reverence, all other sound in the restaurant fading away. Chara missed a puck, and it sailed right through Rask's legs.

"Bloody hell." Frank's voice caused other diners to turn their heads. He lifted his chin to them. "What? Get back to your eggs, you morons." He turned to Henry. "What's up with these people? Is a man not allowed to watch hockey highlights in a restaurant anymore?"

A lanky server came to deliver Henry's French toast and asked Frank to keep his voice down.

"Sorry, mate, couldn't help it. You'd be upset, too, if your team sucked."

"Man, how could Chara not have blocked that?" Henry sprinkled pepper over everything on his plate, including the whipped cream.

"I know. Looked like he was going to cry when he lined up for the handshake. I wonder where my food is?" Frank poked his head outside the booth and motioned to the waiter.

"Poor guy. I would have loved to have seen him win the cup this year." Henry tucked a piece of eggy bread in his mouth.

"Not in the cards. Happiness is not in my cards, either, I'm afraid."

"Frank, no offence, but you can't possibly be in more distress than me."

"I beg to differ. I'm buggered." Frank banged the heel of his hand down on the table. The cutlery jumped.

"Frank, you are talking to someone whose only child went up in flames in front of ten hyper-vigilant parents . . ."

"But . . ."

"Let me finish. I'm also facing kidnapping charges for a baby that magically appeared in my shopping cart."

"I know. Sorry, Henry. It's just the press is getting to me. Ever see *V for Vendetta*?"

"No, but the journalists have always attacked you. What's new about that?"

"What's new is I can't take it anymore. Friday they were on about the meter thefts, and today it's the increased parking fees." The waiter arrived with the Cabot Tower Special, and before his hands had left the table, Frank was spearing a pancake. "I can't bring myself to go in to work." He gestured wildly in the air with his fork, talking with his mouth full.

"Okay, give me a recap," said Henry.

Frank was relieved to hear those words. Henry was the only one who understood him. It was as if the sheer act of verbalizing his stresses to Henry made everything bearable.

"You know in the past three years thieves have damaged or destroyed more than one thousand meters."

"Yes, everyone in town knows."

"Okay, but did you know how much money they actually got out of those meters?"

"No, but I'm guessing not a lot."

"A measly twelve thousand dollars in coin, while I am left to replace them to the tune of one point four million."

"That's the latest estimate?"

Frank nodded.

Henry, stealing a fish cake off Frank's plate, lifted a hand, urging Frank to continue.

"I think the best thing to do is eliminate coins altogether."

"How will that work?"

"I've got an idea. You know how bad I am in live interviews. Why don't you pretend to be a reporter so I can practise?"

"I can't be a reporter."

"Sure you can. You just asked me how a coinless system will work."

"Okay."

"So, repeat the question."

Henry rolled his eyes and held a sausage up to Frank's face. "How will a coinless system work?"

Frank was pleased to see Henry playing along. "We will accept payments in three ways: credit cards, parking cards, or cellphone payments."

"And that will eliminate the parking meter vandalism?"

"Yes, this new system would eliminate the vandalism."

"I assume there will be a fair bit of opposition to this new system. What percentage of parking is now paid for with coins?"

"Seventy-two per cent of parking in this city is paid for with coins, so it would take some adjusting for the public."

"When do you expect to have the new system in place?"

"There is no timeline on when that project will start. But should Council accept the recommendations, then we test the cashless system in certain areas before bringing it in across the city." Frank rubbed a hand over his bald head. "How was that for a sound bite?"

"Too wordy." Henry tied his napkin in a sailor's knot. "Also, you should finish every quote on a positive for the City." He sat back and stroked his scruff.

"Okay, Mr. Media Training." Frank wasn't used to seeing Henry anything but clean-shaven. "Otherwise, what do you think of the plan?" Maple syrup pooled at the left corner of Frank's lips.

"Let it run through the proper channels at the bunker, and then roll it out. People will get used to it if you just introduce one area at a time."

Frank nodded, his mouth too full to speak.

"I think things are on the up and up, now that you have an eyewitness to the meter thefts."

"Yes, but she's in hospital with a head injury. It'll be just my luck that she forgets what she saw."

"Naw, she'll come around. Remember what the doc said last night? She just needs a few days' rest."

Frank felt calmer. He knew now was the time to do the neighbourly thing and ask Henry about his own problems. "What's the latest on the court case?"

"I have to appear before Judge Hiscock sometime next week."

"Is she the one who was reprimanded for wearing sandals to court on the weekend?"

"That's her."

"Is Millie going to represent you?"

"No, her co-worker, Gloria. I hope I can concentrate. Whenever I talk to her, I can't stop looking at her forehead. It doesn't move."

"Her forehead doesn't move?"

"Yeah, you know, most people's foreheads move a bit when they talk? Hers is like it's frozen. Come to think of it, her cheeks don't move, either."

"That's called Botox, Henry."

"Really? Anyway, she's coming over this afternoon so we can practise. She's hoping to dig up something on the mother. Make her out to be a bit of an unfit parent . . . like she had pot in her system or something."

Frank interrupted. "If Trudeau gets his way, that'll be legal soon."

"Yeah, Gloria says she can't ask for a blood test, anyway. I feel bad, but Millie says we have to do something or risk jail time."

"One good thing that might come out of it all is you might not be allowed to go back to Cub Camp." Frank laughed.

Henry pushed his plate away.

Frank stopped his fork in mid-air. "What's wrong? What did I say?"

"It was bad at the camp. All the other parents knew it was me that had taken the baby."

"How? They didn't use your name in the press."

"The head leader must have told them. Witch. How did you know, by the way?"

Frank swallowed. "Mad-Eye told me."

"Figures. He's always been out to get me."

"Why? I've never understood the animosity between you two."

"Long story. You heading down to the bunker?"

"Yes. You should drop in and have a gander at Wiener in his commissionaire getup."

"Saw him when I went in to get my record of employment." Henry removed bills from his wallet and slowly turned them so that they faced the same way. He then smoothed them out and arranged them back inside. He took some hand sanitizer from a dispenser and rubbed it over his palms.

"You saw his uniform? Man, that cracks me up every time I see him."

"Probably doesn't crack him up, losing his job like that with no notice."

"Ah, he'll be all right. No family to support. Hopefully he'll be able to get away for the Big Brothers, Big Sisters indoor golf tournament. A week from today, is it?" Frank pulled a toothpick from the faux crystal holder next to the cash. He peeled off the plastic and stuck it between his teeth, then handed the cashier his credit card.

"Yes," said Henry, "a week from today." He held the door open for Frank. A gust of wind lifted napkins off a nearby table despite the weight of the forks and knives folded inside.

"Finally." A man wearing a monocle stared as the pair headed out the door.

"Tosser," Frank called out over his shoulder. Even if his star witness was in hospital with a concussion, he had to admit things were looking up.

34

Henry's Practice Session with Gloria

"That was Gloria." Millie laid her sleek, pink-rimmed iPhone on the table in front of her plate. Sometimes Henry hated that phone. It was like an interloper with whom he had to compete. He hated the way the ring tone interrupted their lives with its steam train whistle bearing down on the kitchen. "She was worried they might charge you with child endangerment but says they're leaving it at kidnapping." Millie paused, taking a bite of her toast. Ever since Henry had met Millie back in university, she had always started her day with dry toast dunked in black tea.

"Good Lord." Henry stood up.

"I know it sounds bad, but you'll be all right. Gloria will make sure you're prepared for court."

"When is the hearing?"

"This coming Monday."

"That's not going to work. I'm going golfing with Frank on Monday," he said, leaning against the counter.

"I would advise finding a designate."

"But it's the Big Brothers indoor tournament." Henry thought of his old office buddies. At this moment they were down south, golfing in thirty-degree temperatures, their grown children independent and out of the picture. Henry was stuck in a place that had no spring, and his life had gone so far off the rails that he couldn't even manage to get away for one morning to play golf indoors.

"Go golfing if you like," said Millie, brushing crumbs off the table and onto her plate. "I'll arrange for a tour of the penitentiary after your game."

Henry loved his wife, but right now he wished she would disappear. She would normally be at work, but today she was going in late so she could be here to work on defence strategy with Gloria. Henry couldn't help but feel nostalgic about his years at the office, where all he had to worry about were lazy employees and marketing campaigns. He tried to look at the bright side. Answering questions for Gloria would be better than answering questions for Millie. Millie was one of the most intimidating people he had ever met. All the same, he wouldn't want to come up against either Millie or Gloria in court. Vultures were less menacing than those two.

Dash ran in and dumped his backpack in the porch. "Going out to play manhunt with Stella."

Henry hoped Dick hadn't mentioned anything to Stella about the supermarket incident. It was awkward enough when Akela had brought it up at Cub Camp.

Dash was gone less than a minute when Gloria arrived in a cloud of perfume. She came in the dining room and air-kissed Millie, then Henry.

"You smell like Frank when he's vaping."

"He smokes Giorgio Armani Acqua Di Gioia?"

"No, cotton candy."

"Love you, too, Henry."

Gloria was a Latino clone of Millie. With Honduran parents, she was a bit taller, curvier, and always wore outlandish glasses and austere jewellery, whereas Millie was more subtle, but for all intents and purposes, they were the same. He knew that people at the office called them Tweedle Smart and Tweedle Smarter. Today Gloria wore glasses with opaque white frames, lenses as large and round as coasters.

She pulled off her five-inch heels and threw them back toward the front door, where they bounced off the hardwood. "This will take some time, a few sessions at least, so let's get right to it. First, we'll outline what happened, and then I'll question you about the Dilaudid."

Gloria took a folder out of her leather laptop bag and flipped it open.

"Oh, one thing, Henry," said Millie. "I'm telling you this not as a lawyer, but as your wife. Try to avoid using the word 'baby.'" Millie did the air quote thing with her fingers.

"Do you want me to say 'child' instead?" Henry paced around the table. "No."

Henry jumped. "Geez Louise. Why not?"

"Sit down, and I'll explain," said Millie.

Henry sat down on the chair farthest from Gloria. Between her funky glasses and frozen forehead, Henry had a bit of trouble concentrating.

"I figure that you might arouse more sympathy if we avoid talking about the child," said Millie.

Henry raised his eyebrows.

"In the same way, if Gloria asks you if you recognize the young woman seated in the courtroom, she will probably not say 'the mother.'"

"Uh, okay."

"When you first saw the carrier, you didn't know there was a baby in there, did you?" Millie touched his shoulder.

"Not right away, but I peeked in and saw it." He could still see the little pink-clad human. When he gave her the pacifier, she looked like Maggie in *The Simpsons*.

"Where was this?" asked Gloria.

"At the cash." Henry tried to focus on anything but Gloria's forehead. "I plugged in the pacifier."

"Are you sure?" Gloria's eyes locked onto Henry's with an intense focus.

Henry gulped. "Yes, I'm sure. I may have taken medication, but I know what I saw."

"So, I won't ask you about looking inside the carrier. I will only ask you about the carrier itself." Gloria paused and pushed up the preposterous glasses.

Henry scrunched up his brow.

"Henry, listen to me. It's okay to leave out some details in court." Millie rubbed his back. "If it helps your case."

Henry blinked. "Won't I have to swear on a bible?" He thought of his mother, not in the ground pushing up pansies, but rather kneeling before the rail in the Basilica, her head bowed before Our Lady of Fatima, a plastic hat tied under her chin. Her Basilica bonnet, she called it, to keep her hair from getting mussed up in the wind. God, where did that memory come from?

"You don't have to use the Bible, no. Even if you did, just tell the truth and you'll be okay. Answer the question as simply as you can, but the important thing is: do NOT ramble on." Gloria smiled, showing two rows of polished teeth. She reminded Henry of Cruella de Vil. "Okay, let's pretend we're in court and I'm about to cross-examine you. I'm going to walk up to you in the docket . . ." Gloria got to her feet.

"What's the docket?"

Gloria looked at Millie. Henry knew Gloria thought he was on the spectrum. Millie had told him.

111

"That's the little booth you'll be sitting in."

"The penalty box?"

"Yes. Where the sheriff's officer will bring you. I'll walk up and say, 'Mr. Puddester, can you please tell the court what happened in the supermarket?'"

Henry blinked. A posse of kids ran by the window. Henry saw a tangle of Dash's hair whip by. Amazing how he and Millie ended up with a kid with blond curls.

"Go ahead, Henry. I'm not going to bite you. I'm the good guy, remember."

Heaven help me, thought Henry.

"What happened when you were at Sundries?"

"I, uh, I was just there minding my own business and had picked up a few things, and then I couldn't . . ." Henry thought of the frustration he felt down in the dairy section.

"You couldn't . . . ?"

"I couldn't find the goddamned eggs."

"Uh, Millie." Gloria glanced at Millie again.

"Let's not mention eggs, Henry." Millie touched his arm.

"But it's because of the eggs that I was there in the first place. If I hadn't had to buy eggs, I would've been down at Fogtown getting my sides trimmed, just like I do every Thursday morning." Henry's eyes widened. "Shoot, I forgot to call and explain why I didn't show up for my appointment."

"Forget that for now, honey," said Millie. "Let's just focus on your defence."

Gloria clapped her hands, and Henry jumped. "What you were looking for is irrelevant," she said. "Let's just say that you turned around and left your shopping cart to find something, and when you turned back, it was gone."

"Yes, that's right. My cart was gone, and someone had put another one in its place." Finally, someone was catching on.

"That's good." Gloria made a note on her legal pad. Henry took notes on a similar pad himself. "Okay, when did you realize it wasn't your cart?"

"When I got to the cash and saw the baby."

"Henry!" Gloria whisper-screamed.

Henry had no time to react, because at that moment, Stella Turner, all sinew, scentless sweat, and energy, teleported into the kitchen.

"Dash is hurt." She paused to draw breath. "He was skitching, and he fell."

"What? What? Where is he?" Millie was on her feet.

"He's on the path to the park. He hit his head. There's blood everywhere." Stella's face paled. She bit down on her lip.

"Jesus in the garden." Henry started running.

35

Henry Comforts Dash

Stella led Henry at a sprint to the patch of gravel near a big red maple at the park entrance. Dash was half kneeling on the ground, bent at the waist, leaves scattered around him like a Christmas tree skirt. It was impossible to tell where the blood originated. From Dash, of course, but from what upper body part was anyone's guess. Dash's platinum curls were matted with thick red. His favourite Fortnite T-shirt was equally drenched.

"Jesus Murphy." Henry knelt on the crushed stones next to his son. Dash's eyes were pinched shut. He was moaning and strangely crouched so that both feet, due to the slight decline, were competing for the same space. Several other children were gathered around, hands over mouths, whispering between themselves.

"Dash, where does it hurt?" Henry tried to move Dash's legs a little to relax him a bit, but it was like working with concrete. Instead, he tried positioning himself alongside to prop Dash up and reduce the effort needed to keep him in that awkward position. Whatever happened had hurt him bad.

Millie arrived. "Oh, God." She pulled out her phone.

"I already called an ambulance, Mrs. P." Stella took Millie's hand. "Before I came over."

An RNC officer on horseback happened by on his regular neighbourhood jaunt. He noticed the goings-on and galloped over, coming to a halt mere feet from where Dash crouched under the tree. Henry blinked twice to see if he was imagining things. Friggin' Dick Turner, all aftershave and horseshit, hopped off the horse.

"Stella, what happened?"

"Dash fell off the skateboard."

"Is he okay?" Dick passed the reins to Stella—she was as accustomed to the horses as her father was.

"Does he look okay to you?" Dick Turner was not a person Henry wanted to see right now. He hadn't seen him since the day of the supermarket incident, or SI, as Millie called it.

"Stella called an ambulance." Millie looked pale standing next to Stella. She let go of her hand.

Dick crouched down so close to Henry their knees touched and took Dash's hand, the one that was not clutching his shoulder. "Dash, if you can understand what I'm saying, squeeze my fingers." Dick closed his eyes, then looked up and nodded at Henry and Millie. "He's going to be okay."

Dick kept asking Dash questions until the paramedics arrived. The ambulance siren caused Dick's horse to thrash its head a bit but not bolt. Stella rubbed the animal's cheek until it calmed. The first paramedic cut off Dash's Fortnite shirt—right through what looked like a skeletal zombie with tusks—to "ascertain the source of the bleeding," he said. "It's here, behind the ear." The first paramedic reached out his hand, and the second gave him a pad of gauze. "We'll take it from here. Thanks for your help."

Like Dick, the first paramedic talked to Dash quietly in a low, manly voice to keep him calm. Dick moved to one side and took back the horse's reins. "You did good, Stella. Let me know how he is when you get home, Millie."

When the paramedics moved Dash from his crouching position to a stretcher, he inhaled deeply and cried out. Henry went to help him, but Millie pulled him back, clasping his elbow and whispering in his ear. The paramedics loaded Dash into the back of the ambulance like they were making a bread delivery. "You can follow us to the children's hospital."

Henry ran back to 10 Pine Place to get Millie's car. His was still at the impound lot.

36

Kaitlyn's Unexpected Nocturnal Visit

Someone was beating on Frank's front door. He swore and got out of bed, not bothering to put on pants or a shirt. If someone had the gall to wake him up at 11:00 p.m., by God, they would get to see him in his boxers.

He swung open the oak door. Kaitlyn shivered under the porch light. Huge teardrops hung on her lower lashes like melting icicles.

Frank's anger melted away. "Kaitlyn, what's wrong?" His daughter might sometimes be a little self-centred, but when she turned on the tears, she was Daddy's little girl again.

"Dad," she croaked.

"What is it?" He would kill the person who harmed his daughter. So help him, he would do time for murder rather than let someone hurt his baby. "What is it, my Kaity?" He pulled her inside and shut the door.

"I . . ." She sobbed a sob for the ages, her shoulders shaking violently.

"What happened?" Frank led her into the living room, sizing her up for torn clothes and signs of struggle.

"I . . ." she started again.

Outwardly, Frank was calm, waiting for his daughter to explain the atrocities committed against her, but inside he was preparing to do battle. "You can tell me."

She inhaled a shuddery breath. "I got a tattoo, and it doesn't say what I thought it did."

"What? Don't talk tosh." Frank took a step back, an arm's length away from his lunatic daughter, spawn of the devil.

"I wanted a tattoo in Japanese characters. The guy said he was half-Japanese. He looked Japanese." She started really crying, then. Big serious sobs. They made her nose ring pulsate. Frank was speechless.

"The one I chose was supposed to mean 'weed,' but I found out after I got it done that it means 'green vegetable.'" She sniffed and looked up at Frank.

"You want to be a doctor, and you're going to tattoo your body with a symbol for drugs?"

"Don't be so uptight, Dad. It'll be legal in the fall. I know I shouldn't have spent tuition money on a tattoo, but I really, really wanted one."

"Are you telling me you spent the money I gave you for med school on self-mutilation?" Saliva flew past Frank's lips as he spoke.

"It's body art, Dad."

"Pfff. It's not going to look much like art when you're seventy." He found a sweatshirt on the chesterfield and pulled it over his head. It said: PROUD PARENT OF A MEMORIAL UNIVERSITY GRAD.

"All the girls at the Martini Bar have them."

"I don't care if the girls at the Martini Bar have horns growing out of their heads. Have you told your mother?"

"No, you know Mom. She'd be upset with me."

Frank sucked the air in over his teeth. He slumped onto the chesterfield. "Where did you get it done?"

"Devil Inside Studio."

"Where is it?"

"The studio?"

"No, not the studio, you git. The tattoo."

"Here on my chest." She started to pull over the collar of her shirt to expose her formerly unblemished skin. Frank covered his eyes.

"Crikey, Kaitlyn. I don't want to see it. This is a real cock-up."

"I should've gone to Mom." Kaitlyn marched across the room.

"Don't throw a wobbly with me, missy. You're the one who screwed up. I'm going down there first thing tomorrow morning and demand they remove it."

Kaitlyn laughed a wry laugh. "Dad, they can't remove a tattoo. They'd have to do, like, a skin graft."

"But they can't tattoo a minor without a parent's permission, either. Did your mother sign for you?"

"I'm twenty, Dad."

Frank said nothing. Kaitlyn stared him down. She had stopped crying.

"Tell me you will not go down to Devil Inside."

Frank sighed. "I will not go down to Devil bloody Inside."

Kaitlyn went to the door, threw it open, and slammed it closed.

Frank stood up to protest, but it was too late. His only child was gone, the gulf between them wider than ever. He sank down to the floor in the entranceway, his back against the wall. The strength of the emotions exhausted him.

37

Henry and Millie Follow the Ambulance

Henry held tight to the armrest in the Mini while his wife followed the ambulance. Millie, who was a crazy driver at the best of times, careened around corners, all the while tapping her green polished thumbs on the screen of her little pink phone.

"Uh, Millie, you want me to drive?"

She gave him a look that told him to shut his trap. He decided to assess his situation.

His only child, who had caught himself on fire less than a week ago, was now being transported to emergency with blood flowing from his head after skitching—whatever that was. On a positive note, Dash's accident had cut short Henry's review of the baby case with Gloria. Henry didn't get the importance of going over what he was going to say before he saw the judge on Monday. If he told the truth, then surely the judge would see it was a simple misunderstanding. All Henry knew was that it had to get dealt with before May 24, when he was due to meet up with his Triumph in Montreal for the Spring Tune-Up Ride.

Henry tightened his seat belt and recited the prayer that his mother had made him say every night before bed when he was little. "God, grant me the serenity to accept the things I cannot change . . ."

"Henry, what are you saying?" Millie had her phone pressed to her chest while she drove with one hand, her eyes focused on Henry. She almost rear-ended the ambulance when it slowed to let an old woman cross the street.

"Jesus, Millie, watch the road."

"Henry, I'm perfectly capable of driving." She stopped inches from the ambulance bumper and put the phone back up to her ear.

Henry jolted, the seat belt arresting his forward motion. "At least put your four-ways on."

Millie, who was still no more than a foot from the back bumper of the ambulance, didn't answer her husband. Instead, she jabbered apologies to Gloria, who, unlike Henry, did not have her legs almost separated from her torso by a seat belt. Henry's blood pressure spiked as soon as they pulled off the parkway onto the road that led through the university campus to the Health Sciences. He could not believe he was headed back to emergency for the second time in forty-eight hours—albeit this time they would go to the children's wing, which was separated from the adult hospital by the cancer clinic, where he had brought his mother for her chemo treatments.

The attendants wasted no time unloading Dash. He wore an oxygen mask, and his eyes were closed. His blood had soaked the stretcher sheets. Millie pulled into a handicapped spot and jumped out of the car.

"Millie, you'll get towed."

She threw the keys on the ground near the Mini and ran to catch up with the stretcher.

Henry got out, retrieved the keys, and moved his wife's car to a secondary parking lot across the road. He ran back to the children's wing and made his way past Mickey Mouse and Pluto walls to the emergency reception. A nurse led him to a crisp blue-painted room that smelled of disinfectant. Dash lay in the bed, his upper body elevated, while a young female who looked too young to be an intern, let alone a full-fledged doctor, shaved off Dash's blond curls and proceeded to stitch behind his ear. She looked like the girls Henry went to high school with. Her tag read DR. PAYNE.

"Can that be her real name?" Henry whispered and sat next to Millie on a plastic orange chair.

She elbowed him. "Shhh. Henry, when the doctor tells us what's on the go, you have to pay attention, all right?"

"Of course. I always listen to doctors. Why are we whispering?"

"Dash is a lucky boy. He did quite a job on himself." The child doctor smiled warmly at Dash, showing two rows of polished teeth. "He only needed eight stitches. We've given him something for the pain, so he may be groggy for a while. We're just waiting to hear from the surgeon to see what he recommends for the broken collarbone."

"Broken collarbone?"

"Yes. He's lucky that's all he broke."

Dash turned his head to his father, exposing the stitches and shaved portion behind his ear. "My head feels like it's been attacked by a husk."

"What are you talking about?" Henry was genuinely puzzled.

"Fortnite," Millie whispered.

Henry leaned down and touched Dash's cheek. "You gave us a real scare, Dasher."

Dash smiled wearily. *He's like me*, Henry thought. But he wasn't, really. Dash had his mother's gung-ho spirit. He would drive cars with a lead foot. He would fight against injustice. When he entered a room, people would stop what they were doing. Dash was only like his father when he was out of steam. When he was curled under the covers, threadbare stuffed cat under one arm, waiting to hear the next chapter of *Harry Potter*.

Dr. Payne laid a hand on Henry's shoulder and catapulted him back to the present. Shoot, had he zoned out? Millie was kissing Dash's good cheek, saying she'd see him in a bit. What had Henry missed?

"Henry, did you hear the doctor? They want to observe Dash for a few hours to make sure he's not concussed. They told us to go on. Someone will be with him all the time. They'll wake him regularly to make sure he's okay."

Henry blinked. This room with its sanitizing smell masking icky odours, this hospital with its yellow brick road and elevators and incessant beeping sounds, and this child doctor who was now leaving the room. It reminded him of when his mother was sick.

"If you ever decide to wear a man bag, you'll have a lovely knob to hang it on." Dr. Payne waved at Dash and was gone.

Millie took Henry by the arm and led him out from behind the curtain. Henry glanced back at his son and gave him a weak smile.

"I'll be all right, Dad. The doctor says I can play Fork-Knife even if I get a sling."

Henry's eyes were moist.

Millie dragged her husband through the double doors and back into the emergency waiting room. "I know what we can do while he rests." She seemed surprisingly upbeat for the mother of a boy who had just been bleeding profusely from the head. "We can grab a bite in the cafeteria and then find Delores," she said. "She's at this hospital, isn't she?"

"You mean the station wagon woman?" Henry looked at his wife as if she had sprouted a second nose. "I'd rather go out to eat," he said, objecting to Millie's suggestion on two fronts. 1) Eating in hospitals gave him the heebie-jeebies, and 2) He absolutely did not want to visit the blue-haired station wagon woman with her purple purse.

"Come on, Henry. I want to meet Delores."

"How can you think about visiting some woman you don't even know when your son is lying in bed being poked and prodded by a doctor who looks like she's sixteen?"

"After we saw her and Daisy on the news, I did a Google search. Guess how many newspaper articles popped up?"

Henry shrugged.

"A hundred and twenty-three. As well as three magazine features and thirty-seven TV news stories. I haven't had a chance to watch them all." Millie started down the corridor past two surgeons gowned up with masks and gloves.

Henry quivered. He was fed up with this day. He was fed up with this week. In fact, he was fed up with his life. This was not the way it was supposed to be. He was stuck in a bad-luck vortex, and it was too strong for him to fight his way out. He hated hospitals. He hated injuries. He hated misunderstandings. He hated the thought of going to court.

But as usual, he followed behind his wife without saying another word.

38

Henry gets Hospital Indigestion

"You're not eating much." Millie thrust a hand holding a toasted bagel sandwich toward Henry's plate.

"You know I'll have gastrointestinal troubles trying to digest in this atmosphere." Henry rubbed his hand sanitizer into the front and back of his hands.

"What atmosphere?"

Henry's eyes darted around to the wheelchairs, bandages, crutches, and head scarves. "Millie, everything smells like pee."

"Get over yourself, Henry. It does not smell like urine." A man with dreadlocks and a catheter bag glared.

Morsels of half-chewed bagel caught in Henry's throat every time he tried to swallow. He kept thinking of his own mother and the cancer that ate away at her, slowly but surely working its way through her system, creeping along one tiny step at a time toward the horrid end. When Millie said it was time to go find Delores, Henry hopped up and threw away the remains of his lunch. He popped in a piece of gum to cleanse his palate. The elevator bell dinged, and he followed Millie inside.

"Henry, we're going to the fourth floor. I asked, and Delores is up on Four South."

"I don't want to touch anything in here."

"Henry."

He pushed 4 and immediately reapplied his hand sanitizer. When the doors opened, he followed Millie through the maze of pastel-coloured corridors into a spacious four-person room with a south-facing window and fresh yellow paint. The room did not smell of fresh paint, however. It smelled like an outhouse.

Delores looked like the Queen Mother, propped up in bed with a lunch tray rolled in front of her, her blue hair fluffed. She was shovelling in spoonfuls of coagulated gravy and mushy peas. She let out a watery belch.

"You must be Delores. You look just like on TV." Millie took Delores's hand and continued to gush star-struck pleasantries as Henry stared down at the patient's bruised cheek and scabbed nose. The station wagon woman's chin was black and blue like she had been hit with a left hook.

"This is my husband, Henry. He's the one who brought you to the hospital with our neighbour, Frank."

"Ah, my knight in shining armour." Delores stopped inhaling her food for a second and offered her hand. "I wondered when you'd show up." Her gaze penetrated Henry.

Henry nodded but kept his hand in his pockets. Millie nudged him in the ribs.

"Sorry, don't want to touch you. I have a cold." Henry coughed.

"Don't mind him, Delores. I didn't know he was a germaphobe when I married him."

"No worries."

"So, I understand you had a rough welcome to St. John's."

"Yes, ma'am. Daisy's roof got really banged up."

"I heard. What year is she again?"

"She's a 1983 Ford LTD Country Squire. I have her up at the Walmart. She's covered so the rain won't come in, but I'll have to get her fixed soon. The moose peeled it back like a sardine tin."

"Oh, no. Do you have anyone belonging to you here in the city?" Millie was doing something funny with her eyelashes. Semaphore, maybe?

"No, ma'am."

"What about back in BC?"

"No, ma'am. My mama passed."

"Partner? Children?" Geez Louise, Millie was giving the poor woman the third degree.

"No, ma'am. Just me and Daisy." Delores gave Millie a smile that showed the absence of half a tooth on the upper left palate. She winced as though the smile caused her pain.

An older female doctor came in then and smiled broadly at Millie and Henry. Her teeth were whole.

"Nice to see you have visitors, Miss Cowburn." She turned to face Henry and Millie. "I was just explaining that Miss Cowburn is concussed and needs rest and proper care for at least another week. Then we'll reassess. She can under no circumstances continue living in her car."

"Once she's discharged, she can come stay with us." Millie smiled at Delores.

Henry coughed. "Um, excuse me, could you excuse us for a minute?" He took Millie by the elbow and pulled her out into the hall, where the drone of the air conditioning system would cover their words. A hospital worker in baby blue scrubs pushed a squeaking trolley. Henry closed the door, separating them from the fruitcake in the bed.

"Millie, what are you thinking?"

"I'm thinking that that poor woman needs a place to stay till she gets back on her feet."

"There are things called hotels."

"Henry, there's no need for her to waste money on a hotel. She can stay with us."

"Nuh uh." Henry rasped out the syllables as quietly as he could because he knew all ears on the other side of the door were listening.

"Why not?" Millie looked genuinely puzzled.

How could his wife be such a pit bull in normal life, but whenever she met someone downtrodden, she turned into a puppy dog?

"She could bring unknown diseases into the house." A cleaning lady passed by pushing a bucket with a mop handle protruding. What was the politically correct term these days? Support staff, that was it.

"Don't be silly, Henry. You heard the doctor. She can't live in her car with a concussion."

"Then let Frank take her in. He's the one who met her first."

"You know he can't host her. He's off at work all day. She can't be left alone. She might burn the house down."

"If she's at risk to burn down Frank's house, what about ours?"

"No worries, you'll be with her."

"Millie, that lady cannot stay with us."

"Why not? We have tons of living space, not to mention a beautifully decorated vacant mother-in-law suite."

"That suite was built for my mother."

"Henry, your mother is dead."

With this, Henry was silent. It was true, his mother was dead. She had died shortly after New Year's. She had died too soon, and Henry had not had a chance to grant her dying wish—to accompany her on her Ducati on the Spring Tune-Up Ride from Montreal to St. John's. She was born in Montreal and wanted to see the Cross on the mountain one last time. She had her own bike, a tiny black and chrome Ducati Monster. She bought it when she turned sixty. "You gotta live," she'd told Henry.

Henry should get Dash a dirt bike for his birthday. Prepare him for his Ducati inheritance.

"Henry." Millie's face was two inches from his own. He could feel her breath. She smelled like coffee. "It's the right thing to do."

Henry tried his best to look emotionless, but he really felt like he had just been kicked in the guts. It was as if he had just now learned of his mother's passing. There was too much going on between the court case and Dash getting hurt and now this. He wanted to slide his back down the wall that was propping him up, sit down on the corridor floor, and cry despite the swarms of germs. "The right thing to do?"

"Yes, inviting Miss Delores to stay with us is the right thing to do."

"Miss Delores . . ." He said this with a quiver of his whole torso. But by golly, if Millie was serious, Henry was going to use this to his advantage. The wheels in his mind churned forward, coming up with a plan. "Miss Delores can live in the mother-in-law suite if you charge her rent, which I can then use to go on the May 24 Spring Tune-Up Ride." Henry watched his wife's expression change as she weighed the implications of this proposal.

He had no more interest in this woman staying under their roof than he had of getting his toenails pulled out one by one with pliers.

"Fine, I'll charge her rent." She paused. "A hundred dollars a month."

"A hundred dollars a month? The going rate is at least four."

"Henry, there's no rent money coming in now, and we had not planned to rent it."

"But . . ."

"And I'll take care of Dash while you go on your trip."

Whoa, what was that? Henry blinked to see if he was dreaming. But Millie was still standing in front of him in the hospital corridor with its beeping machines and horrid smells. He knew he should be digging in tooth and nail to prevent a stranger from moving into his mother's flat, but this was the golden ticket. Millie had offered what he had been negotiating for months. So, instead of arguing, he followed his wife back into the room and stood by while she explained the rent situation to Delores and reiterated to the doctor that once Delores was released, she would be coming home with them. Henry sidestepped toward the door.

"Is there anything you need while you're here?" Millie asked, her save-the-world gene in full swing.

"Yes, I'd be mighty happy if you'd bring me a little transistor radio. I miss listening to my songs."

"I will if I can find one. Everyone carries their music on their phone these days. I'm not sure you can still buy them."

"Yes, ma'am. Walmart carries little pink ones next to the front cash."

"I'll get right on it," said Millie.

Henry shook his head. "I'm going to check on Dash."

39

Henry, Monday Afternoon in the Shed

By the time they got back to his room, the doctor was ready to release their stitched, drugged, and slinged son into the hands of the unusually quiet parents. They arrived home under a moody sky, and Henry carried Dash to the couch, where he lay unmoving, eyes closed.

"Jesus, Mary, and Joseph. Seeing him all banged up has got me freaked out."

"Ah, he'll be better before he's married."

"Is that supposed to comfort me?" Dash's shorn and sutured head seemed tender and exposed. Henry wanted to cover it up.

"Why don't you go out to the shed? I'll work from home. I'll keep an eye on him while he sleeps off the painkillers."

That was fine by Henry. If he didn't look at Dash, he could pretend nothing had happened. He went out in the yard. The grass soaked his shoes. Somewhere on the cul-de-sac, a lady called for her cat.

Shining the bike took his mind off his beat-up son. The Triumph Bonneville was a 1970, factory new. Henry had bought it off a collector. The burgundy paint was pristine. The only thing he would like to replace were the forks. But they could wait. For an almost-fifty-year-old machine, she ran smoothly and purred like a kitten. Millie begged to differ, but what did she know about antique bikes? A Triumph was supposed to announce its arrival. Henry promised his mother on her deathbed that he would do the Spring Tune-Up Ride even if she couldn't do it with him. It was set for May 24 weekend. He cleaned the carburetor and spark plugs for the third time. All he had to do now was get the bike shipped and book a plane ticket. His was going to be the nicest bike on the run. He owed it to his mother.

Henry hoped the weather was better in the rest of Atlantic Canada. He couldn't imagine doing a bike trip across the Rock any time soon. His mind drifted, as it always did when he was alone in his shed: memories of taking his mother for fish and chips, of golfing with the boys at work, of riding down to South Dakota for the Sturgis Bike Rally.

"Henry." Millie's voice came from the kitchen, wrenching Henry's thoughts back from their happy place. "Come here."

Henry tossed the rag. He was back to real life, where children got hurt, mothers died, and babies appeared in shopping carts. He crossed the yard in ten strides and shot up the steps and into the kitchen. "Is Dash okay?"

Millie had the phone to her ear and held up a finger to shush him. After a few grunts, she dropped the beige receiver into its matching cradle. Why they still had a land line, Henry did not know. He had threatened to get rid of it, but those crooks at the telecom company said he'd have to pay more for Internet and cable without the land line than for all three combined.

"Yes, he's still sleeping. I called you in because of the phone call."

"Who was it?" he asked.

"It"—she emphasized the *it*—"was the impound yard. They said you can pick up the Escape as soon as you pay ninety dollars." Millie began patting her famous dry rub on a small roast.

"I already paid a two-hundred-and-fifty-dollar impound fee."

"The ninety dollars is for a speeding ticket."

"I didn't get a speeding ticket. I never speed." He raised his eyebrows to show his incredulousness. Everyone knew Henry never went more than five kilometres over the limit. Ever.

"They say you got it on the Outer Ring Road. What were you doing up there? I thought you hated the Outer Ring."

Henry rubbed his thumb knuckles into his temples. He had hoped the whole Escape problem would just go away.

"I wasn't up there, but I bet the Escape was."

"Henry, you're not talking sense."

"Remember when we brought that nutbar to the hospital? I parked in front of emergency to get her in. They towed the Escape to the impound yard up on Major's Path." He sighed. "I bet that new speed trap camera snapped a pic of my licence plate going by on the back of a tow truck."

"That's ludicrous. We'll fight it."

Henry nodded. What else could he do? He married a fighter. Henry was tired of fighting. Tired of misunderstandings. Henry was just plain tired.

He went and sat in his plaid La-Z-Boy chair next to where Dash was lying on the couch. Dash was awake now, hands attached to a lime green electronic gadget that emitted beeps and other factory-made noises. He seemed to be making a swift recovery. Or maybe it was just the drugs.

"How're you doing, Dasher?"

"Still feels like I've been attacked by a Gold Star."

"A Gold Star is a bad thing, I take it?"

"Yep." Dash did not take his eyes off the screen. The sling provided no hindrance to his video game addiction.

Henry would never understand these stupid video games. Why would a person need to try to survive for two weeks in a virtual world? Henry was struggling to do it for real.

Millie washed the spices off her hands and dried them on an apron. "Dash, honey, turn that thing off." She was using what Henry called her good news voice.

"Aww, Mom."

"Now." Millie's tone strayed over to her courtroom voice. Dash worked a hundred commands with his thumbs, set the Nintendo DS on the coffee table, and lay back on the satin throw pillows.

"Why don't you watch one of your *Veggie Tale* videos?"

"I'm too old for *Veggie Tales*."

Millie shrugged. "Go read a book, then."

"Can't I just do nothing?"

"Actually, that's a good idea. I wanted to tell you something . . ."

Dash had his head laid back on the pillow, eyes closed.

"Dash . . . Dash, look at me. We are going to have a house guest." Millie sat down in the rocking chair at the other end of the couch.

Dash opened his eyes. "Is it Auntie Mary? I like that song she sings . . . about the canary in her underwear . . ."

"No, love, it's not Auntie Mary. She's in Florida until the end of the month. This lady's name is Delores, and she's from British Columbia, but she plans to live in Newfoundland."

Henry put his hands over his eyes and slowly shook his head.

"Why's she coming to live with us?"

"Because she just had an accident, and we want to help her get back on her feet."

"Can't she go stay with her own family?"

"That's the trouble. Miss Delores doesn't have any family here."

"Where's she gonna sleep?"

"In the apartment."

"But that's Grandma's apartment."

One point for Camp Henry, thought Henry.

"Well, Dash, since Grandma is gone to heaven, someone else can live in the apartment."

"Is she old like Grandma?"

"No, she's younger than Daddy and me."

"Why doesn't she go home?"

"It's complicated. Don't worry. You'll like her."

"Does she like playing Fortnite?"

"You'll have to ask her. But Dash, you know how I feel about you spending too much time on the computer. You should be playing with your friends."

"I am playing with my friends. They're on Fortnite, too. Daddy just got me headphones with a built-in microphone so we can all hear each other better now. It's just like we're in the same room."

Stella's black braids swung into the room.

"Dash, how come you're not on?"

"Mom made me get off." Two ten-year-old heads turned to look at Millie. Then Stella's head swung back toward Dash.

"Cool sling." She had a bag in her hand. It said IT STORE on the side.

"Thanks. Mom said I can tie-dye it. What's in the bag?"

"I got you a new Ragnarok shirt, the blue one with the pickaxe." She passed the bag to Dash and sat on the arm of the couch.

"I love that one." Dash whipped the shirt out of the bag. "Sweet. I'll have to wait until I get rid of the sling to wear it. I can only do these dorky button-up thingies till then." He looked down at the red and blue checked shirt and frowned.

"You look like it's picture day. Do you get to stay home from school?"

"Do I, Dad?"

"Do you what?" Henry looked up from the newspaper.

"Get to miss school?"

"No, why would you miss school?"

"Broken collarbone."

"Maybe we can let him stay home one day." Millie peered out from the kitchen.

"That's nonsense." Henry shook his head. "If he's well enough to play on that stupid machine, he's well enough to go to school."

Dash shrugged and groaned in pain.

"Let's see how he is in the morning." Millie came out and put the back of her hand to Dash's forehead.

Stella stood to leave. "Gotta go. Dad says I'm not supposed to be over here. He'll kill me if he finds out. Let me know when you're allowed back on." Stella tapped Dash on the forehead right where Millie had just felt for fever, swished her arms back and forth in front of her waist a dozen times, and flew out.

"What did she mean she's not allowed over here?" asked Henry.

"Mr. Turner said Stella is not allowed to play with me anymore."

"Why?"

"Dunno. But don't worry, Dad. She's not going to listen to him."

40

Tuesday: Henry Sends Dash to School

"Henry, be a doll and drop Dash at school, will you?"

Dash was typing a message on his iPad, one finger at a time yet lightning fast.

"What do you mean, drop Dash at school? Why can't he walk?"

"We can't have him walking to school wearing a sling!"

"Why the hell not?"

"It's cold. He can't even zip up his jacket."

"He can wear mine. It'll cover the sling no problem."

"Henry."

"Millie, we've had this discussion. Any child of mine walks to school. Plus, I don't even have a car."

"I'll drop you to the impound yard on my way to work. Dash, Daddy and I are going to leave you for half an hour while Daddy picks up his car—Henry, go online and pay that stupid speeding ticket now, and make sure you print the receipt."

Dash smiled. "Dad got a speeding ticket? Sick."

"I wasn't speeding. Millie, why can't you drop him to school?"

Millie was applying cortisone to Dash's stitches. "You have to get your car anyway."

Dash tried to dodge her. "Mom, that stuff is disgusting."

"Sit still." Millie's voice was stern.

Henry grumbled his way to the computer, logged on, and ten minutes later figured out how to pay the fine. He then muttered his way into his coat. Walking to school was among Henry's top ten rules for raising a child. Dash would walk to school come hell or broken collarbone.

"See you in half an hour, Dasher Dude."

"Bye, love. Take care of that shoulder." Millie kissed Dash on top of his head.

Once Henry was safely buckled into Millie's car, she pushed a piece of paper at him. She had printed proof of payment for the fine.

"Make sure you take this in with you. And Henry, will you freshen up the mother-in-law suite after you bring Dash to school?" This was not a question. "Put some fresh flowers in the little kitchenette."

"You didn't ask me to cut flowers when my mother was supposed to move in."

"It was the dead of winter."

"That makes no sense."

"Just pick up some dahlias and arrange them in the vase on the table." Millie pronounced "vase" with an *ah* instead of an *eh*. It was one of Henry's pet peeves. That and when she didn't enunciate her "t's." Innernet. Dennist. Winner instead of Winter. These quirks only got on his nerves when there was some other underlying conflict. Which, ever since the day at the super-market, seemed like every minute of every day.

Millie dropped Henry at the impound yard, which had no fewer than eighty cars waiting to be claimed. A hairy man, more fridge-shaped than human-shaped, looked down at Henry.

"Licence and receipt."

Henry dug in his pocket for his wallet and pulled out his licence. He had far less grey hair in the picture. A massive grease-stained hand took the piece of plastic. Did his knuckles really say "L-O-V-E" and "H-A-T-E"? Henry thought that choice of tattoo lacked originality.

"Receipt."

"What receipt?"

"The receipt showing that you paid the fine."

Ah, yes, the receipt that Millie had printed and reminded him not to forget. He had left it on the dash. "Can't you just look me up in the system?" Henry flashed his best toothy smile.

"Sorry, buddy. That's the policy. No receipt, no car." He pointed his H-A-T-E fingers at the poster behind his head without turning around.

"I'm gonna need a cab."

The L-O-V-E hand passed him a phone.

Back at home, Henry helped Dash tuck his sling under his lined MEC jacket, Velcroed a Gore-Tex hat under his chin, and pushed him out the door.

"I thought Mom said I was getting a ride."

"A brisk walk in the elements builds character, Dash. I walked to school every day and walked home for lunch, too."

By the time Dash disappeared down the path to the park, the sky was a slate grey that announced upcoming snow. All Henry wanted to do was head to the shed to bond with the bike and get it ready to be crated. What he had to do instead was freshen up the mother-in-law suite. Freshening up translated as changing the bedsheets, sweeping and mopping the floor, and making sure the bathroom was the cleanest in the land, freshly stocked with soap, shampoo, rolls of the softest toilet paper, and a small wicker basket overflowing with toothbrushes, toothpaste, Q-Tips, and sanitary napkins. These Henry picked up like they were hydrogen bombs.

He was nothing more than Millie's manservant—a glorified maid in his own home. It could take hours to catalogue his woes. Henry eyeballed the small bedroom. He didn't understand why he had to change sheets that had never been slept in. His mother deteriorated so rapidly that she never had a chance to move in. Everything they had bought for her was sitting there eyeing him like it was he who had murdered her rather than the nasty, overblown cells that just kept on multiplying until no chemo or radiation had a chance to curb their production.

Henry had to put his grief somewhere, compartmentalize it.

He picked up the vase and noticed a piece of orange paper stuck inside. He plucked it out and put it in his pocket to investigate later.

Henry would leave the sheets. Millie would never know. He had no flowers, either. And he sure as hell wasn't getting any delivered. He had a better idea.

41

Henry Heaves in Delores for the Second Time

Millie drove Henry back to the impound lot, accompanied him into the office, and passed Mr. L-O-V-E H-A-T-E the receipt herself. Millie had made it known that she was unimpressed that Henry had left the receipt on the dash after she expressly reminded him not to forget it.

Mr. L-O-V-E H-A-T-E gave Henry a look that said *I know who wears the pants in your house.*

"Now, follow me downtown, and we'll drive to the hospital together."

"Why can't we drive separately to the hospital?" Henry was of the opinion that Millie always unnecessarily complicated things.

"Because this way one of us can stay with the car so it doesn't get towed." Millie practically foamed at the mouth as she ran from the sanctuary of the impound office to her car.

Henry ran toward his own vehicle. Arrowheads of sleet battered his shoulders and back as he dug in his pockets for the keys. They showed up in the last pocket he checked. He raced after Millie and followed the Mini downtown through the wind tunnel otherwise known as Duckworth Street. He pulled up in front of McLoughlan, McLoughlan and Mercer and waited for her to park. Cabot Tower looked down menacingly from Signal Hill. He opened the passenger door and held on tight to make sure it didn't blow off its hinges. Millie brushed the snow off the seat and dived into the Escape.

"I hope this weather clears off soon." Henry turned the wipers on a higher speed so he could see through the wet snow on the windshield. "I can't remember a spring this bad. I feel like I'm being punished by the weather gods."

"Don't be so dramatic, Henry. It's always freezing until the twenty-fourth of May. Your memory is just short." Millie cranked the fan and turned on the heated seat.

"Seriously, maybe I'm being punished for all my fatherly and husbandly transgressions."

"You're the perfect father and husband, Henry." Millie jammed her gloved hands underneath her thighs.

"Are you being sarcastic?"

"Of course not."

"What about that time I dropped Dash at Cubs and I got the night wrong, and he had to walk home alone in the dark?"

"There was that." She pretended to be solemn.

"Or when I locked my only key in the car when he was a baby, and we had to pay fifty dollars for Babb's Lock 'n Safe to come with a slim jim."

"I remember that. I thought you were going to cry. Dash was strapped in his little baby carrier—" Millie abruptly stopped.

Henry cringed at the words "baby carrier." No matter how hard he prayed to make the whole supermarket incident go away, it didn't work. How stupid was he to get himself into this predicament?

Millie brought the subject back to safe territory. "Look, even the dogs are dressed for a January storm." She pointed at a Great Dane wearing a yellow rain slicker.

By the time they reached the Health Sciences, the snow had shrouded the hill that rose up behind the hospital. Mount Scio looked like an iced cinnamon bun. Three men of varying ages and stages of health shielded cigarettes with their hands and inhaled as if their lives depended on it. Speakers barked out the same old recording: "Smoking is prohibited outside the hospital doors." As soon as Henry shoehorned the Escape between an ambulance and a Mercedes, a security guard made a beeline for him, leaning into the wind like a cartoon character. *Oh, no,* he thought, *here we go again.*

"Sir, you cannot park there . . ."

Henry had forgotten Millie was with him. That poor fresh-faced numbskull had no idea what he was dealing with.

"Sir," said Millie. Henry knew what her eyes looked like, even though he did not have a view of them. They said: *Back off or I'll cut out your spleen and have it for dinner.* "Unless you'd like to assist us in getting our friend here into the vehicle, I would advise you to quietly turn around and go back to your post."

Henry stayed with the Ford while Millie went to collect the wing nut. The security guard was giving Henry the hairy eyeball, but he was too afraid of Millie to bother him again.

Ten minutes passed. The spring snow was full assault at the main entrance, and frozen tufts were attaching themselves to the SUV doors like stalactites. Henry wiped down the dash and console to busy himself. Finally, Millie appeared, pushing Delores in a wheelchair.

Henry came around to open the passenger door. The right side of Delores's face was still swollen and puffy as if she had been dragged behind a Mack Truck, but the swelling in her lip had gone down, and her purple hand was now a dark shade of blue. Her right cheek was also purple, with a shocking black circle on her chin. The cuts on her nose had scabbed over.

"The doctors ran all kind of tests and said she's good to go." Millie put the brakes on the wheelchair.

"If the doctors say she's fine . . ." Henry came around and whispered this in Millie's ear.

"Not to be living in a car, she's not," Millie hissed, causing Henry to acknowledge that he had absolutely no chance of convincing his wife that inviting a scrubby into their house was not a good thing.

So now, here he was, faced with a blue-haired lady wearing a floral dress from the '60s and a pair of men's slippers. She had nothing on her legs. Where did she think she was? The Florida Keys? Although she was a decade younger than Henry, she seemed a decade older. Henry forced himself to think of the Spring Tune-Up. He gulped, wondering if the trade-off was actually worth it.

Millie swung the purple bag over her shoulder. She then prodded Henry to pick up the three plastic grocery bags behind the wheelchair. Henry felt in his pocket for his hand sanitizer. He didn't want to touch those bags. Of course, they were Sundries. Henry would never set foot in Sundries again after the baby fiasco. *Please don't let me run into anyone I know*, he thought as he avoided looking at Delores's germ-ridden possessions.

"Put Delores in the front seat, Henry. I'll ride in back." Millie's eyes resembled little tornadoes. Henry guessed she didn't appreciate his suggestion that Delores could care for herself, far away from Henry's family. He tried to ignore the sleety water dribbling up his sleeves as he took off the brake and manoeuvred the wheelchair a bit closer to the passenger door, as close as he could without damaging the paint. He then pulled Delores out and shoved her in the passenger seat. She helped a little, making it somewhat easier than when she was unconscious at the Walmart. He could see the security guard watching the procedure, cowering in his uniform over by the main entrance, where he had blown in among the smokers.

Henry wiped the condensation on the inside of the windshield with a rag and felt inside his coat for his keys. His fingers glanced upon the pocket of his plaid jacket, and it crunched a little, like a candy wrapper at the opera. It was the orange paper he had pulled from the vase yesterday.

He still hadn't opened it. Life was moving too quickly to even see what it was. He withdrew the keys and glanced around to make sure everyone was buckled up.

"Henry, you do not have to do a seat belt check." Millie was blowing on her hands in the back seat.

"Remember that time Dash told me he was buckled, and next thing he came catapulting into the front seat?"

"We are all adults here, Henry."

Henry waited until he heard the telltale click of Delores's belt and the dinging terminated before he began navigating the slushy streets.

They weren't out of the parking lot when Delores piped up, "Excuse me, Mr. Puddester, uh, Henry, sir. There's something wrong with my seat."

"The seats are heated, Delores. You just have to turn this here." Millie leaned forward and twisted the knob. "You can turn the heat down or all the way off."

"That's a relief. I thought I had wet my pants."

Jesus in the garden. What had Henry got himself into?

The wind had picked up something fierce, and at the intersection of Elizabeth and Long Pond Road, a traffic light blew off its metal strap and plunged to the road below, landing three feet from the Escape. Henry swerved just in time.

"I thought it was just the Walmart lot that was windy like this." Delores's hands were both clamped to the door handle. "I hope Daisy is okay."

"I'm sure she's doing just fine." Millie was using her voice reserved for the owners of flattened cats and refugees. "Henry will go get her once things calm down."

Henry rolled his eyes and turned on the radio. "The RCMP are advising motorists to stay home and not venture out unless absolutely necessary," said the female voice. God, was that that scroungy Gillian Gee? Henry flipped the channel to VOCM.

"I can tell you that storm chips are flying off the shelves. I swear we're selling more than in January." Henry groaned and turned off the radio.

As he pulled onto Pine Place, tree branches danced maniacally all around the cul-de-sac. Henry got them home just in time to see Carter, their recycling man, pull his shopping cart up the driveway ahead of them. Bits of ice were lodged in his beard.

"I'll move my Harley out of your way," Carter called, dragging the cart backwards over the ice. As Henry extricated himself from the car, Carter pulled his shopping cart farther underneath the overhang.

"Carter, what are you doing out in this weather?"

"I can't take a day off, Henry. You don't think the Good Lord is going to send me down a case of beer, now, do ya?"

"I guess not." Henry struggled against the wind to get around to open the door for Delores.

"Who ya got aboard?" asked Carter, his azure eyes peering through the tinted glass.

"This is Delores," said Henry as he opened the door. "She's going to be staying with us for a week or so."

"Perhaps longer," said Millie, closing the back with a slam. "Carter, Delores drove her station wagon all the way across the country, and she was living in it until Henry and Frank rescued her when she got a nasty hit on the head."

"Frank?"

"Yes, you know Mr. Parrell next door?"

"You mean the guy who keeps getting bigger?" Carter was looking from Millie to Henry to Delores still in the front seat and running his fingers through his frosted beard. "Hi, Delores," he said. "Whoa, you're pretty banged up."

"I know, but I'm in good hands."

"Yes, Henry and his missus are best kind. They lets me leave my Harley here when the weather's too bad to push 'er home. Like today."

Henry started to say something. Millie elbowed him in the ribs—hard. Choice words had been exchanged between the couple about Carter's "Harley" getting too comfortable on their property. Since Henry had retired, he often saw more of Carter than anyone else. It was not how he imagined his retirement.

"Nice to meet you, Carter," said Delores. "I had a Harley once—1985, black, with monkey bars. What year is yours?"

Carter laughed and gave his shopping cart a loving tap like Henry's mother used to in order to coax their old Dodge up a hill. "This here's my Harley. Some calls it their Cadillac, and I knows a girl in Mount Pearl who calls it her Hummer."

"Make sure you bring it inside the gate and 'round back," said Millie. Henry knew she hated having a shopping cart parked in front of their house as much as he did, but she was too much of a softie to tell Carter he couldn't leave it there.

"See you 'round, Delores. You landed with the right people."

"I know, I've been rescued by angels," said Delores as Millie pulled her out of the front seat.

Henry ran around to make sure Millie didn't collapse under her girth, but Millie just waved him away. The wind picked up Delores's dress, exposing purple ruffed underpants. Then Millie, looking directly at Henry, added the kicker. "I have a feeling this is going to work out really well for us all."

42

Dash Meets Delores

Dash blew in the door from school, yammering on about tree limbs flying off maples in the park, when he spied Delores settled into Henry's La-Z-Boy.

"Who are you and what are you doing sitting in my dad's chair? No one ever sits there except him."

"You can call me Miss Delores."

"I've never met a Delores before." Dash, sling mud-caked around the edges, skirted the La-Z-Boy, taking in the humanity of his new house guest.

"And I've never met a Dash."

"Your hair is pretty sick."

"I take that as a compliment." Delores tentatively picked up a toothpick, skewering a cube of bologna, a cube of cheese, and a pickled onion that Millie had just delivered to the side table. She popped one and then another into her mouth with the gusto of a sumo wrestler. Dash did the same, and the two fell silent for a minute, sizing up one another like two curious puppies that wanted to play but were sidelined by injuries, or two battle-wounded soldiers happily recuperating in a field hospital with efficient nurses catering to their every whim.

Delores swallowed and broke the silence. "How did you break your shoulder?"

"How come you get to ask me about my injuries but I'm not supposed to ask you about yours?" Millie had warned Dash not to comment on Delores's battered face.

Delores shrugged. "You can ask me anything. I got clobbered by a shopping cart. You?"

"I fell off my friend's longboard."

"Longboard?"

"Yeah, like a skateboard but longer. Me and my friends wanted to try skitching. We saw it in a Tony Hawk video."

"What's skitching?"

"In the video game, these guys get pulled on their skateboards by a car. We decided to try it with a bike. But I didn't know longboards went faster than skateboards."

"What happened?"

"My friend said that riding on gravel would ruin the wheels. So, when I came down the hill and saw the rocks at the bottom, I tried to jump off. I don't think it was the best plan."

"Maybe not." Delores raised a third skewer. "What do you call these?"

"Nan used to call them Newfie hors d'oeuvres. Mom makes them for me as an after-school snack when she's home. Dad always makes peanut butter celery. You like 'em?"

"Best thing I tasted since pickled eggs."

Dash picked up another skewer and slid the contents over his bottom lip. "Do you have a favourite NHL team?"

"Yes, sir. I'm a Vancouver fan, although a lot of good that did me this year." Delores was wearing printed flowers on both top and bottom this afternoon.

"I like Montreal, but since they got knocked out, I'm cheering for Washington." Dash stretched his T-shirt so Delores could see the red and blue eagle logo.

"I'm going for Vegas. Can you believe they made the playoffs in their first year? Not only the playoffs, but the finals," said Delores.

"I know. It's discombobulated." Now they were like a couple on a blind date—trying to feel out whether they were compatible enough to go for a second round.

Henry arrived bearing a plate of celery and deposited it on the coffee table. "Bumps on a log. Enjoy," he said and skittered back to the kitchen.

"Do I lie?" Dash picked up a green stick, raisins sticking out of the peanut butter.

Delores laughed and dug in.

"You don't really live in your station wagon, do you?"

"Yes, sir. Me and Daisy are a team."

"Daisy? That's your car's name, right? I named my skateboard Blackie."

"Sounds like a good name for a skateboard." Delores inserted another celery stick between her lips and crunched audibly.

"But if you live in a car, where do you get a shower?"

"Sponge bath at the bathroom sink."

"You mean you don't have to get showers every day?"

"A sponge bath works just fine."

"Dad, Miss Delores says she doesn't take showers. I don't want to take showers, either." No sound came from the kitchen. Dash continued with the interrogation. "Okay, but if you only have your car, how do you watch hockey games? On your phone?"

"No, I don't have a phone."

"Wait a minute. You don't have a phone?" A piece of celery had stopped midway to Dash's mouth.

"No, sir. I watched all the games in the Walmart."

You could almost see the wheels turning in Dash's head. "Okay, so if you watched the games in Walmart, where did you sit?"

"I'd drag a plastic chair from the furniture department to the electronics department. Walmart TVs are always tuned to Sportsnet."

"Did the workers watch, too?" Dash stuck two carrot sticks up his nose.

Delores laughed again. "Usually too busy, but I'd fill them in on any big plays. They said I missed my calling."

"Huh?"

"They said I should have been a TV sports commentator."

Dash saw his father roll his eyes in the kitchen. "Like Bob Cole," said Dash.

"Not sure I know him."

"He's from Quidi Vidi, here in St. John's. He's old now but still calls some games."

"You'll have to introduce me to Mr. Cole."

"Dad, can you introduce Miss Delores to Bob Cole?"

"I don't know him personally," came his father's voice.

"Well, anyway, he's famous." Dash went to the kitchen for a refill of milk. "Can you remember where you saw all the games?"

"Of course."

"Okay, I'm going to quiz you. Where'd you see Tampa eliminate New Jersey?"

"Sault Ste. Marie—their Walmart had the best big-screen TVs. Good game."

"How about when Boston eliminated Toronto?"

"I remember that. Game seven. First round, I was in Toronto. Nice store. Friendly staff. They were sorely disappointed, although I remember one staff member was a Boston fan."

"So, you'd watch the game, and then you'd go outside and sleep in your car?"

"Yes, sir. Come closing time, I'd brush my teeth and head on out to Daisy."

"What about if the store closed and the game wasn't over?"

"Most Walmarts are open twenty-four hours."

"Where is Daisy now?" Dash put his feet up on the coffee table. Three toes poked through a hole in his right sock.

"Hopefully she's still at the Walmart. I'm worried about her with all this wind." Delores's blue hair caught the light.

"I'm sure she'll be okay." Dash put his hand on Delores's shoulder. "You can watch tonight's game with me and Dad. Right, Dad? Daaad . . ."

Henry put down a knife and ran to the kitchen doorway. "What? What? Where's the fire?"

"Bad joke, Dad. Miss Delores is going to watch the game with us tonight."

"Uh, okay, I guess."

"Thank you, Mr. Henry. It would be an honour to sit with you and Dash."

"And Mr. Parrell. He always watches with us." Dash bounced off the chair.

"I knew your father was a good man."

"How did you know that?"

"He drives a Ford."

Henry did not comment on that syllogism. "The game starts nine thirty our time, so Dash, you'll only be watching the first period."

"Aww, Dad."

"It's a school night, and you can hardly drag yourself out of bed in the morning."

"I'll go to bed early tomorrow night. I promise."

"First period or your mother will have both our hides." Henry ran his fingers through Dash's hair. Tiny sprouts poked up around the jagged stitches. The new hair was darker than the sun-bleached stuff at the end of his curls.

"Dad, can I dye my hair blue?"

43

Wednesday: The Ruby Rose Chicken Plant

Some guy was tapping on Tiny's passenger window. He was wearing a black hoodie that had ADHD written in the ACDC font with the lightning bolt in between the D and the H. The font was called Squealer. Tiny knew that tidbit of information because he had once made knock-off ACDC shirts and sold them at school to finance his beer consumption. Tiny pushed the button, and the passenger window descended into the frame.

"Wanna buy a ticket? Twenty bucks a pop."

"Get the fuck away from my truck." Tiny hit the button to roll up the window, almost severing the guy's hand. A quick calculation told him the scalper was selling Chase the Ace tickets at twelve times the original selling price. Were these people out of their minds?

Tiny wished he hadn't agreed to take his co-worker's Wednesday night shift. He had no idea they had changed the Chase the Ace night from Thursday to Wednesday this week to accommodate some bigwig's funeral. Gillian Gee had been on about it before giving an update on the storm cleanup. Thirty-two traffic lights down in the city alone.

Tiny switched off the radio and inched the truck ahead a few feet. He might have to give up night shifts, period, until this insanity was over. He knew he couldn't, though. He needed the money to tide him over until he settled out west. Only three more months before he'd sell his truck and ride his motorcycle out to Fort McMurray and find work in the tar sands. He would not be sad to say goodbye to the chickens.

This morning the wind had done a complete about-face, raising the temperature twenty degrees in twelve hours. The result—the hoards of gamblers, who up to now had stayed hunkered down in their vehicles, tuned to the radio waiting to hear their ticket number being read, were now outdoors, strolling the thoroughfare in the Goulds or lounging like they were at a fair, ensuring that it would take Tiny even longer than last Thursday to get to work. Tiny counted twenty-four blue porta-potties before he managed to navigate through the last logjam and drive the last two miles to work.

He backed his truck into his usual spot straddling two parking places at the Ruby Rose Chicken Plant just as the last of the daylight was disappearing. He unfolded himself from the cab and stretched his spidery legs. The smell of ammonia was almost overwhelming, and he wasted no time getting inside. He punched the clock. 9:03 p.m., the card read. Shit. Late again. Mr. Morgan would have his head.

Tiny spun the combination lock, hung up his coat, and stored his lunch in his locker before turning to the wall that housed the forklift keys. He came to a dead stop. All he saw was a sea of wooden pegs. The keys were AWOL. Nine forklifts couldn't be all working the night shift, even if there was a glut of chickens. That had never happened in the history of the chicken plant.

Tiny checked the back room and saw five forklift operators milling around. The skunky pong of dope hit him as he entered. Two were kicking around a hacky sack. The other three were drinking Rockstar out of tins and passing a joint back and forth between them.

"What's going on?" Tiny's eyes focused on the smokers.

"Dunno," said R. J. Mahone, looking up at Tiny, half his face tattooed with demons. "When we got here, Wally let us in and told us to wait for him. We haven't seen him since. Right, b'ys?"

Grunts of acknowledgment ricocheted off the concrete walls.

"You know you're not supposed to smoke indoors," said Tiny. All movement stopped, and all eyes swivelled to see what the foreman would do next. "So, take your smokes and get the hell out." Tiny knew he was venting his Chase the Ace frustrations on the boys, but he couldn't help it. It had been a trying evening, and he hadn't even started work.

"What happened to Williams?" asked one of the hacky sackers.

"Burst appendix." Tiny felt all eyes on him until he turned to leave the room. He waited until R. J. Mahone wet his fingers and stroked the tip of the joint, putting out the small point of red at the end, and inserted it into the chest pocket of his blue coveralls for later enjoyment.

Tiny's heart rate quickened. This only happened when he was very, very angry. Tiny kicked the door open to continue his search for Wally. Maybe they had done away with him. Weirder things had happened. Just last summer, one cokehead had strangled another in the van on the way out the highway. The first-degree murder trial was due in court any day. Tiny returned to the desk and knelt before the cabinet underneath. He started snooping in the drawers. He would find out who hid the keys and pulverize him. This type of thing had happened before, but never on his watch.

Wally Burke appeared. His big nose preceded him into the room. "Overflow in the boiler room. Did you get the boys straightened away?"

Tiny unfolded himself from under the desk, his XXXL yellow shirt rising up from behind the wood like a cotton sun. Wally took a step back. Like the forklift operators, Wally had been expecting a normal-sized human, not Tiny, who right now looked like a massive rat about to pounce on a tiny mouse. "Happy you decided to bless us with your presence, Gonzo."

"What's your problem?" Wally snarled, not something he often did when talking to Tiny, perhaps his only ally at work.

"We'd have about a hundred crates loaded if you hadn't done away with the keys," Tiny snarled back.

"What the . . . ?" Wally looked at the wall behind the desk. "Where'd you put them, you sneaking son of a bitch?"

"I didn't touch them, you simple-minded ape. I clocked in to find an unmanned reception with no keys."

"The keys were here when I went to check on the boiler." Wally looked a bit sheepish now, grasping one of his gold hoop earrings between the fingers of his right hand.

"Well, they're not here now. And I've got five guys relaxing in the lunchroom like it's goddamned Christmas."

"One of them must have taken them." Wally spat on the floor.

"And I'm going to find out who it was, and so help me God, I'm going to strangle his scrawny neck, and you're going to watch." Tiny turned the fingers of one hand inside the palm of the other.

Wally pushed past Tiny, not an easy feat, and went thirty feet down the hall to where large doors opened into a warehouse. Tiny could hear him counting, one, two . . . nine forklifts. If someone thought that hiding all the forklift keys was a form of entertainment, Tiny begged to differ. He wanted to get his work done and get the hell out of there. He couldn't stand the smell of ammonia that assaulted his nose every time he approached Ruby Rose. Tiny had expected Wally to follow him out to the back room, but Wally was not behind him when he began tearing into the workers.

"If whoever took the keys does not come forward right now, I will feed each and every one of your gonads to the chickens." Bits of saliva punctuated Tiny's words. "If, however, someone comes forward now, I will forget the whole thing and not mention anything to Mr. Morgan. But . . ." he continued, pausing here for effect, "if it ever happens again, I will proceed with the gonad plan. No second chances."

R. J. Mahone did not say a word, simply walked out to the office and showed Tiny where he had hidden the keys behind the printer.

"I want at least five hundred crates loaded by the time I check on you." Tiny was sick of practical jokers. Last week, Randy had stuck chicken parts in his pants and got caught on surveillance camera. He was now looking for other work. Two months ago, a guy got fired after biting the head off a live chicken, apparently inspired by some old Alice Cooper clip making the rounds on YouTube. Or was it Ozzy Osbourne biting the head off a bat? Who knew? Or cared? Tiny just needed his lift guys moving chickens to the trucks so they could all punch their cards at the end of their shift and get home to bed.

Wally was not back in the warehouse when the men finally got to work. Nor was he out back. Tiny shrugged on his coat and headed outside to see what had become of his buddy. First that damned Chase the Ace, then mutiny at work, and now a missing forklift foreman. How bad could things get?

*

141

In a clearing near First Pond, only a few hundred metres behind the plant, a sweet rusty smell hit Tiny's nostrils, and he sensed something foul and wrong.

Come on, Wally, you old bastard, he urged silently. *Come on, pop out of the trees at me.*

He took a few steps forward, and his foot hit something soft, something too soft for nature, something that should not be in the woods. He looked down and, in the dim light of the undergrowth, made out the remains of Wally's mauled body. His co-worker's entire left leg and a chunk of the right were missing, and both bloody stumps were still bleeding out.

Tiny was stunned into near-paralysis. What remained of Wally's yellow Ruby Rose button-up shirt was matted. Tiny's gaze travelled up to what was left of his friend's head—one ear and a chunk of the scalp were missing; the second ear sporting two golden hoops remained attached to his mutilated face. Half a tattoo of a snake was just visible creeping up his bared shoulder blades.

It dawned on Tiny, standing there alone in the woods, that whatever had got Wally couldn't be far off. He backed away, hand over mouth, and then in stunned silence turned and ran back toward the chicken plant.

44

Millie Finds Out Henry Didn't Change the Bedsheets

"Miss Delores, what do you think of the apartment?" Millie was ladling a second round of turkey soup into Delores's bowl. She did not offer any to Henry.

"It's more than I ever dreamed of. Are you sure you don't mind me moving in?"

"Not at all. We're delighted to have you. How is the bed?" Millie noticed that Delores's bruises were fading and the cuts on her nose were almost fully healed.

"Great mattress. I'm wondering if you have any bedsheets?" Delores buttered a dinner roll and passed it to Dash.

"What do you mean? Are there no sheets on the bed?" Millie put the pot back on the stove.

"No, I can pick some up at Walmart if you like."

Millie sat back in her spot and looked directly at Henry. "Henry, did you not put fresh sheets on the bed?"

"The bed was never slept in. I didn't see why . . ."

"Henry, Dash and Stella slept in that bed after we came home late from the movie that night, and they both fell asleep in the car. I washed the sheets and put them in the linen closet."

"Oops." Henry's cheeks reddened.

"I'll put sheets on after supper, Delores." Millie shot daggers at her husband.

"Thank you," said Delores, inserting another load of broccoli into her mouth, showing off her missing tooth. "I really like the dinky cars."

"Dinky cars?" Millie raised her eyebrows and looked at Henry again. Henry shrugged.

"Yes, there's a real nice collection laid out around the vase in the middle of the table. Volkswagen Beetle. A Ford Mustang. Even a red Nash Rambler station wagon."

"Dad, did you take my dinkies?" Dash slopped turkey soup on his sling, which was now a rainbow of tie-dyed colours.

"You haven't played with them in years." Henry pushed his bowl away.

"That doesn't mean I don't want them."

"I'll give them back to you, Dash." Delores lowered her head to her bowl and slurped up the soup as if she hadn't eaten in weeks.

"It's okay. Maybe I can come over and visit them sometimes."

"Any time, Dash. *Mi casa es su casa.*"

"It's not exactly your *casa.*" Henry looked at Delores.

"Henry." Millie gave him a withering stare.

45

Thursday: Henry and Dash Pick Up Daisy

"Come on, Dash, time's up, you're coming to Walmart with me." Henry had descended to the basement to extract Dash from the computer screen.

"Not now, Dad. It's getting really intense. We're in the top three." Despite the sling enveloping his left arm, Dash's hands were working furiously at the controllers. His head lurched with each move, the little shaved bit behind his left ear turning toward Henry one second and away the next.

"Top three what?"

"Top three squads, Dad."

"And we're sneaking up on one of the other squads right now." Delores's disembodied voice came through Dash's mic.

"Yeah, and they don't see us, and I've got an RPG, and Miss Delores has got a purple scar, and we both have full shields."

"I'm not sure what any of that means."

"It's our loot, Dad. We got sick guns."

"And shields are kind of like health bars." Delores again.

Henry raised his eyebrows. "Did I tell you I've decided to convert to Scientology?"

"Dad, you are so weird."

"Dash, turn off the computer. We're going to Walmart. Now."

Henry watched as, within seconds, Dash built a box all around his avatar to protect it before turning to his father. "Is that where you and Delores are watching tonight's game?"

"No." Henry laughed despite his frustration. He could just imagine himself snuggled up in a plastic lawn chair next to Delores in the midst of people buying Bluetooth speakers and HDMI cables. *Excuse me, sir. Could you move over just a little, I can't seem to reach those headphones.* "No game tonight, remember?"

"Oh, right, they're between cities. So, why are we going to Walmart?"

"To pick up the station wagon." As if Henry didn't have better things to do.

"Why do you need me to come? We're winning."

"Your time's up, and your mother is working." Henry noticed that, of late, Dash seemed to be developing an alarming video game tick. He kept putting his right hand up to his left shoulder and touching the sling knot in the split seconds between joystick moves.

"Can't I just stay with Miss Delores?"

Delores called in from the granny flat. "Henry, are you going to pick up Daisy?"

Henry slowly inhaled. *Remember the Spring Tune-Up*, he told himself. "Yes, Delores. Millie gave me your keys."

God knows Henry had argued with Millie. "It's bad enough having her in the house, Millie. But aren't you worried about what the neighbours are going to say when that kitschy wagon shows up in the driveway? Can't we just leave it at Walmart for now?"

"No, we cannot, Henry Puddester. It's a wonder Daisy hasn't been vandalized."

Could this be the same Millie who had freaked out when Mrs. Sampson's son had done garage work in the driveway? "What's the neighbourhood coming to?" she had said. For some reason that Henry could not fathom, Millie was really taken with this station wagon woman. Dash's voice brought him back to the task at hand.

"Why can't you get it, Miss Delores?" Dash looked like a child in spasm, his back swaying with every finger movement, like a pianist on speed.

"Doctor's orders. She said I shouldn't drive until I go back to make sure my head's okay."

"Your head seems all right to me," said Dash. "You were quick taking down that zombie with the PAS."

"Daa-aash. Now."

"All right, Dad. One more round, and then we'll go."

Translation: Three to ten minutes, unless Dash got preoccupied. Then he would conveniently forget that he had been asked to stop playing. How many times a week did Henry hear "last round"?

"Finish up. NOW." Henry rubbed his temples. This was not how he was supposed to live out his retirement. Dash continued blowing up zombies. "Dash, turn it off, now, or I'll unplug the machine."

"Aww, Dad." Dash reluctantly said goodbye to Delores and his other teammates, one of whom was from Nairobi, and promised to be back online later.

By the time Henry got upstairs and took the Minnie Mouse key chain off the elk's head key holder, Delores had made her way in from the apartment and was making a beeline for his La-Z-Boy. He'd been wiping it down twice a day. Soon he wouldn't be able to sit in it at all. Too germy. Delores's face was healing at an astounding rate. She held the small transistor radio Millie had given her in the hospital. She wiggled a couple of dials. Leonard Cohen's voice came out of the tinny speaker. Delores pulled the wooden lever on the side of the chair and reclined the chair. "'Hallelujah Chorus.' *Various Positions*, 1984," she said.

Dash tumbled up the stairs. "Hey, that song is in the Shrek movie." He ran and gave Delores a hug. "See ya later, Miss Delores." He went and met Henry at the door. When they got out to the driveway, Dash gave his father a huge smile showing off a half-grown molar. "Mom says Miss Delores is like the sister I never had."

Good grief, thought Henry.

46

Henry Bonds with Daisy

When they pulled into the Walmart lot, two dozen people were milling around the Ford LTD like they were at a Show n' Shine. Despite the cubed windshield, it was an impressive vehicle. Henry hadn't had a chance to size up the station wagon the night Delores was hit by the cart, but now that he got his first glimpse of the toy-covered pink paint through the crowd, he couldn't deny the bubbly sensation in his stomach. The last of the sun's rays reflected off the metal clasps on a six-inch Clydesdale's harness as well as on a pair of gold-painted praying hands. The licence plate read C4TWMN.

"Wow." Dash was out of the Escape before Henry had a chance to put it in park. He flew over to the Ford like a squirrel shot out of a cannon. Henry watched his son's platinum head disappear into the crowd.

He turned to open the door and jumped. Frank's head was inches from the window, his bald pate covered by a Running Hut mesh ball cap. Henry pressed the button, and the window descended, allowing cotton candy fumes to enter the Escape.

"Evening, Henry. It's been donkeys' years. Crisp?" Frank held out a bag of salt and vinegar chips.

"Yes, déjà vu all over again." Henry stuck his hand out the window and took a chip from the proffered bag. "I wish I could wind back the clock."

"I know. A lot going on. I guess you're wondering what I'm doing here." Frank was wearing a grey jogging suit. It looked new.

"Crossed my mind." He motioned for Frank to remove his arm so he could close the window and open the door.

"Millie said you were picking up Delores's estate car, and you know how much I'd like a ride in the LTD. So . . . here I am." Frank's expression was one of a small child afraid he might be denied a candy treat.

"How'd you get here?"

"I've been dossing all day, so I jogged."

"*You* jogged?" Henry knew Frank had been a track star, but not in the past several decades.

Frank nodded as if this were something he did every day. "I only do it once the sun has set and people can't tell who I am. I figured I could help you by driving one car home."

"I'm going to leave the Escape here, and Millie is going to drop me back up in the morning." Henry approached the crowd.

"I could drive the LTD." Frank followed him.

"Frank, you don't have a licence." Henry had long decided that whatever prevented Frank from getting his licence was none of his business.

"Minor technicality." Frank's smile showed bits of chips on his teeth.

"I think I better stick to the plan. You know how Millie is."

Dash saw his father approaching and announced that Henry held the sacred key, so the crowd parted as if Henry were Jesus Himself.

"Miss Delores's car is even better than Mr. Parrell said. But look at the windshield and roof." Dash was jumping up and down to get a better look at where the moose had peeled back the metal.

"Jesus Murphy. It's like a curio cabinet gone haywire."

"Told you." Frank crunched his chips.

"I can see R2-D2 and C-3PO," said Dash. "And there's Santa and the Easter Bunny. We should do this with the Escape, or your motorcycle."

Henry snickered. "Good one, Dash."

"Hurry, Dad. Open the door."

"Give the man space." Frank directed the crowd to move back. Henry unlocked the driver's door, which opened surprisingly well despite the damage. He leaned over to unlock the passenger door for Frank and turned around to unlock the back door for Dash.

When he turned back, Dash was already in the front seat.

"You should let Dash ride shotgun," said Frank. "I'll get in back."

"No way. I have to keep Millie in my good books for the next little while. She'd have my head if she found out."

"She won't find out," said Frank. "If you stop just before you get home, he can jump in back for the last block."

"Yes, Dad, yes." Dash was bouncing up and down on the vinyl like an Indian rubber ball. "I won't say anything to Mom, I swear."

"If you promise." Henry took his first look around the inside. It was almost too much to take in. Until now he hadn't quite grasped that Delores had glued on things inside the car as well as out. Nothing that would puncture a lung in a crash, he noticed, but still, it wasn't the ride for a Zen Minimalist. Tiny toys surrounded the horizontal speedometer, which was wider than the steering wheel. Knick-knacks lined the brown wood-panelled dash above the knob for the lights and all across the top of the cassette player, radio, and glovebox. Rubbery sea life protruded from the middle of the wheel surrounding the blue Ford symbol.

Frank deposited himself in the seat behind Dash and started belly laughing. "You should see the stuff back here. We got Huey, Dewey, and Louie, Donald and Daisy, some dude with a big green head and funnel ears."

"That's Shrek." Dash's entire torso disappeared into the back seat. "And that's Fiona. They're ogres. And that's Donkey. Eddie Murphy voices him in the movie."

Henry turned back to the front. "What am I going to do about the windshield? I can't see a thing."

"Just tap out a few pieces, enough to have a good gander for oncoming traffic."

"What about if it all comes in on me?"

"Trust me, it won't. It's designed to stay together when fractured."

Henry poked tentatively at the windshield with the car keys. Nothing. He poked harder and a couple of cubes gave way, opening enough of a porthole to see the road.

"Cool. It's like Minecraft," said Dash.

Henry looked in the rear-view mirror. Delores's grey suitcases were standing at alert in the trunk. He figured Walmart must have had their security guys keeping an eye on it because of the steady stream of customers it was bringing to their store. He turned the key, and the engine purred to life. "Wow, sounds new."

"Told you she was mint, did I not?" Frank beamed.

"You did. Come on, Dash. Come and buckle up."

"You sure you won't be too distracted to drive?" Now Frank was leaning over the armrests between Henry and Dash's heads. "Budge up, Dash, and make room. I'll come up front, too, to help your father concentrate." Frank pulled the armrests back into the seat. He pushed Dash into the middle and squished in beside him.

"Isn't this cozy? Seat belt check." Henry waited until he heard the two clicks and put the big boat of a car into drive.

"Looks like you'll be stopping by the gas station on the way home," said Frank.

Henry peered under a kewpie doll to see the red needle pointing at the big E for empty staring at him. "Figures."

"Come on, Dad. What are you waiting for?"

"Dash, you weren't this excited on Space Mountain."

"This is way more exciting than Disney, Dad."

Henry patted his jacket pocket for his wallet. "Okay, we're good to go." He gave Dash's waist belt a tug to make sure it was tight and touched the gas. The crowd parted like the Red Sea to let them advance. Frank rolled down his window. May had arrived, but the air was still cool.

Dash raised his body off the passenger seat to wave at the crowd like the queen. "See ya, suckers."

"*Dash.*"

"What?"

"Nothing." Henry pulled into the Stavanger Drive traffic. "It drives surprisingly smooth for a thirty-five-year-old car."

Henry didn't want to let on to Frank how much he was enjoying himself. He still blamed Frank for the fact that a stranger was right now sitting in his La-Z-Boy, eating his candied nuts, and leaving her tea-stained mugs on the coffee table for him to pick up.

"Hey, I saw Millie posted a picture to CBC's online contest asking for pics of people with their favourite car."

"Yes, she told me. It was her first day of school." Henry knew the shot—Millie's hair in plaits and her little cardboard bookbag at her side. She looked so innocent, no one would have guessed she grew up to crave arguing like Frank craved potato chips.

"They had close to two thousand entries before they shut it down." Frank was now waving at the gawking pedestrians.

"Look, Dad, someone is videoing us." Dash waved at the phone with his good arm.

When Henry returned from paying $57 to fill the tank, the clerk—a teen-aged boy wearing John Lennon glasses—ran out and asked if he could take a selfie with Daisy.

"For Instagram," he gushed as he stretched a gangly arm as far away from his body as he could and clicked.

Henry had no idea what Instagram was.

"Why don't you sit in the driver's seat, and Henry'll take your picture," Frank called to the boy through the window.

"So now I'm a freakin' photographer."

Henry took the black Samsung phone and hit the tiny belly button near the bottom of the screen. He then ushered the clerk out of the station wagon, reinstalled himself, fastened his 1983 seat belt, and began to drive away, narrowly avoiding a rubbernecker who came dangerously close to the three blind mice Henry noticed on the side door. Henry took a deep breath and pulled onto Portugal Cove Road.

"What's NYPD?" Dash was pointing at a rectangular blue sticker on the low glovebox.

"New York Police Department," said Frank. "You kids today. You don't watch enough TV."

Henry turned onto Pine Place just as Dash half-opened the glovebox.

"Hey, that looks like a water pistol." Dash's eager hand had just begun to reach inside when Henry caught a glimpse of black matte metal and stretched across and pushed the glovebox closed.

"Cardinal rule, Dash. Never open someone else's glovebox without permission."

"Why not? I was just wondering what kind of things Miss Delores kept in here."

"People sometimes carry personal things in gloveboxes."

"Like what? Shampoo?"

"No, not shampoo. Before I met your mother, I was hitchhiking . . ."

"You hitchhiked?"

Henry was disappointed his son didn't imagine him the hip guy he once was.

"Dash, my boy, your father was a renegade back in the day."

"Did you hitchhike, too, Mr. Parrell?"

"No, not me."

"Well, I used to hitchhike all the time. This one time a trucker picked us up on the Northern Peninsula. He was going to bring us all the way to St. John's until my buddy popped the glovebox. He was so angry he left us on the side of the road outside Deer Lake, and I ended up missing Mother's Day. Your grandmother almost killed me."

Henry could see the wheels turning in his son's head—trying to digest this new idea of his father. Henry knew Dash thought he was a nerd, and maybe he was, now, but he wanted to impart upon his only child that he used to be something else.

"Henry, we forgot to put Dash in the back seat." Frank looked panicked.

Henry looked at his son sitting in the middle of the front seat. "Jesus, Mary, and Joseph. Millie'll have my head." Henry pulled in six houses shy of their own. "Quick, into the back seat, or Mom'll have a cow."

"Aww, Dad." But Dash slithered over the seat like a snake with legs.

"Don't damage any toys." Frank gave Dash's feet one last push to get him over. "Buckle up." Henry heard the click and pulled away from the curb. "Someone must have alerted the entire neighbourhood." He looked at Frank, who sank a little into his seat.

They were all there on the lawn, cameras at the ready as the LTD inched in next to Millie's Mini Cooper. Henry could feel the eyes on him. Sandy Hickerman and Billy Bruce stopped chatting in Sandy's driveway to openly gawk as the boat of a wagon rolled by. He could see them taking in the trolls and the monkeys, the bobble-head Jesus, and the Smurfs.

Delores occupied a place of honour in one of the egg-shaped chairs that Millie had brought to the front lawn for the occasion. They looked like white macramé. Before sitting down, Delores prodded the white nylon thongs that formed the seat, as if testing to see if they could hold her weight. Millie sat at her side like a lady in waiting. Delores looked down upon her minions; a benevolent smile tickled her lips. All was well in her kingdom today.

Frank hopped out and ran around to open Henry's door for him like he was a small-town mayor greeting a celebrity. "I'm going to ask Delores if I can take her for a drive once the hullabaloo dies down," he whispered.

"You might mention that you don't have a licence." Henry suddenly felt surprisingly possessive of the wagon.

Dash exited the back seat like it was spring-loaded. "Mom," he shouted. "I got to ride shotgun."

47

Tampa Bay Lightning vs. Boston

Delores set herself up on the couch between Dash and Henry. Henry moved himself as far as he could toward the armrest. The warmup had just finished, and the players were lining up for the anthem.

Frank bounded down the stairs in his usual cloud of vaping fumes and squeezed himself in next to Henry. "Sorry, I'm late.

"Jesus on the mountain, Frank. I can't breathe here."

"Jesus wasn't on the mountain. That was Moses," said Delores. "And God told him not to take the Lord's name in vain."

"Are you here to watch the game or lecture me on the Bible?"

"I'm zipping the lip." Delores mimicked locking her lips with a key.

"Good. Anyone else got anything to say?"

Frank shook his head.

Henry looked at Dash.

"I have to cut the cheese."

"Daaash."

"At least you won't smell Mr. Parrell's cotton candy anymore."

48

Tiny and the Black Bear

It had been a long night at the Ruby Rose chicken plant. So long that it was now Thursday morning.

"You lot are going to drive me to drink." Tiny's boss, Vik the Prick, the owner of the Ruby Rose chicken plant, arrived within ten minutes of Tiny's call. He was not in good humour.

Tiny didn't blame him, really—this was the second time in less than a year that one of his employees was murdered on the job. Definitely not good press. "Like I said on the phone, I was trying to figure out what happened to the keys when Wally just disappeared. It looks like something got to him before I did."

"Something?" Vik the Prick rolled his eyes.

"I'm thinking a black bear."

"Surely a bear didn't come in and drag Gonzo—I mean Mr. Burke—"

Tiny's boss was cut off by a knock on the door. A man entered. One of his eyes independently meandered around the room.

"Officer?" Vik the Prick held out his hand.

"Constable Dick Turner. These are Constables Handrigan and Foley."

Tiny hoped the officers wouldn't notice the pong of cannabis that permeated the plant.

"Okay, Tiny, bring them out back."

Once the police viewed the mauled remains of Wally Burke, they shoved the five forklift operators in separate rooms. The head cop, the guy with the meandering right eye, ordered Tiny into the lunchroom and got him to go over the details leading up to Wally's death.

"There's something not right here," said Officer Turner, standing in front of a row of coats on hooks above small lockers. "Mr. Taylor, you're telling me you think a bear did this, but I just got off the phone with a bear expert who says there are no bears on the Avalon." He banged his fist on the table, jangling Tiny's already frayed nerves.

"Listen, I grew up on the Baie Verte Peninsula. It's crawling with black bears over there, and I swear that Wally looks like he was mauled by a bear." Tiny thought back all those years to his friend who took a shortcut through the dump and crossed paths with a hungry mother bear trying to scavenge enough food to feed her twins. The result of that encounter wasn't pretty.

Constable Turner pushed his wireless phone piece into his ear. "We'll find out soon enough. Dr. Hannaford has arrived." Constable Turner opened the door, allowing Dr. Hannaford to enter.

Tiny momentarily saw the keys hanging on the wall behind the desk before the door shut again. He did a double take. Dr. Hannaford was wearing a green neck scarf and pink steel-toed boots. "I thought Dr. Hannaford was a man."

"Do I dare remind you that we are currently in the twenty-first century, Mr. . . . ?" She spoke with a condescension that only academics can get away with.

"Taylor, Tiny Taylor."

Dr. Hannaford's eyes travelled from Tiny's toes up to the brim of his hat. She was not appraising him in a sexual manner. "I repeat for Mr. Taylor's benefit, there are no bears east of Terra Nova National Park." Dr. Hannaford was obviously a woman who liked hearing her own voice. She had yet to see Wally's corpse, which, when Tiny left it, was being guarded by an armed cop while a forensic team photographed the scene.

"If it wasn't a bear that ate chunks of Wally's body, then what was it?" Tiny had quartered a fair number of moose in his day, and blood and guts didn't bother him in the least, but he couldn't get the image of Wally Burke's half-eaten body out of his mind. The shredded shirt and missing swaths of flesh. He shuddered.

"Whatever killed this man couldn't have been a black bear." Dr. Hannaford had this way of scrunching up her nose like she smelled something bad. Tiny thought she looked like a weasel. *Just wait until she gets out in the woods*, he thought. *Then she'll scrunch up her nose, all right.*

"How can you be so sure without viewing the evidence?" asked Constable Turner, his left eye focused on the doctor, the right taking a stroll past the others present.

"Black bears are quite shy. They avoid people, so the Avalon Peninsula doesn't make a good habitat for them. They prefer sparsely populated areas and have no need to move away from them. The closest black bear habitat would be west of Clarenville on the Bay du Nord Wilderness Reserve." Dr.

Hannaford's voice was monotone, and Tiny's brain was starting to fade a bit. He had been up for well over twenty-four hours by this point. *Was Chase the Ace only last night?* His eyes were blinking more slowly, and he let his breathing slow as well. He felt like a reptile.

Constable Turner's voice jolted him back awake. "Well, if it wasn't a black bear, what was it? He's pretty chewed up."

"I can't say. If a bear were here, it would more likely be a polar bear. If not a bear, then perhaps a rabid coyote. As of now, however, we do not have rabies on the island. But it is possible that a coyote could have cross-bred with a Labrador wolf, resulting in a sort of super coyote that came across the Straits on pack ice."

"And you think one of those coyotes could have made it a thousand kilometres from the Northern Peninsula to here?"

"I don't know without examining the scene."

"Let's take you out to the site."

Tiny was happy to sit tight while they escorted the scientist to the clearing in the woods. He needed time to absorb the fact that Wally wouldn't be going home to his wife. Flora was ten years into her journey with MS, and Wally was her reason to get out of bed in the morning. Tiny shut his eyes. If he could just catch a few winks, he'd be able to think straight.

49

Vanessa Is Shocked

Tiny opened his eyes when he heard the group approach. Dr. Hannaford looked slightly pale. Her hands were shaking, either from excitement or from the shock of seeing Wally's mauled corpse, Tiny wasn't sure. The forklift operators had all been questioned by the two female officers who had accompanied Constable Turner and were now seated around the lunchroom table. All eyes turned to the scientist.

"There has not been a bear sighting on the Avalon in the twenty years since I started collecting research," she said, "but the footprints surrounding the deceased could potentially have been made by a black bear."

"So, you're now saying that it was a black bear that killed Mr. Burke?" The cop with the wandering eye was on his booted feet.

"No, I cannot confirm that without further tests. The scene warrants further investigation." She really enunciated the *cannot*. "The footprints surrounding the scene are not clearly discernible, but they could be consistent with those of a black bear. The claw marks on the deceased's neck, however, are not consistent with any black bear mauling I have ever investigated." She held up her finger here, and the fluorescent lights flickered. "And, I repeat, unless someone transported a black bear to the Goulds on a truck, I stick to my word that there are no black bears living in this area." She locked eyes with Tiny, letting him know she was still right even if she was wrong.

"So, let's say someone did transport a bear. Is it normal behaviour for a black bear to kill a human in this manner?" This came from a second female police officer.

"Black bears usually shy away from humans unless they feel threatened. For example, if a human gets between a bear and its food or a mother and her cub."

"If a black bear attacks, besides the claw marks, would the wounds look like what you just witnessed?"

"No, the wounds I saw are not consistent with those normally inflicted by a male black bear."

"Male? Why do you say male?" Tiny tried to keep his head from dropping to his chest like his great-aunt Nel's.

"Normal males weigh between two to three hundred pounds, whereas females rarely exceed a hundred. The claw marks I saw are much bigger than those of a female black bear. Males can be up to six hundred pounds."

Constable Turner tried to say something, but the scientist held up a finger again. "Plus, there were no secondary tracks to indicate the presence of a bear cub. Like I said, the area surrounding the deceased man is grassy and the tracks are difficult to discern. On other parts of the island where bears live, it's the time of year they emerge from their dens looking for food. As you can imagine, after sleeping all winter, they wake up very hungry."

"What do they usually eat?" Vik the Prick had his elbows on the lunch table, chin resting on his interlocked fingers.

"Berries in the fall. In the spring, roots, grubs, and animal carcasses. They have even been known to attack caribou and moose calves. If the spring has been particularly cold and the ground frozen, roots and grubs are harder to come by. In that case, the bears eat whatever they can get— garbage, pet food. A male black bear eating human food can grow obese, up to six hundred pounds, just like humans eating junk food."

"Would it be normal for a black bear to be prowling around at night?" Back to Constable Turner.

"Yes, black bears are crepuscular, meaning they are most active at dawn and dusk. Like moose, most of their activity occurs a half-hour before sunrise, which corresponds with the timeline provided by Mr. Taylor."

"But you're still saying there are no black bears living here?"

"Absolutely. If, and that's a big if, the animal in question was a bear, it would have been transported here. Then, it may have stayed due to refuse from the chicken plant. If a bear has indeed somehow made its way across the isthmus and set up camp, why it attacked Mr. Burke warrants further investigation."

"What do you propose?" Constable Turner had black circles under his eyes.

"I can get a team out this afternoon to search the area to find any evidence of an animal and try to determine its territory. We can set up some hair snag stations and some motion cameras. Once we get samples, we'll see what we're dealing with."

"How long will this take?" asked Turner.

"About a week."

"We don't have a week."

"I can tell you that hair samples provide us the best indication of animal populations and trends."

"We can't wait. You can contact the Department of Environment for your research." Constable Turner stood up.

"Don't patronize me. I know who to contact. But remember, if your men come out here to install motion cameras and the like, keep in mind that if it is a black bear, they can run faster than humans, they can swim better than humans, and they can climb trees a heck of a lot better than humans."

"Thank you very much for your time, Dr. Hannaford. I'll get back to you by tomorrow as to what our plan of action will be."

The police let the forklift operators go home but told them not to stray far. They'd be calling before the day was out with further questions.

50

Delores Does Laundry

"Delores . . ." Henry felt the veins in his neck bulge. He wanted to scream, but he restrained himself. First the washer full of floral shirts and massive bras, and now this.

"Yes, Mr. Henry?"

"Don't call me Mr. Henry, Delores."

"Yes, sir."

"Where are my Cheerios?"

"Can't say I know."

"Well, Dash and Millie don't eat Cheerios, but someone put the empty Cheerios box back in the pantry." Henry came around the corner into the living room brandishing the cereal box like a sword. Delores was sitting in the La-Z-Boy, feet up, clipping her nails on Henry's newspaper, an empty cereal bowl with a spoon and milk stain on the coffee table.

"That's not very good. Would you like Daisy and me to go get you some more? I know how you don't like going to the supermarket. Miss Millie told me—"

Henry flattened the cereal box with a loud bang. "After breakfast, I would appreciate it if you could remove your undergarments from the washer so I can do a load of laundry."

Delores shuffled off to the granny flat, leaving the newspaper and toenails for Henry to clean up. Henry had just put her bowl in the dishwasher and dumped the paper and nails in the bin when he caught a glimpse of a CBC van pulling in by the end of the driveway, effectively blocking his vehicle from moving. The rat-tat-tat on the front door came a few minutes later. Henry rubbed his temples and tried to ignore it, but it became more insistent. Then the bell started, so Henry took off the rubber gloves he used to wash the dishes and opened the door to a petite brunette wearing what looked like a red hockey jacket emblazoned with the CBC logo. He recognized her as the imbecile reporter who had done the story about the supermarket fiasco. Henry was going to give her a piece of her mind.

"I am not answering any questions about the supermarket incident."

The reporter looked a bit confused. Was she simple-minded? "Good morning, my name is Gillian Gee. I'm looking for Delores Cowburn. We went by the Walmart lot, but staff told us that we might find her here at 10 Pine Place. You must be Mr. Puddester?" Gillian Gee did a double take. "Puddester. Henry Puddester. I knew the name sounded familiar. We were here the other day after the supermarket kidnapping."

Henry cringed.

"I left messages on your phone . . ." Gillian made a tiny motion with her wrist, and Henry noticed the broad-shouldered male, standing behind her, hoist a large video recording device onto his shoulder.

"No," said Henry, the only word that came to mind. He was looking at the cameraman's meaty hands holding the camera that sported no lens cap.

"No?" Gillian cocked her head to the left. She looked like a parrot.

"You must have the wrong address." The cameraman moved closer, and Henry started to shut the door.

"Uh, excuse me, Mr. Puddester." Gillian's tiny, childlike shoe was between the weather stripping and the screen door, preventing it from closing. "We're working on a different story today. I see Miss Cowburn's station wagon in the driveway. Is she here?"

"No," said Henry again. He slammed the door just as Carter came ambling up the driveway dressed in flood pants and a Toronto Maple Leafs hoodie. His shopping cart was overflowing with recyclables, blue bags tied on to all sides as if he hoped to take flight.

"Jesus in the garden." Henry shuffled back into the hall, safely out of sight of the cameraman, the recycling man, and the prying young Gillian Gee. Through the door, he heard the reporter ask Carter if he knew where to find Delores Cowburn.

51

Gillian Gee's CBC Interview with Delores

Carter stood off to the side in his Maple Leafs sweater while Gillian Gee's cameraman set up the boom mic. Delighted to have his two minutes of fame, Carter promised not to make a sound during the interview. He gave Delores a thumbs-up.

"Now, Delores, just ignore the camera, and look at me when I ask you questions." Gillian Gee moved the mic closer to Delores's mouth.

"Not to offend, Miss Gillian, but I've done this before." Delores ran her fingers through her cropped blue hair.

"Of course. Let's get started, then. Can you spell your name for me?"

Delores turned her gaze directly toward the camera lens. "D-E-L-O-R-E-S C-O-W-B-U-R-N."

"Thank you, Delores. Now, you say it all started in 2000. Can you bring us back to that time and tell us what led to you decorating your car?"

"I remember it as the summer I fell out of love." Delores's sea-green eyes swung over to Gillian Gee, who remained silent but gave her cameraman an almost imperceptible nod, telling him to zoom in.

"I remember it happened quickly. No fanfare. No warning. No one thing caused it, and nothing could have prevented it. One minute we were holding hands, sharing dreams, meandering along ferny paths. Next minute I'm opening a separate bank account."

"Who are you talking about here?"

"Me and Cordell."

"And Cordell is . . . ?"

"My ex. We weren't married in a church or anything, but we were as good as."

"Okay, so you and Cordell fell out of love?" Gillian Gee threw a quick glance at her cameraman to get a two-shot. He took a step backwards. "How did that lead to your road trip in the Ford LTD?" The cameraman then panned over to the station wagon sitting neatly in front of Henry and Millie's house. He paused on the gold spray-painted praying hands.

"It started with insults about my figure, which I describe as curvaceous. Cordell described it as . . . well, let's not get into that. What got to me the most was the nasty things he said about my toy collection." She paused and looked at Daisy.

"You mean the toys on your car?"

"Yes, ma'am. My collection is worthy of a museum exhibit. I have been collecting since I came into this world. Just small things. Nothin' more than a foot high, we'll say. I have things you can't get anymore, or maybe you can online if you're rich."

"Can you give us an example?"

"Yes, like that German kewpie doll with the real glass eyes. There's one right on the dash—passenger side." Delores pointed her plump finger toward the car. "A man from *Antiques Roadshow* told me mine was worth three hundred American, and that was going on twenty years back. Must be worth thousands now. But no way was I selling my kewpie doll to pay for Cordell's cigarettes. No, sir. I'd sooner be single and living on the streets. And when I told him as much, he went off his head."

"In what way?"

Delores put a finger to the gap in her mouth where a tooth should be. "Let's just say that after I was discharged from the hospital, I knew I had to get out of Dodge. My mama always said marriage is like a berry patch. Sometimes you hit payload. Other times you have to move on to another patch. So, that's just what I did. I picked up kewpie and my other keepsakes, left the blackberry patch with its nasty thorns, and moved on to the blueberries with their nice soft pickin."

"You left Cordell?"

"That is correct. While he was sleeping off a bender, I packed a bag and hitched all the way from Williams Lake down to Vancouver. I had never been to the city before. I didn't have enough money to rent an apartment, but I did have three hundred bucks to buy this 1983 Ford LTD Country Squire station wagon. I painted her pink around the wooden panels—like one of them Mary Kay cars I always dreamed of having. I called her Daisy. I know, daisies aren't pink, but I always wanted a car named Daisy."

"Then what did you do?"

"I had a bit of money left over after I bought the car. I found a place that sold Greek skewers for two dollars a pop. And life was good for a while. Until the money ran out. When it did, I didn't panic. Another thing my mama used to say is have faith, and things will turn out all right. It was August 22. I remember because it was my Auntie Jean's birthday. I had seven dollars and twenty-five cents in my pocket and a half-tank of gas. Didn't need to drive anywhere. I was already in my usual spot in the Walmart parking lot."

"What was that like, sleeping in your car at Walmart?"

"It was nice." Delores looked dreamy. "I had one of those camping mattresses in the back. Sometimes people used to give me stuff to eat, and I could always go freshen up inside the store."

"They didn't mind you being there?"

"No, every Walmart across the nation has been as friendly as can be."

"Okay, so tell us about the day when you began to decorate your car."

"You can call her Daisy. She likes her name."

"Okay, tell us about decorating Daisy."

"Well, this one morning, it was bit cold, but I turned on the radio, and Bobby McGee came on. I always know it's gonna be a good day when I hear Janis singing about Bobby.

"That was me. Free. But instead of free like in the song *with* a man. I was free *from* mine. Cordell could never touch me again. Daisy was my Bobby McGee. It was just after the song ended that it hit me. Glue. I needed to buy me some Gorilla Glue. I waited till nine a.m., said good morning to Betsy, the greeter. She answered: 'How y'all doing today, ma'am?' Betsy was from Miami, Florida. How she ended up in British Columbia I didn't know, and I didn't ask. But we were both outsiders in Vancouver, and I sure was happy to see her welcoming face as she nudged a trolley my way. I nodded thanks and headed straight for the craft aisle. I've never looked back."

"So, you bought glue?"

"Yes, ma'am. It was a balmy day—maybe too humid for adhesion—but it was like I had had a vision. I could picture Daisy all decorated. And this would somehow help my situation. So, I started right then to glue my toys to Daisy's hood. I put Raphael, my favourite Ninja Turtle, right out front over the passenger headlamp. And the big plastic horsie my mama gave me when I was six, closer to the midpoint on the bonnet. Next, I worked my way through my plastic fruit and vegetable collection, sticking a banana up above the wheel well and a cucumber farther back near the driver's door. Finally, I took my family of Trolls, kissed them all on their bare bellies, and told them how nice it was going to be to feel the wind in their hair.

"That's when other shoppers started coming to see what I was up to. Some thought it wasn't right to display my belongings in that fashion. Others, well, they liked the idea of me gluing my favourite things to Daisy. Some of them even brought me new toys when they came out of the Walmart with their oversized shopping bags. That's how I got the gold-coloured praying hands on the roof and the flat pink flamingo on the window. It felt like it took no time, but it must have taken all day, 'cause by the time Daisy was near-covered, the sun was about to drop behind the hills.

"I was bone tired and got a little sad thinking of my mama back in Williams Lake in the cemetery out on Banks Road. I was wishing she could see Daisy all decorated like for a Thanksgiving parade. You could hardly see her pretty pink paint job anymore.

"I remembered my mama's words: 'When the golden sun is setting / And your thoughts from care are free / When on others you are thinkin' / Will you sometimes think of me?' Well, I was thinking of her, and it's like I could feel her spirit inside my soul telling me things would be all right."

"And were they?"

"Well, next thing I know, a newspaper reporter is asking to take my picture. Things got better right after that. That was a year ago. Now me and my pink 1983 Ford LTD station wagon named Daisy have travelled all the way across Canada, through the Rockies and the Prairies. We've been invited into homes of the rich and famous, not that it matters to me what folks got or don't got. We dipped down to New York and spent a night at Niagara Falls. We stopped on Parliament Hill and then on to Montreal and Quebec City. We had French people admiring my handiwork. 'C'est beau. Merveilleux.'"

Delores flung out her hand. "Next, we went through New Brunswick and across the bridge to Prince Edward Island, where someone gave me a little Anne of Green Gables bobble-head for Daisy's dash. Then we drove all the way down to Halifax and up to Cape Breton until we came to the ferry that brought us all the way to *Newfundlund*. We were like Janis Joplin singing Bobby McGee all the way across the country. It was a long haul to get here, but we finally made it to St. John's."

"Well, Delores, we're happy you made it safely. Although I understand you hit a moose just as you arrived."

"More like a moose hit Daisy. It was big enough to feed a large Catholic family for two years."

"Oh dear, are you okay?"

"Yes, we're both okay, thank you for askin'."

"Were you ever lonely on the road?"

"Sometimes, but people were so friendly, and once people got to know me and Daisy, they started bringing us meals. Yep, life is good. And I sure do like St. John's. I think I'm here to stay."

"You're no longer sleeping in your car at Walmart, though. Can you tell us a little about that?"

"Well, after I got hit by a shopping cart last Sunday night . . ."

"Yes, I heard about that. How are you feeling?"

"Much better. Thank you. Mr. Henry and Mr. Frank rescued me and brought me to the hospital. Then when the doctor didn't want me convalescing in my car, Miss Millie invited me to stay with them, so here I am."

"That's a wonderful good-news story, Delores. Do you have anything else you'd like to say to our TV audience?"

"I'd like to thank Miss Millie and Mr. Henry and Mr. Frank for helping me out. And Dash, for being the baby brother I never had."

"Anything else?"

"Yes. Never give up on your dreams." Then Delores started belting out "Me and Bobby McGee" in a husky bluesy voice.

The cameraman brought the camera down from his shoulder, and Carter clapped.

52

Henry Is Traumatized

"Anyone home?" Henry poked his head in Frank's living room. Frank was jogging on his treadmill, bare-chested. His entire torso was covered in black hair, providing sharp contrast to his bald head. A cotton candy cloud surrounded his head.

"Geez Louise. Put on a shirt, will you?" Henry shielded his eyes.

"It's too hot in here."

"Frank, put on a shirt or I'm gonna have to go back home."

Frank slowed the machine and picked up a ratty undershirt off the couch. He got back on the treadmill. "There, you happy now?"

"Much better. I think I know why the boys at the bunker got you a bubble mower for your birthday that time."

"You thought it was for the garden, did you?" Frank laughed and coughed and almost fell off the moving carpet.

"What are you doing?"

"What does it look like I'm doing?" Frank was huffing hard.

"It looks like you're trying to kill yourself."

"Doctor said I should take up exercise. So . . ."

Henry sat on the couch facing him. "Frank, I don't think she meant vaping and jogging at the same time."

"I get stressed if I don't smoke. Doctor said to avoid stress, too." Frank wheezed, and the treadmill beeped. "Did you see yesterday's editorial?"

"Nope, missed it." Henry pulled a bar stool from the kitchen island and set it up next to the window.

"They called it 'Meter Mess,' and I quote: 'Broken meters are testimony to mismanagement.'" Frank could barely get the words out between his jogging and smoking.

"Oh, no."

"Oh, yes. They said if you travel anywhere else in this fine country you will not find the almost total devastation of parking meters by thieves. They said, and I quote again: 'Letting the problem go unchecked has meant multi-million dollar losses for the City and the taxpayers.'"

"But the problem has not gone unchecked." Henry scratched his scruffy chin.

"Exactly. We just can't catch the thieves. They're always one step ahead, and they can apparently strip a meter in seconds. The editorial makes it out like we've been giving them free rein to hone their technique."

"That sucks."

"I know, but I'm not going to let it bother me. How are things with you?"

"I can't take it anymore." Henry pushed his fingers into his forehead.

Frank hit a button on the console to slow his pace to a walk. "What's going on?"

"It's Delores. She's driving me insane. She wanders around with this little radio Millie gave her, and every time a song comes on, she spouts off the name of the artist, album, and year the album was released."

"Hmm, very interesting. But if she's in hers, how can you hear the radio? Is it turned up that loud?"

"She sleeps in the apartment, but the minute she gets up, she hightails it to the house for breakfast. This morning she came in playing 'Bohemian Rhapsody.' I like Queen, but not before I get a coffee in. Dash loves it. He has been quizzing her on artists and album names."

"Does she get them right?"

"Yes, she's never wrong. It's uncanny. Any decade. Any genre. Bowie. Bing Crosby. ACDC. Michael Bublé. She's a walking encyclopedia of useless music trivia."

"Okay, so you're fed up with her. Can't you stay in your room until she goes back to the apartment?"

"The thing is, she doesn't go back. Dash leaves for school. And then Millie goes off to work. Then I'm home with Delores all day serving her tea and picking up her dirty dishes."

"Hmm. That is an unforeseen problem." Frank stopped the treadmill, stepped off, and stretched his arms high in the air. His arms were gorilla long, and the vape pen looked like it might touch the ceiling. He then bent at the waist and lowered his arms over his solid gut. The vape pen banged off the floor.

"And she's taken a liking to my La-Z-Boy chair. I never even get to sit in it anymore."

"Nooo, not the one Millie gave you for Valentine's Day." Frank gasped and coughed. "You're telling pork pies."

"I'm not. Dash even knows not to sit in it. And when I went to do a wash this morning, the washer was full of flowery shirts and massive bras."

"You can ask her to leave, you know."

"Then I don't get to go on my bike trip."

"Ah, the truth comes out. I figured you and Millie must have struck some sort of deal. It's been less than twenty-four hours. I'm sure things'll settle down." Frank began to lift one arm up and over the opposite side. "How's it going between Delores and Millie?"

"Best kind. They're like teenagers together."

"That's good, at least. And I saw Delores and Dash playing a video game."

"Yeah, Fortnite. She is apparently very talented at surviving a zombie apocalypse."

"Interesting. Is that what the game is about?"

"Yeah, you gotta dodge the zombies for two weeks to survive and win the game."

"Or . . . ?" Frank threw himself on the couch.

"The zombies take you down and eat your brains."

53

Friday: Henry Mans the Barbecue

Millie kissed Henry on the lips, slow and sensuous. He closed his eyes. "Wow, haven't had one of those in a while."

She was wearing a sexy white dress that was designed for someone a decade younger, but she carried it off. It was at times like this that Henry couldn't believe that someone like Millie had chosen him. At fifty-six, she still had the ability to turn heads.

"I knew you'd be out here taking refuge." She rubbed his cheek with the fingers of her right hand.

"I'm biding my time till they all bugger off." At least fifteen neighbours had been in the driveway gawking at the Ford LTD.

"Speaking of the neighbours . . ." Millie took a high heel off her left foot and rubbed her sole against Henry's thigh. "This has been a rough week, and I think we need to get our minds off things. So . . . I sent out some emails and invited a few people over for a barbecue."

Henry flinched. *So that's what this is about.* "How many people are you talking?" The westerly wind had done an excellent job of transforming St. John's from an arctic clime to a normal city sitting at forty-seven degrees north. It wasn't Paris, nicely warmed by the Gulf Stream, but they were enjoying temperatures hovering around twenty degrees Celsius. The residents of Pine Place would be on a free meal like flies on roadkill.

Henry knew his wife could sense his protest before it had formulated in his mind. She hissed out her plea bargain. "Listen, Henry, you smile and cook the burgers, and I will forget that you let Dash sit in the front seat. And . . ." She paused for effect. "I'll give you an extra-special good-night rub."

Henry was defenceless. "I look forward to it," he said.

"You can't be buggering off to that shed during the party, though." She gave him another kiss that made him melt.

Henry knew Millie and recognized a fair deal when he heard one. So, he helped her carry in three dozen burgers and three big Costco salads and went in to wash his hands and put on his apron to stoke the barbecue, amazed that the weather was warm enough for an outdoor party. Only a breeze every now and then reminded him of the cold that had cursed the city up until yesterday. At least that explained why so many worker bees had sidled over to Henry's driveway to ooh and aah over the station wagon rather than relax in their own gardens on a fine Friday afternoon. Most neighbours had already been over to examine the assortment of toys glued to the body. Today they had moved on to stories of Delores's accidents and intricacies of the Country Squire itself. Delores was front and centre, answering questions about her trip across the country, moose and shopping carts, and the finer parts of V6 engines.

Millie invited everyone around back. They all followed except the diehards, who were still peering under the hood. She had knotted a child-sized pink T-shirt over her dress like a beach cover. It said DELORES AND DAISY'S GREAT ADVENTURE. Henry didn't know where Millie had found the time to make pink Delores-and-Daisy T-shirts, but by the time he had the first patties on the grill, the yard had transformed into a sea of pink.

"To match Daisy's original colour," she was saying to Billy Bruce, who had just passed her a half-dozen beer. Other neighbours arrived proffering chips and wine and cheese, which Millie arranged on the glass-topped patio table.

"Thank God the weather co-operated," said Delores, following the crowd around the house. "This is the first time I've been warm since I got off the ferry."

The two egg chairs had moved from the front to the backyard and were stationed in the grass beyond the deck. A little plastic table on which sat a plate covered in Delores's favourite Newfie hors d'oeuvres stood between them.

"Anyone who would like an audience with our guest of honour can sit here next to Delores." Millie showed Delores to her chair, and she began working her way through the skewers of bologna, cheese, and tiny round pickled onions.

"These," she said, holding a skewer like an umbrella, "are even better than Mr. Henry's bumps on a log."

Henry rolled his eyes. From his post at the barbecue, he counted over twenty-five adults and at least twelve children. The children were all sporting pink T-shirts, and he found it almost impossible to pick out one from the next as they flitted between the refreshment table and the far reaches of the well-treed yard. He let his mind wander to his upcoming road trip as Delores regaled the crowd with war stories of her journey across the continent.

"Then there was the time Daisy broke down in Manhattan, right in the middle of an intersection."

"Delores takes Manhattan." Henry did not recognize the catcalling neighbour, a small man wearing a white polo shirt and shorts. "What were you doing in New York?" The man seemed absolutely smitten with this woman. *Try living with her*, thought Henry.

"I couldn't bear to cross the continent and not bring Daisy to see the Big Apple. When the tow truck came, the driver did a double take on account of Daisy's accoutrements and asked me where I wanted to go. I told him the nearest Walmart, and could I please sit in the truck with him to go there.

"Next thing I knew, the police were coming lickety-splickety, like. I thought they were going to give me a fine, but when they saw the TV cameras rolling, they offered me greetings on behalf of the NYPD. They came back later with a bumper sticker and a chicken dinner. I had no space left to put the sticker on Daisy's outside, so I stuck it on her glovebox."

The glovebox that houses the pistol, thought Henry. He had meant to go investigate when Dash was not around, but he forgot before he gave back the key.

The first burgers were circulating on a platter by the time Frank arrived wearing a Hawaiian shirt and a big straw hat. In each arm he held a huge bowl, which he set down on the table next to bottles of pop and juice.

"You brought your punch." Henry jabbed a spatula in the direction of the bowls. There were cardboard labels stuck to the sides, peeling off with the condensation.

"Yep, the bowl with a skull and crossbones has the vodka. This one with Mickey Mouse is for kids." Frank withdrew a tin of Bud Light from the chest pocket of his Hawaiian shirt and cracked it open.

"No homebrew?" The burgers sizzled, and grease sprang up in an arc. Henry withdrew his hand just before the hot oil made contact.

"Trying to go easy on it, you know, with the stones and all." Frank nodded toward his gut. "I think I'll stay here and help you man the grill." Frank clinked the tin can against Henry's glass bottle of Black Horse.

Dash and Stella moved in on the drinks table. Dash picked up the Sharpie to mark his plastic red cup with his name. Stella did the same. Henry noticed Dash ripping some cardboard off the plastic cutlery box and handing a piece to Stella. They wrote something on each piece, pulled off Frank's punch labels, and replaced them with their own. Dash's said CHUG JUG in scratchy letters. Stella's read SLURP JUICE. They both poured punch into their cups and moved off to join the growing herd of neighbourhood children.

Henry opened the silver Weber lid, and Millie swept by and took a burger. She added the toppings, splashed a bit of salad on the paper plate, and then poured up some of Frank's punch and delivered it all to Delores.

Delores raised her punch to the crowd and offered a toast. "To Henry and Millie, who invited me into their home. And to Frank, who helped Henry rescue me. Without them, I'd still be on the ground at Walmart."

Everyone applauded and raised their drinks in the air until they heard a fire truck siren approaching.

"Please don't let there be a fire on our street." Millie looked alarmed.

Henry began to sweat. The siren was getting closer to 10 Pine Place. He looked at the barbecue, and he looked at the house. No melting siding. No smoke except from the barbecue. He turned his nose to the sky and sniffed.

"I can't smell anything, either," said Frank, sniffing several times quickly, like a beagle. He laughed. "I just thought of something. Were you on campus that day some loser set fire to the microwave in the TSC?"

Henry shook his head. "Don't think I remember."

"Really? It was a big deal. Classes got cancelled, and all the concerts scheduled for that fall had to move downtown."

Henry shrugged.

"You had to notice the TSC was there one day and gone the next?"

Henry didn't answer. The sirens came to a halt, and Henry watched as Millie put down the plate she was holding and ran. Before she reached the corner of the house, she bounced back. She had run straight into a Mack Truck of a young man wearing navy pants and a short-sleeved light blue shirt with EAST END FIREFIGHTERS embroidered on the pocket. He looked like a Ken doll.

Millie visibly exhaled. "God, Payson, you frightened the life out of me."

Payson's modelling-clay features broke out into a grin. "Dick called me. Hope it's okay. I brought along some of the boys."

Henry's pasted smile turned to a frown as he watched Dick Turner, his wonky eye surveying the crowd, follow Payson into the yard.

54

Dick Comes to the Barbecue

Both Dick and his wife declined Millie's offer of pink Delores-and-Daisy T-shirts.

"What's he doing here?" Henry pretended to keep his eyes on the grill.

"Dunno," said Frank. "Maybe he wants to check up on Stella. Have you spoken to him since the SI?"

"Yes. Guess who was first on the scene when Dash fell off the skateboard? Friggin' mounted Dick. Did you know the RNC had horses?" Henry wanted to make a break for the shed, but he knew Millie would not deliver on the promised rubdown.

"News to me, too." Frank's eyes followed the action, but his body, like Henry's, did not move.

Dash trudged by and threw himself into a deck chair near Delores. "It's too hot."

Delores guffawed from her egg chair. "Honey, you ain't felt heat until you've fried eggs on the sidewalk in New Orleans."

"I thought Delores was from BC." Frank took the last pull on his beer.

"Apparently she was born in Louisiana."

"That explains the 'Yes, sir, no, sir.'" Frank tried to stifle a laugh, but his belly began to jiggle under the pineapples and palm trees on his shirt.

"We used to go visit her people when I was your age." Delores's voice carried to the barbecue. "On a day like today, folks down there be wearing winter woollies, that is if they had winter woollies." That sent her off on another laughing fit. Delores's laugh was infectious.

"You're bonkers, Miss Delores." Dash got up and disappeared around the corner of the house. He, too, was giggling heartily at Delores's words. He always seemed to be laughing in Delores's presence.

Millie turned on some music.

Delores muttered under her breath, "'Feelings,' Morris Albert, 1975."

Frank started singing. "Peelings . . . talking about peelings. Millie, don't you think we need something a bit more upbeat? I feel like I'm back in the Stanley's Steamer circa 1975."

"Feelings" was quickly replaced by Bruce Springsteen's "Cadillac Ranch." Henry cocked his ear to see if Delores would nail it, but before she had a chance to speak, wonky-eyed Dick had ambled over next to Millie and the stereo.

55

Millie Manages Dick Turner

"Dick," Millie said with a scowl and poured him a glass of punch from the children's bowl. "Didn't expect to see you here after my visit to your work." She was trying to keep her voice down. She hadn't told Henry about her trip to the cop shop.

"Wavey got your email and wanted to come. Quite the little get-to-gether." Dick's eye darted to where his wife was shaking Delores's hand.

"Yes, we're thrilled to be hosting Miss Delores."

"Hopefully you won't be hosting that rust heap in the driveway for long." Millie blinked. "Excuse me?"

"You heard me, Millie. It's against City bylaws to house junk in your yard. Have you seen Stella, by the way?" Dick began surveying the posse of nine- to twelve-year-olds who were consuming unhealthy quantities of punch and caffeinated pop and taking turns in the tire swing.

"Not lately. Saw her earlier, though. *With Dash.*"

"They better not be in a tree."

"I warned Dash not to climb anything higher than a countertop, at least until his collarbone heals."

"I didn't hear from you after you got home from the hospital. How's he doing?"

"What do you care? Dash told us you said Stella is not allowed to play with him anymore. A bit harsh, don't you think?"

"Not in light of what happened at that supermarket, Millie. Do you even know who you're married to?"

"Yes, I do, in fact. A smart, loving, upstanding citizen whose mind occasionally wanders."

Millie glanced at Henry. He raised an eyebrow and opened the barbecue cover. A cloud of smoke lifted, revealing sizzling meat. He was just far enough away that he couldn't hear their conversation. Henry gave Millie a thumbs-up to let her know he would keep his cool. Millie always told him to take the high road. But Lord Almighty, it was hard to pretend that this man did not put handcuffs on him and throw him in the back of a police car.

Frank sidled over and tipped his big-brimmed straw hat. "Hey, Millie, I think you might have to coax down your little monkey over there." Frank pointed to Dash, who was attempting to shimmy up the rope that attached the swing to the tree. He had his sling hanging limp around his neck and was relying on his good arm to do most of the work, his feet balanced on knots evenly spaced all the way up.

"Telling that boy not to climb is like telling an alcoholic to stay out of the still. Dash, come down before you break your neck."

Dash looked at his mother, smiled, and slid down. Frank raised his beer and offered one to Dick, who held up his punch and feigned a smile.

"Hi, Frank, didn't know that was you."

"Who'd you think it was? Speedy Gonzales?" A lawnmower started up in the yard backing onto Henry's.

"Wasn't looking. Just trying to find Stella."

"Why? She have to be somewhere?" Frank scratched his chin.

"No, but we have to get ready for my mother's visit tomorrow."

Frank looked to Dick and then Millie and cocked his head. An early-season housefly zipped by. "You're expecting a ten-year-old to leave a Friday night party with her friends to help you clean up? Good luck with that." Frank stifled a burp.

Dick cleared his throat. "Let me know if you see Stella. We have to get her home."

The three stood awkwardly scanning the yard until Dick excused himself. Glass in hand, he moved away from Millie and Frank, toward Payson the firefighter, who was telling Delores how he had just seen her and Daisy on the CBC news before he left the station.

"Asshole," Frank whispered behind the lip of the beer can.

56

Carter Arrives at the Barbecue

Henry momentarily forgot about Dick Turner when Carter, the recycling man, ambled in the yard wearing the Toronto Maple Leafs jersey that he wore every day, rain or shine.

Frank had moved back to the barbecue. "What's he doing here? He's usually two sheets to the wind by now."

"I swear he can sniff out free beer from five miles away." Henry shook his head.

Carter stood on a cedar stump near Delores in her egg chair and smiled, showing off his black teeth. "I'd just like everyone to know that it was me who set up the interview with Delores and Gillian Gee. Did everyone see the news this evening? Delores did a fantastic job."

"Hear, hear." Payson raised his punch glass. "Cheers to Carter. You did well in your interview, too."

"Jesus in the garden." Henry dropped a burger. "Did Gillian Gee interview Delores *and* Carter?"

"Sounds like it." Frank looked down at his shoes.

"Gillian asked how it came to be that Miss Delores is living here. I said I wasn't surprised at all when Henry and Millie invited her to stay with them. They're good people. They've been letting me keep my recyclables in their yard for years. They didn't even get mad when the bottles attracted rats . . ."

Laughter rang through the yard. Payson, the firefighter, choked on his punch. Henry's head dropped to his chest. "Take me now, Lord."

Carter sidled over to the table and poured himself a glass of punch. He raised his glass to Delores. Next thing, Delores, wearing her pink Delores-and-Daisy T-shirt over her floral dress, was balancing on her chair. Millie saw Henry run over to brace himself to catch her when she fell, but she stayed aloft. She shushed Carter. "I propose a toast to Henry and Millie."

"A toast to Henry and Millie," the crowd responded, but Henry noticed that Payson's focus had shifted to the roof. He knew the children were particularly rambunctious, but climbing on the roof was a bit over the top. Millie had laid down the law.

While everyone raised their glasses to Henry and Millie, Henry forced a smile. His eyes followed the firefighter, who went around the corner and climbed up the big red maple to ferry the little monkeys down from the roof. Luckily, everyone else stayed focused on Delores and her latest story about hitting the moose on her way into St. John's. Millie had set out a donation tin to help her with the costs of repairing the windshield and roof. Henry watched in disbelief as someone dropped a crisp $100 bill into the tin. He had heard the moose story one too many times. He squinted to see who the climbing culprits were. Aaron and Aoife McGuire. Twin devils, those two. Whew, Dash was on solid ground. Henry caught his eye as he loped over to refill his punch. He could tell by how nonchalant Dash was trying to seem that he, too, had been on the roof.

"Dasher, you promised you wouldn't climb trees."

"I didn't, Dad. We climbed the fence and the shed roof to get up on the house."

Henry sighed and was just pulling another beer out of the cooler when Carter took it out of his hand and said, "Thank you. Don't mind if I do."

That's when Dick Turner shut down the music on the ghetto blaster. He looked sterner than ever—Terminator with a wonky eye.

He said something to Payson, shot Henry a savage look, and whistled to the crowd. "This party is over," Dick shouted in his best cop voice.

"What?" said Delores, pushing herself gingerly out of her egg chair. Frank hurried over to offer support.

"Because," said Dick, looking at Henry rather than Delores, "under no circumstances should minors, especially preteens, be provided with alcohol."

57

Stella Does the Floss Again

Henry felt the party imploding. He caught a glimpse of Millie's face as she spooned a ladle from each punch bowl into separate cups to conduct a taste test. She quickly ascertained that Frank's skull and crossbone label had been replaced with the SLURP JUICE label, and the Mickey Mouse was now CHUG JUG. As a result, the glass of what Millie thought was virgin punch had left vodka easing its way through Dick's bloodstream. That explained the more than normal hyperactivity of the dozen neighbour-hood children. They were experiencing their first drunk.

Thoughts rushed through Henry's mind. First, he thanked his lucky stars that he had not been tasked with labelling the bowls. Then he thought of poor Frank. His days of potent punch were undoubtedly over. Thirdly—and this thought was far stronger than all the others jockeying for space in his brain—Henry felt an incredible hatred for Dick Turner.

Dick's wonky eye was scanning the yard, his wife by his side. "Stella," he was saying. "Stella, come on, we're going home." There was no sign of Stella.

Henry wondered how he and Dick could remain civil as neighbours. He thought of them as children, how his mother and Mrs. Turner were fast friends, sitting out on the front step while they played with Tonka trucks on the lawn. He remembered back to the day in grade ten when he and Dick had fallen out. That fall, both boys had sworn off trying out for se-nior hockey. Neither had made the team the year before. They were sick of being on the fringes of the hockey clique at school. On a Friday night before the sweat camp, they, along with another boy named Gerry, planned a camping trip for the same dates as the Triple A tournament. They pooled their money and booked a campsite in Terra Nova. Dick bought a new sleeping bag and tent. When sweat camp and tryouts were over, the coach called Henry's mother. *Why hadn't Henry been at the tryouts? Was there anything going on at home?*

When his mother assured the coach that Henry had just decided not to go for the team, the coach asked if he could come over. He called around the next evening. "You have the skills for Triple A, Henry," he said, shovel-ling in a mouthful of potatoes. "We need a defenceman like you to play alongside Hunter. What do you say?"

"But I didn't try out . . ."

"That's neither here nor there. I have the final say."

So it was that Henry became first line defenceman for the Gonzaga Vi-kings Triple A hockey team. He had to miss the camping trip, of course. When Gerry said he didn't want to go with just two of them, Dick was savage.

"How could you?" he screamed at Henry.

So, as Henry was initiated into the closed group of hockey elite, Dick went camping on his own. Henry went on to play hockey while he was in university but didn't pursue it once he met Millie and got the job at the City. Hockey now meant sitting on the couch with Frank holding a cold beer. Dick's grudge, however, was not so short-lived.

Ever since the supermarket incident, Henry had a sinking feeling that Dick was getting his revenge. Sending Henry before a judge on child abduction charges would be Dick's vindication after all these years. Henry couldn't help that he got called up to the A team, nor could he help that he missed the camping trip. He was the one who should have been mad at Dick for not letting him enjoy the glory of winning gold. Regardless, between the incident at the supermarket and Delores's station wagon taking up permanent residence on Pine Place, Henry could feel Dick's judging and wandering eyes just waiting to pounce. Now he had a second infraction to nail Henry on.

"Blimey," said Frank. "I never noticed that someone changed the labels."

"We're doomed. Serving alcohols to minors is a summary offence."

"How do you know?"

"From quizzing Millie back when she was studying in law school." Henry also knew a summary conviction could be punished by up to two years in prison. Summary offences were generally dealt with quickly. It was the indictable offences you had to worry about—like child abduction. "The homeowner might be liable. Millie will know."

"So, you think they'd charge you and Millie as hosts of the party rather than me for supplying the punch?" Frank pursed his lips.

"Who knows?" Henry shot another glance over to Dick, who had his head down discussing what to do with Payson, the firefighter.

Please let no one be injured and everyone laugh it off, thought Henry. He still had his eyes on the two men when something caught his eye from the roof. There was still a pink-clad kid up there. Payson must have missed one. Jesus, Mary, and Joseph. Henry felt an electrical charge through his chest. It was Stella Turner, and she was doing the floss. Just as Henry urgently motioned for her to come out from behind the chimney, she slipped on a piece of moss and tumbled headlong over the side of the house.

58

Saturday: Tiny Talks to Wally's Wife

Tiny sat in the F150 and tried to stretch his legs to full length. Impossible even with the oversized cab. Tumbleweeds of litter blew around the tenement lot. A Styrofoam plate flew past like a Frisbee. Tiny tried to give himself a pep talk before going in. Instead, he ended up talking to Wally, wherever that was. Wherever a good soul goes after being half-eaten by a bear.

That time I said, "Any woman who would have you isn't worth having" . . . I didn't mean it. You know I was just joking. I promise I'll take care of Flora, Wally. I'll call in once a week and make sure she has groceries and . . . Tiny swallowed hard. Enough of this—he was going in.

The door of the truck almost hit a rusty red tricycle intertwined with the remains of a green mountain bike in the next parking space. Tiny walked around the only other vehicle in the lot, a blue Hyundai circa 1985. He walked up the wooden ramp and rapped on the door. Two green garbage bags sat tied up next to the neighbour's entranceway.

"Door's open." Flora's voice was faint.

Tiny pushed the heavy steel, and the stale air hit him, dead skin and mildew. A mouse squealed in a sticky trap. Tiny brought his boot down hard. The mouse was silent. He bent over, picked it up, and tossed it out the door.

Flora looked small in her wheelchair. Tiny leaned down and felt the bones through her sweater. She tried to keep a brave face. "Thank you for coming. Wally valued your friendship. We both did." Her smile showed the beautiful young woman she once was.

Tiny swallowed, tried to talk, couldn't. Instead, he sat on the couch, sank almost to the floor. Springs poked out on the far end. He tried again. "I brought some food for Spike." He removed four tins of blue Purina Friskies from the pockets of his reflective coat and laid them on the arm of the couch. As if he understood, Spike came and jumped on Tiny's lap. Tiny's hand covered his whole back when he rubbed him.

"His favourite." Flora rolled her chair over, took the cans, put three in a cupboard, and brought the other to an electric can opener. The countertop had been lowered so she could reach. You could see the paint line from where the old counter used to be. At the sound of the can opener, Spike jumped down off Tiny's lap. He didn't quite run but wasted no time crossing the room to his dish. The dank smell of seafood offal travelled across the room.

"Decide anything about the funeral?"

"We're going to wait until the summer when the girls can come home."

"They both still in Alberta?"

"No, Allison moved to Toronto a few months back."

Tiny nodded and rose up off the couch, his cranelike frame towering a full three feet over Flora. "I'll be back Monday with groceries. Anything special you want?"

"Two tins of Klik. I like to have a bit of meat on my toast in the evening."

Tiny went to leave but turned back. He leaned down and gave Flora a hug. "I loved him, too."

"I know you did. Go on with you now or we'll both be blubbering like babies."

59

Vanessa, Bear Scat

Vanessa Hannaford had a whale dream again. This time while she was sleeping.

A dead humpback washed ashore in Outer Cove, its gargantuan bloated carcass riding the waves. Vanessa swam alongside the dead mammal. It glided in and out, in and out, never quite making it to the beach. It was in no hurry, as if in death it had all the time in the world. Its tongue, or stomach, Vanessa wasn't sure which, blew up like a Zeppelin and floated alongside the rancid carcass. Vanessa poked it with a sword, and it popped, sending down a rain of fusty whale blubber.

Vanessa woke with a start, her flannel nightgown drenched with sweat. There had been a real dead whale in Outer Cove several years back, and seven days after it appeared, the town council called upon Simon, the resident whale whisperer, Vanessa's father, to do something about the rotting carcass. The smell of rotting whale meat is not one people soon forget. The pong reached the airport kilometres away.

Her father gathered a remediation team, and they went out in a speedboat to determine if they should float it offshore in pieces or attempt to drag the whole thing out with a tug. They were only on site five minutes when a rogue wave overturned their boat, and Vanessa's father was taken out to sea. They sent divers down. Nothing. The whale was believed to be a bad omen. The townspeople wanted it out of there and fast. The remediation team decided to chop it up and tow it out in pieces. Cheaper than renting a tug. Afterwards, they threw away their clothes, even their watches, so permeating and pungent was the smell.

Vanessa was in her first year of graduate school. The week after her father's funeral, she went to her adviser and changed her area of study from whales to black bears. She never wanted to smell dead whale again.

She checked the time. Eight o'clock. Perfect. She didn't have to try and go back to sleep. Vanessa changed out of the soaking nightgown and ate a hearty breakfast. She couldn't wait to get back to the Goulds. She had scooped up a patch of Mr. Burke's shirt while the police were looking at a footprint. It tested positive for bear DNA. Of course, Vanessa knew that without the evidence. She had seen those claw marks on the dead man's neck. She didn't want to admit it after just insisting there couldn't be a black bear on the Southern Shore, but she knew without a doubt that one was there. Vanessa twirled her favourite blue paisley neck scarf in anticipation of the bear hunt.

By ten o'clock she had a team of students waiting in the university field truck ready to comb through the woods for traces of bear scat and fur. Damn that Constable Turner for telling her to wait until their investigation was complete. Phooey. They were taking too much time. If there was more evidence of black bear to be found, beyond the mutilated body of a tattooed dead man, Vanessa was going to find it before it disappeared. Plus, following orders was not one of Vanessa's fortes. She shoved some more sample bags into her backpack and ran to the car.

Singsongy Darryl, who Vanessa had run into at the supermarket, waited on the lawn with Holly, a middle-aged grad student from Holyrood. Darryl climbed in front for the legroom while Holly made herself comfortable in back. Vanessa drove two blocks to pick up two younger students. They were not on the lawn where they said they'd be. Vanessa unbuckled and headed into the basement apartment where she'd picked them up before. They were semi-propped up in opposing corners of the porch, hoodies pulled tight around their faces.

"Must have been some party," said Vanessa. "I've seen more life in a pile of laundry."

"Sorry, Professor Hannaford," said the one called Power. Her first name was Cheryl, but everyone called her Power for some reason Vanessa had not quite figured out.

"Come on. The others are waiting."

While the two students installed themselves in the back of the Civic, one on either side of Holly, Darryl swatted the bobble-head moose on the dash. "Did you hear about the sighting on the Southern Shore?"

"What sighting? When?" This from Holly in the back seat.

"Last week." Darryl tapped the moose again. Its felted head nodded.

"Where?"

"Between Bay Bulls and Petty Harbour." The back seat squeaked under the weight of its inhabitants. Darryl turned to size up his colleagues. "It was on the East Coast Trail website. Professor Hannaford, you should take a peek at the sleeping beauties."

Vanessa glanced in the rear-view. Holly was sandwiched between the two like marshmallow in a s'more. She nudged the younger of the two grad students off her shoulder.

"I am not a pillow."

"Sorry, sorry." A mumbled apology came out of Cody, who was not as well-known to Vanessa. She had only become his adviser in the past two months. His head was back, Adam's apple facing the ceiling, mouth gaping. A snore erupted from the one called Power. Holly rolled her eyes. Vanessa directed her eyes back to Water Street and the Southern Shore Highway.

"I'm sitting up front on the way back." Holly attempted to open her Thermos with arms pinned to her sides.

"No can do. I'll never fit back there." Darryl tickled Cody's nose with a tissue. He responded with a sneeze.

"Who saw the bear?"

"Two hikers."

"When was that?" Holly shifted, her knee hitting the back of Vanessa's seat.

"About a week ago."

A week ago? Vanessa's mind spun as she drove. The Ruby Rose chicken plant, where the dead man was found, was midway between those two trailheads.

"Did anyone get hurt?" Holly again.

"No, but the Association is advising all hikers to be on the lookout for bears."

"What are they supposed to do if they see one?"

"Give it a wide berth." Darryl laughed. "And contact wildlife officials."

Vanessa snaked down Old Bay Bulls Road as her students talked. She couldn't help but replay Friday night at Cub Camp in her mind. What was it that Dash's father had said? *I thought it might've been a black bear.* Maybe it wasn't a coyote at Camp D that night. Maybe Dash's father wasn't off his rocker after all. Vanessa had just come to the Goulds, where they had planned to stop and pick up a picnic lunch. They poked the two young ones awake and went into the supermarket.

"I checked with the Department of Fisheries and Land Resources," said Darryl as they waited at the cash.

"Yeah? What did they say?"

"They said that, except for the hikers, there were no other sightings. They set up a bear trap in Shoal Bay as a precaution."

This comment intrigued Vanessa until she and her crew were in the woods behind the Ruby Rose plant. It took no more than ten minutes from the time they left the car until one of the students found the first mound of fresh bear scat.

"Bingo." Cheryl Power was wide awake now.

All told, in three hours the researchers collected two dozen fur samples and five mounds of scat, three of which contained yellow material consistent with a Ruby Rose work shirt.

This was Vanessa's chance to make history, like her father had done with whales.

60

Day Five of Living with Delores

"I challenge you to a game of Fork-Knife, Miss Delores." Dash's shadow whipped through the kitchen, where Henry sat on a spindle-back chair. Ever since Delores had set up permanent residence in his recliner in the living room, Henry felt like he was an unwanted guest in his own home. The chair had begun to smell like Delores, or like a perfume she wore, which in turn smelled disconcertingly like the scent of one of Henry's old girlfriends. It wasn't a bad smell, but it felt as if she had marked her territory on his La-Z-Boy.

"You're on, Mr. Dash." Delores leaped up and swished off to the granny flat just as fast as her generous back end would take her. She was wearing a signed Marc-André Fleury jersey over her floral pants. The logo was an eagle holding a hockey stick in what looked like a cyclone. She was all set up on Henry's computer that Millie insisted be moved to the in-law suite.

"She needs access to the Internet, Henry."

"What about me?"

"You can use my laptop."

"It's a Mac. I can't use a Mac—everything's backwards."

"Oh, Henry." Millie ruffled his hair and cupped his cheek in her hand. Henry had not received his rubdown after the barbecue Friday night. Once the pandemonium died down, no one was in the mood for anything but sleep.

Henry watched Delores's porky ass disappear through the door. She seemed to have recovered overnight. Her bruises were fading quickly, and she was moving about as if she hadn't been creamed by a shopping cart. He didn't move. He just sat there on the hard oak chair, drinking his camomile tea, going over the details of Friday night's disastrous party. Stella appeared unhurt—the eavestrough and hedge had broken her fall—but she did have some nasty scratches. Dick said he was going to press charges and that Stella, under no circumstances, was to come near any member of Henry's family. And vice versa.

Henry knew Frank felt terrible. He had already called this morning to invite Henry to come watch the Saturday night game at his house. Henry declined, and Frank's disappointment was palpable. "Come on, Henry, it's the first game of the final round: Vegas Golden Knights vs. the Washington Capitals."

Frank said he really wanted to watch the game with a buddy. He was a diehard Marc-André Fleury fan, and the game was in Vegas, so they had home ice advantage. It was also the first time Washington had reached the finals in twenty years. But Henry had had enough socializing for a year last night.

"Dash, use your Boogie Bomb." Delores's voice made Henry slop tea onto his hand. They were on day five of their new living arrangement. He had to hold up his end of the bargain or he wouldn't make it to the Spring Tune-Up. They would send her packing as soon as he was done the ride. He would discuss it with Millie as soon as she came home from her errands.

"Henry, I'm just going out to get some groceries." Millie didn't call it "going to the supermarket" anymore. She knew it set him off. It was kind of her.

From the donations taken in at the barbecue, Delores almost had enough to replace the windshield in the Ford LTD. Millie had booked an appointment at the glass shop for ten o'clock this morning, and where it was just across the street from the supermarket, she offered to take it in.

Delores was so excited about the idea of the windshield being fixed that she was even more vocal than usual in the Fortnite competition. This afternoon, she was supposed to be taking Frank on some sort of adventure. Henry was looking forward to the break, even though he was well aware that the doctor had not given Delores the go-ahead to drive.

61

Frank and Delores Go for a Drive in Daisy

"Mr. Frank? How are you today?" It was Saturday afternoon, and Delores had come right in Frank's house without knocking. "You ready for a spin?"

"Yes indeed. I feel wonderful." It was true. Frank was in a good mood. He'd just had news that on Monday the City would begin installing new parking signs downtown. People parking on the waterfront would have to download an app—Pay-by-Phone, they called it—and pay even if the meter had no head. It was all blue skies and apple pies. "I have decided to ignore the press. Today I read the editorial and didn't even feel the need to vape."

"That's good. You know you can't go vaping in Daisy, don't you? She wouldn't take to all that smoke."

"Don't worry, Miss Delores, I would never smoke in Daisy. I feel so good, I could give up smoking. From now on, I am going to seize the day. You know, always look on the bright side of life." Frank put on his best British accent.

Delores was in the living room picking chips off the chesterfield, her sneakered feet sticking out of her floral pants. She started singing "Always Look on the Bright Side of Life." Then, under her breath, she switched to a speaking voice. "Eric Idle, *Monty Python's Life of Brian*, 1979."

"What did you say?" Frank had heard, but he wanted to see if Delores would comment on her strange habit.

"Nothing. Mr. Frank, do you like my hockey sweater?" It was a signed Marc-André Fleury jersey.

"Not too shabby."

"Vegas's first year in the franchise, and they've made it all the way to the Stanley Cup finals. Are you excited about tonight's game, Mr. Frank?" So, Delores was as savvy about hockey as Henry had said.

"Yes, except for one thing."

"What's that?"

"I won't be watching it with Henry."

"I thought you two always watched the Saturday night games together. Miss Millie says Henry should have married you."

"Yeah, well, sometimes I think I should've married Henry."

"Why did your wife leave you, Mr. Frank?"

"I don't really think there was one reason. We just grew apart and forgot why we fell in love in the first place." He didn't mention the cookies.

Delores nodded. "Why isn't Henry going to watch the game with you?"

"He's definitely not himself. In all the years we've lived next door to one another, Henry has only missed a Saturday night game twice—once he was out of town, and the other time, Millie was in labour with Dash. And he's never missed watching a final with me."

"Shame, because tonight's game will set the tone for the rest of the series."

"I know." Frank shook his head and changed the subject. "Delores, I can't figure out where you stored things like your jerseys when you were driving across the country."

"In my suitcases in Daisy's back end. I just moved them up when it was time to go to bed."

Even though it was no longer freezing outside, Frank went to the back porch for his Mackintosh and glanced out the back window. "Come look at this, Delores."

Delores arrived at Frank's side quicker than he would have imagined. "Well, would you look at that."

A gaggle of kids were playing soccer in Pine Park, Dash's sneakers serving as goalposts. Stella Turner was in net. Aoife came in for a shot, deked her out, and scored. All the children on both teams tackled Aoife and Stella and formed a pyramid of youthful energy. Dash jumped off the heap and pulled Stella out from under the pile, and the two sat to the side, laughing and swatting one another.

Frank's uncharacteristic jubilant mood turned slightly sour as he and Delores started through the house to Henry's driveway to pick up Daisy so they could go for a drive before the game. "Thank God Dick's house doesn't back onto the park."

"Why?"

Frank took one last look out the back window. Stella and Dash were dancing. They were waving their arms back and forth in front of and behind their stomachs. It looked like someone had made a video and pressed fast forward.

"He said that if he caught Stella playing with Dash ever again, he would redden her hide. If he sees them playing in the park together, there'll be hell to pay. For Stella and Dash and for Henry."

"These misunderstandings occur when neighbours don't get to know each other."

"But Dick Turner and Henry have known each other for over fifty years."

"Oh!" Delores gasped.

"Yeah, there's been friction between those two for decades."

"Why does he dislike Henry and Dash so much?"

"I have no idea. I think it goes back to high school, and Stella sliding headlong off Henry's roof into the hedge Friday didn't help matters."

"But Stella didn't get hurt. The eavestrough and hedge broke her fall."

"I know that, and you know that, and Henry knows that. But Dick Turner is not a man you can talk sense to. He has it in for Henry at the best of times, and now he feels he has a reason."

"Does Stella have any siblings?"

"Now, that's a funny story. Dick had three children with his first wife. They're all in their twenties now."

"Dick was married before?" Delores's eyes grew round, as if divorce were something novel to her.

"Yep, Stella is the product of Dick and his trophy wife. You know, Miss Tight T-shirt. Did you meet her Friday night?"

"Wavey, yes, she was sweet."

"Yes, well, that's one word to describe her. Anyway, the funny thing is that when Henry and Frank were both in their late forties, both their wives got pregnant. Henry and Millie said they never wanted children, but Dash was meant to be."

"How so?"

"Henry's fifteen-year-old vasectomy failed. Mutant scar tissue grew a tunnel around titanium clips, and the determined sperm banged their way through. So, Stella and Dash grew up together, and no matter how hard Dick tries to keep them apart, they just become closer. They're inseparable."

"I get a sense that the neighbourhood vibe has been out of whack since the barbecue."

"It's since before that. Henry is having a run of bad luck."

"Miss Millie said Henry has to go to court Monday about the mix-up at Sundries."

"Yes, his court case is on Monday morning. He was supposed to come golfing with us, the Big Brothers, Big Sisters tournament. He's been looking forward to it for months."

"That's a shame."

"Yep, and guess who stepped in to take Henry's place?"

"No . . ." Delores's eyes widened.

"Yep, good old Mad-Eye Turner."

"That's not very charitable of you, Mr. Frank."

"Delores, it was Dick who arrested Henry at the supermarket."

She gasped. "That's not what neighbours are supposed to do."

"I know, but to be fair, Dick had a lot of pressure on, there were all these witnesses, and the girl is a first-time mother and all. If Dick ends up testifying at Henry's trial, he could put a real black spin on things."

"That's why Mr. Henry is in such a bad mood. And to think I thought it had something to do with me." Delores flung her purple tote into Daisy's trunk. "Enough gossip. Let's make our first stop Walmart so I can say hello to everyone." She threw Frank the keys. "Here you go, Mr. Frank, let's see if you can make Daisy purr."

"Ta." Frank caught the keys like a midfielder. He was secretly hoping he'd get to drive Daisy.

62

Frank at the Racetrack

Frank took the wheel and peered out like he was playing Super Mario. "That's great that you got the windscreen fixed. Really helps with visibility."

"Yes, everyone was very kind to donate."

"Wow, you got enough donations to cover the full cost."

"Somehow I suspect Miss Millie bumped up the pot. She wouldn't let me see what was in there, and she took Daisy in this morning to get it replaced." Delores spun through the radio stations, settling on OZFM. Amy Winehouse was singing "Rehab." Delores whispered under her breath. "*Back to Black*, 2006."

"Do you need to pick up any food?" asked Frank.

"No, sir, Miss Millie insists on making all my meals."

More like Henry, thought Frank. Millie was working like crazy to come up with a solid defence for Henry on the kidnapping charge.

The Walmart staff greeted Delores like a rock star. They refused to take money for the gardening shears and the case of Diet Pepsi she had hoisted into the shopping cart. As Frank was busy sliding the Pepsi into the boot, Delores was busy sliding her rear end into the front seat behind the wheel.

"Delores, the doctor said you're not allowed . . ."

"Yes, sir. I know all that. But where's your sense of adventure, Mr. Frank? I'm gonna take you for a ride. Plus, Mr. Henry told me about your lack of a driver's licence."

"That blighter. I'm going to . . ."

"Calm down, Mr. Frank, no need to get your knickers knotted. I'll give you a chance to drive again in a bit."

Frank sulked while Delores whipped onto the Outer Ring Road and passed by the exit for their neighbourhood.

"Uh, Delores, that's where we get off," said Frank, checking his seat belt.

"Not today, Mr. Frank."

They sailed out the Trans-Canada past Paddy's Pond and the Witless Bay Line. They had just passed Holyrood and Salmonier Line when Delores pulled a map out of her door and began to consult it.

"You be my eyes for a minute, Mr. Frank. We're almost there."

"Uh, Delores, eyes on the road." Frank took the wheel and steered the car off the shoulder and back into the lane. The noise from the rumble strips made Delores look up from the map.

"Thank you, Mr. Frank. I know where I'm going now." Delores left the dual carriageway and whipped down the Avondale access road until they came to the entrance of the Eastbound Speedway.

"Oh, crap," said Frank, realizing her intentions. "Uh, Delores, the racetrack is closed for the season."

"Not to worry, Mr. Frank. I came prepared."

Delores put Daisy in park, strode around to the tailgate, and took out the shears. She then proceeded to snip the rope that barred the entrance to the track, which was slick with rain that had fallen in the night. Frank swallowed. He had been here only once to see a NASCAR rally with Kaitlyn before she transformed into the Creature from the Black Lagoon.

"Delores, you can't take the wagon on the track."

"Tighten your seat belt, Mr. Frank. I'm gonna see what Daisy here can do."

They entered the oval, and Delores gunned the engine. Black smoke spewed from Daisy's exhaust. The Ford LTD was surprisingly gutsy. They tore around the asphalt in less than a minute. Delores was hooting and hollering. Frank was pressed back into his seat, his right hand tight to the door handle. "Delores, you're giving her a bit too much welly."

"Wanna do that again?" shouted Delores.

Yes, thought Frank. "No," he said.

Delores ignored his response. They rocketed around the track a second time, picking up speed. The tires spun, and the smell of burning rubber filled the car. It was exhilarating. Just inside the oval was a jump made of brown earth for monster trucks and dirt bikes. Delores saw it the same time Frank did and veered the LTD in that direction. She put her foot to the floor, and the engine screamed in protest. Frank closed his eyes. When he opened them, they were airborne. A moment later, they smacked down, the front end crunched but amazingly rebounded, and they continued through the dirt and back onto the track.

"Good shocks," he managed to say before Delores whipped around and went for another go. Frank wondered what the doctor would say if he could see her now.

That's when they saw the orange-clad security guard coming at them waving the black and white flag. Delores slowed down, rolled down the window, and smiled.

"Nice track you got here, son."

He was gobsmacked.

"You're . . . you're Delores and Daffodil." His tone was reverential.

"Daisy." Delores did not seem bothered by the mistake. "We came to try out your track."

"How did you get in?" asked the guard.

"Just drove on in." Delores fluttered her eyelashes. "Were we not allowed?"

"There's supposed to be a barricade," said the guard.

"You best get that fixed," said Delores, smiling her snaggle-toothed smile. "You want to take Daisy for a go-round?"

The security guard beamed. "Really?"

"Sure." Delores turned off the engine and slid out. Frank followed suit. "If you go over the jump, make sure to gun 'er good."

"Can you take a picture on my phone?"

"Of course," said Delores. "Mr. Frank here will do the honours."

Frank snapped pics as the guard circled the track once cautiously, then, leaving caution to the wind, the guard picked up speed and navigated Daisy over the mound of dirt, bouncing back down and slowing to a halt shortly before reaching them. On his face was a smile for the picture books. Frank had snapped several photos, both on his and the guard's phone.

"You have a good day, now, you hear," said Delores. "We'll be out of your hair as soon as Mr. Frank here gets his turn. You ready to take the wheel, Mr. Frank?"

Frank did not answer. He was in full grand mal seizure.

63

Game One, Stanley Cup Playoffs

The Vegas Knights had taken to performance art in their pre-game shows. Knights in golden armour skated and battled men wearing red capes with black hoods who represented the Capitals of the east. There were projected arrows, robots with illuminated drums and clothing. It was all a bit over the top really. Henry had seen the show last week where a knight with a sword took down a jet. If that's what the shows were like on the Strip, Henry had no desire to go. Dash, however, lapped it up.

"We can't watch the game without Miss Delores." Dash pulled the tab on a can of Coke, the gasses sizzling out. The Vegas players in their dark grey jerseys with gold and red stripes skated out for the warm-up.

"Henry, did you tell him he could drink Coke?" Millie stood with her hands on her hips.

"Only half a tin, Dasher. You'll be bouncing off the wall." Henry passed Dash a glass.

"Dad, you didn't answer my question. Where's Miss Delores?" Dash poured a half-inch of black liquid into the glass and proceeded to drink from the can.

"Delores? I told you, she went for a drive with Frank, and they're not home yet." Henry was still in a bad mood. He always wore his Boston toque to watch playoff games, no matter who was playing, but his toque was being held as evidence. *Do not think about Dick.* He pushed his nails into his palms.

Dash parted the curtains and looked out the window. "Where did she go with Mr. Parrell?"

"I have no idea. Do you know, Millie?" Henry ripped open a large bag of Miss Vickie's salt and vinegar chips and poured them into a plastic bowl.

Millie took the chips before Henry could add the entire contents of the bag. "Delores wouldn't say. Insisted it was a surprise. I thought they'd be back by now, though."

"She said she was going to watch the game with us. She put on her jersey this morning." Dash looked deflated as he chugged his cola. "Mr. Parrell should be here, too."

Henry grunted and turned up the volume. He and Dash settled in on the couch. "No farting while the game is on, you hear me?"

Dash nodded. Millie puttered. She always puttered for the first period.

When they started the American national anthem, Dash stood, hand to chest, and sang along. "Why so proudly we stand at the twilight's last beaming / Shoes with broad stripes, bright stars, through the peril must bite / Or the ram parts we watched were so gallantly dreaming." By the time the puck dropped, the first of the caffeine was coursing its way through Dash's ten-year-old veins, and his legs were jiggling up and down, making the couch cushions bounce. Washington took a penalty around seven minutes in. Colin Miller scored on the power play with a slapshot from the blue line. One-nothing Knights. Dash jumped so high off the couch that he knocked out a ceiling tile.

"Down, boy, down." Henry took the tin of Coke to pour the remains down the drain in the bar sink. It was bone dry.

"Miss Delores is missing it." Dash did laps around the rec room while #6 did his victory lap around the ice.

Eight minutes later, things went sour for the Knights when Washington scored two goals forty-two seconds apart. Brett Connolly first, then Nicklas Bäckström.

Millie came and sat down with them when there was five minutes left in the first period. "Dash, go get in your PJs at the intermission."

"It's not a school night."

"True enough." Millie went to the fridge and got out a beer for herself and one for Henry. "Dash, look at the chips on the couch." She laid down her beer and began scooping crumbs into the palm of her hand.

With less than two minutes left, Karlsson had a breakaway. Henry and Dash moved forward in tandem. The front door clanged open.

"Maybe that's them." Millie stood up to see. One set of rapid footsteps on the stairs. Whoever it was, they were in a hurry.

On the screen, Karlsson moved in on Washington's goalie.

"*Karlsson scores!*" The Knights fans went wild at T-Mobile Arena in Vegas.

"Karlsson, Karlsson." Dash ran more laps around the couch. He high-fived his father. The footsteps arrived, and Delores, breathless and wild-haired, fell into the room. Dash grabbed her hands and tried to spin her around as if playing Ring Around the Rosie. "Karlsson scored. Did you see, Miss Delores? Karlsson tied it up."

Delores freed herself from Dash, bent over, and tried to level her breathing. She crouched down to Henry. "Mr. Frank . . . he passed out."

"What? Where?" Henry was on his feet.

"At the racetrack." Delores steadied herself by putting a hand on the back of the couch.

"Racetrack?"

"Yes, the paramedics said it was a seizure."

"Seizure?"

"Yes, epilepsy."

"Is he at the hospital?"

"No, he said he'd be fine with rest and convinced them to let me take him home."

"Where is he now?"

"In Daisy."

Henry ran up the stairs and out the door in his stocking feet. So that was why Frank didn't drive.

64

Saturday into Sunday: Rescuing Frank

Henry and Delores helped Frank out of the station wagon and into the house while Millie held the door. They struggled to get him to the couch in the living room. His leg scuffed up against the coffee table as they sat him down. Dark circles ringed his eyes.

Dash stood glued in place. "Is Mr. Parrell going to die?"

Frank didn't say anything, but he looked a bit dismayed at Dash's pronouncement.

"No, Dasher," said Henry. "He had a seizure, and now he's really tired."

Millie got Patty on speakerphone. "Have you ever known Frank to have a seizure?"

"Of course, he's epileptic. He collapsed at our wedding, for God's sake."

"Don't bring that up again . . ." Frank croaked, trying to sit up.

Henry pushed Frank back down on the cushions. "We didn't know . . ."

Patty continued. "Right at the beginning of the first dance. It was like he was being exorcised. Can you imagine my embarrassment?"

"Not exactly." Millie put a hand on Frank's shoulder. He had closed his eyes and appeared to be readying himself for a reprimand. "What should we do?"

"About what?" It sounded like Patty had company. Laughter and clinking glasses could be heard in the background.

Delores went to speak but held back. Henry piped up. "About Frank. Should we watch him while he sleeps?"

"What for? He'll be fine in the morning. Oh, by the way, what did you get arrested for?"

Henry covered his nose with both his hands and breathed in.

"I saw Dick taking you away in the cruiser."

"Just a misunderstanding. You know I'd never break the law, Patty."

"I don't know anything. Tell Frank something for me when he wakes up."

"Okay."

"Tell him if he ever gives my daughter money to stick needles in her body again, I will give him something to seizure over. Now you'll have to excuse me. I have guests." Patty hung up.

"What was that all about?" Henry cocked his head.

"I think she was referring to the tattoo that Mr. Frank's daughter got on her titty." Delores whispered the word "titty."

"What?" Henry covered Dash's ears.

"Don't worry, Dad. I've heard worse than that."

"Okay, everyone, let's regroup." Millie was taking charge, but Henry could hear the panic under her words. She was also blowing air out of her mouth in little puffs, like she was in labour. She did not offer anything more.

"Well, what do we do now?" Henry asked.

"Why don't we call Frank's daughter?" Delores sat on the end of the couch on Frank's feet. That seemed to wake him up a bit. He squirmed until he dislodged them from under her.

"Good idea. What's Kaitlyn's number, Frank?" Millie nudged Frank's shoulder.

"Don't bother Kaitlyn. She's too busy." Frank's voice came out a mumble.

Millie ignored him. "Frank, what is Kaitlyn's number?" She was using her court voice.

Frank recited the number. Millie pummelled her iPhone screen.

"Hi, Kaitlyn, this is Millie."

"Hi, Mrs. Puddester, wassup?"

"I don't want to alarm you, but your father's just had a seizure. We have him here at our house. I wondered if you wanted me to come pick you up."

"Why?"

"So you can be with him."

"Uh . . ." Kaitlyn paused. "I can't do anything for him. He usually just sleeps it off."

"Okay." Millie looked to the others. Frank gave a dispirited shrug. "I'll check in tomorrow and let you know how he's doing."

"Sounds good." Kaitlyn was chewing gum as she spoke. Music played in the background.

"Goodbye, Kaitlyn." Millie hung up.

"I'll go get a blanket." Henry scurried to the linen closet and took out two blankets crocheted by his mother. He could feel the upstairs and downstairs of his heart pumping. "I'm going to stay here with Frank. You can all get ready for bed."

"Aww, Dad, what about the game?"

"You can watch Don't Tell Me the Score in the morning."

Millie gave Henry a kiss and led Dash out of the room.

Delores was uncharacteristically quiet. "Good night and God bless." She disappeared into the mother-in-law suite.

Frank was fast asleep by the time Henry had wiped down and installed himself in the La-Z-Boy. It still smelled of Delores, and Henry turned this way and that, trying to settle. His eyes kept going to Frank's prone form on the couch. It was as if both their lives were hurtling off their tracks on separate preordained crash courses.

His court hearing was Monday morning. He reviewed what he was supposed to say. His next practice session with Gloria was set for Sunday afternoon. Gloria and Millie had decided Henry must avoid the topic of Cub Camp eggs at all costs.

"The eggs tend to set him off on demented tangents," he'd overheard Millie tell Gloria.

"That's not fair," Henry protested, but he knew he'd never win any court-related battle with Millie.

When he thought about it, Henry didn't stand a chance against Millie in any aspect of their married life, parenting battles especially. He remembered when Dash was three and Millie had bought a series of Christian videos called *Veggie Tales*. Apparently, the mother of the creator—video creator, that is, not the Virgin Mary—took offence to her son portraying Jesus as a vegetable. To appease his mother, the creator featured no stories from the New Testament in the videos.

It wasn't until the creator's mother was dead and gone that he came out with a *Veggie Tales* nativity set complete with a little swaddled carrot lying in a manger. Henry was thrilled and ran out to the Book and Bible Store. When he arranged the nativity on the mantel that Christmas Eve, Millie ranted, but Dash, three at the time, loved playing with all the figures. He was especially taken with Baby Lou Carrot as Jesus. The following Christmas when they took out the decorations, the *Veggie Tales* nativity had vanished.

Dash howled. Millie shrugged. "Things go missing all the time," she said.

Yeah, like babies, thought Henry, lying there in his chair. When he finally went to sleep, he had an elaborate dream. In it, Bob the Tomato with Henry's face was being dragged to prison by Mr. Nezzer who had a wandering eye. When Bob got to his jail cell, a gang of green onions known as The Scallions told him he had to sleep on the concrete floor. Junior Asparagus came to the window. He was playing Fortnite on Qwerty, the computer, and wanted Bob to play with him through the bars. A sheriff's officer, Larry the Cucumber with Frank's face, came and told Bob it was time to appear before Judge Madame Blueberry. Laura Carrot represented Bob but was unsuccessful. Grandma Gourd cried as Larry the Cucumber led the shackled Bob out of the courtroom, all the while singing, "Oh, Where Is My Hairbrush?" Then, out on Duckworth Street, Mr. Lunt came with a black handgun and shot a hole right through Bob's heart, and red tomato guts sprayed the sidewalk.

Henry woke with a start. Frank was lying on the couch looking at him. "And you were worried about me. You're the one who looks like you're going to pop your clogs."

65

Henry Practises with Gloria

"The Golden Knights beat Washington six to four." Dash closed the iPad. He was allowed to watch Don't Tell Me the Score at the table as long as he wasn't eating. As promised, Henry watched alongside him. And Frank, who had got up and announced he had the appetite of a pregnant elephant, was looking on from the other side. Millie was busy at the stove turning out pancakes like she was a short-order cook in a twenty-four-hour diner.

"Who scored the winner?" Frank doused his pancakes in syrup.

"Tomas Nosek. He scored to tie it up at the end as well." Dash got ready to attack the mountain on his plate.

"Where's he from?" Between flips, Millie was enjoying her usual breakfast of dry toast and tea.

"Czech Republic." Dash's cheeks were puffed out like a chipmunk.

"Dash, Honey. Don't talk with your mouth full. You sound like a bloated woodchuck."

"How do you know what a bloated woodchuck sounds like?" Dash still had his mouth full.

"I met one last week."

"Mom, you're strange."

Talk turned to the racetrack. Henry, Delores, Dash, Millie, and Frank sat around the table like a new-age family. Dash's eyes danced with delight, but Delores was still surprisingly quiet. Except for a thank you when Millie served her breakfast, she hadn't said a word.

"Mr. Parrell, tell me the part again when Miss Delores cut through the rope to get in." Dash's hair was wild. Henry would have to get him shorn soon.

At eleven, Gloria arrived and air-kissed her way around the room. She wore yellow glasses with silver stars.

Henry did a double take. "You and Elton John share a designer?"

Millie batted at Henry's shoulder. "Henry, that's not very nice."

Gloria pulled off her shoes. "Don't worry, Millie, I know he's joking."

Henry wasn't joking. Did she think she was in some sort of stage musical? "Okay, let's get started."

Henry motioned for Millie to come over. She bent down to him.

"I can't practise with Delores in here," he whispered.

"Why not?"

"I just can't. You've got to get her to leave."

Millie stood up. "Delores, why don't you and Dash play a round of Fortnite while Henry and Gloria review some things?"

"Wicked." Dash dipped his last bite of pancake into his milk. "Miss Delores, did you know they just introduced balloons? You can have six balloons, but if you deploy all of 'em at the same time, you float up and can't stop."

"Sounds dangerous." Delores speared one last pancake on her fork. "Thank you, Miss Millie. I've had elegant sufficiency."

"More like elephant efficiency," Henry said as she disappeared into the granny flat.

Frank reinstalled himself on the couch, coffee in hand. Henry stayed at the table while Gloria explained how things would unfold in court. She then began her mock interrogation.

Gloria: "What were you thinking when you saw the car seat in your shopping cart?"

194

Henry: "Who the frig put that thing in there?"

Gloria: "Henry, don't say that. Why don't you say something like, 'I was surprised to find a car seat in my cart, Your Honour.' Now, let's try another one. How were you the morning you went to Sundries?"

Henry: "I was a bit woozy from the medicine I took . . ."

Gloria: "Good. That's excellent. Now, what was it that you took?"

Henry: "I thought it was cold and sinus medication, but it turns out it was Dilaudid, an opioid. Stronger than morphine."

Gloria: "How did the Dilaudid make you feel?"

Henry: "I was thirsty. I couldn't think straight. Sometimes I saw two of something when there was only one there."

Millie: "Great stuff, Henry. Did you have a headache?"

Henry: "Yes, but I had one anyway from the sinus pain."

Gloria: "Okay . . . let's refocus. Just say that you had a headache, and don't mention that you had one anyway."

Henry: "Right."

Gloria: "Did you see anyone at the supermarket you knew?"

Henry: "What difference does it make who I knew and didn't?" Henry wanted to lie down.

Gloria: "Well, someone you know might be able to say that your behaviour was out of character for you that morning because of your reaction to the drug."

Henry: "I saw Dash's Cub leader. I ran into her with my shopping cart."

Gloria: "On purpose?"

Henry: "No, not on purpose. Why would I do something like that on purpose?"

Gloria: "No reason." She looked at Millie. "Anyone else you knew?"

Henry: "I saw Millie's yoga teacher and her daughter."

Gloria: "Maybe we can call them as witnesses?"

Millie shook her head.

Gloria: "Anyone else?"

Henry: "I saw Dick Turner."

Gloria: "The police officer who arrested you?"

Henry: "Yes, I saw him as I was leaving Sundries. Then, next thing I know, he's barging in here and—"

Gloria: "Wait a minute. Back up. Are you saying he entered your home without permission?"

Henry thought hard. "He said, 'Mind if I come in?'"

Gloria: "And you said?"

Henry: "I didn't say yes, that's for sure."

Gloria's lips smiled. Her forehead did not. "Now we're getting somewhere. Okay, let's go through it one more time."

66

Monday: Vanessa in the Lab

Vanessa woke Monday morning from yet another disturbing dream. Why couldn't she just sleep without having to attend a film festival every night? At least she hadn't dreamt about whales. She was halfway up a mountain. A bear appeared at the treeline, hunched over a kill. He snarled and stood on his hind legs. Despite the danger, Vanessa continued up. She wanted a better look. When she got there, the bear was dragging a carcass down into scraggly trees. It wasn't an animal carcass—it was human. It was her own body, her Kelly-green scarf hanging from the bear's jaws.

At least now Vanessa was safe in her lab. Her grad students, Darryl, Cody, and Holly, were working on extracting DNA from the bear scat samples.

"I have a positive for human DNA in Sample Two." Darryl raised his linked hands in the air as if he had just won an Olympic medal.

Cody came over for a fist bump. "Way to go, man. Sample One turned up nothing."

Vanessa kept calm, but inwardly she was conflicted. She and her team had confirmed that at least one black bear was living on the Avalon Peninsula. Of course, they didn't need the samples to tell them that. But nothing is true until science backs it up. That day in the woods, besides the scat, Darryl had found an area with flattened grass and trees where a bear had bedded down, and they had all seen scores of pug marks in the fresh mud.

Darryl laid the clear plastic case containing Sample Two on the table and picked up Sample Four.

Holly let out a whoop. "I got human D in Sample Three."

Vanessa remembered what it was like to be in the lab as a student and shared their excitement. "Troops, I think it's time to call the Royal Newfoundland Constabulary."

67

Henry in Court

When Monday morning smacked him in the face, Henry had to will his fifty-eight-year-old frame up and over the side of the bed. He was so utterly gutted, he had to manually assist each leg.

On top of that, he woke with a brutal pain in his right jaw. He clamped it open and shut a few times to test its working order. It performed like a hinge on a finicky gate. He felt as if the bones in his cheek and jaw were rotting from the inside out.

Could it be cancer, like his mother?

Naw, it must be stress. He always clenched when he was upset. He had spent the night tossing and turning over what would unfold in court. His heart palpitated so much that he woke Millie around 3:00 a.m. and told her he was having a heart attack.

"It's just nerves, love. Go back to sleep." Millie rolled over.

Now, with grey daylight coming through the windows, Henry looked over at Millie's side of the bed. Empty. Of course it was. No matter what haunted her days, Millie slept like the dead every night and hopped out of bed bright-eyed and ready to quash her opponents. Henry could smell the coffee brewing, so he dragged himself to the closet, pulled on the suit he hadn't worn since he stopped working, and limped down to the kitchen.

The court appearance was first thing. On the way downtown, the butterflies in his stomach threatened to lift into his lungs.

"I'm more nervous about seeing Dick than the judge."

"I know, but we had to call him to ascertain that he entered our house without a warrant. But I get what you're saying. You're not exactly the best of pals after Stella fell off the roof Friday night."

Henry sighed. "We've never been the best of pals."

"You two, it's like you're still in grade school. I wish you'd grow up."

"But it's not me, Millie. It's all Dick. He's the one who stopped talking to me."

"And how many years ago was that?"

"Well, we were . . ." Henry started to calculate.

"Rhetorical question, Henry. I think we're lucky that they decided not to call the mother. I suspect they realized she would do more harm than good to her own case."

Henry rubbed his hands on his cheeks. "What about the other people at Sundries? Could they cause damage?"

"We'll see. Just remember what you and Gloria rehearsed, and don't stray away from the script."

When they got to Courtroom Number 4, it was as if the air had been compressed, forcing in on his lungs. Henry had trouble drawing a breath.

The room was packed. He scanned the room for any signs of the media. Gillian Gee sat up front in the press gallery, notebook at the ready. Jesus on the Cross. Did that woman plan to haunt him for life?

The baby's mother sat in the front row. She was wearing a pink number, a short dress topped with a green jean jacket, knee-high black boots.

She shook her fist at Henry. "I hope they put you away for life."

Henry started to respond, but Millie led him away. She turned his face to hers, rolled her eyes in the direction of the mother, and gave Henry a kiss. "Let it go, Henry. I'll be right behind you. Just remember what we went over yesterday."

Henry began to protest. Millie interrupted. "You'll be fine." She then passed him off to Gloria, who brought her lips close to his ear and hissed, "Don't say the word baby."

The sheriff's attendant opened the little wooden door on the penalty box and urged Henry inside. Henry sat down and tried to get comfortable.

His heart was trying to race right through his shirt. If he cranked his head, he could just see Millie sitting behind him to the right. He attempted to give her a feeble smile, but here in the little box, Henry felt the same way he did when his father left for Thailand all those years ago. He felt adrift, no longer certain of his place in the universe.

Millie, of course, was in her element. This is what she did. Although he did see a bit of tension in her jaw. No doubt worrying about whether Henry would remember the correct responses. He imagined her silently mouthing the answers behind his back like a prompt in a school play. He had been trying to bring to mind what they had practised. But it wasn't easy. They weren't his words.

Judge Hiscock entered stage left, trudged up the three brown Berber stairs, and deposited herself behind the bench. Over her right shoulder, a young blue-sashed Queen Elizabeth grinned down at everyone, providing a direct contrast to Judge Hiscock's scowl.

"All rise."

"Good afternoon. We're here for the pre-sentence investigation for Mr. Henry Puddester on charges of kidnapping. Who is representing Mr. Puddester?"

"I am, Your Honour." Gloria stood up to Henry's right.

"Ah, yes, Miss Garcia. And who do we have for the prosecution?"

"That would be me." An Amazon woman rose like a mountain to Henry's left, her cropped hair cut with a silver sheen.

Judge Hiscock nodded and turned to Henry. "Mr. Puddester . . ." Judge Hiscock's voice snapped Henry back to the courtroom. "Are you aware of the severity of this charge before you?"

"Yes, Your Honour." Henry fiddled with his tie. It was tighter than a noose.

Judge Hiscock went on to explain that she would listen to the facts of the case and render her decision before the end of the week. And with that, Gloria came forward. She made her way to the front, black form-fitting turtleneck with a dagger pendant nestled in between two perfect breasts.

Henry closed his eyes—all he wanted was to hide away in his old office. Maybe they would let him come out of his retirement for a month of stress leave. He could close the door and be gloriously alone. Or he could be like the red stapler guy in *Office Space*, out in the cubicles with the worker bees but left to his own devices. He imagined himself there in his happy place, a sunbeam warming his limbs as he flipped through file folders. He must make note to give Oliver a call later today. Shucks, Oliver was still in Florida.

Gloria was positioned in front of him now. Henry tried to concentrate on her weapon jewellery rather than her see-through, blue square glasses frames and unmoving forehead.

A voice filled the courtroom. It was not Gloria's.

"He tried to kill Jade." The lunatic mother started to get up, but the person next to her dragged her back down.

Judge Hiscock did not look amused. "Miss Mooney. I will have to ask you to refrain from speaking while court is in session."

"But he's a monster." This time she got out of the clutches of the person seated next to her and went for Henry.

"Bailiff, please escort Miss Mooney from the room."

Henry watched as the bailiff intercepted a sputtering Miss Mooney and began to drag her toward the door. She spat on Henry as she passed by the penalty box. He took a tissue from his pants pocket and wiped the saliva off his cheek.

"Please proceed," said Judge Hiscock once Miss Mooney had been removed.

For the first minute, Henry tried his best to recall the answers they had practised, but all that came to mind was an image of Delores arriving with a plate of bologna and cheese skewers to share with Dash after school. Then he heard Gloria say "Henry" like a drill sergeant. He snapped to attention, jolting upright so quickly his neck seized. He focused on every word that came from Gloria's lips. He noticed she was careful not to mention that the baby carrier held a baby. He laid out for the court what had happened that morning, explaining how he had taken the baby home for safekeeping and that he had taken medication for his sinuses, as if that explained everything.

"What kind of medication did you take?"

"Dilaudid."

"Why did you take Dilaudid instead of sinus medication?" Gloria held a baggy out for the judge to see.

"It was on the shelf where the cold medication usually is."

Gloria approached a step or two, smiled at him very slightly, and lowered her voice. Someone coughed in the gallery, and Henry looked away for a moment, then back at Gloria.

"How did the Dilaudid make you feel?"

"Thirsty. My tongue was glued to the roof of my mouth. I've never felt such thirst."

"Anything else?"

"Yes, my head felt like it had a jackhammer in it, and I was seeing double. Sometimes it felt like I was hallucinating."

"Did you think you were hallucinating when you saw the car seat?"

"Yes. I couldn't figure out how it got in my shopping cart."

"What did you conclude?"

"First, I thought aliens."

This drew another round of laughter from the spectators but not the judge. "Mr. Puddester. I will not have a mockery made of my court."

"Sorry, Your Honour. But I really did."

"Now, Henry," Gloria said, her voice charged with significance. "What made you decide to leave the store with the car seat?" Her tone suggested there was a reason. Did they practise it? Either way, he couldn't remember what it was. She nodded encouragingly once more.

"I didn't want to abandon the baby."

Gloria's expression changed with lightning speed, from one of encouragement to one of shock and then utter defeat. This was obviously not the answer she had been soliciting. He could see it in the way her cheeks got sucked in toward her rouged cheekbones.

Henry tried again. "I thought it had been abandoned. By that estranged father who was in the news. I didn't want him to hurt it."

"So, what did you do?"

"I decided to go home and ask my wife, but then Dick Turner showed up—"

"Showed up where?"

"First at Sundries. Then at my house."

"Did Constable Turner ask if he could come inside your home?"

"Yes, but I didn't tell him he could."

"But he came in anyway?"

"Yes."

"No more questions, Your Honour."

The mother's lawyer was up next. She stood six feet without the heels. She had wide-set eyes and cropped hair, like Annie Lennox in the 1980s.

Prosecution: "Mr. Puddester, can you remember who was nearby when you noticed the baby?"

Henry's hands trembled. All the answers he had practised with Gloria had gone AWOL. His mind was as blank as windswept sand. Thank goodness Henry had accounted for this eventuality. He pulled up his shirt sleeve and consulted his inner arm. "I didn't see a baby. I only saw a car seat." His voice came out stilted, not his own.

Prosecution: "Okay, can you tell us who was around when you noticed the car seat?"

Henry: "Akela was behind me at the cash. The cashier . . . uh, she was chewing gum. And two men, one wide, one narrow."

Prosecution: "Narrow?" Amazon Woman looked to the judge.

Henry: "Yes. Is the microphone not working?" Henry tapped it, sending a squealing sound through the court.

Some people laughed. The judge covered her ears. "I can assure you it's working, Mr. Puddester. Please answer the question."

Henry continued. "Yes, narrow. Like he hadn't had anything decent to eat in weeks. The other guy was shorter and much, much wider. He had definitely been eating."

Prosecution: "I see. Can you tell the court who Akela is?"

"She's a Cub leader."

"Is she the one you hit with your shopping cart?"

"She was standing in the middle of the aisle like a bowling pin."

Amazon Woman raised her brow. "Can you describe what you did next?"

Henry: "I put my eggs on the conveyor belt."

Prosecution: "Your eggs?"

Henry: "Yes, four dozen."

Henry had to admit things went a bit sideways after that. And when

Miss Amazon asked if she could present a video to the court, every head in the room perked up. It was as if she held in her hands the latest Hollywood movie. She popped the DVD into the player. Henry held his breath. What could possibly be on the recording?

The video showed grainy black and white footage of a man, obviously Henry, waiting for his turn at the cash. He takes the eggs out of the basket and goes around to the side, where he pauses. When he sees the baby carrier, he gently raises the flap. The video has no sound, but in Henry's mind, he can hear the beginning of a scream just as if it had been digitally preserved.

The next part makes it difficult to ascertain what is happening. But Henry reaches into the carrier, fiddles with something, and then withdraws his arm. He then glances back at someone out of the frame and begins to place diapers, wet wipes, bum cream, and baby food on the belt and pays for everything, including his yogourt and fruit. For the climax, he repacks the items in around the carrier and quickly pushes the cart out of the frame.

Prosecution: "Mr. Puddester, what were you doing when you put your hand in the carrier?"

Henry: "I was giving the baby back its pacifier. I . . ."

Henry heard Gloria gasp, and an undecipherable hiss came out of Millie behind him. Henry sat up straighter in the penalty box. Shit, he said it again. Millie and Gloria had coached him, but he had failed. He looked straight ahead, afraid to catch Gloria's expression.

Prosecution: "The baby?"

Henry: "Yes."

Prosecution: "And Mr. Puddester, I'm curious. Why did you then take the baby to your home?"

Henry: "For safekeeping."

Prosecution: "Safekeeping?"

Was the lawyer hard of hearing? Henry should have represented himself. He should have just explained to the judge that he was too old to be a father to a ten-year-old and too old to be buying four dozen goddamned eggs. He was definitely too old to be sleeping in a damp Cub Camp bunkhouse.

The morning he went to the supermarket, all this was weighing heavily on him, and he could not bear the stress. Plus, he had taken prescription medication. He meant no harm to the baby.

Henry: "Yes, for safekeeping until I could ask my wife what to do with it."

Prosecution: "Were you worried that the baby's mother might be worried?"

Henry: "I couldn't see anyone who looked like a mother."

Prosecution: "Did you ask, Mr. Puddester, if the clerk could make an announcement looking for the baby's caregiver?"

"No. I thought someone had abandoned the baby in my shopping cart."

"Why did you think that?"

"Because my wife had told me there had been a child abducted the day before, and I thought the father panicked and left me with his child."

"Did this man, this father you speak of, communicate with you?"

"No."

"No more questions, Your Honour."

Finally, Henry got to step out of the box, and Dick stepped in. Henry's heart somersaulted, but he calmed it. Let him feel what it's like to be put on the spot, Henry thought.

Gloria did a good job of making it look like Dick Turner had entered Henry's house without a warrant. Dick glared at Henry. Henry held his gaze for a few seconds but then looked away.

Finally, it was over, and Henry noticed the sheriff's officer was asking him to stand. Gillian Gee sneezed one of those pitiful little sneezes that are usually followed by a dozen more. She didn't disappoint. She sounded like an old aunt at a tea party.

In his estimation, Henry only forgot his lines once. And apart from saying the word "baby" once or twice, Henry thought the actual court appearance went much better than the practice session. Judge Hiscock had to understand he would never hurt a child. He was sure to get extra points for his honesty.

When Henry saw Millie's Doberman face advancing quickly toward Gloria, however, he reconsidered his positive assessment of the proceedings. Millie's bottom jaw was set against the top, slightly overlapping. He must remember to tell her to relax, or she'd set off her fibromyalgia.

Millie shook her head as she thanked Gloria. Gloria, with her weapon jewellery and frozen forehead, laid her hand on Millie's arm like she was the bereaved at a wake. "Sorry, Millie. I did the best I could, but that was a bloodbath."

Gloria disappeared without a goodbye, and Henry and Millie exited the courthouse together. They crossed Duckworth Street in silence and walked up Church Hill, where they had scored a prime parking spot. Henry noted happily that the meter still had its head and coin box intact. He must remember to tell Frank.

68

Frank Views His Photos at the Bunker

Frank knew it would make Henry nervous if he showed up at his court appearance. Thus he tried to busy himself down at the bunker. His staff had everything under control, so he thought he'd do what he normally did at work when things were slack—he'd play a game of draughts on the computer—but then he remembered the cellphone photos he had taken at the racetrack. He was dying to view them on the big screen, especially the one of the security guard airborne in Daisy. Frank shut his office door and told his secretary, Judy, he was not to be bothered.

He plugged his cellphone into his computer and opened his photo file. The first picture appeared in full 300 dpi glory. The screen was bigger than the floor-model TV screen Frank had grown up with. He scrolled through all the photos but came back to his favourite, the one of Daisy making the jump, security guard at the wheel. He smiled and picked up the phone to call in Judy to help him make it his screen saver. But wait, what was that in the background? Matte grey metal. Digital screens. Frank's mouth gaped. He hung up the receiver.

It couldn't be. Yet it was. How could he have missed them while he was there? They were unmistakable. A heap of parking meter heads lay on the ground to the right of the airborne LTD.

"*Judy . . .*" He bawled out loud enough for her and the next ten offices to hear. "I need a memory stick."

Judy appeared with a tiny lime green plastic rectangle. Frank kissed her hand and danced a jig.

"Nice to see you in a good mood." Judy's eyes widened.

"Things are looking up, Judy. I have to go out for a bit. Will you hold down the fort?"

"Always do." She returned to her desk.

Frank slipped the stick into the laptop. He had to report his findings to Mad-Eye Turner.

69

Stella Defends Dash

Mikey Dawe was the grade five bully. Always impeccably dressed in pressed beige pants and a button-up shirt, Mikey was unanimously disliked by all grade fives with the exception of his two pathetic followers, Bart Corrigan and Cy Connors, who may have hated him, too, but were afraid to show it. Today at recess, they were balling up tiny bits of paper and picking off any classmate who moved. A spitball hit Dash in the forehead and bounced off his shoulder onto his leg. A second one hit his cheek and lodged there, glued to his skin with saliva and pulp. He turned to see the two morons high-five each other while Mikey slowly clapped his hands. Mikey took out a brand new silver metallic iPhone, snapped a picture of Dash picking the spitball off his cheek, and slipped the iPhone into his shirt pocket just before a teacher passed by the open door. One teacher was responsible for patrolling ten classrooms at recess.

Dash decided not to give Mikey and his henchmen the pleasure of seeing him upset. He knew this infuriated Mikey to no end.

Mikey stood on a chair by the windows overlooking the playground, put two fingers in his mouth, and whistled, causing all conversation to halt, except for Jane Avery, who was back-on at the whiteboard drawing a picture of Pikachu. A short "Pica, pica, pica" came from her lips before she turned around to see what drama was playing out.

Mikey cupped his hands around his mouth. "Hear ye, hear ye," he said to the children spread before him like loyal subjects. "In case anyone didn't know, Dash's dad is a kidnapper."

"That's not true, Mikey," said Jane, laying the yellow whiteboard marker on its ledge.

"Is, too, my Dad told me. Dash's dad stole a baby." He paused as if to gauge the reaction in the room. Most children were silent, looking to see what would come next.

Cy Connors piped in. "And his mom's armpits smell like Moisty Mire."

Mikey smiled a perfect smile and stepped down from the wooden chair. Bart and Cy moved into a pyramid formation behind him.

All eyes were on Dash. He started across the classroom toward Mikey, but Stella Turner got there first, hopping two desks along the way, sending papers and at least one water bottle into classroom orbit. Stella stood before a smirking Mikey Dawe. He was taller by two inches. She didn't say a word, but Dash saw the fingers on her right hand clench and knew exactly what was going to happen. He had seen it once before when a kid from the cul-de-sac next to Pine Place called Stella a wuss. Dash watched the action as if in slow motion.

Stella drew back her fist and walloped Mikey square in the nose. She had perfect form. Years of karate allowed her to effortlessly twist her fist at the last second for maximum impact. Mikey staggered backwards but kept upright. Thick red blood oozed down over his top lip. He raised both hands to his nose to stanch the flow. Stella turned and walked to where Dash had come to a standstill. She held her right hand in her left and then blew on her knuckles, which were beginning to bruise.

To his credit, Mikey didn't cry or bawl out, but when he ran to the bathroom for tissue, a cheer went up in the classroom.

Stella started doing the floss, and almost everyone joined in.

Even Mikey's thugs.

70

Henry and the Decorated Triumph

By the time they got home from court, Millie still wasn't speaking to Henry.

"Are you going to stay mad at me all day?" Henry put the kettle on.

"Yes."

"What did I do?"

"What did you *do*? Henry, you said the word 'baby' not one time but two times."

"I did my best, Millie."

Millie sighed. "What were you were doing fiddling with your shirt sleeve?"

"I figured it would look strange if I brought in notes and consulted a paper list, so . . ."

"You wrote cheat notes on your arm? Are you serious?"

"It used to work in high school."

Millie put her hands over her eyes.

"What?" Henry was sure he had aced his court session and convinced the judge he had done nothing wrong.

"Nothing. I'm going to work."

That was fine with Henry. He was going to put the whole supermarket incident and court case behind him. He had appeared before a judge and would be exonerated. The universe would unfold as it should.

And today, this glorious day, he was going to take his Triumph out for a final ride before the shipping company was coming by to load it up Tuesday afternoon for the Montreal bike trip. The weather was finally nice enough to do the Marine Drive loop. He heard there were three icebergs off Middle Cove. Henry was happy he hadn't had a chance to drain the fluids the night Frank dragged him to Walmart.

He skipped over the deck, past the hot tub and up the stone steps, when he noticed the shed door was ajar. Impossible. He may have been absent-minded about certain things, but locking up the shed at night was not one of them. Henry distinctly remembered pushing the padlock together. He approached quietly, expecting to confront a thief slipping his treasured Snap-on tools into a bag and hopping the fence. What he did see was far more distressful.

Delores was busy applying Gorilla Glue to the Triumph's front fender.

"*Aaaah*." Henry felt intense pressure in his chest. The entire gas tank, the magnificent paint job he had saved every penny for last summer, was now covered in tiny plastic toys. "Holy mother of God. Jesus, Mary, and Joseph. Judas in the Garden. Please tell me those things are not glued on."

"Oh, Mr. Henry, you snuck up on me." Delores straightened up from where she was crouching.

"Delores, what were you thinking?"

"I was thinking I would surprise you, but you came out earlier than anticipated. I wanted to congratulate you—it's not easy to appear before a judge. I had to appear before a judge once—"

"Delores." Henry's voice was forceful. "I hate to interrupt—"

"Yes, Mr. Henry. I can answer your question before you ask it. I have finished decorating the midsection of this fine machine, and it should only take about another thirty minutes to secure everything on the fenders." She looked at Henry then and smiled, showing off the gap where the upper incisor should have been. "From the look on your face, I can see you are surprised." The cuts on Delores's face had all healed, and looking at her, one might think she was somewhat sane. Henry knew otherwise.

He spoke slowly. "Delores, the Spring Tune-Up Ride. . . . The men are coming to crate up the bike tomorrow. What are these . . . these . . . ?" Henry was at a loss for words.

"Kinder Surprise toys. All one-piece. Some of my favourites, too. Don't worry, the glue sets instantly."

Henry's legs gave out from under him, and he sank down to the plywood floor so he was at eye level with the gluey fender. Delores was just laying an orange rabbit wearing earmuffs and skis next to an entire congregation of similar rabbits, some with goggles, others with miniature plates of cookies or mugs of hot chocolate. Henry sniffled.

"I can tell you're really moved by my efforts. I wanted to express my sincerest appreciation for you bringing me into your home like your own kin. And for being so gentle with Daisy."

Before Henry could answer, Carter arrived at the door and whistled. Henry couldn't imagine how he achieved this, as he was missing many more teeth than Delores.

"Wow, Delores, you've outdone yourself. Now the TV news will follow Henry around everywhere, too." Carter wore the same clothes he'd had on at the barbecue, a blue and white Maple Leafs sweater that Henry remembered Millie buying one day at Walmart. Did the man have any other shirts? Did he sleep in his clothes?

"Do you like it, Carter?" asked Delores. "Tell me the truth, because I value your opinion."

"She looks good, but I think you need a little more colour on the front. You asked me to be honest, and I'm brutally honest. My mother don't think I is, but I is."

"Thank you, Carter. Now we have to name her."

Henry had lost the ability to speak, to protest. He was caught in a nightmare featuring his shed and zombies from Mars.

"How about Easy Rider? You know, after the movie?"

"I am not familiar with that title." Delores added more glue and spread it with a Q-Tip. "I was thinking something more feminine, like Delilah."

"Delilah?"

"Yes, sir. 'Del' would remind Mr. Henry here of lil ole me, and the 'ilah' part sounds like this island where I have been welcomed and found a home."

Henry regarded this interaction as if he were watching a poorly acted Martian movie.

"De-li-lah." Carter drew out the syllables. "Sounds good to me. Nice shooting the breeze with you all. But I gotta get back at it." Carter removed himself from the shed and began loading his shopping cart with his Sunday bottles that he had neatly stored in the outdoor containers Millie had forced Henry to install for this purpose. Three hundred and fifty dollars at

Canadian Tire for three rat-proof bins so his recycling man could store his empties until Monday when the depot opened again.

"I'll be back in an hour. This load will take at least four trips." Carter gestured to the ten or so bags that filled the courtyard around the bins making it difficult to get through. "And thanks, Henry, for letting me call Mom later. Millie said you'll be here to let me in after my last run."

Henry grinned maniacally. "Sure, Carter, I'll make you a pot of tea."

"You know I'm not into tea," said Carter. "I'd take a nice chilled Black Horse, though. And if you've got any bottled moose kicking around, I'd have a feed of that. See you all later."

Henry watched Carter go off whistling, his legs bowed like he was going to leap on the back of a horse. He then turned to Delores.

"Get. Out. Of. My. Shed."

71

Henry and Delores Go Missing

Henry continued shouting as Delores scurried toward the house. "Delores, you are my worst nightmare. I want you to get out of my house and to stay away from my family. You're a plague . . . a . . ."

Henry had run out of insults. He stormed out of the shed and went straight to his Ford and started driving. He drove past the Holiday Inn and the Dairy Queen and turned left at the lights until he found himself heading up Mount Scio, through Pippy Park, past the Outer Ring Road, until he reached the parking lot next to the golf chalet where he could see the whole city spread before him. It was here he would bring his mother after each chemo treatment before dropping her home to her east-end bungalow. Work had been good, giving him the time off. He couldn't imagine if he hadn't had those days with his mother. His only regret was that he couldn't convince her to stay in the mother-in-law suite, where he could have kept a better watch over her.

Even in the dead of winter, they came up here. He'd turn on the heated seats and let his mother look out over the only city she had lived in. Today, St. John's looked bleak. There was still snow in the hollows, and the tree branches were naked. Not one single bud had dared raise its head to the spring chill.

Henry looked out toward the Narrows and the wide Atlantic Ocean beyond. He tried to comprehend the mess his life was in. He thought he might call Frank to see if he could come keep him company, but he couldn't bring himself to dig out his flip phone. Did he even have his flip phone?

He glanced toward campus. He noticed the shot-glass building they had built on the site of the old Thomson Student Centre. Henry had never admitted to Millie that it was he who had microwaved the burrito all those years ago. Imagine if he hadn't started a fire that day. Most likely he would never have met Millie. They wouldn't have married and had Dash. His whole life would have been different. There wouldn't be some kooky stranger in his house destroying his motorcycle. Henry closed his eyes. He was oh so tired.

Henry must have fallen asleep, because by the time he opened his eyes, the sun had long set behind him. He was quite cold. He started the engine and cranked the heat.

Once he got back to Pine Place, he parked but couldn't bring himself to go in the house. It was past eight. Frank would be home from work. Henry got out of the Escape, but instead of going in his own house, he trudged around the holly bush to Frank's shed.

"Bloody hell, Henry. You're alive. Millie's gone ape shit. Delores disappeared, too. She left a plate of bologna skewers on your kitchen table, and that's the last anyone's seen of her." He paused. "Blimey, you look knackered."

"My Triumph is ruined. I can never ride it again."

"What happened, man?"

"Delores happened, that's what. She ruined my paint job. I told her to get out. I told her . . ."

"Slow down. I'm not following. What paint job?"

"My Triumph. Millie didn't tell you? She glued stuff all over my bike."

"Millie?"

"No, that imbecile, Delores. She glued stuff on."

"What stuff?" Frank looked appropriately shocked.

"Stuff. Crap. Toys like on her wagon. Ever since I clapped eyes on that woman, my life has been in free fall. First, she gets hit by a shopping cart and ends up moving into my house, then Dash falls out of a tree, Montreal gets knocked out of the playoffs, and Stella Turner falls off the roof while intoxicated."

"Hey, that last bit had nothing to do with Delores. That was all my doing. In fact, none of those things have anything to do with Delores—except her getting hit by a shopping cart, of course."

"It has everything to do with Delores. If she hadn't come to our house, we wouldn't have had the party, and if we didn't have the party, you wouldn't have made the punch, and Stella wouldn't have bounced off my roof."

"Come on. You can't blame Delores. Do you know where she is now?"

"No, and I don't care. I never want to see that woman again."

"Okay, does Millie know you're home?"

"No, I didn't go in the house yet."

Frank got out his phone and called Millie. They could actually hear the faint steam train whistle of her iPhone through the shed window. "Millie. He's here." A pause. "In the shed." Frank sighed.

Henry heard footsteps running, and Millie burst in. First, she hugged Henry, and then she started hitting him in the chest so hard that Frank had to haul her away.

"I thought we had lost you. I called the police and filed a missing persons report. Dash came home to an empty house, Henry. No father. You, of all people, know what it's like to have no father. Dash needs you, Henry. Remember that's why you retired? To take care of Dash. I need you, too." Millie started to cry.

"Where's Dash now?" Henry stroked Millie's hair.

"When I saw what happened to your bike, I put two and two together, so I sent him out to play with Stella. That was about half an hour ago."

"Dick might not like that."

"Who cares about what Dick likes or doesn't like? What I don't like is my husband disappearing."

Frank interrupted. "Any sign of Delores yet?"

"No, she's gone. Daisy is gone. All her things are gone out of the apartment, too. The only things she left are the iPhone and the radio." Millie sniffed.

"Millie, why don't you bring Henry in the house while I take another look for Delores." Frank backed away.

Henry followed Millie across Frank's yard and into their kitchen. "Millie, that woman has got to go, and she has to stay gone."

"Why? What's so wrong with her, Henry? I know she ruined your paint job, but we can fix that."

"What's wrong? She's insane, that's what's wrong. It's bad enough to have a strange woman living in my house, eating my food, and clipping her toenails on my newspaper, if she was normal, but she is anything but normal. She sits around in my chair, playing golden oldies on a transistor radio, and quoting the singer's name and when the record came out, and, and . . . she has to go."

Millie took her husband's hand. "Henry, try to think about how happy she makes Dash."

"I don't care. Delores has got to leave this house."

Dash raced into the kitchen. "Miss Delores can't go, Dad. Whenever she

plays on my Fortnite team, we win." His sling was in tatters. The broken collarbone had mostly healed. He showed no signs of favouring the arm at all.

Henry thought he might cry. "Dash, you know how much Daddy likes
his motorcycle?"

"Yes, more than me and Mommy."

"You know that's not true, Dash."

"Sure it is. Mommy says it all the time."

Henry looked to Millie. She shrugged.

"I do admit I like my motorcycle a lot, and I don't like anyone to hurt it."

Dash waited for what Henry would say next.

"That . . . that woman has just covered it in Gorilla Glue."

"What's Gorilla Glue?" Dash asked, eyes wide.

"Gorilla Glue is what Delores used to cover my Triumph in glittery
mermaids and little orange rabbits dressed for skiing."

Dash inhaled audibly. "Are you serious?"

"Do I ever joke?"

"No. But why would she do a thing like that?"

Millie answered. "Miss Delores wanted to make Daddy's bike as nice
as her station wagon."

"Millie, the Spring Tune-Up is in a week. Remember the ride I promised my dying mother I would do in her honour? The shipping company is
coming by tomorrow to pack up the bike. And I am not sure if I will ever be
able to get the glue off. Even if I do, I can't afford to get the tank repainted.
And even if I had the money, there's no time to do it before the men arrive
to crate it."

"Calm down. Frank'll find Delores, and I'll talk to her. We'll figure
something out."

"Millie, look at me. My life is falling apart."

"Dash, why don't you go play Fortnite."

"I already had my video game time at Stella's."

"It's okay, honey. You can have extra time today." Dash disappeared
into the basement.

Millie hugged Henry. He stayed stiff. She whispered, her lips brushing
his ear. "Okay, hear me out. You know Dash will be devastated if Delores
goes. Plus, we have a deal, so let's give it until this weekend. Let's do something special with Delores, and I'll explain to both of them that after you
return from your trip, it'll be time for her to move out."

"Deal—as long as you know I'm serious. I cannot survive much longer
with that woman sitting in my La-Z-Boy. When I get back from my trip, if
she's not gone, I will be. You've got to choose. It's either her or me."

72

Millie Makes Things Right

Henry lay under the covers like a corpse. Millie finished a hushed telephone conversation, threw her iPhone on her pillow, and rubbed her temples. "That was Frank. He's got Delores. She was back at Walmart. He's going to bring her and Daisy back to Pine Place, and she'll stay at his house tonight."

"She can stay at Frank's forever as long as she parks in his driveway and I never have to see her bruised face again." Henry sat up and began tossing throw pillows onto the floor one after the other. Sniffles came through the wall.

"That's Dash." Henry started to get up.

"I'll go, Henry. You stay here."

Millie went into Dash's room and sat on the bed next to him. The NHL night light glowed faintly from below the bookshelf. Dash covered his face with Stinky, his stuffed cat, so mauled some of its spots were worn off and a gaping hole near the rear end allowed tiny plastic pellets to escape. Millie rubbed her son's back. "I thought you were reading." A copy of *The Hitchhiker's Guide to the Galaxy* sat on the headboard.

"I can't read ahead without Miss Delores."

Under her hand, Millie felt his back shudder, trying to stifle a whimper. "Dash, I have an idea to get Miss Delores back, but I need your help." Millie whispered so Henry wouldn't hear.

Dash's head slowing appeared from under the threadbare cat.

"Remember that car show you went to with Daddy in Bowring Park, and he really liked a yellow motorcycle, same kind as his?"

"Yeah, the guy called it Bumblebee, like the Transformer."

"That's it. Do you remember the man's name?"

"Uh . . . he was massive." Dash looked up to the left. "His name didn't suit him. It was Tiny. Tiny Taylor."

"You are a marvel, you know." Millie rubbed Dash's hair. "I'll be back in a minute." She crept back to her own bed and retrieved her phone. Then she went to Canada 411 and searched "Taylor." There were over 200 in St. John's alone. She called every one of them until she found Tiny, the owner of a bumblebee-yellow 1970 Triumph Bonneville.

"Yello." Tiny's voice came through the iPhone.

Millie explained her predicament.

"I'd consider it for a thousand."

"How about five hundred?"

"Seven fifty."

"Okay."

"You got yourself a deal, lady. You email the money, and I'll come down tomorrow with the parts."

"I'll need you here by mid-afternoon at the latest. The men are coming at five to pack up the bike."

"No worries. I'm working in the Goulds, but I can run into town at lunchtime. Text your address to this phone number."

Millie hung up and went back to Dash's room to tell him the news. Dash came out from under the covers and hugged his mother. "I miss Miss Delores," he said.

"I know, honey. I do, too."

"Why is Dad so mad at her?'

"Because he loves his motorcycle."

Dash sighed. "How come all my friends have brothers and sisters and I don't?"

"It just worked out that way. You came into our lives later than most babies. That makes you more special." Millie gave him a kiss on his curly head.

"Is that why Daddy tried to steal a baby?"

"Daddy didn't try to steal a baby, Dash. Where did you hear that?"

"Mikey Dawe said it in school."

"Why, that little . . ."

"Don't worry, Mom. Stella punched him in the nose."

"Did that shut him up?"

"For now . . ." Dash looked up at her.

"Is there anything else you want to ask me, honey? You know you can ask anything at all."

"How come Daddy is retired? Stella's father still works."

"Daddy is older, that's all."

"They're the same age. Stella told me they were in the same class in school."

"Yes, well, Daddy retired so he could . . ."

"So he could what?"

"Take care of you." Millie pulled the covers up around Dash's neck.

"Oh." Dash nodded. "Can you give me a tuck like Grandma Puddester used to do?"

Millie tightened the blankets around the perimeter of Dash's arms and legs with karate chop motions like Henry's mother used to do. "You go to sleep, now. I'll work things out."

"Good night, Mom."

"Good night, love. Don't let the nighttime zombies attack." Millie went downstairs, grabbed three lemon tea bags, and headed over to Frank's. On the way over, she tried to work out rationally why she was so tolerant of Delores's idiosyncrasies. She adopted Henry's method of listing the facts.

1. Dash needed a companion.
2. She, Millie, was too busy trying to keep her husband out of jail to be a companion to a ten-year-old.
3. Henry was too shell-shocked from the fact that he had a child—despite the fact he had a decade to get over it—for him to be in the moment with his son.
4. Delores was a perfect companion for Dash. She was everything Dash needed and wanted. She had all the time and patience in the world. She was funny and enjoyed juvenile games.
5. Henry was having a hard time adjusting to Delores living with them. He had reason to be upset about the glue and his bike.
6. Millie had to fix up the mess with the glue or Delores would have to go.
9. Delores's idiosyncrasies outweighed Henry's discomfort.
7. Henry missed his mother.
8. The Spring Tune-Up bike trip would help bring closure.

Millie had always liked her mother-in-law. She didn't know how she'd feel about living with her, but as it turned out, she never got to find out. To assuage her husband's loss, Millie would allow him to do this bike trip. If the packers were coming tomorrow afternoon, then the bike would be ready, albeit multicoloured. She arrived at Frank's door and knocked. Frank nodded to Millie and waved her in.

"You'll have to excuse the mess. I haven't had a chance to clean up after tea."

Millie hadn't been inside Frank's house since Patty left. She took in the treadmill by the window in the living room. Frank's shed jacket was draped over one arm. Dirty dishes covered the coffee table.

"Hi, Miss Millie." Delores sat among an assortment of laundry that almost fully concealed the couch. Frank started to pick up some of the clothes.

"Don't clean up on my account, Frank. Although a tiny dusting wouldn't go astray."

"Is Mr. Henry still vexed with me?"

"Henry is still pretty upset, but I'm sure he'll calm down. It's been a trying day for him, with court and all. But good news, I found a new gas tank and fender. A man is going to deliver them tomorrow."

"You are going to take off my toys? I thought Mr. Henry would like his surprise."

"I know you did, Delores, but you have to understand that that motorcycle is Henry's pride and joy, and he doesn't like anyone messing with it."

"I was *dec-or-at-ing* it for the trip." Delores pronounced each syllable like they were separate words.

"Why don't we have a cup of tea and figure things out? Frank, I'm going to boil the kettle."

"A cup of rosie would hit the spot right now." Frank dropped the clothing from the couch into a pile at the landing of the stairs. Peter Pan stared down at him from the back side of his wedding photo frame.

Millie followed his gaze. "Why don't you just take the frame down, Frank?"

"I don't rightly know. I figure if Patty comes back I can just flip it around again."

"Makes sense." Delores nodded.

Millie found three mugs in the sink and rinsed them.

"Anyone for apple on toast?" Frank came in the kitchen and began to clear away some of the mess on the table. Delores followed and took some dishes out of the sink and laid them on the counter. She put in the plug to start washing up.

"I have a dishwasher, you know." Frank puffed out his chest.

Delores opened it up and showed the interior to Frank. "I think you forgot to turn it on." She chucked in a tiny pillow of detergent, shut the door, and pressed start.

Frank looked sheepish and went about cutting up an apple into thin slices.

"Miss Millie, tell me about this motorcycle trip that Mr. Henry is going on."

"It's called the Spring Tune-Up, and about two hundred bikes will all start together in Montreal and ride east, stopping wherever they want along the way." Millie put the tea bags in the cups.

"Are Mr. Henry's friends going?" Delores squirted in far too much dish detergent, and bubbles began to float around the room.

"Not really, but he knows a bunch of the riders. He was supposed to do this trip with his mother." Millie turned off the whistling kettle.

"She can't go anymore?" Delores was pulling on blue rubber gloves she found under the sink.

"She died five weeks after she was diagnosed with pancreatic cancer. Before she died, she made Henry promise to still do the ride."

Delores laid down the steaming mugs of tea. "The apartment I'm in was for her, wasn't it? That's why Henry doesn't like me staying there." Delores put a plate in the dish rack to drain.

"It was for her, but Henry is just set in his ways. He doesn't like change. He likes things to go smoothly without a ripple. The past couple of weeks have been a bit tangly for him."

"Like the supermarket incident."

"Yes, the supermarket incident is a big worry. We'll just take each day as it comes."

"Maybe tomorrow I can clean the carburetor. You can hear that bike coming from ten blocks away."

"Delores, *do not touch the bike.*" Millie motioned for her to come sit and have tea.

"All right, I won't, but I don't think a fifty-year-old Bonneville that's not firing on all cylinders is fit for that kind of distance." She kept on washing.

"I know, but he'll be with a group all the way from Montreal. They have a support vehicle with parts and gas. You, of all people, Delores, should understand his love of an older machine."

Delores stayed mum, but Frank piped up. "I think he'd be better off trading the Triumph for a modern Japanese crotch rocket."

"I suggested he get a Suzuki Bandit for his retirement."

"And?"

"He said, 'Pshaw. What fun would that be?'"

"He could ride his mother's Ducati." Frank sat down with a plate of apple slices and four pieces of toast. "I know, not going to happen."

Delores pulled off the gloves with two snaps and came to the table.

"I think you should come back to our house with me." Millie sipped her tea.

"Really? Are you sure?" Delores mimicked Frank stacking the apple on toast.

"Yes. Frank can bring the rest of your things tomorrow."

"Delores is welcome to stay here."

"That's kind, Frank, but Dash was upset when Delores wasn't there to read with him."

"Oh, no. Did he read ahead in the *Hitchhiker's Guide*?" Delores crunched down on the apple and toast.

"No, he wanted to wait for you." Millie paused. "Delores, come home with me, but I have to warn you that you are never, ever allowed to enter Henry's shed again."

"Not even for a peek?"

"No. I'm not allowed in, and I'm his wife."

73

Tuesday: Millie Saves the Day

Millie took Tuesday off work, even though she had a big case to prepare for. Henry was still in a delicate state, so Millie had arranged for Delores to take Dash for groceries when he got home from school. Tiny Taylor arrived at noon. Dash wasn't joking. He looked about seven feet tall. Henry had no idea anyone was coming, so Millie went in the shed first to soften his entrance.

"Henry, I have a surprise for you."

"I hate surprises." Henry was using a metal wedge to scrape a small bunny off the gas tank.

"Yes, but this is a good surprise." She was in the inner sanctum by then. Tiny Taylor followed her.

"Hey, I think I saw this bike at a show once out in Bowring Park. She was burgundy." Tiny stood behind Millie in the door holding two huge brown paper parcels.

Henry looked up, pride showing in his tired face. "She is burgundy underneath all this crap." The bunny flew through the air, and Henry moved on to a dwarf.

"What happened? If my kid did that, I'd pulverize him." Tiny laid down his packages.

"It wasn't a kid. It was my wife's house guest."

Millie caught the full weight of "my wife's."

"What's your name?" Henry wiped his hands on a rag.

"Tiny. I met you last July at Shine 'n Show. I had my Bonneville there, too. Same year."

"Yes, I remember your bike, the yellow one. I liked the colour. It really stood out."

Tiny cleared his throat. "Yes, well, ahem, speaking of colour. I have something here for you that might help your problem." Tiny held out his arms as if presenting an obi to a kimono-clad geisha.

Henry took the package and opened it to see the yellow metal. "You just saved my life."

Millie heard her cellphone ring in the kitchen. She backed out of the shed as the men started to talk about chickens, of all things. She crept back to the house, praying that maybe, just maybe, Delores's expulsion had been averted.

74

Judge Hiscock Moves up the Ruling

Millie swept her purple-nailed finger over her iPhone screen. "Hey, Gloria."

"Judge Hiscock has expedited the sentencing date." Gloria's voice came through the tiny iPhone mic.

"When?" Millie looked out the glass doors to the shed, where Henry was busy removing the toy-covered gas tank with his new friend. He gave her the thumbs-up and smiled the first real smile in a week.

"She has an opening this afternoon."

"This afternoon? That's crazy." Millie smiled back weakly and waved at her husband.

"I know, but she had a cancellation, and she knows you want this to happen as soon as possible. Three o'clock. Can you make it work?"

"We'll be there."

An hour later, the tall man gone, Henry came in for lunch, and Millie broke the news.

"I can't go today, Millie. I—"

"We have no choice, Henry. Come have a sandwich, and then you can shower. I laid out your suit and asked Delores to meet Dash when he comes from school."

75

Court Session Number 3

Henry felt like he might throw up. He could feel the bile rising in his throat. But why? He had nothing to be afraid of. The judge would surely rule in his favour. So, why could he feel the sweat ring widening under his arms?

Millie tried to calm him. "Getting called early might be a good sign, Henry. Judge Hiscock is reasonable."

"What about if the mother spits on me again?"

"She's been warned. Judge Hiscock said that if she does or says anything in court, then the case will be dismissed."

Inside the courtroom, Henry sat down in the front row next to Gloria and scanned the room. He spotted the mother sitting between a man and woman in their fifties. She was wearing a lavender suit jacket with padded shoulders. Miss Mooney didn't say a word, but she held up her right hand, index finger pointed toward Henry. She then bent the finger at the knuckle. He quickly looked away. Henry chanced a glance at Gloria. No air kisses today. She was hard to read behind her yellow glasses frames.

"All rise." Judge Hiscock swished into the courtroom from above like a female Jesus. Henry's mind drifted back to his dream.

"We're here for the sentencing hearing for Mr. Henry Puddester on charges of kidnapping." Judge Hiscock identified the lawyers again just like in the pre-sentence investigation.

Henry gripped the edges of his seat to keep his hands from shaking. His thumb touched a used Band-Aid stuck underneath the chair, and he pulled his hand away, the stress of germ contamination making him momentarily forget where he was. He quickly deployed Purell and felt a bit better.

"Mr. Puddester, you do understand that child abduction is a serious offence."

Henry wiped sweat off his upper lip.

"Mr. Puddester—"

"Yes, but I didn't hurt the baby."

"Just answer the question, Mr. Puddester. Do you understand that child abduction is a serious offence?"

Henry wiped his lips with the back of his hand. "Yes, but I only brought the baby home to keep it safe until I could ask my wife how to get it back to its mother."

Judge Hiscock sighed. "Mr. Puddester, I do not believe you planned to abduct the child. However, you did remove and transport a minor, and that can come with a pretty hefty prison term." Then she dropped the bomb. "Mr. Puddester, I have no choice but to find you guilty of child abduction."

Voices erupted all over the courtroom. Henry heard Millie gasp. He went to turn his head to comfort her, but the judge wasn't finished. "The court sentences you to six months house arrest beginning this coming Monday."

Now it was Henry's turn to gasp.

"That's it?" The baby's mother had hopped up.

"Miss Mooney, would you like to be removed?"

"No, ma'am." She sat back down.

Judge Hiscock turned her attention back to Henry. "Mr. Puddester, do you have anything to say?"

Henry had to pull himself together. He wiped his sweaty palms on his pants. "Yes, Your Honour. I panicked and made a bad choice. I'm sorry I removed the baby from the supermarket. My mind was muddled with the medication I took. Believe me, if I had my time back, I would have left her right there at the cash." Henry knew he was babbling. He carried on. "My wife is always telling me I'm absent-minded, so the fact that I somehow ended up with someone else's shopping cart, whether through my own fault or someone else's, confused me. I've never been good at parenting, but I hope you believe that I meant no harm. I honestly thought I was doing the safest thing for the baby." Henry drew a breath and looked at Judge Hiscock before continuing.

"Are you done?" The judge's eyes were wide.

"Not yet, Your Honour." Henry could see Gloria making cutting signs with her fingers. He continued. "I understand your ruling, and I am ready to abide by it. However, I'm hoping you will reconsider the dates. My mother died this spring. On her deathbed, she asked me to do a bike trip in her honour. It starts next week, Your Honour."

Judge Hiscock sighed and rubbed her temples. "I have heard a lot of excuses in my time on the bench, Mr. Puddester, but I have to admit that is an original one. I will not reconsider the dates, but . . ." She paused. "As an alternative to house arrest, the court will accept a payment of fifty thousand to be paid to Amber Alert by Monday, the day the house arrest is due to begin. If you do not come up with that amount, you must stay in your home for six months, only leaving for work or doctors' appointments."

"You can't let him off." The young mother screamed.

"Miss Mooney . . ." Judge Hiscock was spitting tacks.

The mother sat back down.

The judge turned to Amazon Woman. "I trust this arrangement is agreeable to the prosecution."

Amazon Woman rose to her feet. "I am in agreement. Thank you, Your Honour."

"Does the defence wish to speak?"

"Yes, Your Honour." Gloria cleared her throat and straightened her yellow glasses. "The defence appreciates the alternative sentence but requests that the house arrest be delayed two weeks to allow the accused to go on the Spring Tune-Up Ride if he cannot come up with the fifty thousand dollars by Monday."

"Miss Garcia, I am sure you are aware that it is extremely uncommon, dare I say unheard of, for this court to offer an alternative sentence. If you wish to keep that option open, I suggest you accept the sentence as presented. Any other comments?"

"No, Your Honour. Thank you, Your Honour."

Judge Hiscock banged the gavel. "This sentencing hearing has adjourned."

76

Millie Takes Henry Home after Court

When Henry and Millie arrived home, Dash and Delores were still out. The bike that had been left in the driveway for the shippers to take was gone. A yellow sheet stuck out of their mailbox. Henry passed by without removing it and went in the kitchen. He didn't utter a sound until he sat down at the table. It was as if he could not trust his voice until he was in the sanctity of his own home. "Millie, I'll go snapper cracky if I have to stay home for six months."

"You'll be allowed in your shed."

Henry looked like he might cry. Millie came around and rubbed his shoulders. "We'll come up with the money."

"Yeah, right. Fifty thousand. Where am I going to come up with fifty thousand dollars by Monday?" Henry stood up and opened and closed the fridge door without taking anything out of it.

"You could sell the Ducati."

"No way. It's my mother's." He pulled off his tie and threw it on a chair.

"It's not like she's going to use it, Henry."

Henry looked as if he had been slapped. His cheeks reddened, and his eyes watered. "No, but Dash will."

"Over my dead body."

"What's that supposed to mean?"

"That I don't want my son riding a motorcycle." She watched her husband's nostrils flare. "Henry, forget what I said about Dash riding a bike. But listen to me. How else are we going to come up with the money? The line of credit is maxed. The credit card is linked to both the mortgage and the line of credit. The bank would hardly look at us when we remortgaged to build the in-law suite. It's either that or do the house arrest. What do you say?"

"I say if we weren't living beyond our means we might have a bit of money."

"Pardon me?" Millie didn't like where this was going.

"Millie, I know you took care of whatever was owing for Delores's windshield repair. I know you pay for Delores's phone. You can't be at it, Millie. You can't be buying windshields and cellphones for strangers."

How did this go from the court case and house arrest to Delores?

"She's not a stranger. It's not all my fault. If we didn't have to pay all those years of back taxes on your mother's property, we might be in okay shape."

"Don't bring my mother into this." Saliva flew from Henry's lips. Millie had never seen him so enraged.

"All I'm saying is how could she have stopped paying after your father died? What did she think all of those notices were for?"

"How do I know? All I know is the bank's not going to lend us any more money. They barely gave us enough to pay off the tax bill. Surely this is a misunderstanding. How can a judge sentence me to house arrest for—"

"Taking a baby. Hello? This is what happens when you remove an infant from its mother without asking permission." She knew she was being unreasonably mean, but if he just thought now and then, he wouldn't get himself into such predicaments. Millie remembered the Dilaudid then and felt guilty.

Henry hung his head.

Millie put a hand on his arm. "Listen, we can go with the house arrest. Maybe you can sign up for a different ride in the fall. You always wanted to ship your bike to Boston and ride back from there."

The look Henry gave Millie was not one of love and marital contentment. "Millie, I promised my mother. I have to do *this* ride. Not some other ride. This one. I'm doing it for her."

Millie started to say more, but the side door clattered open. Dash and Delores and grocery bags tumbled into the room. Henry headed the other way. Millie heard the bedroom door slam. Henry did not reappear for the rest of the day.

77

Wednesday: Frank Shares His Good News

Things were so dire Wednesday that Millie had given Frank strict orders to get Henry out of the house. They were squished inside the Tardis in Frank's shed drinking homebrew. "It's not quite as roomy in here as in *Dr. Who*," said Henry.

"I'm working on it," answered Frank.

"I thought it was supposed to look sort of like the *Starship Enterprise*."

"Wrong show, but you've got the idea." Frank pointed toward his laptop screen. It was balanced on his lap as he scrolled through pictures showing a mountain of parking meter heads at the racetrack in Avondale.

"I can't believe it." Henry's voice was low, like he'd had the life sucked out of him.

"I couldn't, either. And I still can't believe Mad-Eye Turner actually investigated and made an arrest. One of the security guards matched the description given by Delores. She's due to pick him out of a lineup in a few days."

"That's fantastic." Henry scratched his stubble. He looked like a sad Paul Newman.

"I didn't actually see them while we were at the track." Frank leaned over Henry for a better view.

"Maybe you did, and that's what set off the seizure?" Henry scrolled down to the next picture.

"Could be. Doctor says they're not always caused by flashing lights."

"Did you tell him about racing the station wagon?"

"No. I left out that tidbit." Frank laughed his big belly laugh. It felt good to laugh again. "You should have seen Daisy fly."

"I thought she only had a V6." Henry looked incredulous that Delores's station wagon actually had enough power to fly.

"Me, too, but Delores added a four-barrel carburetor and a set of headers. We'll have to go for a ride." Frank saw Henry's face fall. "Shit, Henry. I forgot. The house arrest starts Monday, doesn't it?"

"Yeah. I can't believe I just got the bike crated and shipped and then . . ." His voice trailed off.

"I know. It even warmed up a bit." Frank wasn't sure what to say. His hand was on his way to his mouth with his beer bottle, but he changed direction and laid it on the floor of the Tardis.

"Six months? Can you believe she gave me six months?" said Henry.

"So cruel. I'll visit every day. Isn't there an option to pay a fine?"

"Yeah, fifty thousand dollars." Henry smiled unhappily.

"That's a lot of money. Do you think you can come up with it?"

"Definitely not in the cards."

78

Chase the Ace Plans

"Dad, we have to go to Chase the Ace." Dash raced into the kitchen, where Henry was sitting staring into space.

"Dash, what did you do to your sling?" The new sling Millie had picked up at the drugstore was covered in grass stains.

Dash was wilder than ever since the temperature had finally risen to the double digits. Today was supposed to top out at eighteen degrees.

"Dad, did you hear me? Chase the Ace is on tonight. Stella's father is taking her, but he said he can't take me because he's working. Stella's going to meet up with her aunt who lives really close."

"Is he never not at work?" Henry muttered. He knew he shouldn't take out his frustrations on his son. Dash was naturally oblivious to his delicate state of mind. Henry was not only stuck in the house for half a year as of Monday, but he had a bike en route to Montreal, and he wasn't allowed to go meet it. There could be nothing crueller than that. He wished lightning would strike both Dick Turner and the woman in the in-law suite.

"Dash, go wash your hands, and we'll discuss it over dinner." Millie was taking a tuna casserole out of the oven. Dash ran to the bathroom.

"Henry, I know you're not feeling well, but go easy on Dash. None of what's happened is his fault. And you know he's been fascinated with Chase the Ace since it started back in the fall. He wants to be part of it, that's all."

"Millie, there is no way I'm spending one of my last evenings before a six-month house arrest going to a goddamned Chase the Ace night." Henry closed his eyes as if it hurt too much to leave them open. Dash bounded back in the room, water dripping from the sling.

"Come on, Dad, please. All my friends are going. It's my last chance."

"Don't waste your breath, Dash. I refuse to drive through bumper-to-bumper traffic only to waste my money on useless tickets that will make other people rich." Henry watched his son's face contort into a pleading mask. "Maybe your mother can bring you."

Henry could see Millie's lightning-quick mind preparing her case in her head. "Unfortunately," she said after a pause, "I have a big disclosure to-morrow at nine, Dash, love. I have lots to prepare this evening. Otherwise, I would love to go."

"I can take you, Dash." Delores had appeared in the kitchen without Henry noticing. "Daisy and I want to go, too."

"That would be sick, Miss Delores."

Henry had done his best to pretend that Delores was gone from his life. It was a very difficult thing to do when she was standing in his kitchen wearing a pair of pink bell-bottoms with a matching floral shirt and head-band. She had probably been sitting in her favourite spot, Henry's La-Z-Boy, listening to their exchange.

"That's a great idea," said Millie.

"What are you saying?" Henry looked at his wife, daggers for pupils. Had she forgotten that Delores was public enemy number one?

"I'm saying it's a great idea that Delores take our son to Chase the Ace."

Despite his inner turmoil, Henry tried to come up with an excuse that would placate Dash. "The doctor hasn't given Delores the okay to drive yet, buddy."

"I actually received the papers yesterday," said Delores, seemingly oblivious to the hatred emanating from Henry. "I'm good to go."

"No." Henry got up from the table.

"Henry." Millie's voice was slow and deliberate. "This is a perfect solu-tion. Your son would like to experience Chase the Ace. Neither you nor I can accompany him. Miss Delores has her licence back, she would like to go, and I know she'll be extra watchful. So, calm down and recognize something good when it's presented to you."

"Millie, I don't know if you've noticed, but not one good thing has been presented to me since this year started. Plus, they're expecting over fifty thousand people in the Goulds tonight. She might lose Dash in the crowd."

"Dash, honey, do you promise to stick close to Miss Delores?"

"Yes, we can glue our sleeves together with that Gorilla Glue stuff Delores used on Daddy's motorcycle."

Henry took a sharp intake of breath through his teeth. "Delores . . ." He put on his best peaches-and-cream voice. "You'll have to spend hours in traffic. Daisy might overheat. I know you said she's only good for so much stopping and going."

"Not to worry, Mr. H., I've got it all figured out. Mr. Frank explained the best way to avoid the crowds. He told me to drive up through Shea Heights." Delores paused and squinted at a map she had unfolded on her lap. "He said to take that road out near Cape Spear to . . ." She stuttered a bit. "Petty Harbour? Yes, Petty Harbour. And then go the back way to the Goulds. Is that how you pronounce it? We can park as close as we can to the main road so we can get out of there quickly once it's all over."

Henry made note to strangle Frank's doughy neck.

"Delores, you sure do know the lay of the land." Millie's smile disappeared quickly when she saw the look on Henry's face.

"Yep. I figure if I'm going to live here, I'd best learn my way around."

Henry's temples throbbed. He shot Millie a look. She shot him one back to say that she hadn't had a chance to broach the subject of Delores moving out yet.

Henry knew he had lost the fight, just like every other fight in his life. "Dash, you can go, but you have to wear your bright yellow jacket and baseball cap so Delores can pick you out of the crowd if you get lost."

"Aww, Dad."

"Your choice." Henry figured the yellow might also help him find Dash on the TV coverage. He knew these things were televised—ever since the pot reached over half a million, all the main TV and radio stations were out there early, setting up and interviewing the natives.

Henry went to the bathroom and rattled in the cabinet for a painkiller. Dash followed him in a few minutes later just as he was downing a Tylenol.

"Dad, I look like a banana."

Henry looked at his son. He was indeed very yellow.

"That's perfect. You'll stand out enough not to get lost.

"Okay. Do you want me to buy you any tickets?"

"No thanks, buddy. Maybe your mother wants some."

"She does." Dash's smile beamed out from under the baseball cap. "She gave me sixty-five dollars for supper and tickets."

"What?" Henry felt his rage go up a notch. What was Millie thinking giving $65 to a kid who misplaced everything he ever touched? Henry swallowed a second pill dry and stalked to the kitchen.

"Delores, do you have your phone in case you run into trouble?" Millie was opening the door for them.

"Yes, Miss Millie. We'll be off now."

"Bye, Dad. Bye, Mom." And with that, she and Dash were gone.

"Millie, darling. You know that Dash can't even purchase tickets, don't you?"

"Yes, you have to be nineteen, so Dash is going to give the money to Delores, and she'll get fifty dollars' worth for him. Twenty-five dollars' worth of fifty-fifty tickets and twenty-five dollars of Chase the Ace."

"But if Dash wins, he's too young to collect. Then who'll get the money?"

Millie laughed and said, "Oh, Henry." She came behind her husband and directed him onto his kitchen chair at the head of the table he once ruled over. She ran her fingers up under his hairline and down over his shoulders. She kissed the nape of his neck, sending a shiver down his spine. Henry could not eat his casserole. His stomach was knotted like when he was waiting for Dash to be born. Apparently, everyone except him had no problem with letting a ten-year-old boy travel on busy roads at night with a certified nutbar and destroyer of personal property.

An hour after Delores and Dash had set off, Henry still could not relax. He went to the shed, but of course he had nothing to tinker with. He glanced at the Ducati. Even if they sold it, where would they get the rest of the $50,000 to pay off the fine? Henry sighed and left the shed. He had no more mental stamina to deal with the details of his life. It had gotten away from him. He was but a puppet in a play.

79

Half an Hour Later, Henry Worries about Dash at Chase the Ace

Henry paced around the rec room like a bear in a cage.

"Henry, for God's sake, sit down, would you? You're making me crazy."
Millie turned up the volume on the remote.

Henry did not want to watch the live over-the-top Chase the Ace coverage. But he did want to make sure his only child was okay. There was no way around it. He'd have to watch. Maybe if he turned the sound down and ignored the host, he might catch a glimpse of Dash's neon yellow jacket. He picked up the remote and pressed mute.

"Honey, why did you turn down the sound?"

"I want to concentrate on finding Dash."

"You know they probably haven't even arrived yet, don't you?"

"Millie, how could you have let him go off with a stranger?"

"Delores is not a stranger, Henry. She adores Dash. Have you seen her reading to him?"

"That's called grooming. For all we know, she could be pulled off on the side of a deserted road chopping our only child into bits."

"Oh, honey, Delores wouldn't hurt a fly." Millie took his arm and pulled him close. She kissed his ear and clicked unmute.

While the TV crew waited for the 8:00 p.m. draw, they played a piece that had aired earlier in the day saying that the Goulds crowd were on top of logistics. Everything from security to porta-potties had been addressed.

Next, they played a time-lapse video from that morning, when thousands of people snaked through the residential streets in the Goulds. The journey took over two hours on foot for the cameraman. CBC had sped up the footage to show it all in sixty seconds. It was an epic journey through scores of people in shorts and tank tops who were willing to wait more than five hours for the chance to part with their money. Some of them had arrived in the Goulds on Tuesday night and set up trailers so they would be the first to buy tickets and then hang out and enjoy the festivities, the buskers, and people selling soft drinks from their tailgates. By noon the line had reached several kilometres.

"These people are out of their cotton-pickin' minds." Henry got up and took a beer from the mini-fridge. The camera was now inside the parish hall focused on Dot Rogers, the woman who had been the voice of Chase the Ace since the first night twenty-eight weeks ago.

"Five minutes left before sales shut down for the evening. I repeat, only five minutes remain before ticket sales shut down." Dot's voice boomed out of the wraparound sound system. "We have run out of fifty-fifty tickets, but we still have Chase the Ace tickets. The pot is now over two point five million."

"She sounds like a trucker." Frank came down the stairs. A whiff of cotton candy smoke came with him. "Sorry, I was ringing the bell, but you couldn't hear me." He was wearing a long-sleeved cotton T-shirt showing the St. John's subway system. Last time Henry checked, St. John's did not have a subway system.

"It's now eight p.m. All sales must cease."

Henry muted the TV.

"I just saw Dash." Frank lifted his arm to the TV. "He looked like a crossing guard."

"Where? Where did you see him?"

"He was right underneath the big Cross outside St. Perpetua's."

"I didn't see him." Henry stared at the silent TV. All Henry could see on the screen was a long line of people waiting to buy tickets.

Millie went to the beer fridge. "All we have are these Labatt Max Ice." She handed a black tin to Frank.

"Oooh, I like this stuff." Frank pulled the tab, which emitted a satisfactory whoosh.

"I never saw Dash," Henry repeated.

"That's 'cause you got it on NTV. Flip the channel."

"Easier said than done." Henry struggled with the two remotes. Millie took the bigger one to help, but before she had a chance, her train whistle ring tone sounded. Henry jumped. "Millie, you've got to change that ring tone."

"Shh, shh. It's Dash." She stood up. "He's on Delores's phone." Then louder: "How's it going, honey?"

"It's wild here." Dash's voice was loud enough for Henry and Frank to hear without the benefit of speakerphone.

"Did you get something to eat?"

"Yes, I had poutine and a deep-fried Mars bar."

"Lovely. Where's Miss Delores?"

"She just went to get us ice cream. I'm waiting for her under the big Cross on the school. She told me not to move."

"Jesus in the garden." Henry felt faint.

"Will you put her on the phone when she comes back, darling?" The background noise was alarming.

"Sure, Mom. You should've seen how crazy people went when we showed up in Daisy. They almost tipped her over with us in her."

"What?" Millie blessed herself.

"What did he say?" Sweat trickled down Henry's scalp.

Frank imitated Millie using his beer tin to make the sign of the Cross. "Spectacles, testicles, wallet and watch."

"*Fraaank.*" Millie went to punch him, but he dodged her.

"I can hear Mr. Parrell," said Dash. "Is he there, too?"

"Yes, mate, I saw you on TV," Frank shouted.

"That's sick. Where's Dad?"

"I'm here." Henry wished Millie's phone could show him a video of their son.

Frank went to the fridge and passed Henry a beer.

"Lots of people were taking pictures of us in Daisy. They wanted us to drive all the way up to the parish hall, but there are cars and trucks parked everywhere, and we couldn't get through."

"What did you do?" Henry stood up to get his mouth close to the phone. He bawled into it.

"Whoa, Dad, not so loud. We had to leave Daisy out by a pond and walked in. I memorized the closest house number so we'll be able to find our way back in the dark."

"Good thinking, darling." Millie turned to Henry. "See, he memorized the house number."

"Give me the phone." Henry tried to grab the pink iPhone out of Millie's hand. She batted him away. The TV showed drone footage of the swelling masses. Henry could see a large group eating what looked like a Christmas dinner on someone's front porch on the main street. "Ask him if he's seen Stella."

"Have you seen Stella, darling?"

"Nope, haven't seen anyone I know 'cept Miss Delores."

"Ask him how he knows which tickets are his." Henry nodded vigorously.

Millie rolled her eyes. "Daddy asks how you know which tickets are yours. And which are Miss Delores's."

"Oh, easy. When Miss Delores bought the tickets, she put mine in her bra and hers in her pants until we got out of the parish hall. Then we both wrote our names on the stubs. They haven't drawn one of our tickets yet. But I know they're going to. Miss Delores says . . ." The connection faded but picked up again. "The person who has the winning ticket has fifteen minutes to get to the parish hall to get their ticket verified—that's the word, right?"

"Yes, honey. That's the word."

A huge whoop went up in the crowd on Dash's end of the line.

"What's going on?"

"Oh, they're just announcing who won fifty-fifty. I helped Miss Delores check all our numbers, but we didn't win."

In a parallel TV universe, Dot Rogers was barking out the same news. Henry struggled with the remote. Frank took it from him and switched it to CBC.

"Can you see Miss Delores yet?"

"No . . ." Dash's voice faded.

"What happened? Why can't we hear him anymore?" Henry looked crazed.

"Calm down, Henry, Delores's phone must have gone dead." Millie sat back on the couch.

"*Ahhh.*" Henry raised his hands in the air. "Now what do we do?"

A huge cry came from the crowd on TV. He watched as a forty-something-year-old man sprinted through the crowd into the parish hall. Henry wished the TV camera angle would swing over to the left a bit more so he could see Dash under the Cross. Henry could picture exactly where the school was in relation to the parish hall if you were looking from the road. All he could see besides the door and the crowds were a martial arts booth that appeared to be selling cotton candy.

The camera followed a couple inside. Henry did not care that the man and woman, who owned a farm a mile up the road, were pocketing a cheque for $390,000 and change. He lay his head back while Dot Rogers went through the motions like some hyped-up American game show host. Then Henry heard a voice he recognized and popped his head back up.

"How long have you been playing?" CBC reporter Gillian Gee was larger than life in Henry's rec room.

"Jumpin' Jesus. Is she everywhere?" Henry shook his head. Frank patted his shoulder.

"We've been chasing the ace for a long time, ever since we put the plastic on the corn," said the woman. "Our daughter is supposed to be getting married out in the field next week. Now we can go to the Dominican."

"Congratulations to you and your daughter. I hope you enjoy your trip down south." The couple moved off the stage to do the paperwork associated with claiming their winnings.

Despite bouncers on the doors, the camera showed throngs of people continuing to spill into St. Perpetua's parish hall behind Gillian Gee.

"It's like a freakin' Rolling Stones concert." Henry felt sweat roll down his brow.

"Move away from the stage. I repeat, move away from the stage." Dot Rogers bawled at the crowd that kept advancing toward the microphone. The 50/50 draw had them in a frenzy. "We cannot have you this close when we do the draw."

"What happens next?" asked Henry, pressing the black tin of Labatt beer to his cheek.

"The person who has the number gets to try for the Ace of Spades." Frank had gone to the mini fridge and got a second beer for Henry, who chugged half of it down in one go.

"And what about if they don't turn it over?"

"It all happens again next week." Millie took Henry's beer from him and had a small gulp.

"I can't take the stress." Henry thought he might throw up. "We should never have let him go." He paced the floor, wringing his fingers.

"He'll be okay, Henry." Millie got up to get a beer of her own. "You want another one, Frank? Oh, you're not quite finished."

Frank chugged the remains and held out his hand. "Thanks, Millie. Good stuff, this. Pass another for Henry, too."

"He just started one."

"That's nothing."

Millie passed another tin.

"Henry, keep watching. Maybe we'll catch a glimpse of Dash next time the camera goes outside."

Henry opened the beer Millie tossed him, even though he had yet to finish the one he was drinking. The foam poured out when he pulled the tab. He sucked it off the side of the can. Gillian Gee was finishing up her report. "With crowds hovering around seventy-five thousand, I'd just like to remind all the parents here in the Goulds to be extra vigilant this evening . . . given recent events." She screwed up her face in fake sincerity. "Keep your children close. We don't want to see any more abductions. For *CBC News*, this is Gillian Gee."

80

Henry Sees Dash on TV

"That woman is a monster." Henry tried to get up off the couch. Millie pulled him back down and held his hand. The camera had left Gillian Gee and swung back to Dot Rogers. It made Henry dizzy.

"In late January, the jackpot sat at four hundred and forty-seven thousand dollars. By March, it was over a million, and tonight it has surpassed two million. And folks, tonight some lucky person may walk away more than two million dollars richer." Dot Rogers was in her element. "And remember, you have to be on site with your ticket physically in hand to win the chance to flip a card. That's why we have approximately seventy-five thousand people here in the Goulds tonight. Wait, I think we may have found the lucky ticket holder." She pushed her earpiece farther in her ear. "What's your name, sir?"

"William Williams the fifth."

"You're pulling my leg. No? Well, Mr. William Williams, come on up and turn over a card to see whether you are the province's newest multi-millionaire." The camera panned to William Williams, whose face was getting redder by the minute. "Mr. Williams, please hold up the card you have chosen." The camera zoomed in. "Oooh, so close. Right suit, wrong card. Mr. Williams has chosen the ten of spades. That means he will take home the consolation prize of. . . . How much is it tonight, Chedley? Ah, yes, four hundred thirty-seven thousand, five hundred and fifty-six dollars. Not too shabby. Congratulations, Mr. Williams. I believe you'll find that the press will want to speak to you."

Henry felt relieved. At least they were done and his ten-year-old could get away from the freak show. That is if he ever managed to meet up with the nutbar who had taken him there. Dash looked younger than his age, and the sling made him look even more vulnerable. "A kidnapper is probably leading Dash to a car at this very moment. All it would take is the promise of a puppy. Even a chocolate bar would do it."

Millie shook his arm. He knew that shake. It was the one she used to bring him back to the planet he occupied with her. "It's going to be okay, Henry."

"It'll be okay once Dash is safe at home."

"Looks like that might be a while," said Frank, gesturing at the crowds.

The coverage switched back to the inside camera, but Dot Rogers's grating voice was drowned out by a siren.

"Jesus in the garden." Henry felt an electric shock to his heart.

"Calm down," said Millie. "There are seventy-five thousand people there. There's bound to be some old man who overexerted himself and needs assistance."

"Or an abandoned ten-year-old boy who's been abducted."

Henry watched, helpless, as Dick Turner's face filled his TV screen. "If everyone could please move off the road. We need a clear path to let the emergency vehicles through." Speakers were positioned up and down the main street so the people outside the parish hall could hear the coverage in the streets or on their car radios.

"I can't take it." Henry grabbed Millie's pink iPhone, and his big meaty fingers were frantically pushing at the screen trying to reach Delores's phone.

"Here, give me that, Henry. You have to tap the screen gently. It's not like your flip phone." Millie took the device and located Delores in contacts and waited for her to respond. "Nothing. Her phone must still be dead. I should have gotten her to charge it before she left. I'll have to pick up one of those external battery chargers."

Henry's heart rate quickened. The sirens were moving off. The camera showed the back end of an ambulance speeding away. "How do you know it's not Dash in there?"

"I just know. Dash is fine." Millie took Henry's face in her hands and turned it toward her. She did not look like she knew.

Dot Rogers's face came back. "Ladies and gentlemen, in light of events this evening, we have been advised by the RNC that this will be the final night of Chase the Ace." The people in the crowd erupted. It was chaos. "Please, may I have your attention. Because of the crowds and the difficulty we are having maintaining a clear path for emergency vehicles, we have decided that tonight we will keep calling numbers until the Ace of Spades is chosen."

"Nooo," said Henry.

"We will draw a card every ten minutes until we find a winner. Each person who flips a card that is not the ace of spades will win twenty-five thousand dollars."

"Half my court bill." Henry took a gulp of beer and hiccoughed.

"Yes, there're only seven cards left. Look, they're drawing the next number already." Frank pointed at the screen.

"Ticket holder number four hundred and three. You have ten minutes to get to the hall for your chance to flip the ace of spades." As it turned out, the woman, Sarah Mahoney, was in the hall already and took no time making her way to the table to flip the card. "Sarah is about to turn over the card. It's the . . . aww, it's the king of hearts, ladies and gentlemen. Sarah doesn't go home empty-handed. She's an extra twenty-five thousand dollars richer."

"Will it never end?" Henry finished the beer and put the cool can to his forehead and checked his watch. All he wanted was to see his son. He prayed that Dash had not been injured. "I hope Delores has enough sense to just pack it in and come back."

What was Dot Rogers saying now? She had drawn another number, and the winning ticket holder still had three minutes to check in. "Millie, let's turn it off. I can't listen to her anymore. I'm going to implode."

"Let's wait another five minutes." Millie stretched. Henry groaned and shut his eyes. Frank burped and patted Henry on the head.

Dot Rogers was back. "I think we have found the lucky ticket holder." Henry stared as his son, wearing the fluorescent yellow jacket and baseball hat, made his way to the stage followed by their house guest, wearing her signature floral-print top. He heard Millie inhale next to him. She did not breathe out.

"Holy frankfurter." Frank spit a mouthful of beer on the carpet.

"What is your name?" Dot Rogers was holding out her hand to Delores.

"Delores Cowburn." Henry had never even heard his house guest say her family name before, although he had seen it on hospital forms.

"Congratulations, Delores. How many weeks have you been chasing the ace here in the Goulds?"

"This is my first time, ma'am. I only just arrived here in Newfundlund less than two weeks back."

"Well, now, what brings you to our fair province?"

"I travelled across the country in my Ford LTD station wagon, and now I'm living with this young man and his family." She gently prodded Dash forward, and there he was, slinged and as yellow as a lemon. Millie still hadn't exhaled. Henry turned up the volume.

"Hello, young man. What's your name?"

"Dashiell Puddester." He smiled. Were his teeth blue?

"Is this your aunt?"

"No, Miss Delores is sort of like my sister. She lives with us now." He smiled again, showing off his Gatorade-stained incisors. "Miss Delores told me she knew she was going to win."

"Really? How did she know?"

"She said ever since she got knocked out by a Walmart cart and got rescued by Dad and Mr. Parrell, her life has been nothing but one lucky thing after another."

"That sounds like a story we'd all like to hear after the draw. Well, Delores. Now's your chance to see if you're going to walk out of here a millionaire tonight. It's time to turn over a card. Which one are you going to choose?"

The camera zoomed in on Delores, who made her way closer to the cards, which lay face down on the table. She sized up each of the six remaining cards before her, and a gaudy floral sleeve reached out to take the second from the left. Her hand hovered over it for a split second but then seemed to float farther down the table to the last card. She picked it up and turned it over. The camera did not have a view.

"What card did she get?" Millie raised her neck to try and see what the camera could not.

"Jesus in the potato patch. I don't know."

Before the camera could get to the card, Delores's knees buckled under her, and she fluttered to the floor. The undisclosed card went with her.

The camera was all over the place then. Dash dropped to her side and started fanning her with what looked like a Frisbee. Dot Rogers was calling for paramedics. Millie had jumped up off the couch and moved to the flat screen. Henry had to stand up, too, in order to properly see what was transpiring.

"Henry, what card did she draw?"

"I only know as much as you do. Jesus Murphy, where's Dash?"

"He's there. He's got Miss Delores sitting up." She motioned to the screen.

And there was their house guest in her full floral glory, weakly holding up the ace of spades.

81

Delores Is a Millionaire

"Oh my God. She won." Frank was jumping up and down. His rectangular beer gut was moving up and down with him.

"She won?" Henry felt dazed.

"Yes, Delores won. Can you believe it?" Frank continued jumping. Then he urged a little. "Too much beer," he said.

"You'd best take it easy, Frank." Millie eased him back down onto the couch. "We do not need you seizuring here tonight."

Henry felt deflated. "If she won, that means she can afford to go live somewhere else."

Frank looked at Millie, who shook her head.

"I don't think Henry has fully embraced the idea of having Miss Delores live under the same roof."

"I long for the day she disappears," said Henry.

"Henry, listen to me." Frank was always trying to be the peacemaker. "Because of Miss Delores, they have the meter thief in custody. He's admitted the whole thing. There may have been a few other thieves, but he had over a hundred meters in his possession. I haven't been this happy in months. The lottery could not have been won by a more deserving person."

"Let's hope she's lucky enough to get the hell back here with my son." Henry stared at the swirling crowds on the screen. He could feel tears welling up. He put the beer can to his lips. There was none left. Millie passed him hers and started poking at her phone screen.

"Delores's phone is dead. But we know Dick is there somewhere. I'll see if he can find Dash. Frank, go get yourself and Henry another beer." She made big eyes at Frank and nodded toward Henry. It was almost imperceptible, but Henry saw it. Then she exited the rec room.

Frank grabbed two black tins of Max Ice out of the fridge and sat down next to Henry. His presence relaxed Henry a bit. Henry leaned back into the couch cushions.

By the time Millie came back, she had Dash on the line. "They're all good," she shouted to Henry. "Dick and Stella will drive them back to the station wagon."

"Don't you think Dick Turner has done enough?"

"We have to get past that now, Henry. I think he feels bad about the verdict. No one expected it to be so harsh. Plus, Dick's car is much closer to the parish hall. He'll drop them to Daisy and then follow them home to make sure they get here okay."

"It'll take hours." Henry could no longer feel his teeth.

"He says half the cars have cleared out already. By the time they get the paperwork done with Delores, the roads should be clear." She got a fresh beer for herself and sat down in a nearby chair, taking a sip. "These things taste strong." She looked at the label. "Good grief. Make no wonder, it's seven point one per cent."

Frank raised his tin. "Here's to Delores." He slurred the last bit.

"To Delores." Millie clunked hers off Frank's and Henry's. "If I drink all this, I'll be looped." She laid the tin on the coffee table.

Henry said nothing, just kept drinking.

82

Thursday: Two Weeks after the Supermarket Incident

It was close to 1:00 a.m. Dash bounded into the living room and jumped on his father's lap as if he were still only forty pounds. He weighed more than ninety. Dash's bony elbow hit Henry in the ribs. He held him close despite the pain—that film of tears rising again. "Dasher, you came home."

"Dad, you're slurring like Mr. Parrell."

Delores sashayed in behind him.

"Delores, you're a millionaire." Frank attempted to get to his feet but fell back on the couch laughing.

"She doesn't look like a millionaire." Henry blinked at the floral Walmart shirt and pink bell-bottoms.

"Your father and Mr. Parrell have been celebrating." Millie hugged Dash and opened her arms to welcome Delores into the huddle.

"I can see that." Delores looked down at the two drunken men, her rosy cheeks aglow. "Dash and I had quite an adventure. He's a good-luck charm, for sure."

"Miss Delores said she'd buy me some V-Bucks." Dash wiggled away from Millie and began bouncing on the couch in between Henry and Frank.

"V-Bucks?" Frank tilted his head.

"Vindertech Bucks. That's what you use to buy things in Fortnite." Dash put one hand on each man's head and sprang off the couch.

"You lost me, kid." Frank rubbed his bald scalp.

"You can use them in Battle Royale or Save the World. Stella buys Llama Piñatas."

"Delores, what else are you going to do with your millions?" Frank squinted up at her.

"Pay more rent, hopefully," said Henry.

"Henry Puddester, don't be so rude." Millie had her hands on her hips.

"That's okay, Miss Millie. Sure, I can pay more rent. And . . . I think I'll get Daisy some studded tires for winter driving. Also, some undercoating. Oh, and get the bumper and headlight fixed."

"That's living on the edge." Frank pushed himself up off the arm of the couch and started making his way to the door. "Henry, it's probably time you got rid of your land line."

"What are you talking about?"

"Patty's sister won six hundred thousand on Lotto Max once. They found her within two hours of the announcement."

"Who found her, Mr. Parrell?" asked Dash.

"The vultures." Frank had trouble twisting the handle on the door to let himself out. Dash went to open it for him. Frank fell out onto the step.

"What does he mean, Daddy? The vultures?"

"Not sure, Dasher. I think Mr. Parrell is feeling no pain, and the synapses in his brain may be misfiring somewhat. Now that you're both safe at home . . ." At the word "home," Henry coughed and tried to glare at Delores but did not do a convincing job. "I think it's time we all went to bed."

Delores took the hint and skittered as fast as her floral-wrapped body would carry her.

83

The Calls Begin

The calls began Thursday morning just after 6:00 a.m. Henry was dreaming. He was in a station wagon with thousands of vultures stuck to it. There were vultures on top of vultures all over the hood. They were inside, too, on the steering wheel, making it hard to drive. He was bouncing through a desert. Delores was in the back seat telling him which way to go. He looked through the station wagon window. Dash was hitchhiking next to a sign with an arrow pointing toward GOULDS. He was smiling and waving a lottery ticket. Henry pulled in to pick him up. He could hear a bell ringing.

Henry woke up with a raging thirst. It was worse than when he had taken the Dilaudid. "Oh, God." He rolled over to see Millie pick up the portable phone on the bedside table. The movement made his temple throb.

Millie looked at the number and pressed it on and off in quick succession.

"Who is it?" Henry's voice came out a croak. He felt like he had swallowed caterpillars.

"Don't know. Didn't recognize the number, so I hung up. They've been calling here for ten minutes."

Henry's flip phone began to ring. He found it on the floor next to the bed and picked up.

"Mr. Puddester, this is Gillian Gee from CBC."

"What do you want?"

"I'm looking to speak to Delores Cowburn."

"Never heard of her." Henry shut the flip phone, eliminating Gillian Gee.

"Who was it?" Millie propped herself up on one elbow.

"That stupid Gillian Gee. Where did she get my cellphone number?"

In Henry's hazy memories of the night before, he remembered Frank had said something about getting rid of the land line. The memory swept over him like a tsunami. Chase the Ace. Delores was a millionaire. He stumbled out of bed and went in the ensuite, stuck his head under the faucet, and drank like he had never experienced piped-in water.

The phone started again. Millie picked up the receiver and laid it alongside the phone. Within a minute the incessant beeping noise that comes when you leave a phone off the hook began. Henry moved to the side table and unplugged the little beige carcass. "Millie, how many beer did I drink?" He crawled back under the covers.

"Not sure, but I think we had a dozen of those strong ones, and they're all gone."

The land line downstairs started ringing.

"Jesus at the landfill." Henry shoved his head under the pillow.

Millie got up and went on a mission to unplug all the phones in the house. How many times had Henry threatened to do away with the land line? He would put in a request as soon as the office opened.

Frank appeared—had he even made it home? Henry remembered him falling out the door. Frank lay on Millie's side of the bed. The mattress sagged down an extra inch. He was wearing green plaid pyjama pants and the same faded subway shirt he had on last night.

Henry looked at the clock. "Jesus, Frank, it's six thirty a.m."

Frank hoisted his stainless-steel coffee mug in a salute. "I know, but the trucks woke me up."

"What trucks?"

"Vans, actually. The third one just pulled in."

Henry crawled over to the window. He separated two rows of the blind with his thumb and forefinger and peered through. Blinding sunshine poured in. "Jesus in the garden. How do these people know that Delores is here?" Henry flopped back onto the bed and covered his head once again with the pillow.

"They must have seen the station wagon parked in the driveway."

Henry thought of Carter leading Gillian Gee to Delores in the apartment. "That still wouldn't give them our number."

"Reverse directory," said Frank. "All you gotta do is punch in the address, and you can get the rest of the info online."

"They're calling my cellphone, Frank."

"Journalists have their ways, Henry. What do you think I've been harping on about? The press still won't leave me alone. I changed my number, and they were calling the new one within two days. And my sister-in-law said the people who call asking for money are worse than the journalists."

"What do you mean? What sister-in-law? What people looking for money?"

"Patty's sister won Lotto Max last year. People started calling right away. Anyone she ever met. Strangers, too."

"I thought only charities would ask for donations."

"Not just charities. Anybody who feels like they want a piece of the pie. Shameless gits. My sister-in-law said this bloke called her from Wyoming. Said he was her kin. He had done the DNA test. And by the way, could she spare two grand?"

"What did she do?" Henry twisted the sleeve of his pyjama shirt.

"She ended up moving. And she only won six hundred and seventy-five thousand dollars. You're going to have to get out of here while this dies down."

"But I didn't win the lottery. Delores did. I should just send her packing."

"Don't do that to her," said Frank. "I know you want her out, but wait until things settle. I can watch the house for you. But take Delores with you."

"Are you out of your mind?"

"Come on, Henry. She's got such a big heart. She'll probably end up giving it all away to the first person who tells her the children need boots."

Millie appeared, yawning deeply. She laid her silent pink iPhone on the table.

"Morning, Frank."

"Morning, Millie. Sorry to be here so early. I just wanted to warn you not to go outside in your dressing gown."

"I saw from downstairs. How'd you get in here?" Millie sat in the plush chair by the window.

"I came through the backyard so they wouldn't see me." Frank nodded his head toward the window. "You should really keep your sliding door locked."

Millie rolled her eyes. "I expected a few calls and the odd media request, but I had no idea we'd be inundated like this." She gestured to the blinds separating them from the nation's TV screens. A moan came from under Henry's pillow. "Henry, come out from under there. I have an idea," said Millie.

"I don't like your ideas." A swatch of Henry's hair appeared from under the pillow.

"We can go on a camping trip. If we sneak out with Delores today and leave Daisy here, they shouldn't even know we're gone."

"Splendid idea." Frank pulled the bedcovers over his legs. "Where will you go?"

"The Spout."

A groan emanated from Henry. Millie had wanted Henry and Dash to do the Spout with her ever since her brother had done it with his kids. Camping reminded Henry of Dick and missing his birthday. He refused to let his mind go there. He felt Frank's big hand pat the top of his head.

"What the heck is the Spout?" Frank continued with the patting.

"The Spout is a geyser on the East Coast Trail. It spits up sea water every few minutes. It can reach thirty feet on good days."

"Oh yeah," said Frank. "I remember something about it back in the

242

nineties. They came to the City looking for funding to remove a big boulder that had stogged it up."

"Did the City contribute?"

"No, they said it wasn't a project they could support financially. I think I remember a team of Hibernia engineers and a group from the East Coast Trail Association got help from O'Brien's Boat Tours in Bay Bulls to pull out the rock."

Henry raised his head. "Millie, if you think I'm spending my last days before six months of house arrest . . ."

Millie sat on Henry's side, shoving him closer to Frank. "Come on, Henry. It'll be a fun bonding experience."

"Millie, the Spout is the hardest hike on the East Coast Trail."

"So?" said Millie. "We can walk thirty-two kilometres no problem."

"*Thirty-two kilometres*? Seriously? Dash can't do that."

"What can't I do?" Dash ran in and jumped on the bed between Henry and Frank, jolting them both. Frank banged his coffee mug off his teeth.

"The Spout, honey. You know that hike your cousins did?" Millie rubbed Dash's feet. "You can do it, no problem. We'll spread it out over two days."

"But he's in a sling, Millie. He can't carry a backpack for two days."

"We can carry all the heavy stuff."

"Can't we just go check into a hotel?" Henry wiggled out a few inches from under Dash's weight.

"They'll find you there." Frank was nodding solemnly and rubbing his teeth.

"My back hurts just thinking about slogging the tent, stove, and food for two days."

"Don't forget sleeping bags and self-inflating mattresses," Frank added helpfully.

"You can do it, Henry, if you take it slow. It's either that or stay home with the monsters."

"What monsters, Mom?"

Millie pulled up one blind halfway. Henry could just see a mild frenzy among the troops outside.

"Are they here for Delores's car?" Dash started toward the window.

Henry pulled him back. "Don't let them see you. They're not here for her car. They're here because she won Chase the Ace."

"Delores will come with us, of course. That'll share the weight. She and Dash can use the new pup tent, and me and you will use the old one."

"You have got to be joking. Millie, please tell me you're joking. I can't spend two days on a trail with that woman."

"You don't detest Delores, darling. You're just mad at her. There's a difference." Millie sat on Henry's side of the bed and rubbed behind his ear.

"How would you feel if someone destroyed your Mini?"

Millie recoiled.

"Last week Delores was in a hospital bed, and now you think she can hike thirty-two kilometres with a thirty-pound pack on her back."

"You're mixing metric and imperial, Henry."

"I'll go to Churchill Square and pick up some freeze-dried meals," said Frank. "Eight should be enough. Anything else you need?"

"Yes, a couple of cans of compressed gas. I'll get one to show you the kind." Millie left the bedroom to fetch a canister in the basement.

Henry put the pillow over his face and screamed.

"It's gonna be okay, Dad. You said things would be better once the weather got warmer. Look how sunny it is."

Frank, as always, must have known what Henry was thinking. "Delores needs to get out of here, too, Henry. She'll never survive this."

As if on cue, Delores sashayed into the bedroom wearing what appeared to be floral leggings and an oversized T-shirt with a piece of cardboard pinned on the front. Written in pink marker, it said: IF I HAD A MILLION DOLLARS, I'D BUY A FORD LTD.

"I wondered where everyone had gone," she said and clambered onto the bed with the rest of them.

84

Frank, the Getaway Driver

"Have you looked out the window?" Frank moved over to make more room for Delores.

"No, why?"

"There's a mob of journalists out there."

"And you think they're all here for little old me?" She batted her eyelashes.

"You and your money." Frank checked the window. "They're like a bunch of bloodthirsty wolves staring at your front door." He jumped in glee. "Here's the plan. I'll take the Escape and get supplies. Henry, you get the camping gear. You gotta be quiet and bring it all to my house through the backyard. When I get back, I'll park the Escape under my overhang. That way those wankers won't see us loading up."

"Are you hiking with us, too, Mr. Parrell?"

"No, Dash, but I'm to be your getaway driver. And if you get your mother and Miss Delores to disguise you real good, you can be my shopping accomplice."

"Can I wear my gorilla suit?"

"I was thinking more of dressing you like a girl."

"A *girrrl*? Ew."

"Stella is a girl, and she's all right." Frank raised his eyebrows.

"True. But I'll only do it if I get to pick out a bag of gummies."

"Deal," said Frank, holding out his hand. "Maybe Miss Delores will let you borrow that fancy jacket she always wears." Dash ran off with Delores. Frank called after him. "Remember, you have to be quiet. You can't let them hear you going back and forth."

Frank turned to Henry. "Henry, are you feeling okay?"

"I feel like I've been left for dead in the desert. How are you so bright-eyed?"

"I have the ultimate hangover cure."

"What is it?"

"Two raw eggs washed down with apple cider vinegar."

"You're not serious."

"Would I lie about something like that? Come over and I'll whip up some."

"I'd rather drink a two-four of cod-liver oil."

"Have it your way. Just get the camping gear ready. Now."

Millie passed Frank a slip of paper. "Here's the list."

"You're fast." He began to read. "Eight freeze-dried meals. Two pounds GORP. One pound oatmeal. Two dozen bagels. Peanut butter. Two gas canisters. Hot chocolate. Gatorade powder. Four double A batteries. Any particular kind of meals?"

"I'll leave it up to your discretion."

"Perfect. I'm on it like a car bonnet."

"Don't forget to pick up the trail maps." Millie had her head stuck in a closet looking for the first aid kit. She popped back out with a canvas bag embossed with the Red Cross symbol and a pink Boston Red Sox ball cap. Dash reappeared dressed in flowery cotton.

"Hey, Mom, can I wear that?" He snatched the hat out of his mother's hand and put it on his head, his blond curls cascading around his ears.

"Dash, you look simply . . . dashing." Frank took out his phone to snap a picture. "Okay, let's go. We're on a mission."

He drove out the cul-de-sac with Dash in the front seat wearing cat's-eye sunglasses as a final touch.

An hour later, they were back.

Frank's plan worked like a charm. They loaded up the Escape under the overhang, which didn't have a view of Henry's driveway. With the tinted windows, the journalists wouldn't be able to tell who was aboard.

"Quick, shove the backpacks in the boot. You can add in the food once you get to Bay Bulls. Delores, I picked up those frankfurters in a tin you like so much."

"I think they're called Vienna Sausages, Frank."

"Whatever. Hurry."

Delores was outfitted in spandex pants and a fleece featuring a large purple kitten head. "You've a coat, I presume, Miss Delores?"

"Dash is wearing it. I assume he'll wear his own once we set out." Delores looked at Millie.

"Oh, yes, I've got it right here with the bags."

"Speaking of jackets . . . Henry, haven't seen that jacket on you since the last fishing trip."

Henry looked down at the red plaid. "I wore it to camp just last week. It's reserved for special wilderness events." He closed the back hatch.

"Well, wild is what you're gonna get." Frank laughed his belly-busting laugh. "Okay now, Delores up front and Dash in the back between your parents." Frank loved being sergeant major.

"Why does Delores get to sit up front?" Henry sounded like a sulking teenager.

"Oh, Henry," said Millie. "Come on." She pushed him in the back seat, closed the door, and ran around to the other side."

"Frank shouldn't be driving. He doesn't even have a licence."

"Really, Mr. Parrell? But you just drove me shopping."

"I can drive, Dash. It's just the doctor doesn't like me to."

"Oh. What was it you said, Mr. Parrell? We've got a full tank of gas, half-pack of cigarettes, and . . . what was it about the sunglasses?" Dash tapped the cat's-eye rims.

"It's dark out and we're wearing sunglasses." Frank laughed. "And we're on a mission from God."

"Too bad you can't come, Mr. Parrell."

"Next time, Dash." Frank pulled into the parking garage at the bunker and hopped out.

"How are we going to get home if we leave the Escape at one end and we finish on the other?"

"Don't worry about that, honey. Once we're in cell range, we'll call Frank, and he'll come pick us up."

"Goodbye, Mr. Frank," Delores called.

With his new regimen, Frank could jog back home in under thirty minutes. Up to now, he was too ashamed to jog outside in daylight. But not today. Today he would jog outside where people would see him.

85

Henry Takes Over

In the parking garage at City Hall, the inhabitants of the car switched places. Millie took over the driving, and Dash moved over to her spot. "It's like a Chinese fire escape." Dash was still wearing his mother's glasses.

"You can take them off now, honey." Millie went to remove the glasses, but Dash jerked his head away.

"No way, Mom. I like 'em. They're like Stella's."

With Millie at the wheel, they made it to Bay Bulls in under thirty minutes. They would leave the Escape at the trailhead and pick it up later.

Delores proved to be astoundingly nimble. She shouldered her pack and appeared to have no difficulty hiking the first few kilometres toward the Bull Head lighthouse. Henry was not quite so agile. His head throbbed. His throat needed moisture. He had all the cookware and heavy food along with his tent while Millie and Delores split the other food and supplies, one carrying the poles and fly while the other had the tent.

"How can she be so fit when she doesn't look fit?" he whispered to Millie.

"I don't know. I'm certainly feeling my age." She adjusted her shoulder straps.

The walk from Bread and Cheese to the lighthouse was magnificent. The sun warmed their faces, and a light breeze propelled them forward. Delores distracted Dash so he didn't complain about the distance covered. "Dash, do you know the alphabet game?"

"The one where you go through the alphabet and name something starting with each letter?"

"That's the one," answered Delores. "We'll start with hockey players. You can use their first or last names."

"How about nicknames?"

"No nicknames. You start."

"Okay. Anderson, Craig." Dash was fast.

"Bourque, Ray." Delores was, too, but Dash had played this game with Henry a hundred times.

"C. That's easy. Coffey, Paul. Chara, Zdeno. Crosby, Sidney."

They kept up a swift pace, the earth spongy underfoot, and reached the lighthouse before noon. Dash doffed his backpack, pulled open the heavy iron door, and disappeared inside.

Millie dropped to the ground and wiggled out of her pack. "Dash, I'm not sure you're allowed in there."

"Too late." Henry sat down and rubbed his neck.

"Henry, go after him."

"I can't move."

Dash was already at the top, looking down at them from the catwalk.

"I'll go." Delores trotted after Dash into the metal tower.

Millie opened her pack and pulled out lunch: Georgetown bagels with peanut butter and bananas. Delores coaxed Dash down, and they ate with gusto.

They packed up, donned their packs, and headed north. After about ninety minutes, they stopped for a snack at Shag Rocks.

"That sure was nice of Mr. Frank to buy us these bars." Delores bit down into crème brûlée–flavoured milk chocolate.

By the time they reached Drop Cove, the trail had taken on a sinister air with steep rises and overgrown paths on teetering cliffs. But they powered on with Delores in the lead. Finally, around four hours in, they saw the glazed-wooden East Coast Trail sign announcing Bald Head Campground.

"Praise the Lord and the puppies in Heaven." Henry barely had the strength to remove his pack. He saw Millie gingerly undo her straps and went to help her. He dug around for the cookware and backtracked to the stream to fill a pan for their supper: four freeze-dried meals that Frank had picked up for them, two pasta, two rice.

Dash dropped his pack and tore after his father, energy renewed now that they had arrived. Half an hour earlier, he had moaned that he couldn't make it. While Henry put the water on to boil, Millie wrestled with the tent.

"Let me help you with that, Miss Millie." Delores clearly knew her way around a tent and had the two assembled in jig time.

Henry poured the boiling water into the freeze-dried meal packs and zipped them closed. "I can't believe I'm excited to eat something out of a foil bag." He applied his hand sanitizer, and they all ate supper in relative peace. Henry was too exhausted to be bothered by Delores.

"I have to go the bathroom again." Dash stood up, jumping from one foot to the other.

"Dash, that's your third time since we arrived. Is your stomach okay?" Millie furrowed her brow into deep lines.

"He just likes the facilities." Henry accompanied Dash up the winding path to the privy. The toilet at Bald Head campground had three plastic sides offering privacy, yet the user was perfectly exposed to the elements. "I'll just be over here, Dash."

The moon was full and the sky perfectly clear with thousands of twinkling stars. It was pretty out here. But Henry couldn't enjoy it. He always had trouble enjoying camping. It was the guilt of abandoning Dick all those years ago. Plus, it wasn't like he was out here of his own accord. He was out here because some nutbar Millie had dragged home had ruined his life. How had he come from marketing cruise ships for the City to hiding in the woods? How could a judge sentence him to house arrest? He hadn't done anything wrong. How far had he fallen through no fault of his own? Henry pressed in Frank's number on his cellphone. No service. He knew they could not go back until the press had moved on to another story.

Dash ran past him on the snaking trail and did a cartwheel in the clearing, crashing solidly into Henry's tent.

"I'm hitting the hay." Henry kissed Millie on the cheek when they got back and crawled inside the tent.

Once in his sleeping bag, Henry ate a Nutella sandwich he had snuck in his pocket, and as he chewed, he reviewed his mental files once again.

This was what he knew. It was Thursday night. He had one more day on this trail. Monday, his house arrest would begin. And Millie would get rid of Delores. He had to figure out what he was going to do with his bike, which was now sitting in a garage in Montreal waiting for him to arrive for the Spring Tune-Up Ride. He had never been so disappointed in his life when he heard he wouldn't make the trip. How could life be so cruel?

Boom. Something hit the tent. Henry jolted.

Millie's voice penetrated the nylon. "Dash, stop throwing sticks at your father. He's trying to sleep."

Boom. Another direct hit.

Dash giggled. "Aww, Dad, don't be a party pooper. It's too early to go to bed."

"Dash, you need to get rested so tomorrow morning we'll not only see the Spout," said Millie, "but we'll walk out to Petty Harbour, and Mr. Parrell will come pick us up. Come on, I'll tuck you in."

Boom. Henry discarded the last of the purloined sandwich. "Dash, don't make me come out there."

"Quick, in your sleeping bag. See, Miss Delores is already in hers." Millie gave him a shove in the tent. "Good night, Miss Delores."

"Good night, Miss Millie. Good night, Mr. Henry."

"It sounds like we're the freakin' Brady Bunch." Henry slid lower in his sleeping bag. Millie crawled in the tent.

"Henry, did you put the food bag up in the tree?"

He pretended to be asleep.

86

Surprise Visitor

Boom. Henry sat bolt upright. He checked his watch. 10:47 p.m.

"Dash, go to bed."

Boom. "Dash . . . so help me, Millie, I can't be held responsible for what I might do to our child."

"Wha? Wha?" Millie had drifted off.

"Dash is still out there chucking things at the tent."

"He's not, Henry. It's just the wind."

"The wind does not hit me in the head."

"Dash, honey. If that's you, go back to bed. You need to get a good night's sleep."

No answer. "Not Dash." Millie snuggled deeper in her bag.

Henry concentrated. A crack. Like someone walking on a stick. He poked Millie. "There is something out there."

"I don't hear anything. Go back to sleep."

Henry moved his eyes to the side to indicate where the sound had come from. "No, there's something. It sounds like something breaking sticks in the underbrush."

"It's probably just Delores going for a pee." Millie lay back down.

Something musky-smelling started snuffling outside their tent, scratching and rubbing its bulk against the fly. Millie sat up, suddenly wide awake. "Henry, go see what it is," she hissed.

"Are you joking? I'm not going out there."

"Why not?"

"It could be a skunk."

"We don't have skunks in Newfoundland."

"Still . . ."

"Henry, whatever it is, I don't want it eating our porridge. We need that porridge for energy. It'll be frightened as soon as it sees you."

"So why don't you go?"

"Henry, be a man."

Henry had slept in his T-shirt, so he pulled on his hiking pants and padded plaid shirt and quietly unzipped the tent. He glanced back at Millie. She was sitting up with the sleeping bag pulled up to her chin. "Go on," she urged.

Henry unzipped the fly, and light flooded in. The moon was huge and round, like in a children's painting. Henry crawled out into the clearing. He turned on his flashlight and shone it under the trees. It caught the red eyes of an animal. "Millie."

"What is it?" Millie crawled outside just in time to see a giant coyote run into the undergrowth. She swallowed. "It's gone. Come back to bed."

"That's a relief." Henry turned off the flashlight and crawled in after his wife. Within minutes he could hear the sleep start to envelop Millie's words.

Scratch. Something struck the tent again.

Henry couldn't take it. "I'm going to get rid of that stupid coyote." He crawled back through the vestibule. A large rock was silhouetted against the moon. Funny, Henry didn't remember a rock there before. He looked around when he noticed the rock's shoulders moved. Henry gulped. The rock moved close enough for Henry to feel its warm, rank breath on his face. The rock turned so that Henry could see the curve of its yellow teeth.

"Holy Mother of God." A piece of moss was stuck between the canines. "Millie!" he said, voice trembling. "It's not a coyote." His voice was a whisper. He was motionless for a second, trying not to breathe. Henry closed his eyes, opened them again. He thought of Akela's mantra at Cub Camp. *No bears on the Avalon. No bears on the Avalon.* This thing eyeing him was still there and sure as heck looked like a black bear.

"Millie," he said, louder.

"Henry, what is it?" Millie whispered from inside the tent.

It was bigger than any black bear Henry had ever seen—he had only ever seen bears in a zoo. It paused and sniffed the air, its pointed nose rising toward the night sky.

"Henry?"

Henry felt a rustling in the tent behind him, Millie's hand on his back. Millie knelt forward until she could see Henry's line of sight.

"*Henryyy!*"

Her scream startled the black mass, which backed away and moved across the clearing. The coyote appeared, and the bear clambered to get at it, but the coyote was too quick and disappeared into the night.

"Jesus in the garden." Henry tried to remember what he was supposed to do to scare a black bear. Stand tall, look him in the eye, and assert his dominance? Or was that for a grizzly?

The bear moved to Delores and Dash's tent and began pawing at the flap. It looked like it weighed over 500 pounds.

"Dash! Delores!" Henry could not let the bear get his son. He picked up a rock the size of his fist and pelted the bear's butt. The bear turned and reared up on his hind legs, turning away from Dash and Delores's tent and sniffing the air. Its ears flattened like a cat before it pounced on a bee. In the sea of black fur, two beady eyes narrowed in on Henry. The bear flattened its ears back even farther and opened its mouth, exposing pink gums around razor-sharp teeth.

"Shit." *What should I do? Lie down and play dead? Climb a tree?* Black bears could climb trees. Henry's neurons were firing too quickly. He could almost see the air filling the bear's lungs. He could see muscle under fur. The bear gathered its strength on its hind legs and sprang forward. As it left the ground, Henry could see the pads of the bear's feet, its massive paws thudding toward him, sending twigs flying. Millie screamed.

The bear had him pinned on his back in seconds. Henry fell hard under the black bulk. He felt the massive claws ripping through his red plaid jacket. The bear's can opener of a muzzle growled in Henry's ear. Henry had read somewhere that bears broke their opponent's jaws to incapacitate them. He tweaked the bear's nose. That shocked the bear enough to give Henry time to flip over and cover his face with his arm. The bear was breathing hard. It was trying to roll Henry to get at his face. Its breath smelled like rotten tuna.

Dash's screams combined with Millie's.

With his face still covered, Henry tried to grab something hard in order to beat off the animal. The bear lifted him off the ground, playing with him. It swung him around by his plaid jacket like a dog shaking a toy. Henry felt like he was on a roller coaster, his neck snapping back and forth. Just as abruptly, the bear dropped him. The hard ground came up against Henry's ribs. Winded, he looked up to see the bear come down on him again. Its jaws clamped around his ribs, and it began gnawing. *A bear is chewing on my body*, thought Henry. He felt the crack as the ribs snapped. The bear let go and reared up on its hind legs once again. Henry tried to back away. He could hear Dash crying. He managed to get a few feet away, but the bear wasn't finished with him yet. His eyes locked with the bear's. This time its saucepan-sized paws approached Henry's face at full bore. Henry put his arms up to protect his face and steeled himself for the impact. No time to turn away. *Is this it, then? Is this how it all ends?*

A shot rang out and echoed off the rock face. Henry watched in disbelief as the bear's paw stopped in mid-swing. The big animal growled and then fell on top of Henry. The bear's muscles relaxed, and its full weight collapsed across Henry's chest and legs. The bear's panting slowed to a rocking-chair rhythm. Henry struggled to fill his lungs with air. His breath came in gasps—not enough to sustain life. His vision blurred, but he thought he saw Delores standing over him holding something in her left hand. The matte black in Daisy's glovebox zipped through Henry's throbbing brain. He could hear Millie and Dash crying. Another shot rang out.

Delores began to pull the animal off Henry. It was too much for her. "Dash. Millie. I need you here."

They joined in, grabbing handfuls of black fur until they managed to extricate Henry. Henry lay where he was in the dirt and felt his ribs. He moaned in pain as he looked down at blood soaking through his jacket and hiking pants. Millie and Dash were on either side of him. Delores was on her feet.

"No service." Delores held up her pink iPhone, the twin of Millie's. "I'm going to run to get reception." She grabbed her hiking boots and jammed her feet inside. She pulled her food bag out of the tree and stuffed granola bars into the pocket of her floral jacket.

In Henry's field of vision he could see his food bag lying on the ground alongside his tent. The food he was supposed to have suspended before he went to bed.

Delores called over her shoulder as her spandex-covered legs set off into the dark night. "You'll be okay, Mr. Henry. I'll get help."

The last thing Henry heard before he lost consciousness was Delores's fading voice singing, "I Am Woman."

8 7

Frank Sees Kaitlyn's Feet

Frank removed his shed coat from the treadmill and made sure it was positioned for the best possible view of the reporters who were still fanned out in front of Henry's house. He hoped Henry was enjoying the quiet of the woods, because there was no way he'd survive this. The number of journalists had doubled since yesterday. They milled around, but they did not appear frustrated. The nice weather helped. They were happily biding their time until the next big story pulled them elsewhere. They looked more like strikers on a picket line than journalists, but news of the Chase the Ace winner was on everyone's tongue, and the public wanted more details about Delores. And they had to deliver. They had already done stories on Delores and Daisy and the cross-country trek, but now she was a superstar, and everyone wanted a piece of her. The reporters were civil, though. Rival news agencies were chatting. Cars came and went bearing takeout food.

Frank took off his shirt. There was no Henry to bother him about his manly chest. He should have told him to sod off. Women liked Italian men, and they were hairy. He upped the tension on the treadmill and adjusted the headphones attached to his phone in the cupholder. He had downloaded the CBC app and could listen live. Through the window, he saw Gillian Gee doing a stand-up. The camera's light illuminated her face. Frank turned up the volume so he could hear better over the noise of his banging feet.

"We are still trying to determine the whereabouts of the winner of last night's Chase the Ace in the Goulds. It's a real rags-to-riches story. We have brought you stories about Delores Cowburn before. She's the woman who crossed Canada in her Ford LTD decked out in over four thousand toys. She was living in the Walmart parking lot until she moved here." Frank saw the camera pan over to Henry's house and Delores's wagon. "We do not fear for her safety, but we would like to hear from anyone who knows where she is. As soon as we find her, we will ask her how it feels to be an overnight millionaire. For *CBC News*, I'm Gillian Gee."

The cameraman switched off the light. Frank could no longer hear Gillian Gee's words, but he saw her indicate toward his house, and she and her cameraman began making their way to his front door. Frank opened the door and smiled. Sweat glistened on his rug of a chest.

"What can I do for you folks? You need a washroom?"

Gillian Gee took a step back but kept her composure. "No, we don't need the washroom. We were hoping you might know where we can find Delores."

Frank used the towel around his neck to wipe the sweat from his face. "Sorry, I'm a bit ripe." He smelled under an armpit. "Ah, yes, Delores. I heard she hightailed it to the neighbours' cabin in Hants Harbour."

"Where's that?"

"This side of Trinity Bay."

"Are you sure?"

"Heard it from the horse's mouth."

"Which horse?"

"My neighbour, Henry."

"Do you know him well?"

"No, don't know him at all."

"Didn't I see you going in and out of his house?" Gillian Gee held a microphone in Frank's face.

"Ask me no questions and I'll tell you no lies." Frank took his vape pen from his pocket and exhaled a cloud of cotton candy smoke at the microphone.

"Do you know when they'll be back?" Gillian Gee waved her free hand in front of her face.

"No idea."

"You sure?" Gillian tilted her head and looked him straight in the eyes.

"Cross my heart." Frank crossed the vape pen over his lips.

"That's not your heart."

"Toodle-oo."

Frank shut the door and went back to the couch. He watched Gillian Gee and her cameraman putter off back to the van and begin packing up. The other journalists followed suit. Frank should be doing another half-hour on the treadmill, but he decided he'd done enough for the day. He patted his belly and stood up and posed sideways in front of the floor-to-ceiling mirrors on the hall closet doors. He sucked in his gut. "Looking good," he said. He went back to the couch to pull up the pictures from the racetrack on his phone and see if he could tell what brought on the seizure.

Facebook pinged. Frank only had seven Facebook friends. He opened the app. Ten toes with nails sporting blue and yellow polish filled the screen. He turned his phone sideways to enlarge the image. The second toe on the right foot sported a gold ring with a dangling heart. A twenty-year-old wouldn't take pictures of her feet and post them online, would she? Apparently a twenty-year-old would.

Frank creeped his daughter's Facebook page. The second post was a typical soft-porn bathroom selfie. Kaitlyn, his 4.0-GPA daughter, stood in front of a mirror wearing only underwear. She had her body contorted at an impossible angle. Her cheeks were sucked in, and her gel-enhanced lips were stuck out. Frank had paid for those lips. Was he out of his mind? The picture's pièce de résistance, however, was the left breast, where the tattoo of the Japanese kanji was prominent. The hash tags read: #newtat #whosaiditwouldnthurt. Frank turned his head away.

It actually wasn't as bad as one picture she had posted last summer. She was belly down on a pool floatie, ass to the camera, wearing nothing but a dental floss–thin G-string, with the hash tag #niceviewfromhere

Frank decided to give Kaitlyn a call. He hadn't seen her since the tattoo incident. Perhaps he needed to be more of a presence in his daughter's life. Maybe if he tried harder, she wouldn't feel the need for self-promiscuity.

"Hi, honey."

"Hi, Dad."

"I just got a picture of your feet."

"I thought I had blocked you."

"Nope."

"I'll go do it now."

"Uh, Kaitlyn?"

"Yes, Dad." She sighed.

"My birthday is coming up soon." Frank shared a birthday with Queen Victoria.

"And?"

"I was wondering if you could come by for cake?"

"I usually go camping May twenty-fourth weekend."

"I know, honey. But that's the weekend before the actual twenty-fourth."

"I'll let you know. Pretty busy here, Dad. Gotta go."

"Kaitlyn, I have a question."

"Yes?"

"Last year, did you send me a card?" Last May, Frank had received a birthday card signed "Love, Kaitlyn." It looked suspiciously like Patty's handwriting.

"Not that I remember. Why?"

"No reason." He laid the phone on the table next to his feet and closed his eyes. He prayed his daughter would revert to the girl he had raised to be caring, kind, and loving."

88

Millie Tends to the Patient

"Don't worry, Henry. Delores will get help." Millie smoothed Henry's hair. There were twigs in it. Henry's unconscious body did not move.

Dash hopped around, full of fear and raw energy. "Dad, you were awesome." Dash picked up a stick and began jabbing at the bear carcass.

"Dash, stop poking it." Millie was half expecting the bear to get back up, even though it had a gaping hole in its head and another in its back. Where did Miss Delores get a gun? And what was it doing with her on a camping trip? For the first time, Millie questioned her decision to invite Delores into their home.

"We're lucky Miss Delores had her gun, aren't we? I told you she had good aim. Wait till I tell everyone on Fortnite that she's just as good in real life."

"Dash, come and help me get Daddy back in the tent. You take his feet."

Millie dragged Henry's upper body into the vestibule while Dash helped with the legs. Once inside, it was a little easier to assess his wounds. There was a tremendous amount of blood on his upper body, but as far as she could tell, the bear's teeth had just grazed his chest through the plaid jacket and T-shirt. Millie patched up the bloody spots as best she could. Henry came to and grimaced every time she touched him.

"You'll be out of here in no time." Millie touched his cheek with the back of her knuckles. To Dash she said, "Quick, go fill a water bottle at the stream and bring it here."

Dash arrived back in minutes. "Dad, do you think this is the same bear we saw at Cub Camp?"

Henry's eyes flickered, and he tried to say something, but the words were too weak and faint to make out.

"Shhh," said Millie. "You rest." She held up Henry's head and had him open his mouth. She inserted two Tylenol and put the water bottle to his lips. He swallowed and then turned his head to one side, eyes still closed. She felt his pulse. It was strong. She covered him up and backed out of the tent.

Dash was back to poking the bear with a stick. "This is just like Fortnite, 'cept with bears instead of zombies. Mom, what if there's more than one bear out there?"

Millie hadn't thought of that. "Come on, Delores." She brought her hands together and raised them to her chin. "We're counting on you."

89

Friday: Frank Hears the News

Friday morning, Frank was pleased to see the crowd of journalists had dwindled down to CBC and VOCM. He decided to hear what VOCM was saying and turned on the radio.

"Breaking news: VOCM has learned that an adult male has been attacked by a black bear on the section of the East Coast Trail known as the Spout. Details are scanty, but VOCM has learned that the injured man has been airlifted to the Health Sciences Complex. We will be following this story and updating you as we learn more. For VOCM news, this is Price Phillips."

Frank jumped in a cab to the hospital.

The aseptic carbolicky acid smell hit his nostrils as soon as he entered. He found Millie in emergency. A second helicopter had ferried her and Dash and Delores and their gear. The RNC and wildlife officials were on their way to the site to investigate.

Just as he made his way toward her, he saw the ever-present Gillian Gee enter from a side corridor, mic in hand, and approach Millie. *Uh oh*, thought Frank.

"Mrs. Puddester, we'd like a word with your husband."

Millie stood up and squared off against Gillian Gee. "Haven't you done enough already?" Millie was using her most menacing courtroom voice. "The reason my husband is here is because he was trying to avoid you lot. You're like the freakin' paparazzi."

"The public . . ." Gillian Gee started.

"I don't give a flying fuck about the public." An elderly male doctor passed by. "Excuse me," said Millie. "Could you please see these people get escorted out of the hospital. They are harassing my family."

"Hospital security to emergency." The doctor spoke into his phone. Gillian Gee, her cameraman, and three other journalists who had followed them began making their way down the long corridor. Hospital security arrived within minutes.

"Make sure they don't sneak back in," said Millie.

Frank watched the CBC logos disappear. "Where's Dash? And Delores?"

"I sent them home. No need for us all to be here."

Frank gave Millie's shoulder a squeeze. "How is he?"

"I haven't seen him since they took him in. The surgeon should be done soon."

"Surgeon?"

"Yes, he was pretty ripped up. The bear was chewing on his chest like he was beef jerky."

"Blimey." Frank looked into the middle distance. Two men passed by pushing a gurney. "So, you know, will he recover?"

"They say he'll recover physically. It's his mind I worry about. You know that ever since his mother died he's been pretty delicate. I thought that the incident at the supermarket and Delores ruining his bike was bad enough, but this bear attack may just drive him over the edge."

"I know what you mean. Will he be well enough to do the Spring Tune-Up?"

"Doesn't matter if he's got twelve cracked ribs and ten feet of stitches. He's not allowed to go on the ride, anyway."

"Oh, right, the house arrest starts tomorrow, doesn't it?"

"Yes, that or pay fifty thousand dollars, which we can't afford."

"What are you going to do?"

"Nothing we can do. He'll have to get the bike shipped back home or have it held in a warehouse in Longueuil until the fall. Then once the house arrest is up, he can fly up and ride it home."

A flustered-looking intern appeared. He looked like Peewee Herman with his pants hiked up to his ribs. "Mrs. Puddester? Millie Puddester?"

Millie stood up.

"You can see your husband now."

He opened the door and allowed Millie through. Frank followed.

Henry was taped up like a hockey stick, chest covered in gauze, one arm in traction. He looked up, and Frank could tell by his eyes that he was heavily sedated. The airy inhalations of the blood pressure machine droned on. Millie gave him a kiss, careful not to hit the IV attached to his arm.

"Millie . . . don't have to go on bike," he croaked. "Just . . ." He coughed. "Happy to be alive."

"Shh," she said.

90

Gloria Checks in on Delores

Millie asked Gloria to go check on things on Pine Place and, in particular, to ask about the handgun. "She saved Henry's life, Gloria, but I'm worried. I mean, who carries a gun on the East Coast Trail?"

Gloria put on her lucky pink glasses and drove to Millie's. She arrived to find Delores playing Fortnite with Dash. "Hi, Delores. I heard you ran ten kilometres to get help."

"Yeah. Mr. Henry was pretty banged up, but he's going to live." Delores didn't take her eyes off the video game. "Dash, pick up the double-barrelled shotgun."

"Where?" Dash sounded frantic.

"There. By your left foot."

"Uh, Delores, speaking of guns, I didn't know you packed a pistol . . ." Gloria dispensed with the welcome kisses.

"I keep him in Daisy's glovebox, just in case," said Delores.

"Just in case what?" asked Gloria.

"Just in case my good-for-nothing ex-husband shows up. Plus, I always take him with me in the woods."

"Why do you take it in the woods?"

"Grizzlies."

"We don't have any grizzlies here, Delores."

"No, but you do have man-eatin' black bears. Jeepers. That thing was taking bites outta Mr. Henry."

"Is your gun, you know, legal?"

"Registered in British Columbia."

"Even if registered, the gun is not allowed to be carried in a glovebox or on the East Coast Trail," said Gloria.

"Did I tell you I had a premonition the night I won Chase the Ace that I might need Flick? So, I brought him into the house with me."

"Flick?"

"My Glock."

"Oh, you have a name for your gun, too?"

Delores looked incredulous. "Doesn't everyone?"

"Well, without you and Flick, Henry probably wouldn't be alive. Still, he's going to be pretty down. Hospital is a helluva way to spend your last day before house arrest." Gloria looked out the window.

"What are you talking about? House arrest?" Delores kept her eyes on the screen. Gloria was surprised she hadn't heard about the judge's ruling before this.

"You didn't hear the judge sentenced Henry to six months of house arrest? Unless he can come up with fifty thousand to donate to Amber Alert."

"Well, that's a no-brainer. I got more money than I could ever spend," said Delores. "I can pay whatever it takes to make sure Mr. Henry is on a plane for Montreal and riding his bike back for his mama."

"Really?"

"Yeah. Why not?" Delores glanced up. "You're a lawyer, right? What would you need from me?"

Gloria smiled, already going over in her mind the paperwork for $50,000 to be transferred from Delores's bank account once her winnings cleared.

"That's a lot of damage," Delores said. She was talking to Dash, not Gloria.

91

Henry Finds the Note

Millie and Frank had been ushered out, and beyond the drip, drip of the IV and the buzz of the fluorescent lights, all Henry could hear were faraway voices rising and falling outside the door. He must be near the nursing station. Nurse Belinda came in to take the lunch tray that Henry had nudged away when he woke up.

"You haven't eaten anything?"

"Can't stand the smell."

"Fair enough. I'll take it away, but I'll be back in a second. I have something to show you."

She returned carrying a bag of Henry's hiking clothes. "I figured you might want to have a look at these."

"Jesus in Jerusalem." Henry's voice was still faint. His lips were parched, and his whole body felt immensely heavy. "I won't be wearing that jacket any time soon." The jacket and shirt were completely shredded down one side.

"I dare say not." Nurse Belinda passed him the bundle and went out into the corridor. "You're lucky to be alive."

Henry fingered the red plaid shirt. He ran his palm over the decimated material on the one side and then the soft flannel of the other. He felt something in the breast pocket. Henry took out a folded piece of orange paper. It was the note he had taken from the vase in the mother-in-law suite. It felt like a lifetime ago. *Was it only last week?* He unfolded it and read.

> Dear Henry, my precious son. I wanted to explain why I cannot stay in your beautiful apartment. I know I don't have long in this world, and I fear that if I were to leave it in this space you lovingly prepared that it would be forever tainted. Dash might be uncomfortable with that. I hope you understand.
>
> Your loving mother
>
> PS Think of the good times when you do the Spring Tune-Up. I'll be right there with you.

Henry folded the note, blinked slowly, and lay back on his pillow.

Nurse Belinda poked her head in again. She had a small tray with one tiny paper cup and a larger one. She told Henry to hold out his hand and shook an itty-bitty blue painkiller from the smaller cup. He put it in his mouth. She then held a straw in the larger cup of water to Henry's lips. He noisily sucked up the fluid. He was so thirsty. His mouth and lips had never felt so dry, and licking them only made things worse.

"You have a visitor. I let him in even though visiting hours are over."

Dick Turner filled the door frame. He walked toward Henry's bed and stopped at the pillow, his wandering eye well-behaved. He took something out of a brown paper bag and laid it next to Henry on the bed. Henry opened it with one hand. A yellow and black Boston toque with a pair of gloves were inside.

"Thanks, Dick." Henry's breathing was light and fast.

"Sorry, Henry. I shouldn't have arrested you."

"Just doing your job." Henry inhaled and gathered his breath. He looked straight at his old friend. "I'm sorry I missed your birthday camping trip, Dick."

Henry flashed back to that weekend. That Sunday night he came back from the Grand Falls tournament with a medal around his neck. Dick came out of the woods and was immediately flown to Halifax for emergency eye surgery. He had chopped into a log with the axe Henry had given him as a birthday gift and hit a cheap nail. Metal shards flew into his eye. Dick never forgave Henry. When Henry went over to visit him after the surgery, Dick told his mother he didn't want to see him. When Dick recovered enough to come back to school, he asked to change homerooms.

Dick swallowed, his Adam's apple bobbing up and down. "I'm sorry that I blamed you for my eye. I should have worn the safety goggles."

Henry closed his eyes. He remembered the weight of the axe in his hands as he passed it over before he left for the hockey tournament. The goggles were taped to the wrapping paper. His mother had insisted he add them.

"I want to start over." Dick looked at the floor.

"Does that mean Stella can hang out with Dash again?"

"Yes, I'll tell her, but she is, anyway. Nothing changed when I told her she couldn't see him. That girl has a mind of her own." His eyeballs whipped back and forth like a TV about to go on the blink.

"It's better to be feisty than to follow the crowd." Henry held out his good hand.

Dick shook it, his eyes settling into alignment. "I want to invite you over once you're back on your feet. Actually, my mother wants to see you. Nothing as wild as your party."

"Oh my God, I haven't seen your mother in years. Remember how she used to keep her cigarettes in the living room curtains?"

"Yeah, she'd stand at the window and smoke until Dad showed up, then she'd douse the fag and fan her arms around like a demented chopper."

"I used to watch her. She'd stick the pack and matches back in the hem of the sheer before he got inside." Henry smiled at the memory.

"Remember how she acted as if Dad was crazy when he asked about the smell? 'What smell?' she'd say."

"Export A." Henry could smell it as if Mrs. Turner had just now lit one up. He could see the smiling Scottish lassie on the green pack as if she were there in the room encouraging their first hacking draws. "We used to steal the odd one in grades seven and eight, before . . ." He stopped mid-sentence.

"Enough of that. Let's let bygones be bygones. Mom knew it was us pinching her smokes, you know, but she couldn't say anything to Dad because that would be admitting what she had been denying for years." Dick was quiet for a minute. Then he started speaking again.

"I'd like you to get to know Wavey. She makes a mean lasagna. We'll just invite a few people. You and Millie. And Frank, as long as he doesn't bring any punch."

Henry laughed. "Frank is a good guy. I heard you made an arrest in the parking meter case."

"Yes, in fact we made two. And they retrieved over three hundred meter heads from the racetrack. I have to say I never would have thought of searching out there."

"What's going to happen to the track?"

"Nothing. The boys admitted the owners had no idea what they were up to. So, some new staff, but business as usual."

"That's good to hear. I know Delores really wants to go see some racing."

"I have to apologize to Delores . . ."

"Did I hear my name?" Delores walked in the room then, wearing a fairly tame, mostly green floral ensemble, a change from the pink. She must have been shopping. Millie followed. She was wearing sneakers, so Henry hadn't heard her coming. Even though she was wearing yoga clothes, she still looked like she could be on the cover of a magazine.

"Speak of the dangerous driver. I don't think we've been formally introduced." Dick held out his meaty paw.

"I know who you are." Delores looked him up and down and did not offer her hand in return. "I saw you at the party. You're the one who's been causing Mr. Henry so much worry. Whatever happened when you were children, can't you just get over it?"

Dick let his arm drop to his side. "Done deal," he said, adding, "Sorry not to have been more welcoming." Then to Henry, "I'll call around and let you know details of when we'd like you to come over." Dick walked out.

Millie raised her eyebrows.

"Dick says he's having us 'round for drinks."

"Marvels never cease." She kissed Henry on top of the head, avoiding the tender parts.

92

***

Monday: Reconciliation

Henry came home from the hospital with strict orders to take it easy for at least a week. His leg was okay, but his torso wounds needed healing. Three ribs were broken. He had trouble inhaling and shifting in bed. He wasn't doing much laughing, so he was safe in that department.

Everyone, except Dash, tiptoed around him as he reclined in his chair. Dash bounced around, recounting the bear attack as if Henry hadn't been there. "And then he started chewing on you, Dad. You should have seen it. It was so cool."

Millie walked in, a tray in one hand. "Here's your tea and newspaper. Just call my cell if you need anything. Dash, Miss Delores will be here in a minute." Henry saw Millie take in Dash's shirt. "Dash, you look like you slept in the yard. How many days have you been wearing that shirt?" It was the Fortnite shirt that Stella had bought him. "Didn't you have that on hiking?"

"Maybe."

"Dash, you have to wear a clean shirt to school."

"It is clean." He pulled it away from his body and scanned first the front, then the sides. The chocolate stains on the chest didn't seem to register with him.

"Go on, Dasher, change it for your mother."

"Aww, Dad." Dash turned and went back to his room.

Delores arrived and knocked on the door, something she had never done. Henry knew she was here to walk Dash to school. Up until last December, that had been Henry's job in the morning. But after Christmas, Dash had told Henry and Millie he was too old to be accompanied to school by a parent. "Dave the crossing guard would never let anything happen to me."

Henry had felt the pang all parents feel when their children grow up and let him go off on his own. Lately, though, he let Delores walk him to school. According to Dash, she was a bit of a celebrity in the schoolyard.

"Because of Daisy?" Henry had asked.

"No, because of Fortnite. Everyone wants to get a pumpkin-head skin like hers. They think they'll be as good as she is with a new skin. I told them they're crazy. They didn't believe me when I told them I saw her shoot a gun for real."

Millie opened the door to Delores. "You know you don't have to knock."

Delores was quiet. She looked at Henry and then at the floor. What in heck's name was going on? Delores was never quiet.

Millie went out. "See you after work, everyone."

"Mr. Henry, I heard about your dilemma."

"Which one?" Henry's head hurt thinking about the downhill slide his life had taken.

"I heard that you can't go on your motorcycle trip because of the baby . . . I mean supermarket incident."

Henry closed his eyes. He did not want to discuss his house arrest with Delores. This was day one. He had five months and twenty-nine days to go.

"Miss Gloria told me that you won't have to stay in the house for six months if you pay fifty thousand dollars. Well, as you know, I came into a considerable amount of money last week, and I've already made arrangements with Miss Gloria to pay the fine. She says it won't take more than four days for the money to clear at the bank. You should be able to fly to Montreal as planned. As long as the doctor says you're good to go."

Henry stared at his tenant. He shook his head. "You . . . you can't do that."

"It's already done."

Henry started to jump out of his chair before he remembered how the slightest movement hurt his ribs. "Delores, that is too kind. I don't deserve it. I haven't been nice to you. I'm sorry. Also, I caused that baby's mother to worry. Plus, I realized I can't just up and go on a trip. I have to be here for Dash. I know Millie said she'd take time off work, but that's not fair."

"First of all, it would be an honour to help you out by paying the fine, Mr. Henry. Second, I can stay with Dash while you go on your motorcycle trip. I want you to be happy. I am sorry for gluing things on without your permission."

Henry grunted. "Maybe I could put one of your toys in my saddlebag."

"For good luck."

"Yes, for good luck. Thank you for saving me from the bear."

"Well, I guess we wouldn't have been at the Spout if I hadn't won Chase the Ace."

"We didn't really get to see the Spout, did we?"

"No," said Delores. "Maybe next time." Then her face turned serious. "I told Miss Millie I'll move out before you get back from your trip. I wanted to let you know you all can come see me and Daisy any time you like at the Walmart."

Henry swallowed. "You don't have to go, Delores."

"Really? I can stay?"

"Sure, but maybe you can buy yourself your own recliner out of your winnings."

Delores laughed a great hiccoughing laugh as Henry gingerly lay back in the La-Z-Boy.

93

Vanessa Visits Henry

Vanessa knew she had to go see Henry Puddester. She'd heard about the bear attack on the news, but it was Baloo who told her it was Dash's father. She waited until she figured Dash had left for school and pulled up in front of 10 Pine Place. The wooden door was open. She called through the screen.

"If you're not a reporter, you can come in."

Henry was sitting in a recliner when Vanessa entered. She slipped off her shoes and padded over to the couch.

"Akela. What a surprise."

"You can call me Vanessa, Mr. Puddester . . ."

"Henry."

"Henry, I owe you an apology. When you saw the bear that night at Cub Camp, I didn't believe you. I am sorry for dismissing what you said and for telling the other parents about what transpired at Sundries."

"Water under the bridge," said Henry. "I would appreciate if you would talk to Dash, though. He was pretty shook up about the bear."

"I plan to, as well as the other Cubs. I will explain that I was wrong."

"I'm interested . . . the news reports haven't mentioned how the bear ended up on the Avalon . . . ?"

"As far as we can ascertain, it hitched a ride on a Ruby Rose chicken truck that had been doing a delivery in Clarenville. The driver said he thought the truck was empty coming back to the Goulds, but he heard banging in the back shortly before he reached the chicken plant. He pulled over, and when he opened the doors, a non-chicken smell hit him. Something big started coming toward him, so he ran. He told his wife but thought the boys at work would make fun of him so didn't mention it to them."

"That explains it, then." Henry paused. "You know my friend killed the bear."

"Yes. It would have had to be put down, anyway."

"Was there a cub?"

"No, it was male. Males never travel with cubs."

"One of the doctors in emerg was from BC. He said my wounds were more consistent with a grizzly attack than a black bear. Why do you think that particular bear was so aggressive toward humans?"

"Someone mentioned that there was a coyote at the campground shortly before the bear attacked you."

"Yeah, so?"

"Often black bear attacks start with an altercation with a dog or another animal. Also, I think he must have been extremely hungry. He was massive, six hundred and twenty-four pounds, and his jaw was inches bigger than any black bear jaw ever recorded in the province. Still, we've never seen this kind of behaviour from a black bear. Samples have gone to be tested for rabies."

"You said bears don't live on the Avalon . . ."

"They usually don't. Like I said, we think this guy crawled out of his den, hitched a ride, and got out in the Goulds. There was not much in the way of food except for chicken offal, which is locked up. We found scratch marks all over the locked dumpster, and the unlocked garbage buckets behind Ruby Rose were ravaged."

"But I wasn't near any chicken plant."

"I know, but a man was killed when he went walking near the dumpster behind the Ruby Rose chicken plant last week."

"Killed?"

"Yes, mauled by a bear."

"You think it was the same bear who got me?"

"Yes, after the attack, there was an incredible amount of noise and activity around the plant, and I think he got spooked and moved farther south to try for food. Where you were camping is very near two large farms. The Cub Camp is not far away, either, and probably had been supplying him with dropped hot dogs and the like."

"We didn't have a fire, remember?"

"Exactly. That's probably why he moved off."

Henry blew out through his teeth. "Imagine if he had come when the Cubs were outside."

"I thought about that. We're lucky all we had to deal with was a boy on fire." Vanessa smiled.

Henry returned the smile. "Vanessa, I appreciate you coming by."

"Henry?"

"Yes?"

Vanessa looked toward the door as if to see if anyone would overhear. "Did you kidnap that baby?"

Henry raised his eyebrows. "No. What in God's name would I do with a baby? I can hardly manage Dash."

Vanessa smiled. "I believe you." She went back to the lab happier than she had been in months.

94

Tuesday: Henry Sends Cordell Packing

It was just after two in the afternoon on Tuesday. Delores had left no more than ten minutes earlier to pick up Dash at school. Henry had settled in his chair with the paper to read the story about the meter thieves. The doorbell started ringing. Henry ignored the bell, but the person started rapping their knuckles on the door. The news vans had moved off to the next story, but they did keep calling. Henry had disconnected the land line.

Whoever was at the door this time was incessant. They must have bloody knuckles. "I am going to call the police," Henry muttered. He got up with effort and took a look out the window to see what news organization it was this time. Instead, a Spiffy Cab sat at the end of the driveway.

"Delores here?" asked a short, muscular man before Henry had a chance to open the screen door. He had wiry eyebrows, some of which curved downwards to cover his eyes. Although he was attempting a smile, his default expression seemed to be a frown.

"She's out. Who are you?"

"Her husband." The man's expression was hard.

Henry glowered. "Ex-husband, if I'm not mistaken."

"Misunderstanding," said the man. "When's she coming back?"

"No idea. Why don't you just leave me with a number where she can reach you, and I'll give her the message?"

"I'd rather wait." He crossed his boxy arms.

"I don't think so, buddy. You'd best be moving on."

"Why? What's it to you?"

"Delores is a part of our family now, and she does not want some sleazebag emptying her wallet."

"What are you talking about?" The man rubbed his nose with his left palm.

"You know what I'm talking about." Henry could see the muscles twitch in the man's face.

"Tell her I was here." Just as he turned and moved down the driveway to the waiting yellow cab, Delores arrived out of the laneway from the park. She was carrying the small transistor radio Millie had bought her. That putrid song, "Seasons in the Sun," was playing.

"Terry Jacks, single, 1974," Delores said, looking up just in time to see Cordell.

"I see you haven't changed." Cordell smirked without changing his lips from the frown.

"You slimy-tongued snake." Delores turned off the radio. "How dare you show up here."

"I just want to make sure you're okay, baby."

"I see. This has nothing to do with money?"

"Of course not."

Delores walked toward her ex but instead veered off and unlocked Daisy's passenger door and leaned in to open the glovebox. "If you know what's good for you, you best leave, and fast. Go crawl back under a rock, where you belong."

Cordell jumped in the cab. Henry applauded as it drove away.

"Delores, you weren't really going to shoot him, were you?"

"Naw, the police still have my gun."

Henry laughed, but it quickly turned to tears. It was the first time he had laughed since the bear attack. "You only won Chase the Ace Thursday night. How could he get here so quick?"

"That connivin' son of a bitch can smell money a thousand miles off."

"You sure told him where to go."

"I told him a long time ago that if he ever came near me again, I would kill him."

Henry laughed nervously—he wasn't sure she was joking. "Where's Dash?"

"He and Stella are playing at the park." Delores turned the radio back on and went past Henry into the house. Henry held his ribs and breathed gently. He had no idea how long the pain was going to last.

What he did know was that things were going to be all right. He had just survived the worst two weeks of his life. He and Dick had made amends. Akela apologized. Millie and Dash loved him, and he loved them. Even Frank was doing much better since the police had arrested the meter thieves, but the best thing of all was that on May 24, he would be on a plane for Montreal to meet up with his bike and ride all the glorious way back home, thanks to his house guest and newest family member, Delores Cowburn.

95

Friday the Next Week: Mystery Solved

Tiny was called to the inquiry into Wally's death.

The university woman spoke. She wore beige field pants with pockets on the thighs and a pink swirled neck scarf. "Rest assured, that bear was a one-off. He came in on a chicken truck, and now that he's dead, the Avalon Peninsula is once again free of bears."

After the inquiry, Tiny went straight to see Wally's wife, Flora. Ruby Rose had agreed to pay for Wally's funeral and tombstone. At least Vik the Prick was good for that.

"I'll stick around until the summer when the girls get home for the funeral service," he said.

"Then what?" she asked.

"Then I'll ride my bike out to Fort Mac. I need a change of scenery."

"I guess you do." She smiled up at him from her wheelchair.

"I'll write to you, though." Tiny sat down on the couch and pulled a pen from his pocket. "Here, I know you've got my number. I'll let you know if it changes. I'll give you my email, too." He wrote it on the inside of the phonebook.

"Thank you, Tiny."

He stooped to give her a hug and took some things from the shopping bags he had brought. "Shepherd's pie in the fridge," he said.

He wanted to say more but found his throat too dry to speak. He nodded as he went out the door into the warmish wind and saw a dandelion poking its head through the broken blacktop.

96

Two Weeks Later: Frank Gets His Groove Back

It was the twenty-fourth of May, the Queen's birthday. Frank's, too. His paunch had gone down an inch, and he hadn't heard a parking meter complaint in weeks. He wandered over to say hello to Millie and Delores. Despite some lingering injuries, Henry had left for his motorcycle ride and was due to call after lunch.

Dash ran out the back door straight into Frank's midriff.

"Mr. Parrell's here. Can we cut the cake?"

"Not yet, Dash," said Millie. "After lunch."

"Aww. Can we go hang out in your Tardis, Mr. Parrell?"

"Yes, after we eat." Frank raised his nose to the ceiling. "Sure smells good in here."

"Have a seat, Frank," said Millie.

Frank sat at the end of the table in front of a rectangular gateau covered in chocolate icing with dinky cars flying over a ramp. He swallowed. Delores patted him on the back and offered him a plate of bologna skewers.

"It's okay, Mr. Frank. You can cry if you want."

"I'm not going to cry, Delores. Just got dust in my eye."

Millie came to his rescue. "Frank, did I see you jogging *outdoors* this morning?"

"Yes, I went to Fort Amherst and back for sixteen K."

"Frank gets his groove back." Millie smiled.

"We have a surprise for you, Mr. Parrell," said Dash. "One, two, three . . ."

Kaitlyn appeared from the kitchen wearing a bright yellow apron. "Happy birthday, Dad." She passed him a card.

Tears welled up in Frank's eyes. He opened the card and saw his daughter's handwriting inside: *Please be my Facebook friend again.* She went to him, and he enveloped her in a hug. "I'm cooking your favourite, roast leg of lamb with mint sauce."

Frank inhaled, his eyes really watering now. "Sunday joint. That smell brings me back to the old country. I can picture my mother nursing a gin and tonic and serving the veg."

A pink iPhone vibrated on the table. "Is that mine or yours?" Millie looked at Delores. When Millie's ring tone was off, it was impossible to tell.

"That one's yours, Miss Millie." Delores fished hers out of her blue jeans. "I added some flower stickers to mine so we can tell them apart."

"It's Henry." Millie pushed her finger to the screen.

Dash snatched the phone from his mother. "Hi, Dad. We're getting ready to eat Mr. Parrell's cake."

Millie tried to retrieve the phone. "Put it on speaker, Dash."

Everyone crowded around the phone. Henry's tinny voice came out of the speaker. "Wow, that's great, Dasher. Wish I was there."

"Don't worry, Dad. You can go away and leave me with Miss Delores any time. She took me and Stella mini golfing yesterday, and she's taking us to the Thunderdome today."

"How is Delores?"

"Dash, pass me the phone." Millie sounded stern.

"Why? It's on speaker." He hopped out of his mother's reach.

"Hand it over. You're hogging it." Millie caught his arm, grabbed the phone, and held it out like a torch. "Hi, honey. Delores is right here."

"Hi, Delores. How are you and Daisy?"

"Never been better. Daisy is going to be the main attraction in the car show at the Avalon Speedway in October. All proceeds go to ChildFind."

"Dad, you should enter your Triumph, too."

"Maybe. I'll get myself home in one piece first."

"How are the ribs?" Millie asked.

"They're all right as long as I don't laugh, cough, or sneeze."

"You'd better not overdo it," said Millie. She switched the phone off speaker and moved to another room, pushing Dash out and shutting the door. "I wanted to let you know I got a card from Britney Mooney. She says thank you for the money you gave her. She's going to put it away for Jade's education. Where did you get money, Henry? You didn't ask Delores for more, did you?"

"No, I sold the Ducati."

"What?"

"I felt bad about what happened. I caused that poor girl so much grief."

"Who am I speaking to, and what have you done with my husband?"

Henry laughed. "I'll tell you all about it when I get back."

"I love you. I'll take you back to the others now." Millie went back to the kitchen.

"Where are you now, Henry?" asked Frank.

"We just reached the New Brunswick border. It's beautiful out. Almost too warm for leather. You having a good birthday?"

"Yes. Kaitlyn's cooking."

"That's great. Hi, Kaitlyn."

"Hi, Mr. P."

"Dad, did you know Kaitlyn got a tattoo on her chest, but she won't let me see it?" Dash asked.

Kaitlyn put Dash in a headlock.

"Uh . . ." said Henry.

Frank changed the subject. "We're also celebrating my retirement."

"What?"

"Yep, finally bit the bullet. I'm leaving the bunker."

"Wow, that's big stuff. When?"

"A month from Friday."

"What are you going to do with yourself?"

"I joined a running club. They say I have potential." Frank did a twirl.

"That's fantastic, Frank."

"That's not all."

"What else?"

"I'm looking at buying the old fire station on Duckworth."

"What the heck are you going to do with a fire station?"

"Kaitlyn thinks I should open a brew pub."

"Get outta here."

"I'm serious. It was actually Patty who put me on to the owners. They're leaving the province and need to sell quickly. We're going to cash in some of our RRSPs and go in on it as partners."

"Wow, that's great, Frank."

Voices called out to Henry. "I'm going to have to go. The boys are about to leave."

"Okay, call me later," said Millie. "Love you."

"Bye, Dad."

"Bye, Mr. P."

"See ya, Henry."

"Bye, Mr. Henry. Take care of your ribs."

97

May 24: Henry Is in the Zone

They had just drifted into Matane, the main hub on the north side of the Gaspé Peninsula. Forty-eight riders in staggered formation. The Triumph was performing better than ever. The old twin never missed a beat—she was practically purring. Henry thought of his mother. He knew it was her watching over him.

After fuelling and a washroom break, the leader decided that they had time to keep heading east around the Gaspé Peninsula. Henry settled in about eight riders back. The Great St. Lawrence opened up in front of them. The river seemed to be rising up to meet the road, at places just a few feet from their wheels. A vertical rock face towered on the right, a hang-glider drifting overhead like a soaring eagle.

Henry was like the hang-glider. For the first time in months, he hadn't a care in the world. He loved having no responsibility. When someone said stop, he stopped. When someone gave the five-minute warning before heading out, he put his helmet on and stood by his Triumph.

They continued east toward Campbellton, New Brunswick, crossed the bridge, and turned south. Henry pulled up his visor and patted his mother's picture in his pocket. A gentle breeze tickled his face. He would be home to Millie, Dash, Delores, and Frank by week's end. And he was looking forward to seeing them all. Even Delores.

Fin

Dolores's Playlist

1. "I Am Woman," Helen Reddy, *I Don't Know How to Love Him*, 1971
2. "Me and Bobby McGee," Janis Joplin, *Pearl Album*, released posthumously, 1971
3. "Levon," Elton John, Madman Across the Water, 1971
4. "When the Lights Go Down," Journey, *Infinity*, 1978
5. "Hallelujah Chorus," Leonard Cohen, *Various Positions*, 1984
6. "Losing My Religion," REM, *Out of Time*, 1991
7. "Achy Breaky Heart," Billy Ray Cyrus, *Some Gave All*, 1992
8. "Jumpin' Jack Flash," Rolling Stones, released as a single, 1968
9. "I Want to Hold Your Hand," *Meet the Beatles*, 1964
10. "Piano Man," album same name, Billy Joel, 1973
11. "Respect," Aretha Franklin, *I Never Loved a Man the Way I Love You*, 1967
12. "Bohemian Rhapsody," Queen, *A Night at the Opera*, 1975
13. "Feelings," Morris Albert, 1975
14. "Cadillac Ranch," Bruce Springsteen, *The River*, 1980
15. "Seasons in the Sun," Terry Jacks, single, 1974
16. "Always Look on the Bright Side of Life," Eric Idle, *Monty Python's Life of Brian*, 1979
17. "Rehab," Amy Winehouse, *Back to Black*, 2006

Questions and Topics for Book Club Discussion

1. The entire action of the novel takes place in a two-week period just like Dash's favourite game, Fortnite. Did you find yourself rooting for Henry to survive the nightmare?

2. Dash is involved in the twilight world of video games in which he's "socializing" with people he knows nothing about. Henry and Millie sometimes tell Dash to go play Fortnite to get him out of the way, and Dash considers Delores a star because of her skill with Fortnite. What do you think of the role video games play in the world today?

3. Delores is a catalyst, the stranger who brings about change, uncomfortable at first, but finally healing. Were you surprised to learn Delores had been married? Why? When Delores uses a gun, it is Millie who has second thoughts about Delores while Henry doesn't ask questions. Is this surprising? What do the song references tell you about Delores's character?

4. Big changes occur in Henry's household with the arrival of Delores. Do you think Millie did a good thing by inviting Delores to stay with their family? When Henry points out his house is not Delores's "*casa*," do you feel sympathy for Delores? When Henry laid down the ultimatum—*It's Delores or me*—did you think he means it?

5. Henry, perhaps due to his late start, is ill-suited to the demands and expectations of parenthood, and his garrulous misunderstanding of children provides comic relief. Do you think Henry is a good father?

6. When Henry and Dash arrive at Cub Camp, Henry has no idea that the other parents know about the supermarket incident. What did you think of Akela when you realized she had told the other parents about Henry and the supermarket? All the Cub leaders and other parents at camp are female, echoing the young mother in the supermarket. Do you feel Henry is the odd man out in a bunch of mother hens looking after their brood?

7. The novel *Supermarket Baby* is essentially a small-town drama, with media reports making it sound as though St. John's has fallen prey to a serial abductor and a general panic is in the ether. News of kidnappings pop up on radio and TV and in newspapers. For example, Gillian Gee notes the extra vigilance needed to watch children at a large event. How does this serve to heighten the panic? Do you think the media have blown things out of proportion? Henry is frantic with worry when Dash is at Chase the Ace, making him the mirror image of the worried supermarket parent and all the other members of the public. Is this ironic?

8. In the classroom scene, Dash is the collateral damage of his father's actions. Is this realistic?

9. Frank has reason to be angry with the media. Are journalists justified in making him out to be a doofus?

10. In the tattoo scene, Frank turns from sympathy to thinking his daughter a she-devil. How can Frank improve his relationship with his daughter?

11. Henry describes Millie as a "pit bull in her work and puppy dog with the save-the-world gene whenever someone is downtrodden." Does this explain how Millie ended up with Henry? Henry's character is a mixture of good intentions, fussiness, and incompetence, whereas Millie is ultra-organized. How does this create conflict?

12. Millie has to remind Henry that his mother is dead. What impact do you think Henry's mother's death has had on him?

13. When Akela says there are no bears on the Avalon, do you believe her?

14. Kaitlyn's treatment of Frank is extremely harsh. Is it warranted, or is she just finding someone to blame for the divorce? Were you relieved when she came to see Frank for his birthday?

15. The grudge Dick Turner has against Henry originated in high school. Is it realistic for a simple grudge to continue for decades? Were you surprised to learn that Henry was responsible for Dick's wonky eye?

16. In the opening chapter, Henry's bike doesn't work. In the final chapter, it's purring along. Is this a metaphor for Henry's life?

17. Shopping carts play a prominent role in this novel. Delores gets hit by a shopping cart and ends up in hospital; Carter uses a shopping cart (his Harley) to collect recyclables; and of course Henry inadvertently switches carts while shopping and ends up with a baby, landing him in jail. Have you ever pulled a shopping cart switch?

Acknowledgements

While writing *Supermarket Baby*, I felt the positive vibes of an entire community. I would like to thank my family, especially Declan, for providing fodder for this story and special thanks to Liam Flanagan for binding the first copy and Ryan Flanagan for designing the first cover.

I would also like to thank Jerry, Garry, and Margo Cranford, Ed Oldford, and the super support team at Flanker Press; Graham Blair for cover design; my beta readers Yolanda Wiersma, Cathy Smallwood, Kim Todd, Corinne Breen, Kelly Anthony, Kate Benson, Clare Thorpe, Mary-Lynn Bernard, Andy Jones, and Conor and Marie Flanagan; my editors Paul Butler, Edward Riche, Charis Cotter, and Robin McGrath; Ernest Hadley and Annie Mullins in Nova Scotia; and fellow writers Marie Wadden, Glenn Deir, Françoise Enguehard, Terry Fallis, Gerard Doran, Sharon Bala, Lisa Moore, and Carolyn Morgan for helping me on my journey toward publication.

Thanks to Edward Roberts, Maria Clift, and Michael Levine for legal assistance; Marie Snippa for my author photo; Matthew LeDrew for website support; Chris Flanagan and John Marshall for answering motorcycle questions; and Gerry Marshall and Jason Coombs for helping with criminal justice questions. Any mistakes are my own.

I especially thank the Government of Newfoundland and Labrador's Arts and Letters Program for the Percy Janes First Novel Award, the Writers' Alliance of Newfoundland and Labrador (WANL) for their manuscript evaluation service, and Katrina Rice and the ArtsNL Professional Project Grants Program for their financial assistance.

Finally, thanks to Terry Kelly, my personal guru, who had faith in me long before I had faith in myself.

AUTHOR PHOTO BY MARIE SNIPPA

Susan Flanagan has worked as a freelance journalist in St. John's for more than thirty years. She graduated from King's College in Nova Scotia with a Bachelor of Journalism in 1991, and her non-fiction works have appeared in *Canadian Geographic*, *National Geographic* (maps), *Canadian Running*, *Newfoundland Quarterly*, *Hockey News*, *Doctors' Review*, *Atlantic Progress*, *Atlantic Business*, *Saltscapes*, and many others.

Susan contributed a biweekly column, "48 Degrees," to the *Newfoundland Herald* (2002–04) and a weekly column, "The Kids are Alright," to the *Telegram* (2011–15). She has been a contributor on CBC Radio (St. John's), *The Point*, *Out Front*, *Radio Noon*, and *Definitely Not the Opera (DNTO)* and has worked for both NTV in St. John's and CBC TV in Halifax and St. John's as reporter, producer, and researcher.

She lives with her husband and two of their five children in St. John's.

Also by Susan Flanagan:

THE DEGREES OF BARLEY LICK
(Running the Goat Books and Broadsides, 2021)

www.susanflanaganauthor.com
www.facebook.com/susanflanaganauthor